# Bundled Up

**Books by Annabeth Albert**

Portland Heat novellas:

*Served Hot*

*Baked Fresh*

*Delivered Fast*

*Knit Tight*

Perfect Harmony series:

*Treble Maker*

*Love Me Tenor*

Published by Kensington Publishing Corporation

# Bundled Up

## Annabeth Albert

LYRICAL SHINE
Kensington Publishing Corp.
www.kensingtonbooks.com

LYRICAL SHINE BOOKS are published by

Kensington Publishing Corp.
119 West 40th Street
New York, NY 10018

All Kensington titles, imprints, and distributed lines are available at special quantity discounts for bulk purchases for sales promotion, premiums, fund-raising, educational, or institutional use.

Special book excerpts or customized printings can also be created to fit specific needs. For details, write or phone the office of the Kensington Sales Manager: Kensington Publishing Corp., 119 West 40th Street, New York, NY 10018. Attn. Sales Department. Phone: 1-800-221-2647.

Lyrical Shine and Lyrical Shine logo are trademarks of Kensington Publishing Corp.

First Electronic Edition: January 2016
eISBN-13: 978-1-60183-871-1
eISBN-10: 1-60183-871-9

First Print Edition: January 2016
ISBN-13: 978-1-60183-872-8
ISBN-10: 1-60183-872-7

Printed in the United States of America

Served Hot
1


Baked Fresh
95


Delivered Fast
215

# Served Hot

# June: Vanilla Latte

# Chapter 1

My nooner was late. Well, technically, David was my 11:50. Without fail, ten minutes before twelve every work day, David P. Gregory bought a vanilla latte from my coffee cart in the Old Emerson building in Portland. I only knew his name because he used his debit card to pay, and I knew the time because of the old-fashioned, massive brass clock directly across the atrium from my cart.

I knew David banked at a local credit union, knew that he worked somewhere that required a tie, knew that he had a smile that made his mouth crinkle up at the edges when I handed him his coffee, and knew that he was an excellent tipper.

What I didn't know was whether or not he was straight. We'd had this weird dance for months now—he'd arrive for his coffee, stilted and uncomfortable, relax into a bit of small talk while I made his drink, and then he'd take his coffee to one of the metal tables out in the atrium to have with the lunch he packed in a blue bag. I liked watching him eat because he gave it his entire focus—no smart phone or gadget, no newspaper or book, no folder of work. A few times I'd caught him looking back in my direction. But his gaze never lingered and either my flirting while I served him was more subtle than I'd thought or he was simply immune.

Today David was late. Unexpected disappointment uncurled in my stomach, souring my caffeine buzz. It was a good day—a steady stream of customers at my cart and bustling business for the pizza place and the vegan sandwich bar on the other side of the atrium. The hundred-year-old office building had been renovated to include a few small eateries in the newly added skylit atrium. Plenty for me to look at, but my eyes kept returning to the double brass doors that opened onto Ninth.

David pushed through the heavy doors at 12:45 just as I was finishing up a caramel soy latte for one of the Goth girls who worked at the jewelry place across the street. I hid my smile behind my espresso machine. Eager for it to be his turn, I tapped my toes against the linoleum.

"The usual?" I figured it would freak him out if I mentioned I'd noticed his lateness.

"Hmmm." He studied my specials sign. I'd glued a chalkboard panel inside a silver frame from a secondhand place on Hawthorne and put the whole thing on a silver-painted easel. Classy on the cheap.

Today I had a half-price tuxedo mocha—white chocolate with dark chocolate swirls. David had never paid any attention to the sign before, but today he gave it a long stare, consideration tugging his mouth back and forth. God, I loved his mouth—full pink lips, a hint of stubble on his upper lip like he'd missed a spot shaving.

After a few seconds, he shrugged, broad shoulders rippling the fine cotton of his dress shirt. "Yeah. The usual."

"Sure thing." I grabbed the cup for his small vanilla latte.

"Wait." He held up a hand as I started to ring him up. "Iced. It's sweltering out." He'd rolled up the sleeves of his crisp white shirt, revealing muscular forearms and a heavy silver, antique-looking watch.

"Meaning it's eighty-five degrees in Portland and everyone is freaking out. You know . . . it's good to try something different once in a while."

"I'll keep that in mind." His mouth quirked. While his brown eyes were often unreadable, his expressive mouth provided more of a window into his emotions. "But my day's had enough excitement. I'm not sure I can handle much new right now."

*Darn.* I wouldn't mind providing something *new* for him. "Rough morning?"

"Budget crisis." A sigh rolled through him, pushing his shoulders down and making his lower lip stick out. My arms tensed with the need to give him a hug. Of course, I wanted to do a lot more than hug. I wanted to nibble on his lip, lick my way into his mouth . . .

"—so everything we did three months ago has to be undone."

Hell. He'd kept talking and I'd missed part of it while I was fantasizing.

"Sucks." *In more than one way.* I'd known he was a corporate type, but knowing he was a number-crunching guy in charge of big dollars pushed him further out of my league.

"Yeah. Wasn't even sure I'd get my coffee fix today."

I looked up from making his drink, hoping to see a telltale bloom of pink on his cheeks. Eagerness. Anything that would give me a teensy-tiny bit of hope. But his paler-than-usual face only showed exhaustion, revealing little lines around his mouth and eyes that I hadn't noticed before.

"At least you get the weekend to recover, right?"

"Hah." His forced exhalation ruffled the brown hair that tumbled across his forehead. "If I'm lucky."

Over the months, I'd watched his haircut go through several cycles—close-cropped enough to hide his natural curl, waves tamed with lots of product, and overgrown fluff that defied any attempts to restrain it. My favorite look was def-initely the latter—my fingers ached with the need to grab hold and never let go—but I knew his hair would be shorter within the next few days. Fluffy and cuddly never lasted long with him.

"That's too bad. It's too pretty out to stay cooped up all weekend." *Great.* We were back to talking about the weather, but I was happy to grasp at anything to keep the conversation going. Sunlight flooded the atrium, lighting up the large planters in the center of the room and making the brass of the clock gleam.

"I know. I'll try to get out at some point." There it was: his rare half smile that on someone else might have been flirtatious. On him, it looked more like he'd surprised himself by letting a joke creep past his usual seriousness. "How about you? Big plans for the weekend?"

*You.* An invitation crept to the front of my tongue, only to retreat before I opened my mouth. I sucked at this. For all that I loved my customers and loved what I did, I wasn't good at taking banter beyond the superficial. I hadn't dated anyone for two years and my last boyfriend, Brian, had been the one to pursue me, slipping me his number with a tip and following it up with an invitation that felt more like a command.

"You could say that." I smiled nervously, not sure how much to reveal. Oh, what the hell. "It's Pride weekend."

"Didn't realize that was going on." Darn it, judging by how wide his eyes popped, he'd genuinely had no clue. Well, at least my question about him had an answer, even if it wasn't the one I wanted.

"Not like I'm going to have as much fun this year. Working one of the coffee stalls for my old boss a big chunk of the festival." I shrugged, like Pride was just another workday, but the motion came out as wooden as the conversation.

"Eh. Have fun." David's voice was weak. He coughed in that awkward rumble guys make when someone's overshared.

"Here you go." I handed him his coffee, making sure my smile didn't seem forced.

Cursing myself with every salty putdown I'd learned from my Navy dad, I watched David walk away. It wasn't the first time I'd come out to a customer, but I didn't make a habit of it. Portland was one of the most accommodating cities I'd ever lived in, but my cart was right in the heart of the business district, and with all the suits running around being all professional, it seemed best to keep things . . . professional.

David went right to his usual table and pulled out a sandwich and a Baggie of chips. Most of the suit-and-tie lunch crowd got coffees on their way over to one of the atrium's overpriced eateries. There was something endearing about a guy who got a four-dollar coffee to go with his daily PB&J on whole wheat and potato chips. Made my insides go all fuzzy. His Spartan lunch was the main reason I'd been optimistic he'd been coming around for more than coffee. Seeing him sitting there in his white shirts and boring ties, looking deep in thought over a lunch most people left behind in grade school—well, it made me want to be the thing on his mind. But of course it was highly unlikely it was me causing the furrow in his brow and the faraway look in his eyes. So what the heck was he thinking about? Numbers, probably. Budgets and columns and spreadsheets.

I got lost in deciding whether David was an accountant or a manager type and inventing a whole fantasy life for him. For long stretches of my day I had no customers and nothing to do but wait and people watch. Usually I kept half my brain on the cart, but this afternoon it took the distinctive *snick* of fingers snapping to break my daydream.

Sheila smiled broadly at me. She was another regular, a businesswoman with short eggplant-colored hair and a penchant for purple business suits and skinny mochas. "Big weekend, huh?"

"Yeah." My disappointment over David faded a little in the face of her excitement. Shelia occasionally brought her graphic designer girlfriend around. Said girlfriend had figured me out in under a minute. It was probably my glasses. They were a bit of a splurge, but hipster glasses seemed to yield higher tips, so they stayed.

"You and . . ." I struggled to remember the girlfriend's name. "You going to any of the events?"

"Laura. Laura and I will be around to watch the parade, but we're getting too old for the rest of it." She winked at me, making me feel like a high schooler getting a free pass to stay out late. I wasn't *that* much younger than her—twenty-seven to her late thirties. And the lease I'd signed for the coffee cart space a year ago made me feel plenty adult.

"Your loss."

"Hey! Someone left their wallet." Shelia held up a brown wallet.

*David.* "Heck." I jerked my hand, dribbling a bit of mocha on the side of the cup. I shot a glance toward his regular table. It was empty. Damn. I'd have to move fast to catch up with him. It was Friday, and I didn't want him to go the whole weekend without his wallet.

As soon as I handed Shelia her coffee, I opened the wallet to verify it was David's. My fingers itched to thumb through the contents, but I pinched the wallet shut as soon as I saw his debit card.

I stuck my BACK IN FIVE MINUTES sign on the counter and speedily navigated through the seating area. If I was lucky I could catch him before—I caught sight of him at the doors leading out onto Ninth.

"Hey! Wait up!" I sped after him, red apron flapping in front of me like I was trying to run down a bull. Actually, a bull wasn't a bad metaphor for him, what with his broad shoulders and wide chest and deep scowl.

"Yeah?" He said the word as if I might be about to toss a coffee on him. Or, worse, ask him out. *Great.* As I'd suspected, I'd totally mucked things up with my word vomit about Pride earlier.

"You left your wallet." I sounded breathless and way too unsure.

"Thanks for spotting it." His expression softened a little, mainly around his eyes, but it was enough to make him look more approachable. Our fingers brushed as he took the wallet from me. A deep sizzle ran from my hand all the way up to my mouth, forcing me to grin.

"No problem."

"I appreciate it—it's got my security card for work and my MAX

Pass. I'd have had to hightail it back to try to catch you before you close." His smile made his soft brown eyes dance. And made my pulse race, but I'd keep that fact to myself.

"No problem. I'm usually around, even after five. Gotta clean up." The business traffic dictated our hours. I hadn't been able to justify evenings or weekends. The odd tourist or Saturday shopper wasn't enough to keep us afloat. We weren't in a residential area, and we were a fair hike from most of the touristy stuff.

"Good to know. Not the first time I've left something important behind." He looked sheepish, and my chest expanded. I liked knowing that little hint of a weakness about him; it made him more real, less of a fantasy dude.

A little idea niggled at my brain—like an evil elf had tapped me on the shoulder. "You know, if you give me your card, I could call you if you leave your wallet behind again."

There. His cheeks went dusky pink. I finally got a blush out of him, but hell if I could decipher what it meant. I could predict people's taste in coffee, down to preferred syrup flavor, but I still sucked at decoding anything as complex as human emotions.

"Ah. Um." He did the nervous cough thing again.

"Never mind." I wiped my hands on my apron. "I'd better get back."

"Wait." He opened the wallet, plucked out a white card with a blue logo, and offered it to me. His broad fingers brushed mine again as he handed it over. Another barely there touch, but I felt the charge all the way down my spine, like I'd chugged a triple shot.

My breath tripped with wishing he'd add a "call me anytime." Brian would have. But David just stood there silently. Straighter than the Fremont Bridge and denser than a concrete pylon.

"I'm Robby, by the way," I offered, mainly as a way to fill up the awkward silence.

"Thanks . . . Robby." David said the name like it didn't quite fit. And I guess it didn't—people expect to hear an Asian name like Kim or Jae, not Robert Edwards Junior. I was Robby, Dad was Bob, and we hadn't spoken in weeks. Dad was actually cooler with the whole gay thing than my Korean mom, but it was an uneasy acceptance, punctuated by uncomfortable phone calls and infrequent visits.

The pink had returned to David's cheeks and I almost said something else, but then he pushed through the doors and was gone.

As I walked back to my cart, I glanced down at his card.

David Gregory, Finance Director
Library Trust

Huh. Not so very corporate after all. And he'd been walking six blocks—past a Starbucks, a Tully's, and two other buildings with coffee carts—to *my* cart. Those two small facts made my stomach all quivery again.

# Chapter 2

Waterfront Park was ablaze with rainbows: banners, sidewalks, T-shirts, tattoos, wigs, face paint. I felt positively monochromatic as I brushed my hands across my black apron and peered around the balloons—rainbow-colored, of course—bobbing cheerfully from Chris's People's Coffee trailer. My old boss, Chris, had scored a primo spot in the park's food vending area for Pride weekend. Since he'd helped me get my current cart, I didn't really feel I could turn him down with "Gee, I'd rather watch the parade and find a willing stranger to make out with."

Not that making out was likely to happen. I could count on one hand with fingers left over the number of times I'd gotten laid in the last year. Purchasing my cart, recovering from Brian, and my general awkwardness with the dating and hookup scene kept my bed cold and my wrist sore.

The line for coffee was at least six deep. I got back to work, not sure if I should feel grateful I didn't have time to linger on my painfully single state. Even with five baristas, the line stayed long for the entire Saturday shift. By the six o'clock close of the festival, I was too beat even to enjoy the people watching. The night offered tons of parties and celebrations. But my feet ached and I could only manage going through the motions at Slaughters before giving into exhaustion and collapsing into my bed, in a quiet house.

My roommates rolled in around dawn, reminding me that I still had to get through one more day of Pride. So much for getting laid. My new goal was simply to endure. Something about being an employee again—albeit it a temporary one—made even my smallest bones ache. I'd stumbled into the coffee-cart business the same way I did everything else in my life, but it was *mine*. I'd come to Portland for college, stayed for Brian, and had a tiny inheritance land in my lap just in time to get in on the coffee-cart opportunity.

When I arrived for the Sunday shift, I was grateful to find the crowd was lighter and more hungover, which meant fewer fancy drinks and a lot more Americanos and triple shots. Lounging against the table with the blenders, I was about to let one of the younger baristas take the next customer when I caught sight of a familiar dark head.

The hair on the back of my neck perked up. David's appearance was far more energizing than the iced soy latte with two extra shots I'd been sipping. "I've got this one," I murmured to the blue-haired barista.

"Whatever," she muttered with a classic teenage eye roll.

I sidled up to the counter. "Didn't expect to see you here. What can I do you for?" Even though I'd already established that flirty didn't work with David, I went for it anyway. After all, he was *here,* right?

He studied the limited menu, scratching his smooth chin. He had the sort of complexion that could easily go scruffy, but even casual he still exuded a nerdy-prep look. His green polo shirt and khaki pants with a canvas belt and loafers made me think of fancy boat parties. And of things people could get up to *on* boats. But then, something about his too-serious eyes had always made me think of sex.

"Vanilla latte. Iced. Another hot one today." He made a vague gesture at the sunny skies.

"Gotta love June in Portland. I want to bottle up the sun and save it for January."

"June makes monsoon season totally worth it." He drum-med his fingers against the metal shelf of the order window.

The weather. We were back to talking about the freaking weather. I wanted to let out a full-on diva scream.

I hadn't missed Brian in ages, but I did right then. He'd always had a way of moving things along to their natural conclusion—us included. And of course his bossy self would have taken issue with my too-spiky hair and too-flashy glasses and shy smile. Brian never would have *let* me be the one to move first. *Be bold,* I lectured myself. *Clearly David's not going to be.*

"So. You enjoying the festival? See any interesting booths?"

"Not sure." He colored an adorable shade of pink. "Just got here. Came for a coffee mainly."

I couldn't help it. I beamed. *Did he come for me?* My heart leapt a little, even though it shouldn't.

"This your first Pride?"

"That obvious?" He did that nervous cough of his again.

"Just a little." I tried to keep my voice light, even as my smile tightened up. *A tourist.* I should have figured. After Brian, I didn't have much interest in closeted guys or being someone's science experiment, even someone as endearingly bumbling as David.

The barista working the machine slid me David's drink and I gingerly handed it over.

"Thanks. Guess I should . . . look around a bit. I've still got some work to catch up on later." After he paid, he lingered at the window, his mouth twitching like he wanted to say something else.

Hope, stupid and unwarranted, reared its head again, taking over my better sense.

"Wait. Want me to show you around? I can take my break."

"You don't have to do that."

"It's no problem. Be fun." *Please don't make me play some sort of offer-and-refuse game.*

"Really? Um. Okay. That would be . . . nice."

*Thank the flying spaghetti monster.* The distant beat of the music stage thrummed through me, muscles twitching with nervous energy. I hadn't taken many breaks, so when I asked to be cut loose for a while Chris waved me off without looking up. I exited the trailer through the rear door. An awning had been erected to cover the trailer's extra supplies and I tossed my apron next to a big carton of cups.

Running a quick hand through my hair, I made my way to the front of the trailer, where David had taken a seat at a folding picnic table.

"Hey." *Hell.* I didn't have a clue what to say.

David blinked a few times, like he'd stared too long into the still-new June sun. His gaze held a whole lot of scrutiny and nowhere near as much heat as I'd wished.

"What?" I asked.

"Nothing." A faint flush crept up his neck. "Just realized I've never seen you without your apron on."

"Guess not." I resisted the urge to preen. Since it was Pride, I'd worn my tight red KEEP CALM T-shirt and wriggled my ass into my tiniest black jeans. My boots had thick lug soles but, even so, when

David stood he had a good two inches on me. He wasn't crazy tall, which was good because I didn't like being with dudes who made me feel like a midget. David's wide shoulders and sturdy, capable build made him seem substantial without teetering into overpoweringly ripped.

"So . . ." He fiddled with his straw, and I half-expected him to bolt any second.

"What would you like to see first?" I gestured at the booths surrounding us. I needed this conversation to move out of awkward land and walking around could only help.

"I have no idea really. I'm not picky."

"Easy to please, huh?" I raised an eyebrow.

"I guess." His cheeks went ruddy and he looked away. Hell. I had no idea what to make of that blush. For the millionth time I wished I were better at interacting instead of merely observing.

"How about the music stage?" I wasn't much in the mood for visiting the same vendors I saw each year. There were only so many T-shirts one could own after all. If I hadn't been working for Chris, I would have spent most of the day watching the bands.

"Sure." He followed me as we headed toward the main stage, winding our way through the crowds and tents. After we made our way out of the rows of tents, we had an impressive view of the waterfront and the bridge. While we walked, I kept glancing over to see what David was thinking about the rainbow explosion.

*Exuberant* is the best word for Portland Pride. It's not the spectacle of San Francisco or the statement of New York and Boston. Hamburg's Pride had been my first, almost a decade ago. I'd snuck away from the German base where my dad had been stationed to attend the parade. I hadn't been out to my parents yet, and I barely knew enough German to get around public transit and buy food. It didn't matter— merely being around so many out, happy people had given me a rush I'd felt for weeks afterward.

Ever since, I'd made a point of attending Pride regardless of where I lived. Portland was my favorite because of how laid-back yet unabashedly happy everyone was. It was a little like a giant family reunion, only with a lot more color, and everyone liked each other or at least pretended to for the weekend.

Even as I told myself not to care, I found myself watching what made David's eyes go wide, like a quartet of drag queens who towered over both of us and a woman holding a poodle dressed in a rainbow tutu. Skin—half-naked people like the guy on a unicycle with a seat shaped like a dick wearing nothing but a G-string—earned a double take from David, as did couples draped over each other.

Guess I was watching for more clues about who David was. Freed from the counter between us, he felt more . . . real.

"So how is it that this is your first Pride?" I asked. It was a clear fishing expedition, but I *needed* to know more about the status of his closet door.

"Up until two years ago I lived in Idaho—and Small Basin isn't exactly a hotbed of Pride activities." His half grin didn't provide nearly enough answers to the questions that abruptly formed on my tongue.

"You move here for your job?" What I wanted to ask was whether he'd moved here to be out. But I kept dancing around the things I *really* wanted to know.

"Something like that." Damn cryptic man, making things twenty times harder. I couldn't ask and he couldn't tell. My inner Navy brat gave a snicker.

David and I stood at the edge of the crowd; some people sat in folding chairs, others on blankets, and plenty of people stood too. The areas closer to the stage were tightly packed. Back where we stood it wasn't as crazy crowded and we could still hear each other speak.

"How about you? You a Portland native?" David's desire to move the conversation away from himself was almost palpable, his eyes going more eager and his lips turning upward.

"Nah. I'm from everywhere."

"Everywhere?" Ordinarily when people ask me if I'm from *here* they pause expectantly, their tone not unlike when they compliment me on how good my English is. But David's tone held nothing but genuine interest, and that made me more talkative than usual.

"Military brat. Born in South Korea, then we hit Maine, Florida, Japan, and Germany before my dad got his twenty years."

"What was his job?" David moved closer to me as the music swelled, giving me an almost light-headed sensation.

"He worked as a Naval medic, but he's a nurse now. Met my mom in Korea, but they live in Virginia currently. She owns a clothing store and . . ." I was rambling, but being around him was a strange mixture of giddiness at his nearness and nervousness that I would screw things up. The dueling emotions were par for the course for me, but I still had to take a deep breath. Not that it helped, because I could smell David—faint ocean-scented soap, a little sweat, and something unique to him that made my blood hum like a MAX train.

"What are you doing in the Northwest?"

I was tempted to give as cryptic an answer as he had, but the warmth in my chest made my tongue loose.

"Came for college at Reed. Stayed for an evil ex-boyfriend. Decided PhD track in linguistics wasn't for me. Lucked out on landing the coffee business."

"Evil ex, huh?" His lips twitched. Oh, man. I loved that he'd latched on to the ex bit almost as much as I loved the way his lips moved. Warmth spread from my chest farther south.

"Yeah. Very evil and very ex. And he's probably wandering around here somewhere." I sighed, having long resigned myself to the relative smallness of the Portland gay scene and Brian's ability to turn up where I least wanted him.

"Really?" David craned his neck as if Brian might pop up at any moment. It was a ridiculously cute, almost protective gesture. His shoulders seemed wider, his hair more ruffled. Jealous? My insides bubbled up like an Italian soda, all sweetness and giddy anticipation.

"Who knows?" I shrugged. "Probably somewhere avoiding people with cameras. He's out in Portland, but not Provo." That part of Brian I hadn't made peace with, not during our four years together and not after. It was especially hard because after we broke up I'd watched him cannonball into the bar scene, making a desperate splash by sleeping with anyone and everyone, all the while drowning in dishonesty, undoubtedly hurting himself and a lot of other people.

And here I was standing with a guy who was quite possibly *more* closeted than Brian. David's nervous glances said the entire scene was new to him. Of course the Portland scene was usually a bit more subdued, but Pride was special, bringing out skin and body paint and screaming-loud outfits. A guy in front of us was wearing pink briefs and rainbow knee-highs and nothing else. To our left, the Portland Leather Men were all decked out, complete with chaps and studded harnesses.

I adored this sort of people watching, but I could tell it unsettled

David. He kept shuffling his feet, his face alternating between horrified and fascinated.

"Want to walk a bit more?"

"Sure." He shoved both hands in his pockets as he walked next to me.

*Well all righty, then.* Not that I'd been planning on holding his hand or anything, but his very clear keep-your-distance signal deflated whatever stupid hope had been brewing in my brain. My skin felt chilled, despite the unseasonably balmy breeze.

We walked the perimeter of the concert, still able to hear the music as we traveled the park's sidewalks. I asked him about his job and some of my tension eased when I saw a little smile tug at his lips.

"I love what we do at the Library Trust," he said. "I've loved libraries ever since I was a kid. It was my favorite building in town. One of the only brick buildings and one of the few air-conditioned public spaces."

"Me too. Always loved when we lived places with a good library."

"Can't imagine moving as often as you."

"Eh. It wasn't terrible."

"I lived my whole life in Small Basin, except for two years of graduate school in Spokane. And then I moved here." His eyes darted away from mine, but not before I saw a flash of pain. It made me want to hug him, but his hands were still jammed into his pockets, his shoulders stiffer than a new recruit's. No hugging happening here.

I plopped down on a nearby bench. From here we could see the river as well as the sea of festival tents. I needed to be getting back to the coffee trailer, but I was reluctant to walk away from David.

Even as frustrated as my libido was, the rest of me really liked hanging around David. I felt calm, my usual frantic mental life slowed to his meandering pace. I was nervous, sure, but I was *always* nervous. With David, I wanted to work past the nerves and frustration over how hard he was to read because of the undercurrent of *rightness*—like we'd sat like this a hundred times. He was a fabulous listener, and gradually my nervous rambling slowed to a leisurely talk about our jobs. Budget cuts across the country were affecting both of us, although inadequate funding for summer reading programs felt a bit more urgent than my inability to shake free of my roommates. We were both dependent on how much spending cash people had.

I thought again about his bagged lunch and the contrast of his coffee habit. He loved his job—that much was clear even if nothing much else about him was. Could it possibly be that he'd been coming for *me* and was just shy? Or was I merely a convenient gateway to a community he had a passing interest in? Or maybe he was lonely and open-minded and not in the least bit gay? I hated the chaos in my brain. I had studied words for years, and yet I still couldn't find the ones I needed to ask what I *really* wanted to know.

"I should be getting back." My words hung heavy with regret, giving him ample opportunity to—

"Me too."

*Hell.* I couldn't flirt and he couldn't pick up signals. Quite the pair.

As if our bodies were determined to prove how mismatched we were, David stretched his arms over his head at the same moment I stood to leave and inadvertently whacked me in the head. I stumbled backward, forehead smarting, as he jumped to his feet.

*Bonk.* Our heads collided. I started to giggle—because, really, what else was there to do—as we ended up sitting on the bench again wincing and face-to-face. He didn't move. He didn't return my semi-hysterical laughter. Instead, he breathed deeply, like he'd been waiting for a chance to . . .

*What the hell.* I closed the last inches between us slowly, willing him not to pull away. I brushed my lips over his in a whisper of a kiss. Compared to the stuff happening around the stage back at the festival, it was laughably tame. But it was also the single most significant moment of my last two months. My nerve endings thrummed with anticipation—a clear, crisp train whistle signaling oncoming change, making every cell in my body sit up and take notice.

I didn't have to figure out when to deepen the kiss—he solved that, kissing me back as if I was an offering at Portland's famed Voodoo Doughnuts and he'd been waiting in line for hours to sample some sugary goodness. His arm came around my shoulder, hauling me closer. Tongue sweeping inside my mouth, he took control.

The way he kissed was the way he walked and spoke and ate—earnestly, and with a single-minded focus. *This* was why I was attracted to him—there was a quiet desperation lurking behind his calm façade, a sense that when he did a task, he did it *well*. Like *Ohmyfuckinggawwwwwwwwwwd* well. My spine lit up like a pinball game, electricity zooming everywhere and David earning all sorts of bonus points with his strong hand massaging the back of my neck, anchoring me.

Like I was going anywhere. I grabbed fistfuls of his cotton shirt, my fingers on a mission to get our bodies closer—

A wolf whistle cut through the haze of sensation. David jerked away from me. He slid to the opposite end of the bench so fast his khakis likely left scorch marks.

"I'm sorry." Resting his head on his hands, his breath came in ragged gulps. He looked as shaken as I felt, but those were *not* the words I wanted to hear from him.

"No one cared. It's Pride, after all." I forced myself to laugh.

"I meant that shouldn't have happened." He still wasn't looking at me. He hissed air between his teeth, a sad, low sound that hit me right in the sternum. "Shouldn't have gotten that carried away . . . I better head back."

"Wait." I grabbed his arm as he stood. I didn't want things to end like this.

"Yeah?" He looked down at me, his expression wary and guarded.

Logic said to let him walk away. But my hand held tight. While I hadn't done nearly as much kissing as most of my friends, I'd kissed enough to know lug-sole bending, willpower-unraveling kisses didn't come along very often. Especially not with a guy as intriguing and confounding as David. I felt like my body had been drugged—brain fogged over, feet and hands all clammy, muscles aching.

I forced myself to say what I'd wanted to say for the last hour. "Come over to my place tonight. No audience . . ." I gestured at the park while giving him my most friendly look—the one that usually earned me bigger tips or a dance partner at the clubs. I couldn't pull off seductive, but I could do a very good I'm-fun-and-nonthreatening face.

He didn't say anything. He was looking over my head at the sky-line behind me. He sucked in a huge lungful of air and held it. And held it.

"I live close to the Lloyd Center MAX stop. Easy." I remembered his relief at getting back his TriMet pass.

Chewing on his lip, he looked . . . wistful. Conflicted maybe. But not disinterested.

"Or dinner? Something casual?" The air felt charged, like he was *this* close to saying yes.

"I can't," he said finally.

My breath escaped in a loud hiss. I felt my muscles deflate, my shoulders slump, my head come down. I knew I looked like a kicked puppy, but when I tried to smile I failed miserably. "It's okay."

"No, it's not. I'm sorry . . ." He brushed his hands off on his pants. "I . . . I can't." He walked away at a fast clip, away from the festival, away from me, away from any chance of this being something more than the strange little dance of two dudes over coffee, a counter forever between us.

# Chapter 3

My coffee—fair-trade, hand-roasted, and god-awful expensive in bulk—tasted like it was dipped straight from the Columbia River. The sounds of people passing through the building grated against my ears like a whining weed eater. But Monday didn't care that I had a splitting headache and the worst hangover I'd had in years.

I had still rolled out of bed at 4:30, rolled up the cart's metal grating at 5:45, and served my first customer of the day at 6:14. That's the thing I hated about owning my own business: I couldn't call in sick. Of course it would have only made me feel sicker to bail on work because I was heartsick over some guy who'd been little more than a crush and was now . . .

Nothing.

Monday came and went and Tuesday should have been easier but wasn't. No big surprise that David stayed away. Then Wednesday, just before noon, I spotted him holding the heavy brass door open for some older ladies. He'd cut his hair and his shirt looked brand-new— icy blue, starched into submission, and topped with a silver tie. Tiny changes.

When he approached the cart my chest got tight, my heart clattering with ridiculous optimism despite dark clouds of logic swirling around my brain.

As luck would have it, I had three customers ahead of him. The wait to talk to him felt torturously slow, made worse by him not meeting my gaze. Not that our eyes could say everything that needed saying, but I wanted *some* sort of sign as to how this was going to go down.

*Finally.* His turn arrived and thank the goddess there was no one behind him.

"Hey." He met my eyes. Sunday hung between us, heavy and cold, like laundry someone had been stupid enough to hang outside in November.

"What'll it be?" I struggled to keep my voice even, keep this casual.

He glanced at my specials sign. Berry season had officially arrived and I had a blackberry smoothie on offer, as well as a blackberry mocha. Personally, I wasn't one for mixing fruit with coffee, but they'd been among my better-selling specials.

He took a very long moment, breathing hard, like a test loomed. And maybe it did—not from me but from himself. I waited. And waited.

"The usual?" I sighed as I grabbed a cup. "Hot?" The teasing June weather had slipped back to cool.

"Yeah. Wait." He held up a broad hand. "I'll try the blackberry thing. Hot. And a short."

*I've got hot and short right here.* I wished I could be that kind of flirty. But I wasn't, so all I managed was "Really?"

"Sure." His shoulders straightened, making him seem taller. "I think it's time for something new."

"Yeah?" I had to busy myself with making the drink to keep my hands from shaking.

"Yeah. Look, I'm sorry about Sunday—"

"No biggie," I lied. My heart thumped out a beat worthy of a dance track.

"Yeah. It was. Or at least to me it was." He raised his eyebrows, his shrewd gaze calling me on the lie. The queasiness in my stomach increased, but behind it was a pleasant tingle. He wasn't going to let me escape behind bland niceties. He *cared* how I felt.

"Okay, it was. But it's also okay that you weren't into it or into it in public or whatever . . ."

"I've been doing a lot of thinking the last few days. I'm sorry if I've led you on."

"You haven't." My heart attempted to touch my toes—emotional yoga. I hated this. Hated everything about this. I accidentally gave him too much syrup, but my hands shook too badly to fix it.

"I like you. A lot." He was a shade of beet red that my complexion could never manage, but on him it looked adorable, making him more vulnerable, more touchable than his always-professional exterior.

"Yeah?" I grinned at him. "I like you too." I tossed the drink and started over. When he didn't say anything I said, "But?"

"But I was with someone for twelve years."

I did some fast math. He'd likely been a teenager when he got together with a nameless guy he'd obviously been deeply involved with.

"And?" I nodded, encouraging him to keep going.

"And now he's gone. Dead. And I'm here. And I've spent two years and a whole lot of cash on grief counseling, trying to make sense of that. And coming here the last few months . . . it helps."

*Dead.* He'd said the word in a rusty voice that seemed to scrape against his throat on the way out. My Brian problems suddenly felt ridiculously self-centered and petty. So what if I had a lousy ex I'd never loved quite as much as I'd pretended? I'd been the one to walk away.

"I can't imagine . . ." I whispered.

"I don't think anyone can." His laugh was as brittle as sugar crystals. "And we weren't out. Not until after . . ."

"Geez. That sucks." A whole bunch of things started making sense.

"But he was a sheriff's deputy and I was an accountant and . . . it made sense at the time. But now . . ." he trailed off.

"Now you're here."

"Now I'm here. And the grief counselor my sister found for me—"

"Your family knows?"

"Everyone knows. Now." He rolled his eyes like that distinction wasn't supposed to matter, but it kind of did to me, and the heaviness of his words suggested it wasn't exactly a small deal to him either.

"Sorry."

"It's . . . it is what it is. My grief counselor says I should start small. Ask you out for coffee—"

I couldn't help it. I burst out laughing, big peals that helped erode my nervous energy.

He smacked his head. "Heck. I rehearsed what I'd say all the way over here. All the good it did me. Obviously going for coffee would be completely stupid—"

"Hey, just because I sell the stuff doesn't mean I can't drink it recreationally." I reached across the counter and touched the sleeve of his crisp dress shirt. Man, I loved him in dress clothes. Blood rushed south and I had all sorts of ideas that had nothing to do with "starting small." I told my overeager dick to behave.

"Yeah. So maybe we could . . . uh . . ." He inhaled sharply.

"Brunch? Is that small enough? My friend Chris—ex-boss, actually—his place does a vegan brunch buffet on the weekends. Still coffee, but with scrambled tofu."

"That is *so* Portland." He laughed. "I think that might work."

"It's a date." I smiled up at him. He smiled back, revealing his perfect white teeth. I wanted to feel them sinking into my shoulder. . . . *Oh hell.* Behaving was going to be a tall order.

"Yeah." He looked both terrified and excited, not unlike how I was feeling. "It's a date."

"It's on the house," I said as I handed him his drink. After all, he wasn't only a customer anymore. I could take on the risk of giving away more than I should. He'd be worth it.

# August: Turtle Mocha

# Chapter 4

I officially hated TriMet. Thanks to stupid construction on MLK, I was over twenty minutes late for my Sunday brunch with David. Narrowed lanes and slow drivers were screwing with what should have been the best day of my week. I drummed my fingers on the cool glass of the bus window.

I didn't think he'd leave; we'd been doing this too many weeks for him to worry I'd stand him up. But he hadn't responded to my text about the bus being late. Little things like delays made David twitchy. The last thing I wanted was David uncomfortable; I had big plans for this week's date.

Finally, the bus pulled up to the stop near People's Coffee. As I'd feared, the line stretched past the entry of the narrow brick storefront. David and I liked to get there early enough to beat the worst of the brunch rush. For six Sundays now this had been our thing, and my heart did a happy little thump as I spotted him.

He was hanging to the side of the line like he couldn't quite decide whether he wanted to join the queue or not. I waved, but David was on his phone and didn't look up. He was scowling, his phone jammed between his shoulder and his ear, but the sight of him still made my chest lighten.

His hair was in a growing-out phase, and the August breeze made the fluff dance. He was way overdressed for brunch on Alberta, but I secretly loved him in preppy stuff like today's baby blue short-sleeve dress shirt. I didn't like it *on* him so much as I wanted to unbutton it with my teeth, slide my hands against his warm skin. I wanted—

"Hi, you!" David finally spotted me and waved me over. Giving me an awkward one-armed hug, he wrapped up his phone call with an "I'll call you later" and a heavy sigh.

"Everything okay?" I stepped closer to encourage him not to drop his arm.

"Sure." His eyes followed the traffic on Alberta, where cars jockeyed for the few remaining parking spots. "Just my sister. Usual family drama. And she's coming next week."

"Your sister's coming?"

"Her biannual trek." David rolled his eyes. "She *says* it's for back-to-school shopping, but really it's to check up on me. Make sure I haven't withered away. Food in the fridge. Typical bossy big sister." Affection underscored his complaints.

"She's staying with you?" I knew what neighborhood he lived in, but I didn't know his address. Six weeks into our erstwhile relationship and I still hadn't seen the place.

"God no." David laughed. "Her husband's a surgeon. She's staying at the Sentinel Hotel. Her husband's lucky Melanie doesn't come shop more often."

"My mom does the same thing. Always brings a cooler full of food for my fridge and acts like I can't tie my own shoes."

"Mel was great right after . . ." He wiggled his hand and I knew he meant the seldom-discussed death of his lover. "She's the one who encouraged me to move and make a fresh start. But now she acts like the rest of the family—like I'm a million miles away and in constant big-city danger."

"My folks live outside of DC. Way more congested place than here, yet they act the same way. Mom's sure everyone here is smoking pot and in poly relationships."

David laughed, rich and full. Looking into his brown eyes felt like sinking into my favorite leather easy chair.

"You want me to testify that you're eating your veggies and locking your doors?" I worked hard to keep my tone joking. After all, we were hardly in the meet-the-family stage, no matter how much I wanted it.

"You would?" His eyes popped wider. Then he seemed to shrug off his startled reaction, his shoulders slumping. "Trust me. You don't want to be anywhere near Mel and her endless game of twenty questions."

"Sure I would." But my reassurance only seemed to make David more antsy; he craned his head to see the front of the line and shuffled his feet forward.

"Never mind." I squeezed his arm. Being around him felt comforting, like butterscotch candy, and I didn't want to crunch up that feeling by being too pushy.

"Yeah," David said, his attention diverted by the moving line. A group of college kids exited the restaurant, tasty aromas wafting from their reusable coffee cups and plates overflowing with baked goods. They claimed one of the wrought-iron tables in the outdoor seating area. The clatter of dishes and the hum of voices made me more impatient to get inside.

My muscles felt heavy, like I'd slogged through a rainstorm despite the happy, sunny Sunday crowd, my shoulders stiffened with familiar misgivings. Was I ever going to see David's place? Was I ever going to meet his family? Was I the world's biggest chump for holding on to hope with this guy?

"Um, David . . ."

"Yeah?"

He looked down at me and, like he knew I was about to blurt a bunch of worries about what the hell we were doing here, he did that David thing that always kept me hanging on. He sent me a smile. *The* smile. The one where his lids went droopy and his eyes went dark and his mouth quirked in a sly smile. There was nothing "just friends" about the quiet seduction in his eyes.

My rigid shoulders went limp and liquid and I swayed toward him. He took my hand, squeezed my fingers, and, okay, I wanted a lot more from the guy, but holding David's hand made me feel as bright and sweet as the fresh-squeezed orange juice on the end of the buffet.

"Sorry again for being late," I offered.

"It's okay." He shrugged, his big shoulders tugging on the cotton of his shirt in a way that made me want to see that shirt on the floor. "Hopefully we don't end up squished in with a big group."

"Hey, I don't mind being squished in with you." Understatement. I'd *love* to be squished in with him in my ancient single bed.

But that wasn't happening anytime soon. Six weeks of brunch, the occasional quick dinner, three movies, and a few games of disc golf, and the best I could hope for was some passionate parting groping.

David moved at such a glacial pace that he seemed almost indifferent to sex. Me, though? I was going nuts. My palms sweat, my dick hurt, and my brain played a never-ending loop of porno-riffic possibilities.

I knew that David was slowly winding his way past his grief and out of his self-imposed closet. Each week brought something new—like us holding hands right there on the middle of Alberta. And David hadn't even turned pink. With David, I was learning to savor the little things like the weight of his hand in mine, the slide of his thumb against the sensitive groove above my wrist.

"You find a spot to park?" Where he'd parked dictated what sort of good-bye I could expect. Right then, with his hot eyes and delicious spicy scent, I *needed* something more than scrambled tofu to look forward to.

"Right there." He pointed, and I saw his Civic a block down the street.

"Great job scoring a prime spot." Too bad the spot on the busy street meant the most *I* was scoring was a quick peck. This stretch of Alberta was a gentrified mecca for weekend foot traffic, Salt & Straw bringing in the tourists and the little restaurants and shops claiming the locals. Maybe I could talk him into an afternoon movie. The dark theater should be good for some quality groping.

"You wanna catch a movie after this? That new superhero-in-space thing is supposed to be good."

"Can't. Got a report due tomorrow." He made a sour face.

We finally got inside the coffee place. It had a distinctly northwestern vibe—long narrow space, with big wooden communal tables lining one wall and a few smaller tables shoved to one side. The vegan brunch buffet was set up in the space usually occupied by two ancient couches.

"Want to come over tonight after you finish?" *Please.* As we approached the battered wooden counter, I put on a puppy face that had worked to get me laid in the past. "My roommates might be gone."

I'd managed to convince him to come over twice, but both times we hadn't ventured farther than the living room couch.

"Ah. Uh. I'll probably be late. In fact, I think I'd better order an extra shot in my coffee." He stepped up to the counter, oblivious to having cock blocked me. *Again.*

He paid for my coffee and food—something he'd done from the beginning. No matter how many times I offered, he always gently shoved my wallet away.

"Hey! They have the raisin toast you like so much." Making his way down the buffet, David leaned over to load three slices onto my plate. That. That right there was why I put up with my dick being in knots. Didn't matter if it took us another three months to get to second base. David took care of me in a way that no other boyfriend ever had. He was sweet and old-fashioned and held open doors and remembered my favorite foods. He shepherded me to a spot at the end of one of the tables. He fussed, making sure I was happy with the spot before seating himself. No one had ever really fussed over me before, and I liked how warm and squishy it felt to let him take care of me.

"So. Tell me more about your Mom." He leaned forward, his eyes bright over his coffee. "What sorts of food does she bring?"

Yeah. He really *was* the best part of my week. My dick could wait.

On Monday I had a line five deep when he stepped up to the counter, so all I could manage was a sexy smile and comping his drink. He went over to his usual table, but I knew he would keep his eyes on me through most of his lunch. We'd gotten to the point where we could hold entire conversations with our eyes.

Like when a young secretary placed a seven-drink order, David's eyebrow quirked as he watched me scurry for the cup holders. He glanced back at the bank of elevators leading to the upper floors and shot me a look that said, *Law firm upstairs must be working on a big settlement.*

*Too bad they never tip.* I sent a rueful head shake back.

*At least you don't have to work with them all day.* He smiled and toasted me with his cup.

We both watched her juggle the cup carriers across the atrium.

David and I spent a lot of lunches like that, people watching. It made me feel connected to him in a surprisingly good way. Made me feel . . . well, *bonded* felt like a silly emotion for such an ordinary exchange, but I was used to working on my own. I had a college student assistant a few hours a week, but otherwise my days were largely my own. Having someone to share even a small slice of my day felt like an indulgence. With David I had someone to tell funny customer stories, someone who would counter with stories of eccentric donors, someone who genuinely cared about the answer to "How's it going?"

Things quieted down toward the end of David's lunch. He came back over, tossing his garbage in the can near my cart.

"Busy day?" I asked.

"Crazy. And not just work. This thing with my sister has thrown a wrench in my week. I swear, one more text from her and I'm going to

toss my phone. And this without her even here yet." He sounded ex-
asperated yet affectionate—the sort of way people talked about beloved
siblings. I wouldn't know. Life as an only child had been lonely, and I
envied him the siblings, even meddling as they appeared to be.

"Let me know if I can help."

"Will do." Reaching across the counter, he ruffled my hair, grinning at me like he'd kiss me if we weren't in public. My heart did a
little flip and I wanted to bottle up the moment.

"You want to grab a slice of pizza after work?" He grinned, a sheepish
smile that turned my insides to caramel sauce. "Maybe about five-
thirty?"

"Can't. Supplier meeting. How about I come by after?"

"Eh." He looked away. "Better not. We've both got early mornings
tomorrow."

"Yeah, but I make killer pancakes." I winked at him. That got an
impressive blush from him, red spreading from his neck all the way
up to his ears.

What it didn't get, however, was a yes.

"*Wellllll . . .*" He studied my menu like it held the key to a tactful
decline.

"Never mind." I grabbed a dish towel and vigorously scrubbed my
already sparkling counter. "Was only a thought."

"A nice one." He gave me a sad, crooked smile. "Another time
maybe?"

"Yeah." Hope and doubt played a frantic ping-pong game in my
gut as he walked away.

Tuesday I got a text from David around 11:50: *Stuck in a meeting.
No lunch* ☹ ☹ The frownies made me grin because David *so* was not
an emoticon sort of guy. My shoulders lightened a bit too. Wasn't like
I had a clue what to say to him, how to get things moving to the next
level.

*Don't you want to make love?* I could ask. Or maybe, *Why don't
you want to make love?* would be the better question. I knew he
wanted me—it was in his eyes whenever he looked at me; it was in
the hard press of his body against mine when we kissed good night; it
was in his tight grip on my shoulders as he reluctantly pulled away.
And that was the part I simply wasn't getting: the reluctance. Was it
the dead lover? Was it some internal timetable he had? Was he wait-

ing for some sort of signal from me? I wanted to be patient because
David was kind and funny and an incredible listener. He deserved to
move at his own speed. However, it didn't matter how many times I
told myself that; my lust kept revving like an impatient sports car at
each new stoplight.

I still didn't have a clue what to say when he appeared at 3:15,
during the slowest part of my day.

"Where's everyone?" David's wide smile cut past all my frustration. He glanced around the deserted atrium. The heading-home traffic would justify my afternoon hours, but this time of day was my
dead zone.

"I ate them." I grinned up at him. No pissy mood could withstand
the sight of David in a suit. Dark gray with a subtle stripe, it made
him look like a very expensive truffle waiting for me to unwrap. And
a David who'd broken his routine just to squeeze in a visit with me?
Yeah. I was mush.

"Have a drink with me?" He gestured at the espresso machine.

"Sure." As usual, I was overcaffeinated, so I made myself a mint
tea. "You want your regular?"

"Let me see . . ." He studied the specials board. "What the heck?
No one *really* drinks banana caramel coffee, do they?"

"It's a latte, not coffee." I adopted a fake snooty voice. "And it was
big-time popular this morning."

David gave a fake shudder as he turned back toward me. "How
about you make that mocha thing you talked me into last week?"

"A turtle? It's got caramel too. Better watch out: next thing you
know, you'll be begging me for all sorts of crazy."

"Never know. I just might," he said softly, and my heart fluttered.

"Yeah?" I put up my BACK SOON sign and followed him to the closest table. "You're in a good mood this afternoon."

"One of our biggest donors sent over box tickets for Saturday's
Timbers game. Whole office gets to go."

"Neat." I tried to match his level of enthusiasm. I wasn't much
into sports. David was the nerdy type of fan, waxing poetic over statistics and advanced analytics. My dad was more the yelling-at-the-
TV type of sports fan, but thanks to him I had a working vocabulary
to discuss David's favorite teams. Luckily, David was happy to listen
to me go on about this season's *Design Star.* It all balanced out.

"You want to come?" He cocked his head to one side, waiting.

My heart skipped a beat as I realized he'd walked over to the atrium just to ask me.

"Sure." I'd endure far worse things than a soccer game for this man.

"Good. My boss said we could bring family or a friend or whatever."

"So tell me," I said, unable to resist, "do I qualify as a friend or as a whatever?"

"Friend," he said, nodding. "You could never be just a whatever to me, Robby." David gave one of his patented smiles—lust in his eyes, tenderness around his mouth. I was toast. How could I argue with the Smile?

Mutely, I nodded my agreement.

# Chapter 5

As expected, David introduced me as his friend. I really was grateful he'd telegraphed his intent earlier in the week; I'd had a chance to focus on the bright side of meeting David's work friends. It helped that we'd had a nice long chat on the phone the night before—one of those meandering conversations in which we ended up swapping childhood summer vacation stories before noticing we'd been on the phone for two hours.

The party atmosphere in the box helped too. In addition to the seats overlooking the field, the space included a catered buffet and a cash bar. A microbrew and a veggie burger made me a cheerful guy.

"A vegetarian option all it takes to make you happy?" David asked. His green Timbers polo gave his brown eyes a hazel cast that I found very sexy.

"I'm easy."

"That so?" David arched one bushy eyebrow, holding my gaze as he took a long sip of his beer. For all he'd "friended" me, he wasn't exactly playing things closeted. He'd been more flirty than usual, and his second beer had him standing closer to me, brushing against my shoulders.

It was almost like he was . . . testing the waters. Easing into something. The idea made my chest tighten. It was easy to forget that this was all new to him—being out, big-city living. On the phone, I had asked if he was out at work.

*"Um. It hasn't really come up before. There are other gay people there, though, so it's not like it's some big issue like it would have been back home."*

That answer hadn't given me a lot of clarity to go on, but I didn't want to break the spell of casual touches and loose laughter. This side of David—the giddy boy getting to watch the game from the fancy seats—made my heart all warm, made me want to cuddle him up.

"You want another beer before we sit down?" he asked.

"I can get it," I offered since he was one of the few people paying any attention to the game. Most people loitered to the back and sides of the box, gossiping or chasing kids who refused to stay seated.

"Nah. I need to find the facilities too." *The facilities.* That was my old-fashioned man. I hid a smile as he walked away.

I spotted a two-mom couple trying to corral twin toddlers. My gut did a weird flip and my neck got all prickly as I got a glimpse of a future I hadn't realized I'd wanted. Lord knew my ass of an ex hadn't been the settle-down type. Hadn't even been the live-together type. I couldn't exactly bring up adoption to a guy who let his parents believe he had an overseas missionary girlfriend. But for the first time, I wondered if I would ever be a parent. Be partnered together with someone for decades, not a few months or even a couple of years.

I hadn't ever met someone I could see keeping around for decades, but David had this solidness to him. A steadiness that made me want to lean into him. Yeah, I could picture him painting walls or mowing grass. His dependability was a huge part of the attraction for me.

I hadn't been able to count on a lot in life—all the moves as a kid, grad school that never panned out, boyfriends who moved on, an uncertain business climate. David seemed like the sort of guy to be as unwavering as a Douglas fir. His trust might be a tad difficult to earn, but there was never any question for me of whether it would be worth it—loyal guys like him didn't show up every day.

I didn't realize I'd been staring at his retreating form until a feminine voice said, "You guys are so cute."

"Well . . . um . . ." I honestly had no clue what to say. "Thanks" was on the tip of my tongue, but I had no idea how David would feel about her comment.

"I'm Carol." The midforties blonde saved me from more floundering. "I work with David in accounting. I'm so delighted he brought someone." She gave me a conspiratorial smile—one I wasn't sure whether to return.

"Fun night." Stunning conversationalist I was not.

"We had a bet." Carol's hair was swept back in a gold clip and her

Timbers shirt with matching scarf and denim skort gave her a youthful look. I could totally picture her as a cheerleader, trying to ensure all her friends had *fun*.

"A bet?" My stomach sank.

"Oh, not a mean one." She lightly tapped my shoulder. "Betsy in public relations and I decided that David *must* be seeing someone. He's seemed so much happier lately."

"He has?" I forgot I was supposed to be playing it cool.

"Totally. Lighter. He jokes even. Before . . . well, even now sometimes, there's just always this seriousness about him. Like a sadness almost, you know?"

"He's a great guy." I did know exactly what she meant—it was the deep weariness that dogged even his widest smiles, but it felt disloyal to admit it.

"How about I introduce you to some of the girls?" Carol, my new, self-appointed BFF, herded me over to a group of women. I felt both welcomed and a bit like an exhibit at the gay petting zoo. I collected multiple invitations to go shopping. No offense to the ladies, but I'd rather get my eyebrows waxed off than shop for women's shoes.

But I smiled and made nice and tried not to overtly out David, walking a tricky line between flattery and reticence.

"There you are." David clapped me on the shoulder, an affectionate squeeze that rippled all the way down my back. "Come watch the game."

I made my good-byes to the ladies and followed him back to the seats.

"You making friends?" he asked as we settled back into our seats. Although we were up high, we had a killer view of the soccer field, supplemented by the huge Jumbotrons.

"You mind? Carol kind of dragged me over there."

"Why would I mind?" He laughed. "Carol's great. Bit pushy, like my sister, but I was hoping you'd like her."

Fresh warmth flooded my chest and his words gave me something new to obsess over as the game got underway. David tried explaining what the stats flashing on the Jumbotrons meant, but I was lucky I could tell which team had the ball—though the roar of the crowd was a pretty good clue. The antics of Timber Joey kept the green-and-yellow-clad crowd active even though Portland was trailing. Since the mascot was a larger-than-life, bear-tastic lumberjack, I didn't mind watching him one bit. As the lazy August night descended over the stadium, the lights went up and the crowd thinned out as sleepy children were carried out and tipsy partners rounded up.

David leaned forward, studying the field, still invested in the game. I was only too happy to soak up the evening, rubbing ankles and knees with him, enjoying my beer. This was the most datelike outing we'd had, and I hated to see it end. He grabbed my knee when Portland tied the score at 2 even. Timber Joey revved up his chainsaw to celebrate, but my own motor was already humming from David's touch. When they pulled out the win on a last-second play, David tossed an arm around my shoulders, and for a split second I thought he might kiss me.

"You drive?" I asked as we headed for the exits.

"You kidding? Parking around here?" David laughed like I was insane. Which I was. "No. I'm only a few MAX stops away."

*Damn.* I'd been counting on a long good-bye, one that wasn't happening at the well-lit rail stop. Spotting a narrow service hallway, I tugged on his hand until we were deep in the shadows, far removed from the rest of the postgame crowd.

"What are you up to?" He offered me a bemused smile, one that said he had a pretty good guess. Heat rushed through me.

"Saying good night." I stretched up to kiss him.

Meeting me eagerly, he took over the kiss with quick nips at my lips before his tongue slid over mine, heavy and insistent. My dick went instantly, painfully hard, and I moaned into his mouth. Hands sweeping down my back, he sucked on my lower lip.

"Good night," he said before kissing me again. We traded kisses for several long minutes, time stretching out like a river of honey, thick and sweet.

"I should go." He broke the kiss, resting his forehead against mine. "But I wish we could do this all night."

"Me too. How about I ride up to your stop? We can say good-bye again there."

"You'd ride in the opposite direction just to say good night a second time?" His husky voice sounded confused but not disinterested. Sweat beaded where our foreheads touched, and his hand was warm against my back.

"Absolutely." Hadn't he realized that there wasn't much I wouldn't do for him? "For more kisses with you? I'd ride all the way to Hillsboro."

"Well, all right then." He smiled shyly as we resumed our trek to the MAX stop. He was quiet on the walk and the train, but when he touched my arm or brushed my side, anticipation crackled between us. As we exited the train, he looked around, craning his neck in an exaggerated sweep of the area.

"This is still kind of public for . . . good night." His cheeks turned bubblegum pink and I wanted to gobble him up. He was lucky I didn't jump him right there.

"I'll walk you to your building." I was happy to accept whatever flimsy excuse he needed to get me to his doorstep. Fortunately, he lived only a block and a half away in a small mid-century apartment building.

"This is still pretty out in the open." I gestured at the flat façade of the brick building. "I better walk you up."

"All right." His reply was so soft I had to strain to hear it. After typing an access code, he led us into a tiny marble lobby that had a flight of stairs and a wall of mailboxes. I brushed up against his back. I wanted to melt right into his solid bulk. Stretching up, I dropped a kiss on the back of his neck.

"I'm on three."

*Oh, goody.* I'd feared he'd settle for the relative privacy of the lobby, but he grabbed my hand, pulling me toward the stairs. I was out of breath by the time we reached floor three and not entirely because of the climb. His apartment sat at the back of a narrow hall, fluorescent lights struggling to reach the deep shadows around his door.

"So." His eyes darted around.

"So." Tugging him closer, I wrapped my arms around his neck. I kissed him softly on the lips. "Good night."

Not letting go of him, I crushed my body against his like I'd been dying to all night. Chest to chest, the collar of his polo shirt brushing my neck, our belts clinking together, finally feeling the heavy pressure of his dick next to mine. At that moment I wanted nothing more than a long, slow grind together, the kind that took hours, edging close and backing off until we were both left boneless.

I let out a soft huff as he abandoned my mouth to tongue along my jaw and neck. Goose bumps broke out down my back and my dick strained against my pants. His erection pressed against my hip. Forget slow. I was fast becoming obsessed with the idea of quick and dirty.

"David?"

"Mmm?" he mumbled against my neck, sending tingles all the way down my spine.

"Invite me in." Leaning into him, I made my point with slow rocks of my groin against his. He paused so long I had to brace myself for the rejection. I stiffened my shoulders and pulled away, telling myself that he had to move at his own pace.

But *finally,* he turned and dug a set of keys out of his pocket. Unlocking the door, he held it open for me. Once inside, I did a quick once-over of the space, registering a sea of neutrals—brown leather couch, brown curtains, brown rug.

"Oooh." His hands roaming all over my back cut my perusal short. His motions were hurried, almost frantic. My wish for leisurely lovemaking vanished. I pulled his shirt loose from his khakis and slid my hands along his bare back. The satin of his skin and the subtle ridges of bone and muscle felt so good I almost purred.

His breath came in harsh pants, like he'd raced the length of JELD-WEN stadium. His head fell back against the door. Moving my hands before they got trapped against the wall, I ventured to the fuzzy softness of his stomach. I knew exactly what I wanted next— what I'd been craving for weeks. Lust clearing away my usual reluctance to take charge, I undid his belt and his fly and dropped to my knees.

Not waiting for permission, I freed his hard cock from his boxers. They were the old-fashioned kind—crisp, light blue cotton. I spared a smile before licking the plump head of his cock.

"Ehhh. Um . . . wow." *Wow* was exactly what I was going for. I lapped all around the slit and the sensitive underside. "You . . . don't have to . . . wanted . . . for you to . . . oh, *fuck.*" The last was a strangled sound as I swallowed him deep. Darn near incoherent was even better than wow.

There were a few things in life I knew I was good at: pulling espresso shots, making pancakes, packing for a road trip, and giving head. I loved the weight of him on my tongue, the tremble in the thick vein snaking up his shaft, the salty slick taste. Making sure he knew how much I loved doing this, I moaned on the down stroke, running my hands up and down his thighs.

Wide enough to give my jaw a pleasant stretch, he was just long enough to test the limits of my deep-throating skills. But his muttered curses and whimpery moans were more than enough incentive to try to get him deeper. Wrapping my hands around his hips, I pulled him closer, using every trick I knew to relax my throat and take him all the way down to the base.

"Oh *fuck* . . . so good." David never cursed—not when we got poor service, not when he got cheated out of a prime parking spot, not when his team lost. Knowing that I could unleash his dirty side made me giddy and I laughed as I pulled back.

"*Please.* Do that again." His hands tangled in my hair, the sort of tugging and petting that made my pulse jump and my dick leak. I wanted to put a hand on myself, ease some of the pressure building in my balls, but this was too perfect, too right to move.

Besides, I could tell from the hitch in his breathing and the tremor in his cock that he was close, and I cared more about tipping him over the edge than about easing my own discomfort. I took him all the way to the root again, holding him there and swallowing hard around him.

"Jesus." That trick got him moaning loud and clenching my hair. *Almost there.* Anticipation raced through me, and I pulled back only enough to get a quick breath before diving deep, this time milking him with my throat until he groaned, his voice Barry White deep. Needing air, I slid back up, working the base with my hand while I sucked hard on the tip. That did it. A couple of quick pulls and he came on a stream of curses and full-body shudders. He tasted salty and musky and perfectly male, and it took everything I had not to join him in shooting.

"Oh. My. Word." Yup. There was my quaint dude again. Offering me a hand, he hauled me up next to him. "Wasn't expecting that when I unlocked the door."

"Complaining?" I kissed him under the ear.

"Never."

"What were you expecting?" Still concrete-pylon hard, I rocked against him. "I take requests."

"Yeah?" His voice still sounded rough.

"Totally. Whatever you want." Even though he'd come, I still wanted to indulge him. I didn't think he'd be up for anything too kinky—and even if he was, I was turned on enough to be down with just about anything he could dream up. Now that I'd handled his impressive dick, what I really wanted was to fuck, but I wasn't sure if that would be too much, too fast for him.

But if he asked? Oh, hell yes, I'd wait for him to get hard again.

His eyes took on a half-lidded, dreamy look. "This way."

Taking my hand, he led me through the sea of beige, down a narrow hallway and into his bedroom, which was a study in gray—gray comforter, gray carpeting, gray curtains. Someone needed to get this man some aqua throw pillows or something. And look at me, not even in his place fifteen minutes and already redecorating. A laugh escaped my throat.

"What?" he whispered, looking at me like I was the winning lottery ticket. The giggle died in my throat. I didn't think anyone had ever looked at me as reverently as he did right then.

"Nothing." The word was little more than a breath. I reached for the hem of my T-shirt.

"No. Let me. That's what I want." Skimming his hands down my sides, he gently pushed my hands aside.

"Sure."

Undressing me slowly, he pulled off my shirt, then folded it. I bit my lip to keep a smile back. His broad palm skimmed down my back, a meandering trail of heat. Dropping a soft kiss on my collarbone, he stroked my chest. Judging by his little smile, he liked my smooth look. In my case, it was genetic, not a waxing studio, and personally, I much preferred fuzzier men like David. He unzipped my pants but didn't go for my aching dick. Instead he motioned for me to kick free of them.

"I just . . . want to look at you." He took a half step backward and tilted his head, like I was a snapshot he'd been waiting to capture and couldn't quite figure out the angle.

"That all?" My dick strained against the stretchy cotton of my boxer briefs. The disco-beat thrum of my pulse made it hard to stay still.

"Well . . . not *all*."

"Good." Stretching up, I captured his mouth in a soft kiss. I pulled at his shirt. "You gonna let me return the favor?"

"Sure."

Removing his clothes was more of a joint effort—him pulling things off and me running my hands over every bit of exposed skin.

His dark hair contrasted with his pale skin. As I'd suspected, he had a decent pelt of chest hair smattered across his pecs, then a thicker trail down his stomach. It crinkled against my palm, but his gasp was even more gratifying. Like me, he didn't exactly have gym-rat muscles, but he had a lot of lean definition that created interesting lines and places to kiss.

Somehow we collapsed together onto the bed, both still in our underwear. We kissed for several long minutes, a slow dance of tongues that defied the raging insistence of my dick. My pelvis wasn't touching anything more than air, but I was still a heartbeat from coming.

With anyone else, the destination would already be clear at this point—hell, most guys were quick to assume that I'd bottom, and I was usually only too happy to go along with it. A fast conversation about the where/when/how subbed for foreplay with plenty of hookups. But this was different. There was no destination. We were already there, hands tangled in hair, lips dragging across stubbled skin, mingled breath, synchronized heartbeat.

We rolled on the bed, him ending up sprawled half on me. Each movement was infused with so much . . . joy. *Joy*. That was it. I didn't think I'd ever had that—the almost giddy pleasure of simply being in this place at this time, knowing that we'd actually made it to this moment. His touch held a sense of wonder I didn't think I'd ever had, even as a teen. He smiled down at me, a shy expression, as if he was amazed I hadn't disappeared.

I wanted to tell him I wasn't going anywhere, but words failed me when he circled my nipple with a blunt fingertip. Sucking on my shoulder, his hand skated down my torso. The air-conditioning in his apartment was cool, but his mouth was hot and his skin scorching. The press of his chest against mine spread heat throughout me, a delicious lick of pleasure that made me shift against him until our groins aligned. All at once, the room seemed brighter, the sound of our breathing louder, the scent of our sweat stronger—everything lit up as our dicks slid against each other for the first time.

"*Fuck*." David gasped against my mouth.

"Love it when you say fuck." I chuckled against his neck. He could take that as an invitation if he wanted, but this was pretty damn perfect. My fantasy earlier in the evening paled next to the reality of his big body rocking into mine, his weight balanced on his elbows.

"You make me wish I knew a lot more dirty words." Stretching, he uncurled one arm to link hands with me. Desperate for more skin, I snaked my free hand down to the waistband of his boxers. He got the message, and we both wiggled until the last scraps of fabric were gone and we were down to nothing but skin. And then perfect shifted, redefined to this, us, hands linked, hips slowly undulating against each other, his silky hot length dragging against my own, a slow wave of pleasure building from deep inside, every cell humming.

I could read his pleasure in the little huffs of breath against my cheek, in the tension in his palms, in the shudders racing through him every time our cockheads dragged against each other.

It was the most leisurely climb of my life—my balls throbbed with the need to come, but neither of us picked up speed. Just kept kissing and rocking. Small movements became everything; he sucked on my tongue and my balls lifted. I squeezed our interlaced fingers and he groaned like I'd put a hand on his dick. Tonguing my ear, his breath felt like licks of fire down every nerve ending in my back.

"*Robby.*" My name was husky and tender on his lips and the sound was almost enough to push me over. "So. Close."

And then that did it—knowing he was right there, that the desperation and hunger wasn't all on my side, that he was riding the same wave. I pushed up, grinding hard against his flat stomach as the first spasms hit me. I felt him go seconds later, a harsh groan and splash of heat against my belly.

Pressing a kiss against my forehead, he flopped next to me. I drifted along on the last of the heady wave of pleasure, muscles getting heavy as sleep threatened to claim me.

"Let me get a towel." David didn't seem to be suffering from the same near-brain-dead fatigue I was as he hopped off the bed and went to a bathroom across the hall. Tossing me a brown towel, he pulled on fresh boxers.

"Holy moly. I'm not sure I've *ever* come twice in an hour before."

"Was it seriously only an hour?" It felt like days had passed, or at the very least like the clock should read 4 A.M., like we'd ridden out the darkest part of the night together, drowned it in a river of kisses. But no, it was barely 11 according to the alarm clock next to David's bed.

"Heck." He slapped his head. "I didn't think. How late does TriMet run?"

"Eh?" I opened an eye to assess him. He didn't seem to be joking—his voice still sounded fucked out, his face still all soft and pink.

"Don't want you stranded." Leaning down, he ran a hand through my hair, affectionate smile at odds with the glass shards nicking my heart.

"Oh, uh. It's till midnight or one A.M. on Saturdays. And not like my roommates will be waiting up." I tried to joke, but the moment was lost.

"Good." He grabbed his pants and slipped them back on, leaving his belt and shirt on the floor.

Well. This was . . . unexpected. I mean, I'd had plenty of hookups not turn into sleepovers, and this wasn't even the most obvious you-can-leave-anytime hint I'd ever gotten, but it still stung how ready he seemed to be for me to leave.

"Um . . . I really do make good pancakes. We could skip the brunch place . . ."

"Wait." He turned back toward the bed. His forehead wrinkled and his eyes narrowed. "You want to stay?"

"Um. No." *Not when he so obviously wanted me gone.* Gee, this was a one-way ticket to awkwardville. "Guess I'd better get dressed." I hauled my creaky muscles out of the bed and stumbled to my clothes, which, unlike his, were neatly folded on a side chair.

"Hey." Sitting next to me on the bed, he took my hand. "Sorry. I didn't think—"

"No, it's no big deal." I tried to push off the bed, but his arm stayed me.

"I like pancakes." He kissed me softly on the lips. "A lot. I just wasn't thinking. . . . Sleepovers are kind of new to me."

"Seriously?" I mean, the guy had been with someone for twelve years. If I'd been with someone that long there would be a shared bed with a premium mattress and chichi monogrammed sheets.

"Yeah." He looked away, his eyes cloudy and distant. "Wasn't exactly a regular occurrence in my past relationship."

"I'm sorry."

"Ancient history." He waved my sympathy away, seeming to make a deliberate effort to brighten his expression. "And no, you're not getting dressed." He shook his head as his eyes raked over me with enough heat to make me forget about our sudden landing in awkwardland. "You're gorgeous, you know that?"

He kissed his way down my chest, pushing right past all the discomfort of the last few minutes. Yeah, I was staying. And, yeah, I was going to show him all the good parts of sleeping over he'd been missing out on.

# Chapter 6

David woke up first, foiling my plan to rouse him with a blow job. Whereas I had to drag myself up every morning at oh-dark-thirty and relished my sleeping-in days the way a sailor treasures leave, David was downright chipper at six-thirty.

"It's okay. You sleep longer." He kissed my shoulder. "I usually go for a run, then come back and shower."

"How about you get your workout here? Then we shower together?" I held the covers open for him to crawl back in. Round two last night had left me boneless, my usual nerves too blissed out to overthink things like usual.

"What did you have in mind?" He slid back in beside me, fuzzy legs rubbing against mine, sending heat straight up to my groin. He rested a hand on my chest.

Last night, we'd ended up rubbing off together a second time. And that was lovely, long and slow and oh so sweet, with lots of kissing until he'd finally wrapped a hand around us both and stroked us over the edge. But right now, sleepiness and leftover good juju from last night had me a bit bolder.

"You feel like fucking?"

"Didn't we . . . ah, you mean . . ." His face turned dusky red.

"It's okay if you're not ready." I stretched to kiss him. I could feel his heart thumping under my palm.

"That really what you want?" Cupping my face, he gazed into my eyes like he expected to find deception there.

"I'm dying to feel you in me, but I can be patient. Whenever you're ready."

He inhaled sharply, his eyes going hotter. Yeah, he definitely wasn't repelled by the notion. I rolled so I was more on top of him and could kiss him easier. Nipping at his lips, I let the kiss build slowly, licking my way into his mouth, sucking on each lip in turn. This was more than enough, and I tried to tell him that in my kiss. Frot and oral and David could make me a happy guy for a long, long time.

"I want you," he whispered as he pulled back. "But I . . . uh . . . don't have condoms."

"I do." I scampered off the bed before he could change his mind and retrieved my wallet from my pants. I'd come prepared. Hope and hard-up dick sprang eternal. By the time I got back to the bed, David had retrieved a bottle of lube from his nightstand. The idea of him beating off with a slick fist had my blood rushing to my already painfully hard dick. Condom in hand, I straddled his waist.

"How do you like it?" he said against my jaw. "Want it to be good for you."

God, he was sweet. "You on top."

Not that I was adverse to playing cowboy, but I really wanted to be surrounded by David, to feel him straining above me, to grab his shoulders and pull him close like I was never letting him go. For once in my life, I knew exactly what I wanted, and it was him.

"Show me what you like." He grabbed the lube with one hand and my hand with the other. His near reluctance worked like an odd aphrodisiac for me, made me more assertive than usual. Raising one leg up, I worked some lube around my rim.

David's eyes never left me as he knelt in front of me. He watched me for a few seconds, then his finger joined mine. "This okay?"

"*Yesss.*" My breath whooshed out as the tip of his finger penetrated me. Together we worked me open, and I had to keep reminding myself not to hold my breath. This strange, intimate space made me afraid to breathe lest I disturb this beautiful new landscape we were charting together.

"Now?" he asked, his hand trembling as he withdrew it.

"*Please.* Want you."

His thighs were tight against mine and I could feel the tension in his muscles as he slowly pressed forward.

"Don't . . . want . . . to hurt you."

"You won't." I breathed around the tight pinch, trying not to let it show on my face. David's expression was so earnest, eyes wide, mouth open—like it would kill him to stop, but he'd do it in an instant for me.

It wasn't my body he was at risk of hurting; it was my heart. It felt like my heart beat in time with his thrusts. Beat *for* him. Like he was my sole reason for existing right then.

The rub against my gland was exquisite; David's thrusts found the right angle effortlessly. Everything about the fuck was fluid—his motions, our kisses, my hands running up and down his back.

Sweat pooled between us and our breath came in synchronized pants, both of us pushing toward release even as we tried to make it last. We didn't need words or even eye contact; our bodies followed each other like this was a dance they'd long since memorized. I reached for my cock at the same instant he did, and David laced our hands together so that we both stroked me off. The pull of our hands, the pressure of him slamming against my gland; it was all too much.

"Ooooh. *Fuck.*" I came in thick ropes that squished between our fingers. I was still shuddering when David's hips stuttered, pushing deep a final time as he came too.

"*Robby.*" Head thrown back, his face scrunched up, he gave a helpless shout. The sight was so intensely erotic that it made my cock pulse again, made a deep aftershock wave pass through me, the after-burn of my orgasm intensified by the sight of his.

After a nap and a mutual shower that ended up in more sex, we finally had pancakes about the same time we usually had our Sunday brunches. I liked this sans shirts version way better. We sat at his tiny table and I educated him on why his drip coffeepot had to go and he told me about the huge breakfasts his grandparents would host.

He insisted on doing the dishes, and no longer powered by last night's lust, I took a moment to peruse his place. The small living room ended in a pass-through to a galley-style kitchen that had a breakfast bar open to the living room. The room was pretty much spotless—David's clean-freak routine had ensured that. The whole place felt sterile as naval barracks; there wasn't a lot of David's personality to spot. No wall art. No bookshelves.

"You play the Xbox much?"

David looked up from the sink and I nodded at his flat screen TV, which had both a DVD player and a game console attached. Below the TV were several pull-out drawers, the kind that could hold a whole library of DVDs out of sight.

"Some." He looked up from the dishwasher. "Just downloaded a really cool snowboarding thing. Wicked runs and neat soundtrack."

"SSX Tricky? I love that game."

"Yeah? We should play sometime."

"Want me to cue up a game?"

"Sure." There was the sound of the dishwasher kicking on and then David joined me. I reached to turn on the console but stopped, my hand hovering above the on button. Next to the DVD player were the only other personal items in the room: three framed photos. One of a smiling female version of David and two toddlers—dark hair, long noses, reluctant smiles. Definitely the sister and her kids. The second photo showed the same kids but older, more like five and seven, with David, holding up a giant fish.

"You fish?"

"Not lately." Like me, his eyes weren't on the fishing photograph; they were glued to the third photo. Blond dude, couple of years older than me, David off to one side. They weren't touching in the picture or even looking at each other, but I knew instantly who it was. Dead boyfriend whose name I didn't even know. He looked like a young Brad Pitt playing a sheriff's deputy. All dark blond hair and blue eyes and sun-kissed skin and an all-American smile. Cockiness radiated from him like a search beam. *He* probably had no problem telling David exactly what he wanted.

Next to me, David's eyes were distant, and he chewed on his lip. I didn't want to think about where his thoughts had gone, but I had a pretty good guess. I'd been feeling all smug about the sleepover and giving David something he hadn't had before, but now that smugness turned into self-doubt. Didn't really matter that the dude had apparently treated David like shit; the David in the picture practically glowed with love and happiness, eyes crinkled, no worry lines like my David had. David had loved the jerk, and nothing, not even me, could ever make that loss okay.

"I should probably get dressed." My voice felt all tight and thin.

"Yeah." David's voice sounded faraway. I crossed quickly to the hallway, not able to stand there doing some sort of weird penance a second longer.

"I should probably think about heading out."

"Wait. You don't want to play?" Catching up to me at the bedroom door, David grabbed my shoulder. He touched my face tentatively, like he hadn't spent the night becoming intimately acquainted with its contours. "You okay?"

"Yeah. I'm fine. It's later than I thought and . . ." I was scrambling and David's raised eyebrows said he knew it too. I pulled away to go hunt down my shirt.

"I'm screwing this up, aren't I? Just like last night." David sat on the edge of the bed.

"No, you're not." As much as I was frustrated and confused, I hated the sad puppy look on his face, the way his eyes turned down and his chin drooped. I shrugged into my shirt. "I just got cold."

Cold feet was more like it. The picture of the dead lover had been like ice cubes landing in a perfect cappuccino, ruining the cozy, snuggly feel of the morning. Now, though, I wanted that feeling back. I wanted that look off his face. Wasn't *his* fault I had issues about the ex.

"It's okay." I went and sat next to him on the bed and took his hand. "I'm pretty sure I'm screwing this up too. I just . . . you must have loved him a lot. You looked so different in that picture. Happier."

"Crap. I *knew* I should have put the pictures away—"

"You don't have to hide that part of your life from me. I *want* to know more."

"You really want to know about Craig?" His foot swung back and forth over the gray carpeting.

"I do." I squeezed his hand. Much as I already hated the dude, I was desperate to know the whole story, to finally open the part of David that had been locked away. My blood felt like it had been run through a milk frother: equal parts anticipation and wariness.

"He was closeted. I *thought* I was happy with what he could give me. But I wasn't."

I nodded. I'd figured as much.

"Like he didn't even think of us as a couple per se. Never used that word. And what we did . . . we were friends, sure. But it wasn't dating. He saved dating for women. I tried to get over him in college. But I just kept ending up back in the same place." He gave a bitter laugh, his fingers tensing. "He even got married briefly. And I . . . I was an idiot."

"No, you weren't. You loved him." It killed me to say it, but I could tell from the flashes of pain in his eyes it was true.

"Yeah. Yeah, I did. We were kids together. Played baseball, hung out—he was my best friend. And it was a tiny little town and I didn't see a way for us to really be together. Not when it first started, at least. And later . . . we'd kind of already established bad habits."

"I get that." Lord, did I ever. Brian and I had created a whole slew of bad habits from the start of our relationship, not the least of which was me following all his stupid rules about making sure his family didn't find out he was gay.

"Anyway. It wasn't like what you and I have. No standing dates. No public outings. Never any touches where people could see."

It warmed my chest to have him admit that what we'd been doing was different from whatever he and the asshole had gotten up to. I nodded, encouraging him to keep talking.

"It was all so damn ironic how he went. All that work he'd done to keep us a secret." He shook his head.

"How . . ." I'd assumed it had been a line-of-duty thing. Some noble exit for Sheriff Perfect.

"In bed."

"Say what?" My face did the whole cartoon bugging-out thing.

"Well, not *in* bed." He was beet red now, but he kept going. "It was one of the first nights we'd had together in weeks. And he'd had a headache when he arrived and kept saying he felt sick. But it had been a while and I was all 'I know how to make you feel better, so we . . . uh . . .'"

"I get the picture."

"Anyway, right afterward, he pukes. Doesn't even make it to the trash can. Just falls to his knees. Grabs his head. And it's bad. I can tell right away that it's heading to a bad place."

So could I. Wrapping an arm around David, I pulled him closer.

"I start to dial 911, but he stops me. Says he doesn't need the ER. But he can hardly get the sentence out. Tries to make noises about how we have to get dressed first, but he's barely making sense. I call it in because I'm just so fucking scared."

I kissed his forehead because I didn't know what else to do. Despite the sunshine filtering in, the room felt chilled, bathed in hospital-grade antiseptic. My nose tingled and my hand trembled against David's back. I would have given anything to be able to take away his pain.

"Somehow I managed to get boxers on before the EMTs arrived, but Craig was still naked . . . and they knew. I could tell they knew as soon as they walked in. Small town. I'd gone to high school with two of them. They weren't going to keep their mouths shut."

"Assholes."

"Damn right. And it didn't matter. Craig flatlined on the way to the hospital. Brain aneurysm. He was dead and the whole damn town knew how, when, and where he'd died within hours."

"I'm sorry." They were the most useless two words ever, but I had no idea what else I could offer him. "I get why you wouldn't want to try sex very soon—"

"I didn't. Not for the longest time. To be honest . . ." He played with the edge of the comforter. "I wasn't sure I *could* have sex again. Wasn't even sure I could get off."

"Not even . . ." I made a vague gesture below my waist. I had a hard time imagining a planet where I didn't jack off regularly, but David's story was all kinds of fucked up. I could see where he'd be messed up for a long time. My heart felt too big for my chest, a deep ache for all the agony he'd endured.

"Even . . . doing things myself felt awful. But then I met you . . . and that problem cleared up in a hurry." He stammered through it, but I suppressed a smile. I'd inspired him to jack off. More than once. Apparently, he wasn't made of steel after all—just an ice-encrusted man in need of a good thaw.

"That's why you didn't want to . . . do stuff sooner?"

"Yeah," he whispered. "I didn't want to hurt your feelings if I freaked. Like I freaked last night. Mainly because I didn't know the protocol. I just assumed you'd leave."

"Because he always did?" I hated Craig for stealing David's trust, for taking advantage of his placid good nature. Everything I loved about him, Craig had taken advantage of. Deep rage built behind my sternum, threatening to erupt in angry words. I had to swallow hard.

"Yeah."

"I'm . . ." I'd run out of things to say. I shrugged. "It's okay."

"No, it's not. I keep feeling like I'm a step behind—like there's a manual for being in relationships and I haven't even cracked the cover—and when I saw Craig's picture just now, all I could think of was how much we missed out on."

"It's okay to be angry." Lord knew I was angry enough for both of us.

"I know. That's what Mel and my grief counselor both tell me too.

I'm not sure if I'm angry so much as . . . sad and confused. But I don't want to hurt you."

"You feel what you need to feel." What did I know about grief? *I* would be pissed, but I wasn't David. And if David's sadness made me feel smaller, I didn't think it was intentional. I'd just have to work past it. Same as him. I wanted to trust in us both.

"And sometimes I'll realize that I'm just assuming things because of how things used to go. Like, I could have just introduced you as my boyfriend last night." He said it slowly, like he was still figuring something out in his head.

"Of course. Um . . . Carol and a few of the others totally guessed. Is that terrible for you?"

"No. I . . . I wanted that." He grinned sheepishly.

"Me too." I kissed his head again, relief coursing through me. "I want to be boyfriends. I want to meet people who matter to you. I want to hear about *what* matters to you. Even Craig."

Eyes widening, he cocked his head to one side, studying me. "Is that why you seem . . . off sometimes? Because you're not sure we're boyfriends?"

I nodded. It felt rather petty now, in light of everything I'd learned in the last few minutes. Here I was, all concerned about labels, while David wrestled sumo-sized guilt and grief.

"I . . . I think I want that too. But it all feels so strange. And I feel like I'm lost in the Sawtooth Forest without a map. I don't know how to be a good boyfriend for you. But I want to try."

"You just have to be you."

"I'm still . . ." He made a vague gesture in the direction of the living room. "Still working some things out. About Craig. About me. Can you be patient with me?"

"We'll figure it out together." I leaned in and kissed him, a feather of a kiss across his lips, before retreating. "Now about that game . . ."

# February: Mexican Mocha

# Chapter 7

The February chill had seeped into the hallway outside David's apartment. I stretched out my legs, wiggling my toes. My wool pea coat wasn't enough to counter the cold snap and make the wait for my boyfriend comfortable. He wasn't *that* late—maybe fifteen minutes. But each minute served as a reminder that I needed to ask him for a key to his place.

And I *knew* that it was mainly my fault; if I had asked, I was pretty sure he would have given me one. But I wanted him to offer. Wanted him to *want* me there. And so we were stuck in this strange place where I spent most nights at his place but didn't keep more than a toothbrush there, didn't have a key, and didn't count on an invitation. For the most part, I was happier than I'd ever been in my life, but this strange, unsettled feeling had descended, along with the temperature, made worse by a truly crap week.

"Sorry!" David came rushing up the stairs, Whole Foods bag dangling from one wrist. His thick wool dress coat and gray scarf made him look like a dapper 1950s businessman. He took the narrow hallway in quick, easy strides. "Been waiting long?"

"Nah." Heaving myself up, I took the bag while he unlocked the door, juggling it along with my messenger bag. "What'd you get?"

"Carol at work was going on about this vegetarian butternut soup she had the other day and how easy it was to make. Thought I'd try it."

Just like that, affection chased out the chill in my bones and the frustration in my brain. Neither of us were great cooks. David had a whole drawer of take-out menus we made liberal use of, so him going out of his way to cook for me made me feel all cozy.

"You don't always have to do vegetarian just for me. You can eat meat around me," I said as we unpacked the groceries in his tiny kitchen.

"I believe I'm well aware of that." Arching one eyebrow, he held my gaze until I was the one blushing for once. "You want to chop the onion?"

"Sure. Hacking something up sounds perfect." I grabbed a knife and cutting board.

"Bad day?" He reached over and squeezed my shoulder. The kitchen was small enough that our hips touched as he grabbed a stockpot.

"Saw you at lunch." I gave him a weak smile. "So not *all* terrible. Just more roommate drama at home."

"More?"

"Oops. I forgot to tell you." The onion aroma stung my eyes like a penance for the lie. It wasn't an accident that I hadn't told him. "Seth and Mark want to buy a place in St. Johns. Small two bedroom row house."

"Where does that leave you and Sarah?" He put down the box of vegetable broth and came up behind me, rubbing my shoulders.

"Sarah's been itching to move to the Pearl, and she's got a lead on a friend who might need a roommate. But Seth and Mark gave notice without telling the two of us, so we've got to scramble for something by March."

"That sucks. What are you going to do?" David's fingers worked magic on my shoulders, but his question hardly had the same effect.

"Not sure," I mumbled. I leaned forward to chop, not shaking him off exactly but also not giving in to the urge to sink into him. "Guess it's time to get a listing on Craigslist and start checking bulletin boards again."

"You don't want your own place?"

*I want a place with you. Badly.* I wanted to bring color to his brown and gray universe. For Christmas I'd gotten him a bright green picture frame with a picture of us at a Timbers game. It was now the lone spot of color in the room. I wanted to drag him to the little shops on Hawthorne I loved. Pick out paint and sheets together. Cook dinner together like this every night. But I couldn't get those words out. As happy as I was, I wasn't sure whether David felt the same way. He'd asked me to be patient and I wasn't sure whether expressing my deepest desire would be too much pressure for him.

"Can't afford my own place. As close as my business margin is

most months, I need roommates." There had been more than one
month when I'd been late getting money to Seth, but he'd been far more
understanding than the average landlord. "But man, I am *not* looking
forward to sorting through ads and trying to find sane people."

"Well . . ." He trailed off, and I waited, my heart in my throat.

"Yeah?"

"Doesn't Portland have some roommate matching services? Some
place that sorts out the crazy people for you and matches you with a
list of places?"

"Not sure." I minced the onion into a pulp and started in on the
celery, chopping hard enough to make the board shake.

"I'll ask Carol at work to check for you. Her husband's a Realtor."
He nodded, like it was all settled. Asking his friend to use her Realtor
connections *should* have made me happy—he wanted me safe and
not living with crazy people. But my stomach felt sour and I wasn't
sure I'd have room for soup with all the disappointment churning in
my gut.

He reached around me to grab the cutting board, dumping the
contents into the pot before adding a package of precut squash and
some herbs. The kitchen smelled like sizzling onions and pungent
rosemary and home—like the promise of comfort on a cold night. *I
need this.*

"Um . . . David?" I really needed to simply tell him. "I was
thinking—"

"You need a distraction," he said at the same moment.

"You want me to flip on the Blazers game?" I asked, chic-kening
out on telling him what was happening in my head. I watched far
more sports these days. My dad would be so proud. Heck, he'd probably trade me for David. He and David had talked more about sports
when my folks came for Christmas than I'd talked to my dad in total
in the last year.

Thanks to a number of holiday fund-raisers, David hadn't gone
back home to Idaho for Christmas, but my dad had snuck in a Blazers game with us while they were here, and we'd had a cheery Christmas Eve meal in Portland's small Chinatown. I'd suffer any amount
of sports talk for more cozy holidays like that.

"Wasn't what *I* was thinking." He wrapped his arms around me,
pulling my back against his front. He dropped a kiss on my neck,
right in the spot that always made me shiver. "I was stuck in a long,

boring meeting all afternoon. Very, very dull. Had plenty of time to . . . think."

"Think, huh?" I leaned into him with a big sigh. Being pissy wasn't nearly as much fun as this—and flirty David was still a rare treat, one to be savored.

"Uh-huh. Thought about you the whole way home too."

"I thought about *you* last night." I tilted my head to give him more access to my neck. "All alone in my tiny little cold bed."

"You could have come over. My work thing was over at about nine."

"Mmm." I couldn't speak as he idly licked along one of the tendons in my neck.

"Next time you should uh . . . text me while you're thinking of me." I swore I could feel his blush against my skin.

"Yeah? How about I call you instead?"

"That . . . might work." He was hard against my back and he sounded more than a little excited at the prospect. And nervous. Which just made me want to try it all the more. Edging him past his comfort zone was my new favorite hobby.

"Tell me what you were daydreaming about." I spun in his arms, the cabinets digging into my back.

"How about I show you instead?" Claiming my lips in a scorching kiss, he went from gee-this-is-nice to must-fuck-or-die in less than ten seconds. Whenever he took charge like this happiness hummed through my senses, canceling out all the worries and thoughts usually clogging my brain.

"David."

"Yeah?"

"Tell me the soup has to simmer a while."

"The soup needs to simmer." He flipped the burner control to low and threw a lid on the soup with a loud clatter.

He returned to me with a growl, diving right back into the kiss. The assertiveness had my toes curling. I sucked on his tongue, trying to insinuate what I'd do to his cock if he moved this to the couch. But he didn't move from our cramped spot between the cabinets. Instead, he kneaded my ass and hauled me closer.

"Couch. Now." I broke away. The way he was going, another thirty seconds and I'd be coming in my jeans.

"Bedroom." Grabbing my hand, he hauled me through the living room.

"Too far." I stopped by the couch, trying to move Mt. David onto the couch.

"Couch doesn't . . . uh . . . have supplies."

"Well, why didn't you just say that?" I gave him a flirty wink before skipping down the short hall. "Race you."

Usually, David didn't ask me to bottom unless he'd had a couple of beers. Made my stomach go all tingly how he always asked so haltingly for something I was only too happy to give.

"So tell me about this fantasy of yours." Forget waiting for him to unwrap me like a late Christmas present. I stripped off my clothes with surgical precision before hopping on the bed.

"Um." Going all pink, he stumbled out of his pants. My dick jumped at the sight of him shedding his dress clothes. Pulling off his tie was a huge turn-on for me, and the thunk of his belt hitting the floor and the rustle of his crisp dress pants was more effective than a double shot of Jack at loosening up my muscles.

I already knew I'd be down with whatever he had in mind, anticipation thrumming through me like a heavy bass beat. There was a trust level with David that I'd never had before—a comforting reassurance that he wouldn't push for more than I wanted to give.

"Hurry up and show me." I patted the bed. Our bodies moved together with a fluid familiarity—a rasp of hair as our legs tangled, a glide of muscle as our chests met. Kisses that dragged on for long minutes, him working my cock with a practiced hand.

"Gonna . . . come if you keep that up," I warned.

"Tell me what you want." Oh, yes. Toppy David was out in full force and my whole body shivered with eagerness.

"Fuck me," I whispered in his ear. His dick leapt against my hip at my words. He might not be able to force the words out himself, but he sure loved me talking dirty.

Grabbing a pillow, he maneuvered me until I lay on it, facedown.

"This okay?" He dropped kisses down my spine.

"Totally." I suppressed a laugh. His big idea was predictably tame and I loved him for it. Loved *him*. Of course, I hadn't managed to tell him that yet. He hadn't said the words either, and I wasn't about to be the only one with the words hanging between us, out of place and as awkward as jeans at a black tie dinner.

"Is it okay if I come this way, though? You gonna care if the pillow gets spooge on it?"

"Not at all." He kissed the dimple right above my ass before reaching for the lube. He knew exactly what I liked, how hard to work me with his fingers, exactly what spots to hit to open me up. I shuddered as he found the perfect rhythm. There were definite perks to having a detail-orientated boyfriend. I loved his big, strong fingers almost as much as I loved his dick.

"Please." I humped into the pillow. I'd come from just his fingers before and my body was hurtling toward that point. "Can't wait."

"Okay, baby." Thank God he didn't make me wait. Slowly, he pushed in, breath hissing out between his teeth. The position forced him deeper and I rocked back into him, needing more. The hard press of his body limited my motion, intensified even the smallest wiggle. Slipping one arm around my chest, he cradled me as he stretched out along my back.

"Kept . . . thinking about . . . angles all morning."

My laugh strangled in my throat as his dick grazed my gland. God, I loved my left-brained, math-obsessed man. Only he could make geometry so fucking sexy. We settled into a rhythm of him stroking into me, me pushing into the pillow, cascading waves of pleasure spreading out with each thrust.

"Love that," he groaned. My head collapsed onto the mattress as I let him surround me, let my senses tunnel down to just this, just his scent, his warmth, everything collapsing into this cozy, safe space where I could let go of everything except him. *Never letting go of him.*

He nipped at my neck, his teeth sending jolts of electricity down my already lit-up spine. Wedging a hand beneath my chest, he rested his palm over my heart. His other hand grasped mine, leaving no spot unconnected. Energy spiraled through us, and all I could think was that I wanted this to last forever. Didn't even want to come. Just wanted to be here like this, breathing the same air, sharing the same skin, feeling the same pleasure.

"Jesus, I love you," he breathed against my neck. I knew what he meant—he loved the sex, the connection, the sheer awesomeness of surging together like this, but the words gave me a thrill that pulsed through me, inched me closer to the edge.

"Me too. *More.*" I pushed back hard against him.

"*God* . . . do that again," he moaned, and I obliged, rocking faster against him, tightening my muscles to intensify the drag of pleasure with each thrust. His chest hair tickled my back and sweat pooled between us. The room reeked of sex and man and the scent got me hotter. His heavy weight on my back, his low grunt every time I pushed up against him, his thighs tense against mine—all the sensations intensified with each thrust.

"Oh, fuck. *David.*" Much too soon, I felt orgasm sneak up on me—not an explosion as much as a flood of emotion and sensation, rushing past every neuron in my brain, leaving my body limp and exhausted. Three quick thrusts and David joined me with a low groan, collapsing on me.

Pulling out, David rolled onto his back, dragging me against him so that my head was on his chest. My eyes drifted shut, sleepiness winning out over all other impulses.

"You know what's funny?" David asked, almost chipper.

"Yeah?" I cracked one eye open. Unlike most normal dudes, sex didn't make David sleepy. If anything it revved him up, made him all talkative and full of plans. One Sunday morning he'd bounded up out of bed to start vacuuming moments after an epic fuck session that had me taking a two-hour nap. *Crazy, lovable guy.*

"Sorry. You can sleep." His cheeks turned pink.

"Oh, now I'm curious." I raised my head to smile at him. Even brain dead and blissed out, I wasn't going to miss out on his candor.

"It's just . . . before you I never really thought of myself as someone who liked to top."

"No kidding?" I tried and failed at keeping the sarcasm out of my voice. I'd already figured out that Sheriff Perfect had been all things toppy and butch. "Wait. Had you never . . ."

"Uh. Yeah. I'd topped." He turned even pinker. "I . . . experimented some in college. And there were a couple of times with Craig, but it wasn't really his thing."

I had a feeling that the "couple of times" in twelve freaking years involved Craig drunk off his ass, but I wisely kept my snark to myself. Dear old Craig had been seriously missing out because David was the best lover I'd ever had—the whole attention-to-detail thing helped, but it was also the way he created such a safe space for me to let go. He was instinctively toppy without any of the asshole side effects that often came with it.

"But you like it, right?" Worry crept past all my post orgasm fuzzy happiness. Being good at something didn't always translate to fulfillment; my aborted grad school attempt was proof enough of that.

"Oh, *yeah*." He laughed. "That's the thing. First time I saw you, my first thought was 'Man, I want to fuck him.' Sorry. That's crude."

"No, it's sweet." I propped myself up on an elbow, stretching to kiss his cheek. "But . . . do you miss it?" I wasn't sure if these were just idle postsex observations or if he was trying to ask to switch in a very David sort of roundabout way.

"Not really." He rolled his shoulders. *Thank goodness.* I hadn't offered to switch mainly because I had no desire to compete with Sheriff Perfect. It wasn't that I never topped, but I definitely felt most comfortable fucking a guy who knew how he wanted to get done and kept charge of the scene, as opposed to a guy who wanted me to go all toppy and commanding. I wasn't anywhere close to the throw-him-down-and-ride-him-hard cowboy I imagined Craig to have been.

"If you ever want to . . ." It took a lot to offer, but if that *was* what he needed, I'd try. There wasn't much I wouldn't try for him.

"I'll let you know." He kissed the top of my head. "But it's kind of like mashed potatoes."

"Like potatoes?"

"Like liking mashed potatoes and being convinced it's the perfect food but never having tasted steak." He scratched his jaw. "Sorry. Wrong metaphor for a vegetarian—"

"No, I'll take being your steak." I kissed his flushed cheek. Suddenly the whole moving thing seemed rather petty. Why begrudge him his slow pace when it got me this? When things *were* pretty much perfect, every single time we got together?

"Hey. You know what?" I asked. "You want to come check out some places with me this weekend? Help me weed out the crazies?" I could do this. I could embrace another roommate situation, put my desire for us to live together on hold.

"I would, but I'm going home this weekend. My dad's birthday."

Just like that, my zenlike peace burst. His hometown was at least nine hours away; spending the weekend there would likely be a big deal. Something you'd mention to your boy-friend.

"But . . . it's Valentine's on Sunday." I sounded like a freaking girl, but I couldn't help it. My first time having an out boyfriend at the right time of year—yeah, I'd been looking forward to it. I'd gotten him a pair of Winterhawks tickets. Nothing cheesy or sentimental, but I'd been planning on our usual brunch, maybe a little extra cud- dling in line.

"That's right. Totally slipped my mind." He ran a hand through my hair. "Not surprising, I guess, since I've never really celebrated that day. Is that like a thing for you? You one of those guys who digs the hearts and flowers?"

"Not really. Overblown commercial crap," I lied. "We can do something when you get back. How old's your dad turning?"

"Seventy. Whole family's descending. Probably a hundred people, all crowded into the Grange. Trust me, I'd rather be spending the day with you."

"Me too," I said softly. *You could.* Huge family gathering like that, I'd bet there would be other girlfriends and boyfriends dragged along. And okay, probably not same-sex ones, but still, the fact that going together wasn't even on the table stung. I felt a bit like I had with Brian: a dirty secret, not fit for his family. It rankled that the holidays had come and gone and he'd met my parents, but no mention had been made of meeting his. Frankly, he'd seemed almost relieved that his schedule had precluded a visit home. Maybe he had no plans to make this more permanent. Sometimes waiting for him felt like an actual weight—a heavy iron thing hanging around my neck, pulling me down.

"Hey, maybe it'll be the perfect time to try out your phone idea." He was all kinds of flustered suggesting it, but I couldn't enjoy his cute discomfort. Phone sex was a pretty empty substitute for a boyfriend who thought I was steak yet still seemed to want to save me for special occasions.

# Chapter 8

I wasn't sure we wanted the same things. I was depressed and unsure what to do about it. Still, my pulse leaped when I saw his name on my incoming call. His number showed with a selfie I'd snapped of us at brunch one Sunday. I took a moment to stare at him, deep longing coursing through me.

"Hey, stranger." Giving up on the laundry I'd been sorting, I plopped down on my bed.

"Hi, sweetie. Sorry if it's late." I could tell from the *sweetie* and the languid tone of his voice that he'd probably had a few beers. I could also tell he was alone, most likely stretched out in a childhood room I'd never seen, but wanted to know everything about.

"Never too late for you." I kept my voice light, trying to match his relaxed tone. "How was the party?"

"Long. Boring. Too many kids."

"You have anyone to talk to?" I wanted to volunteer for next time, but I couldn't find the words. Instead, I stared at my Portal poster, wishing I could tunnel right to David's side.

"Not unless you count my redneck cousins who wanted to talk elk hunting." He chuckled, the sound vibrating through me. "What about you?"

"I watched the Blazers game earlier. Look what you've done to me." Sorting three weeks of laundry while watching a ball game and missing my lover like crazy—yep, I really knew how to have a wild Saturday night. "But that center guy is pretty cute."

"I haven't looked at the box score yet. What was his stats line like?"

"I have no idea. He's got a new tattoo on his left calf, though." My guy watched sports for the numbers. I watched sports for my guy. And the occasional eye candy. "But he did a wicked block in the fourth quarter."

"Knew I'd convert you sooner or later." His voice was like salted caramel sauce—smooth and sweet with a hint of grit. "That's not all I'd like to do to you."

"Yeah?" I stretched my legs out on the bed, glancing over to make sure I'd shut my door.

"Miss you. It's nine degrees here and even with a space heater, this bed is darn cold." It was the closest he'd come to saying he liked sharing a bed for more than just the obvious, and warmth bloomed in my chest. My own room was none too hot. Portland didn't get many of these bitter cold snaps and our drafty old rental wasn't prepared to fend off the chill. I had a small space heater supplementing the ancient radiator that worked better for drying socks than heating humans.

"Wish I were there too. I could heat you up quick." Undoing the top button of my jeans, I starting spinning out a fantasy involving me, David, a pile of quilts, and warm flesh.

"Trust me, you don't want to be here." His emphatic tone threw ice water all over my rising lust.

"Sure I do." I tried to keep the light, seductive tone going, but it sounded forced even to my own ears. My hand fell away from my fly and I went back to mentally categorizing my posters.

"Nah. Too much . . . never mind." There was a scratching sound, and I could picture David tugging at his hair, the way he always did when stressed.

"Tell me about it." The moment for sexy play had evaporated, leaving only concern behind. Didn't matter how frustrated I was; I still wished I was there to rub his shoulders, make him tell me what was bothering him.

"Oh, nothing new. Just same small town, big family stuff."

"They give you a hard time for being gay?" My neck tightened at the memory of the last family reunion my dad had dragged me to. Lots of military types and southerners who'd been all nice-nice while my dad was around and gossipy harpies as soon as he was out of the room.

"Some of them. Most of them pretend it's a nonissue. But it's always hard at things like this, where my parents' friends show up too."

"Ah." Somewhere buried under all his subtext and careful inflection, the real issue revealed itself like a crack in a freshly painted ceiling. "Craig's family was there?"

"Yeah. Not a big deal." His words said one thing, but his weary tone revealed the truth. "Our fathers grew up together. Hell, even our grandfathers were friends. They've always come to family parties and stuff."

"Even after . . ." My fingers fiddled with the buttons on my duvet cover.

"Yeah. I mean, there were a couple of months when Earl didn't talk to my dad."

"And that was easier?" I guessed.

"A little." He sounded like he felt guilty for it. "But somehow they put it behind them. Our folks are at least social to each other."

"But not to you?"

"I don't exist to Earl and Dottie." His voice was quiet. "It's not a question of civil. I simply don't exist to them. At some point they decided that whatever went down was an aberration and that denial was a great place to take up residence. So they did. And they ignore me altogether."

"Geez. That sucks." A chill raced down my spine.

"And every time I see them . . ."

"What?"

"I can't help thinking that he should be there too. That he should be right behind Earl, slapping my dad on the back, getting his mom's coat . . ."

"That has to suck for you." I didn't know what else to say. I inhaled slowly, caught the scent of baking cookies. Sarah was busy testing new recipes. Usually the aroma lured me to the kitchen, but right now my stomach was churning and all I wanted to do was stay behind my closed door.

"It does. But not as much as it used to. Knowing I'd get to call you later helped." He sounded like he was forcing the good cheer past a huge boulder of guilt and sadness.

"How about I come next time?" He sounded so down that my desire to wrap my arms around him trumped my reluctance to raise the topic.

"I . . . don't know."

*Damn.* I called myself thirty-seven kinds of idiot for thinking he might go for it. Kicking at the lump of blankets at the foot of my bed, I sat up.

"You don't want that. Trust me."

That stung. I'd heard similar words from Brian a dozen times. *You wouldn't like them anyway. You'd be bored. I don't want you feeling uncomfortable.* And then, finally, the truth. *We'd need to be just friends for them. I don't think I can play it that way. You don't want to lie.*

"It's not *you.*" He tried to reassure me, his voice like an invisible pat on the knee. "It's them. Some of them are . . . a little racist. The things they say, you know."

"Oh." I'd heard those excuses from Brian too. In Portland, the whole half-Asian thing was a complete nonissue, something I only really dwelled on when my dad dragged me to one of his family things back in Virginia. Mom got all stiff and nervous around my dad's very white, very southern family. But I'd always caught more heck from my cousins for the whole short, nerdy, and queer thing than for who my mom was. "I wouldn't care." I'd told that same lie to Brian, and just like then, it didn't make any difference.

"I would." His voice was tight, and I sensed he was sitting up now, any trace of his buzz gone. His leg would be swaying restlessly, a hand on his knee. "But hey, it's not all a downer. My coworkers love you."

"I like them too." It wasn't really enough and it wasn't the same as meeting the family, but it was all I had. Probably all I was going to get. I told myself not to be a baby about this. My getting all needy wouldn't solve anything.

"Carol talked to her husband the Realtor for you. And it's actually good timing for me too."

"How so?" I couldn't help the uptick in my pulse.

"Yeah. Property management company sold our building. Apparently, it's the season for apartment hunting in Portland."

"You're not thinking of using the roommate service for yourself, are you?"

"Of course not." His dismissal was emphatic. "No. I haven't had a roommate since college. Last thing I want is another. I've been on my own too long. Too set in my ways and all that."

*Last thing I want.* I had to swallow hard, my throat feeling doused in Super Glue. For a moment, I'd let myself believe I'd found the perfect segue to talking about us sharing a place. For an instant, my chest had vibrated with stupid hope, but he'd extinguished all that in four words. Us living together seemed like little more than a pipe dream, especially on a night when he seemed to miss his dead lover's presence more than mine.

"Oh." My voice was way too soft, so I took another breath, needing to get the hurt out of my tone. "You're going to use Carol's connection to find another rental. Still in Northwest?"

"Sure. That or the Pearl."

"Of course." Great. Two of the highest-rent areas. I couldn't even take solace in the idea of living closer to him. With my luck, I'd be stuck out in Beaverton, with a forty-five minute commute to work and David.

"But we can totally look together, like you suggested. Maybe next weekend. Check out some places for me and some roommates for you."

Oh, no. Just no. This I could not do. I couldn't go out looking at little one-bedrooms with him, fresh blank canvases of a future we wouldn't be having. And to have to turn around and hope our next stop didn't yield a smoking cat lady with an angry boyfriend.

"With any luck I'll find a place before then." My mouth was on autopilot, disengaged from the hurt and frustration raging through me. I smacked a pillow hard enough to send it skittering to the floor.

"Sure. Whatever you want." David sounded tentative, and somehow that made my heart break even more. I threw my other pillow at the door.

"I should probably be going." I needed off this call. My control over my voice was slipping and the last thing I wanted was to go all whiny on him. Not when I knew it wouldn't help anything. *Last thing I want.*

"So soon?" I could hear him shifting about.

"Yeah. I've got a load of clothes on downstairs and I promised Sarah I'd try her cookies." The clothes could rot in the washer for all I cared, and Sarah's hemp-nut cookies weren't exactly high on my must-haves list, but I was willing to seize any excuse.

"Oh. I thought . . . never mind."

"Sorry." I knew what he'd been thinking, and five minutes ago I'd been all for it. God, even now, I wanted to give him that release, wanted to erase all the tension I heard in his voice, wanted to undo his shitty day. Wanted to be the best part of his life.

But I was the coward who couldn't even tell him I loved him as we hung up, and he was so used to being alone, I wasn't sure there would ever be room for me in his heart.

# Chapter 9

On Monday, I got the college student who worked some hours for me to stay through lunch. I had a plan.

"So, you planning a nooner with that hot boyfriend of yours?" Suz was twenty with a penchant for roller-derby chic and an assumption that the whole planet was having more sex than she was.

"Not exactly." I sidestepped around her to refill the cup dispenser. It always felt weird working the counter with someone else, even someone as nice as Suz. The space behind the cart was narrow and there wasn't an easy way to avoid conversation.

"You're so lucky." She got that dreamy look that all younger girls get when they see a cute cat—or a sappy couple.

She also had a case of the 10:30 A.M. restlessness that came from having no customers and an empty atrium without people to watch. I usually cured the boredom by cleaning, but Suz got all chatty. "Mmm hmm." I gazed longingly at the double doors, willing a flood of customers to arrive. "I guess."

"You *guess*?" She grabbed my arm, spinning me around. "Wait. You guys aren't fighting, are you?"

"We're not fighting." I tried to sound blasé, but a weary sigh escaped instead.

"Oh. My. God. You're not breaking up with him, are you? That's why you wanted me to cover lunch?"

"I asked you to cover because I could use the help." My stomach flipped as I scanned the atrium. Thank God a whole two customers arrived right then, putting Suz's inquisition on hold. Two mochas to go and a reprieve for me.

"Yeah. Right. We've had maybe a half-dozen customers since the morning rush," Suz hissed at me as she added dark chocolate syrup to a cup. Raising her voice, she flashed a pinup grin at the Armani-suit-wearing guy who was all expense account swagger. "Whip?"

"I've got my own."

And they were off on a flirty little exchange that netted Suz a five-dollar tip on a four-dollar drink and let me focus on the middle-aged dude who'd accompanied the vice pre-sident of swagger. The tip jar got zero moola for my efforts, but I was simply happy with the silence.

"All right. Dish." Suz didn't even wait until the dudes were out of earshot before rounding on me. "Why are you unhappy with David? I mean, have you *seen* how he looks at you? It's the cutest thing ever. I can't fucking *wait* to have someone look at me like that."

"How he looks at me?"

"Like you're holding tickets to Cancún and you just cured cancer. Every. Single. Time. He'd do *anything* for you."

"Not quite." I couldn't keep my mouth shut.

"Wait. Is he terrible in bed? Because those studly nerdy types can go either way; either they're freakishly good or flat-out terrible."

"So not discussing that with you."

"Freakishly good it is." She gave me a grin that was all teeth. "If he were bad, you'd be happy to complain."

"He's a great guy, okay? Fabulous. Perfect. We're just . . . having some issues."

"Come on." Suz hopped on the counter, her feet dangling, as she gave me a sad puppy face. "Don't make me keep guessing. Knowing you, I bet you haven't told anyone anything about your *issues*. You need to clear your energy before you go all Dear John on the poor guy."

"You know, you don't have the psych degree yet. I'm not sure you're qualified to analyze me." I tried to keep it light, even though she was right. I'd lived with Seth and Mark for three years, but they knew more about my coffee business than about David. Sarah and I shared a love of deep-fried tofu, but deep conversation wasn't really our thing. Talking wasn't really my thing with anyone; I'd never really opened up with anyone about what went down with Brian either.

"It doesn't take a degree to see you're on the verge of making a shitty mistake."

"It's not a mistake." I'd been over and over this in my head all weekend. I had to tell David what I really wanted. Had to stand up for myself. But I was almost positive it was going to end badly.

Frustration bubbled up in me, made worse by Suz's concerned eyes. "I'm pretty sure he's still in love with his dead boyfriend and I'm . . . in love with him and I have no clue what he wants and I can't get in any deeper with him because it hurts too freaking much already."

"Oh, sweetie." She got down off the counter to hug me, which did nothing to counter the broken-glass feeling inside me. "Is it really that bad?"

Then it was like the ancient Hawthorne Bridge creaking open inside my soul and the whole story came lurching out—Craig, wanting to move in together, more Craig, his family stuff, and even more Craig. It was hard to articulate that my biggest worry wasn't that he'd say no but rather that he'd say yes and then things would get all weird between us because he didn't *really* want it.

"Give him a chance. You're just assuming David's still hung up on the dead guy. I've seen how he looks at you. You need to at least ask him what he wants instead of deciding for him."

"I will." Every time I pictured telling David what was in my heart, icy sweat gathered at the base of my spine. I didn't see this ending any other way than with us breaking up. But maybe Suz was right. Maybe I needed to have more faith.

Articulating wants usually led to disappointment—moves happened anyway, deployments dragged on, grad school requirements changed regardless, boyfriends kept right on lying to their families. My preferences seemed irrelevant and speaking up led to awkward conversations and magnified the hurt. Keeping pain private kept the wounds smaller, helped me buck up and move on. And maybe that was part of it; it seemed inevitable that David would hurt me too. Why speak up and make it hurt that much worse?

But at some point in the last few days, I'd decided that I couldn't let my aversion to conflict and inability to talk sink the best thing that had ever happened to me. I had to give it a shot. And maybe Suz was right; maybe everything would work out fine.

An hour later, I made a large vanilla latte and headed out into the frigid morning. It seemed important somehow to step out from behind the counter, meet him on his walk over. Downtown Portland was gray and dingy, the sun having fled months earlier. February always seemed far longer than twenty-eight days as the rainy season turned frigid, with a breeze that stung my cheeks and made me wish I'd grabbed my hat.

I met up with David on Ninth. And I watched as he caught sight of me. Suz was right—his whole face shifted, all the tension he usually carried replaced with light, little smile lines lifting up the corners of his mouth and eyes. Somehow, some way, I was going to have to find the right words.

"Hey! This is a surprise!"

"Suz stayed later this morning." I held out his drink. "Thought I'd meet you partway."

"I don't mind coming to you. But thanks." His words felt like punches, hitting me in the stomach, reminding me of how kind and sweet he was.

"You want to walk?" He studied my face, clearly confused about why I was there, but the softness in his eyes said he was willing to go where I wanted.

My KEENs felt dipped in concrete, every step heavy as I followed him around the block. We ended up at a little plaza tucked between two office buildings. Come April it would be buzzing with people, lunchtime picnickers in business suits jockeying for space with street musicians and black-clad teenagers, but right now we had our pick of benches. I headed for one tucked under the building's overhang, slightly shielded from the wind.

"Want to sit?"

"Are you okay?" he said as he settled in next to me, leaving a space between us that made my bones hunger for his warmth and nearness.

"I . . . yeah. I'm fine. But we need to talk."

David fiddled with his coffee cup, his eyes on the cobblestone patio. "Are you breaking up with me?"

*Damn.* Of course he chose right then to get perceptive.

"No," I said, but uncertainty crept into my voice. "I don't *want* to break up. I want a real relationship."

"A real one?" He frowned and his question was edged with what sounded like anger. "This isn't real? I mean, I know this is all new to me, but I've had *not* real. And this feels pretty darn real to me."

"It does to me too. It's only . . . I want more than just dating." There; I'd said it. My heart pounded like I'd run to the riverfront and back. "I want a partnership. I want to deal with your crazy family. I want to hear about when Craig's family acts like dicks. I want . . . I want to look for an apartment. Together."

Despite the freezing temperatures, sweat slid down my neck and my hands turned clammy.

"You want to move in together?" He chewed on his lip and I hated that I couldn't tell whether he was surprised or repulsed or maybe a little of both.

"Yeah."

He didn't say anything for a long minute. "And you want me to tell my family about us?"

"You haven't?" My worst fear confirmed. No matter what he said, this wasn't real to him.

"It's irrelevant." He tried to squeeze my hand, but I pulled it away.

"I'm *not* irrelevant." I stood up.

"I didn't mean . . . look. Robby. This is . . . sudden."

I could see the lie in his eyes. "You guessed, didn't you? Last week. You knew I was thinking about living together."

"Maybe." His answer was all breath and zero volume, but it hit me like a right hook to the jaw. Any hope I'd had that this was all just miscommunication withered away. Deep inside, I'd believed Suz. Believed that all I needed to do was speak up—

"But I . . . I can't, Robby. It's too soon."

"I can't keep wrestling a dead guy for you, David. I won't."

"I . . ." His face squished up like he might cry. And God help me, I was on the verge of tears myself, my eyes hot and itchy.

"I *love* you. And I want a future with you."

"I need time." It was the worst thing he could have said. Not *yes, I love you too.* And not putting me out of my misery with a firm no either. He needed time and patience and probably a better guy than me because I had run out of both.

"I need *you.* I need you in this thing with me. One hundred percent." My voice broke. My cheeks stung as the wind slapped against my tears. I couldn't stand for him to see my tears, so I fled. He let me go, still sitting there with his coffee.

*This* was why I'd wanted to keep silent. Because before I'd had faith, even if it was foolish and unwarranted, and now I had nothing. I had taken Suz's advice. Told him exactly what was in my heart. Given him a chance, and he'd given me . . . nothing except more waiting.

Somehow I made it back to my cart, kept it together long enough to tell Suz she was covering the afternoon too. And then I did what I hadn't done since I'd bought my cart two years ago. I took a sick day. Went back to my house, threw myself on my bed fully clothed, and pulled the covers up over my head.

# Chapter 10

I made it through the rest of the week. It wasn't pretty, and more than one regular customer asked me if I was ill. And I was. I was bitterly heartsick. Broken inside like a shattered espresso cup. Useless little shards of glass where my heart and brain used to be.

Finally, Suz cornered me after Friday morning's rush. "Maybe you shouldn't have walked away."

"What?" She'd dragged the whole story out of me, of course, making soothing noises and telling me how sorry she was.

"I'm just saying . . . would it be the worst thing in the world to wait on living together? To keep dating? I mean, Robby, I'm in your corner here, but you're miserable. And I saw him on the street yesterday and he looked gutshot—"

"You saw him?" My throat threatened to close up. I wondered where he'd been headed, if he'd been going elsewhere to buy his coffee.

"Yeah. He's miserable. You're miserable. And he didn't exactly say no to what you asked—"

"He might as well have." I surprised myself. A few weeks ago, I would have agreed with Suz. Would have accepted whatever David wanted to give me, anything to keep him around. A few months ago, I would have kept quiet, not finding the courage to speak up at all. But now I'd found a resolve I hadn't known I had. I'd laid myself out there. I needed David to do the same.

He absolutely was a guy worth waiting for, but I needed to know we were at least headed to the same place. I couldn't give David my heart and dream that someday, maybe, he'd give me a part of his life—the part he chose to share with me.

\* \* \*

Sunday morning was even colder than the last two weeks. Good. It matched the deep freeze in my heart, gave me an excuse to sleep in. That's what I did lately. I worked and I slept and I tried not to think about David. Tried not to check my messages eighty-five times a day. Tried not to look up at every person through the doors, hoping to see his dark head.

Maybe later I'd feel up to streaming some old episodes of *Battlestar* or *Firefly*. Do some comfort-TV wallowing. But right then, all I could do was stare at the cracked, chipped ceiling.

I had no idea how long I lay like that, adrift on my own thoughts, almost but not quite awake.

"Hey." My roommate Seth pounded on the door. "You home? Your boyfriend is here."

"What?" I managed to get off the bed and come to the door. *He's not my boyfriend.* I had no idea *what* he was, but I did know that I couldn't face him right then. My lungs seized like I'd chugged a quadruple shot on an empty stomach.

"Tell him—" I opened the door to tell Seth to make an excuse, but David was right there behind him.

"I'm gonna take off, man." Seth gave me a mock salute as he backed up down the hall, almost tripping over himself to get away from us.

"Can I come in?" David asked all formally—like I was a coworker in an adjacent office. Unlike his voice, his face was uncertain—eyes weary, cheeks flushed. His hair was a mess and his usually perfectly pressed clothes were rumpled. Looked like he hadn't slept since Monday. He shifted his weight from side to side, as if his feet were considering following Seth.

"Sure," I said, only because it beat having this conversation in the doorway.

"I brought you some of the raisin toast you like so much from People's Coffee." He held out a small package, carefully wrapped in napkins.

Eyes stinging and throat tight, I accepted it. "Thanks."

I had to perch on the edge of my bed because standing felt too strange. My hands flopped about as uselessly as my vocal cords. I felt as if I should be touching him but couldn't, should be inviting him to get comfortable but couldn't, should be shutting the door but couldn't.

"I don't know what to say. I rehearsed on the way here . . ." He plopped down next to me. He was too close. He smelled woodsy and freshly showered and my senses kept remembering what he'd smelled like sweaty and straining. My body wanted to push him down on the bed, forget everything other than the silky feel of his skin, while my mind wanted to run.

"This week has sucked," I said, mainly to fill the silence stretching between us.

"I hate Craig." David's tone had surprising vehemence to it. "I hate him because he's not even here and he's ruined everything between us. And I hate . . ."

"Me?" I asked softly.

"No. Never." He grabbed my hand. "But for a bit there, I hated *us*. I hated how what we had kept reminding me of what I'd never had with Craig. And I tried to pretend it was because of his job or our town or our families. . . ." His voice broke.

I squeezed his hand, lacing our fingers together.

"But instead I kept . . . I kept seeing everything he'd cheated me out of. We could have had this. We *should* have had this."

"You deserved it," I whispered.

"And when I could tell that you were wanting to live together . . . everything came to a head. All this . . . rage I'd been suppressing. And I was an asshole to you."

"You were hurting." I could see that now.

"And sometimes I get so *scared*."

"Of what?"

"Of losing you. Of loving you and living with you and building a life with you and then you disappearing. Gone. Some nights I'll lay awake worrying about what could take you from me."

"I'm not going anywhere." I wasn't. "And I get scared too."

I took a deep breath, searching for courage but only coming up with stale air. "I just worry . . . I'm not Craig. I'm not like him. I'll never be him."

"You're right. You're not him." His voice was firm but not unkind. "You're nothing like him. And that's probably what I love most about you. *Everything* with you is different."

"But you said it makes you sad—"

"It makes me angry that I wasted decades on someone who couldn't give me even a fraction of what you do. It makes me sad that I never got this with him. It makes me sad for Craig that he never got to experience this." He shook his head. "But you? You don't make me sad. You make me whole."

"I do?"

"You do. It took walking around this week like I'd lost a leg for me to realize it. But you . . . you've brought me back from a dark place."

"I meant it when I said I love you."

"I know. And I think that scared me the most. Too scared to get the thing I've always wanted."

"I can see that." My anger was draining away, like a river washing into the vast ocean of potential happiness.

"I don't want to lose you, Robby." He held both of my hands. "I'm still not sure what the next step is. But I love you. And I don't want my fears to cost me you."

"I was maybe rushing you a bit. We don't have to decide right away about living together." Talking to him made me see what a huge jump he had made coming after me. He loved me. I wasn't fighting a ghost for his heart. Some things could wait.

"If it helps, my sister says I'm an idiot for not jumping at the idea."

"You told your sister about us?"

"Yeah. I should have told her this weekend, but . . . I didn't want to share you."

"Share me?"

"Yeah. I know it sounds crazy. But what we have here is . . . special. Magical even. And I didn't want to take it out and look at it back home. Like it would get mud all over what we share."

"Are they really *that* bad?"

"Mel's not. She wants to meet you. And my mom's not so bad either. Talked to her too. She's happy I found someone. Said I should bring you to Easter. But the rest of them . . ."

"My dad's family is full of conspiracy theorists and has annual BB gun shooting contests. My uncle was on *Punkin Chunkin'*. Trust me, I can speak rural too. Why not ask me to go?"

"Ask you to drive ten hours to go eat bad barbeque and lukewarm potatoes?" He frowned. "And be around my redneck relatives, who will tell you how much they like sweet and sour chicken and compliment your English? Or the other ones who will ignore us both? No. I love you *way* too much to ask you to deal with that."

"But I want to." I squeezed his hand back. "Not for the relatives. For *you.*"

"Really?"

"I don't only want to share the happy parts of your life. I want to share *all* of your life. Even the uncomfortable parts. Even the sad parts. Even Craig. You wouldn't be here right now without him."

"I should have been honest with you that I was struggling more with my grief recently. Maybe I should go back to that counselor . . . but I don't think even I realized what was happening until you were walking away."

"I'm sorry." I kissed his neck. "I'm sorry for leaving."

"No. You were right to. You say you want to share everything; I want you to trust me more. I want you to trust that you can speak up."

He was right. I'd been so worried about him pushing me away that I'd kept quiet far longer than I should have. I'd tiptoed around subjects and left a lot of stuff unsaid. I had my own baggage and trust issues. I kept thinking he might bolt when I too had one hand on the door, afraid to come all the way inside.

"You're not going anywhere?"

"I'm right where I want to be." He leaned in to kiss me. And I let go of fear and doubt and indecision and met him halfway, my tongue snaking into the heat of his mouth, my heart fully opening for the first time.

I was more than a little groggy for work Tuesday. David had kept me up late, and my muscles protested the load of coffee beans I had to haul in. Suz kept grinning at me and teasing me her entire shift until I shooed her out at ten. I was pretty sure I still had a goofy smile on my face as David strolled in a little before noon.

He had to wait through a cluster of corporate women, all ordering skinny lattes and leaving even skimpier tips. We exchanged secret smiles over their heads, and my heart went gooier than my big bottle of dark chocolate syrup.

"Your usual?" I said as the ladies departed.

"I'll take the special," he said, leaning on the counter.

"You sure?" I hadn't seen him glance at my sign. "It's a Mexican mocha. Has a tiny amount of chili pepper in it."

"I'm sure. I trust you." Our eyes met and held and I felt the power of his trust.

I set about making his drink but looked up at a clanking noise. He'd dropped something in my tip jar.

"What's this?" I set aside the drink to fish a gold object out from the bills and change. "A key?"

"To my place. I should have given you one a lot sooner. I just . . ." He shrugged. "Not good at figuring these things out."

"It's okay." I smiled up at him, happiness lighting me up like the sunlight filtering through the atrium's skylights. "I'm not either."

"We can figure it out together."

"Deal." I slid the key from hand to hand, savoring the weight.

# April: Coconut Frappé

# Chapter 11

"I hope you can live without coffee for two days."

"What? You didn't tell me *that* was part of the bargain." I faked outrage.

"That right there is the only place to buy coffee in town—" David pointed at a gas station across from the solitary stoplight. "And it tastes like boiled gym shoes. Mom has drip coffee, but it's usually decaf store brand."

"Decaf! Take me back to Portland." I took on a princessy tone to make him laugh. Anything to get him to lighten up. As soon as we'd passed the SMALL BASIN, POP. 1,112 sign, David's back had tensed up, his knuckles turning white on the steering wheel. It was Easter weekend and someone had put two large wooden eggs in front of the sign. A piece of poster board taped to a street pole pointed the way to an egg hunt. Downtown was a single street, half the buildings shuttered, others looking like their last good coat of paint was thirty years ago. A couple of knickknack shops and a used bookstore. Big feed store at the end of the block with pickups lining the lot.

It was quaint and homey and made me want to check in a mirror to make sure my hair wasn't sticking up too much. David was dressed as preppy as ever, so I'd tried not to fret too much about how Portland I looked. David had laughed when I'd gone back and forth between glasses or contacts that morning.

"That's the school over there." He pointed out a small cement-block building with a red metal roof. I looked over at the sports fields, trying to picture a young David there, chasing after Craig. The high school undoubtedly still had trophies and pictures of him. Somewhere in this town was a cemetery with a headstone that had

Craig's name on it. I'd asked David if he wanted—needed—to visit it, but he'd shaken his head. "Nothing left to say," he said. And I'd believed him. The last few months, David had seemed happier, freer with his emotions, and the cloud of sadness that used to follow him around seemed to have evaporated.

His Civic didn't exactly fit with the town full of trucks and SUVs. It was a cute little valley town, surrounded by gorgeous evergreen scenery and mountains in the distance, but every corner seemed to underscore what a lonely life it had been for someone like David.

"So, don't take this wrong, but there's a lot more flannel and denim here than in your closet."

"You noticed?" He raised an eyebrow over his sunglasses.

"When did you start the whole business attire thing?"

"You saying I'm preppy?" David swung the car onto a narrow road leading out of the town. "I had this math teacher in high school. Mr. Gold. He always said a man should dress like the job he wanted to have."

"So you took that as permission to get your inner accountant on?"

"Something like that." He laughed. "My mom always called me her odd duck. I was always begging to wear my church clothes to school, even in grade school. In middle school, I made her teach me to iron so I could iron all my own stuff."

"You're cute."

"You're biased." He reached across the console to squeeze my knee. "And you need to stop worrying about who's wearing what."

"Hey. I only made you look at three different shirts."

"My point."

He could joke, but I wasn't the only nervous one. We'd been invited for Easter dinner, but I didn't kid myself that Mel would probably be the only one happy to see us there. I'd met her a few weeks earlier, when she'd come to Portland. Several years older than David and several times more talky, she had a broad smile and a bossy, good-hearted nature.

She'd liked me, though. Told me I was good for David. And she was probably behind why David's mom had pushed for him to come home for Easter dinner. I didn't care how awkward it was; I was just happy to be making the trek together.

The car bounced down the country road before David turned at a metal gate, taking a long driveway up to a low-slung ranch house.

"Well. This is it." He took a deep breath as he parked the car. "I'm . . ."

"It'll be okay." I grabbed his hand. I wanted to say more, but Mel was coming toward the car, black Hunter boots picking their way across the swampy, still-thawing yard. Two elementary school–aged kids trailed behind her.

"Uncle David!"

"See?" I said before we got out of the car. "You've even got your own welcoming committee."

David's mom stood at the door as we came across the yard. She was tall and broad-shouldered, with a sturdy build that said she'd had no problems corralling four kids. In addition to David and Mel, there were two older brothers. I'd meet them—and a whole bunch of David's cousins—later. The Gregory family was expecting more than forty people at Easter dinner tomorrow. My dad's side of the family wasn't exactly small, but it seemed like David must be related to half the county with the list of relatives he'd rattled off to me on the drive up.

David's mom hugged him for a long time. It was easy to see in her misty eyes how much she missed him.

"So. Let me look at you." She stepped back, still holding his shoulders. "Are you sleeping better? Eating more than bean sprouts and rice?"

"Portland *does* have meat, Ma."

I had to repress a very inappropriate snicker. Then his mom turned her appraising eye on me, looking me over like I was a calf she was considering buying. Finally, she gave a slow smile.

"So. You must be the coffee guy?"

"I'm the coffee guy." I smiled back, and I knew then that no matter how awkward things got later, we were going to be okay.

After the greetings, we headed into the house, David's mom leading the way.

"So tell me, Robby," she said over her shoulder, "how do you feel about venison?"

"I'm sorry," David whispered next to me.

"It'll be fine," I whispered back, leaning toward him a little. "But I'll let you make it up to me later, if it makes you feel any better."

"You sure I'll like this?"

"Of course I am," I lied.

"Well, I suppose I do owe you."

"You do." I grinned up at him, all teeth and sass. It was good to be home.

"Well. It's only paint. And only one wall." David glared at the living room wall like he was daring it to object. Three of the walls were a pale cream shade called Coconut Frappé that I'd fallen instantly in love with—and named this week's drink special after. However, all cream would be as boring as beige, so I'd talked David into a light teal accent wall. Of course, by *talk* I meant *arrived home with paint*.

Home. It was still such a fragile, new word. We'd lucked into a rental off of Alberta—walking distance to our brunch place and close to transit for me. And when the landlord offered us a chance to paint the place in our own choice of colors, I did a little happy dance right there in the property management office. The past owners had made some seriously bad choices. We'd painted the blood-red bathroom pale silver and the dank gray bedroom a cozy taupe. Now, here in the living room, it was time for some *color.*

"You'll see. You'll love it." *I hope.* I smiled encouragingly as I pried open the paint can. "You can take out your stress on the paint rollers."

"Flinging paint as therapy?"

"If it works." I dipped a fingertip in the blue paint, threatening to flick a drip at him before he captured me in a hug.

"It's my legs that need a workout more than my arms. All that driving. I'm still stiff."

"I have a cure for stiff." I leaned into him. We'd gotten back from Easter with his family the day before.

"I know you do. But you're the one who wanted to paint. Three days with no sex and *you* would rather hang out with Benjamin Moore here."

"Three days? Does this morning not count?" We'd collapsed into bed together after the long drive but had ended up rubbing off together before I'd had to leave for work and David went back to sleep.

"Not nearly enough."

"Hey, I'm just happy your mom let us share a room." She'd turned bright pink when she'd shown us to David's old room, but at least his folks hadn't insisted on separate rooms or something equally archaic. But separate room or no, convincing David to do more than cuddle in Idaho had been a no-go.

Lack of sex aside, it hadn't been nearly the ordeal David had feared. No one force-fed me venison or any of the other seven meat dishes on display at Easter dinner. I'd eaten my mashed potatoes and listened to David's siblings tell stories about how he used to wear ties to elementary school. Sure, there were plenty of people at the dinner who didn't talk to us. And there were more than a few stupid questions. But they were David's town and David's family and David's past, and because they meant so much to David, it mattered a lot that he had shared them with me.

And I was David's future. So was this house. It had challenges like horrible paint—which we were taking care of—and a backyard with some sort of weird six-arched pagoda thing happening, along with some funky raised garden beds, but there was room to grow here.

"Are you sure we have to paint?" David hugged me tighter, snuggling into my neck.

"We could paint really fast first—" I ended on a squeak as his hand snaked down the front of my pants. "Or paint second. Second totally works too."

As he pulled me toward the newly taupe bedroom, I thought, *this is what hope feels like.* Since David had come into my life I'd learned a lot more about hope. It looks like ivory sheets and stacks of paint cans and two pairs of shoes next to the bed. It sounds like rustling bedcovers and murmured endearments. Hope tastes like skin and soap and victory and coffee. And I can say now with absolute certainty that hope *does* come in a paper cup and smells an awful lot like a vanilla latte to go.

# Baked Fresh

# Chapter 1

"So, what's your plan this year?" Cliff asked as we unloaded pallets of food for Victory Mission. The stinging December wind whipped through the loading dock, howling against the concrete walls. I had to strain to hear Cliff's booming voice. "Sky diving? Marathon? How you gonna top last year, Vic?"

"Dunno." I hefted a box of tomato sauce cans. That's what everyone wanted to know—how I was going to top last year's resolution to lose a hundred pounds. Truth was, I was pretty good at resolutions. Four years ago, I'd resolved to go to culinary school. Three years ago, I gave up smoking. And last year I lost 111 pounds. But this year I had a smaller, simpler goal in mind.

"Thought I might try dating."

"Dating? As in a boyfriend?" Cliff snorted, a dry sound that echoed off the metal loading bay doors. "I'd go with a marathon."

My stomach churned as I grabbed another box of rolls. I had my own doubts. I was hardly a prize catch. I hadn't dated anyone in the four years I'd been working for Cliff. Never had a boyfriend beyond the rare three-peat hookup. 'Course, Cliff didn't know about my hookups, but I hadn't even had one of those in eight long months. Up until a few months ago, I hadn't realized what I was missing. Ever since then, this weird, restless longing had plagued me. New Year's was the perfect excuse to do something about it. Get out there.

"You guys done out here? Whole stack of boxes waiting inside. We don't have all day." Robin bustled out onto the dock, bringing a shit-ton of bad mood with him. A far cry from the sunny, talkative guy who made me think crazy thoughts, like that maybe dating wasn't a terrible idea. He was gone before either Cliff or I could reply.

"What's up with him?" I asked Cliff once I heard the pantry door shut inside.

"Melissa said Paul broke up with him." Cliff always found the gossip. The food bank volunteers were like bored high schoolers, passing rumors around their shifts like joints at a party.

"Finally." I didn't realize I'd said the word aloud until Cliff laughed.

"Aha! On second thought, I highly approve of your resolution. I'm gonna have to get a bet going with Trish about whether or not you can land your man. Talk about aiming high though, kid."

"Didn't say anything about dating Robin," I mumbled into a sack of rice. The last time Robin was single, I had spent months thinking about him. Wondering if he was out of my league. Knowing he was out of my league but trying to work up the courage to ask him out anyway. Coming to volunteer more often just to be around him. Then Paul swooped in like a star pitcher and sent me back to the minor leagues, where I belonged.

I readjusted my grip on the sack so I wouldn't accidentally tear the darn thing in two. No, I wasn't stupid enough to make a resolution to date Robin. I just wanted to get out there. Give myself a chance to maybe meet a nice guy who wouldn't care about my food issues and my loose skin and my bald-by-choice look.

But now that Cliff had planted the dating-Robin idea in my brain, I couldn't stop thinking about it. Which irked the hell out of me. I'd worked hard to deep-six my crush on him. Finding out he was single was a stupid reason to unearth it. Robin *was* the nice guy of my fantasies. And fucking gorgeous. He was sex walking around in KEENs and hipster T-shirts. He was everything I wanted and everything I wasn't ever going to have.

I ran into Robin an hour later in the pantry room, where he was doing inventory. The pantry room was where the shelter stored all the supplies needed to provide two meals a day for the ever-increasing numbers of Portland's homeless.

"Sorry 'bout earlier." Robin looked up from his clipboard, giving me a sheepish smile. A Robin smile was like sun glinting off the Columbia: it never failed to dazzle me. The pale pink of his lips was a soft contrast to his honey-colored skin. When his wide lips curved, revealing perfect white teeth, my stomach did a happy little flip. The sun had returned.

"No biggie. Heard you're having a rough day." I lined up cans of tomato soup, trying hard not to look at him. I didn't want him to feel uncomfortable. I'd be climbing the metal shelving or hiding behind the stacks of boxes if I were the one being gossiped about.

"Yeah. Sorry. I shouldn't be taking it out on people here." He passed me the clipboard so I could log in what I unpacked. While I started logging, he grabbed a box cutter and opened more of the boxes Cliff and I had unloaded.

"Hey, you're allowed to be human." I shot him what I hoped passed for an understanding smile. "And go you for tossing that pompous ass."

"Actually, it was the other way around." Robin's expression was tight, pained.

"Shit. Sorry. Didn't mean—"

"No. It's okay." He waved away my apology. "He *was* stuck up. I think Melissa was relieved when he didn't show up with me today."

I nodded, not sure what to say. I didn't want to trash the dude if Robin still had feelings for him.

"You're better off without him." When in doubt, go big on cliché. I fell back on my ma's old trick.

"Eh. I figure I had it coming. Better now than later, though, you know?"

"Yeah."

"Anyway, I'm done with boyfriends now. D-O-N-E. Done." He punctuated his words with jabs of the box cutter into the box he was opening. His actions and words were firm, but the look in his eyes was uncertain.

Having a boyfriend had suited Robin. He'd been all smiles and lightness around Paul the Jerk. Seeing them together had made me start to want someone, too. Someone to share inside jokes with, someone to watch TV with, someone to sneak little touches and dirty looks with in public. Hell, someone to talk to would be enough of a novelty for me. Every now and then I'd get to chatting with a guy on-line and think maybe we'd hit it off. But then we'd hook up, and as soon as the fucking was over, he'd beat feet to get out of my place. It seemed like the more good-looking the dude, the faster he was on his feet.

But Robin was fucking gorgeous and most days he liked talking to me. We both liked action movies and blues music, and somehow we always ended up gabbing politics, but there was always this easiness to our conversations, like we'd been having them for years and years.

As usual, thinking about Robin and what a great guy he was had me asking my favorite question: what would he be like in bed? He'd probably talk to me there, too. He'd be the type to hang out and talk after the sexing was done. He'd ask about my day and tell me about his, and maybe we'd even talk about making plans and about when we might get together next. I got hard just thinking about it. I had to distract myself with straightening soup cans.

*Bingo.* That was what Robin needed. A distraction.

"Hey, you got plans for tomorrow night? Got a New Year's party to be at?" I asked. Wouldn't surprise me if he had some fancy shindig to attend. I didn't know a whole lot about Robin's life outside of volunteering, but I knew he came from money; his high-end clothes and the Beamer he drove said that.

"Nah. I'll probably come down here for part of the evening. It's always crazy here New Year's."

"You can do better than that. How about you come out? Some of my buddies are doing a pub crawl. Get out there. Get over what's-his-face. Party at CC Slaughters's supposed to be epic."

"Oh. Uh." Robin swallowed hard, his hands moving restlessly against the row of oatmeal containers he'd been counting. "Thanks, but parties really aren't my thing. Don't drink anymore."

I fumbled the can I'd been stacking. *Hell.* I'd known him two years now, and for all he liked to run off at the mouth he'd never mentioned it, but still I should have guessed.

"Shit. I'm sorry. I didn't think. You in recovery?"

"Yeah." Robin went back to unpacking. The fluorescent lights made his honey-colored skin look sallow—or maybe he was turning green because of what I'd said.

How had I missed the clues? He'd never once mentioned bars—and he'd never once missed a shift. A lot of the most dedicated volunteers at the shelter were former homeless themselves, or recovering addicts seeking to pay back help they'd gotten. While open to all, the shelter had a particular focus on teens and young adults who often slipped through the cracks at the larger organizations. I'd discovered the shelter through a booth at Pride and convinced my boss Cliff to participate; the bakery always had food to donate.

We worked without talking for a few minutes, and while the silence wasn't exactly uncomfortable, I felt the sting of a blown chance. I shoved the cans a bit harder than I should have and a stack collapsed. *Time to start over.*

It occurred to me—too late *again*—that I'd never really done this. Never asked a guy out. Never liked a guy enough to try. Oh, I knew my way around an Internet chat room, but real world? Robin was the first "real-life" guy I'd ever felt inspired to ask.

But now I'd blown it and I didn't know how to fix it. Not to mention my timing was really lousy; I should have waited until Paul was a distant, bitter memory, but I reserved patience for drop lines and sugar flowers, not social conventions.

"How long?" I asked.

"Two years, 363 days." He winked, a trace of his usual humor shining through. "Best resolution I ever made."

A fellow resolution keeper. My chest felt warm with empathy for his hard road. My successes were like speed bumps to his Mount Hood of triumph.

"That's awesome, man. And good on you for coming down here tomorrow."

"It'll be a long night." He shrugged, showing off his surprisingly delicate collarbones, matched by eyes filled with an unexpected fragility.

"I bet." I wanted to ask if he'd be okay, but we weren't really that kind of friends. I wasn't sure I could ask without looking like even more of an ass. But I knew how brutal anniversaries could be.

Later, as I walked out to my beat-up old Civic, I hunkered into my jacket to ward off the chill and told myself to go back to my previous plan. Make a profile on an actual dating site, not one of the quick hookup places. Find some guy, one who wouldn't be anything like Robin, with his wide smiles and silky brown hair and …

Fuck it. My hands clenched tight around the door handle. I knew exactly what my resolution was. Come hell or high water, I was going to be Robin Dawson's rebound guy. And I was going to change his mind about boyfriends.

# Chapter 2

Next day I had a plan, but I played it cool, surveying the racks of bread and pastries waiting for their turn in the too-full front cases. As I'd hoped, the oven-room staff had been overzealous again. We were closed New Year's day, so a lot of stuff would have to be marked as day-old or tossed.

"Want me to make a run over to the shelter?" I asked Trish. "I can do it after I deliver the Russo's cake." She was finishing up the groom's cake for the Russo-Smith wedding.

"Didn't you guys take them stuff yesterday?" Trish didn't look up from the chocolate fondant she was positioning over the diamond-shaped cake.

"Oh, he's got good reason to go back," Cliff butted in. He stopped cleaning the middle worktable and smirked.

"Shut your trap," I ribbed him in our usual good-natured way, but I shot him a look that said I could make all sorts of revelations of my own if he didn't shut up. With the Russo-Smith cake finished and safely stowed in the walk-in, I started putting away my decorating tools.

"You still coming out later? James'll be disappointed if you bail." Cliff ran a hand over his thinning hair. James was Cliff's brother—a sweet guy with an even sweeter husband who always tried to include me in their social circle. I was the Delgado family pet as far as Cliff and James were concerned.

"I'll be along." I wanted to check on Robin to make sure he wasn't too down, but I didn't expect him to give me a reason to skip James's annual New Year's Eve pub crawl.

"Speaking of bailing, I've got Blazers tickets next week. Thought Eddie and me would go, but he's got a school thing. You want them?"

"Sure. Both? You don't want the second?"

"Why don't you see what sort of magic you can work, resolution boy." Cliff kept his voice oh-so-light and innocent, like he wasn't matchmaking hard.

Gray-streaked red hair bouncing, Trish laughed like she was in on the joke; she was good at that, picking up on Cliff's signals. She'd pull the whole story out of her husband five minutes after I was gone.

And while I didn't doubt that sixteen-year-old Eddie had better things to do than hang with his old man, Cliff's reasons for offering the tickets were obvious. He was checking up on me, same as I wanted to do for Robin. Cliff knew how hard January sucked for me. Despite my resolution successes, January was filled with soul-sucking loss for me. It was the month I'd lost my dad three years ago. The month I'd landed alone and uncertain at culinary school, missing my old friends from the mortgage industry and not sure why in the hell I'd believed I could turn an unemployment check into a new career.

And last year it was the month I'd lost Manny, my cousin, my best friend, the brother I should have had. Manny had a heart attack the day after Christmas. Died on the operating table on January 7th, thirty-three years old. I'd been at my surgeon's office three days later. First my dad. Then my uncle. Then Manny. I didn't need a crystal ball to tell me the heart disease gene was coming for me next. Letting a surgeon put a band around my stomach was a radical way of dealing with grief, but I'd always been a go-big kind of guy.

I left the bakery without killing Cliff for his meddling and headed out on my delivery route. Two hours later, I arrived at Victory Mission still in my bakery whites. I carried a stack of three large pink bakery boxes and two smaller ones with treats for Robin and Melissa. Melissa was the director of the mission and plenty nice, but honestly, her treat was the decoy. I couldn't waltz in there with a treat just for Robin.

As luck would have it, she and Robin were both in the staff room when I came in. Robin wasn't staff, but he was there so frequently that Melissa often joked about him being employee of the year.

"This is a surprise!" She greeted me with a big gardenia-scented hug. I hugged back gingerly, careful of her pregnant belly. She set the boxes on the metal folding table in the center of the room, lifting the lid off one of the big boxes. "Pastries! And we can sure use these tonight!"

"Here, this one's just for you." I held out one of the smaller boxes.

"Oh, wow!" She opened it to reveal one of our famous oversize cupcakes buried under a ridiculous pile of buttercream icing and topped with one of my sugar flowers. Those were my specialty. I had large ham hands with thick fingers, but give me a piping bag or some spun sugar and I went into a weird zone where everything slowed down and it was just me and the sugar and the quest for perfection.

"The baby's going to like this." Melissa patted her round belly. Her smile was worth all the hours I'd put in last night, getting the flowers perfect for the Russo wedding cake and making sure there were extras for the goodies in the display case.

"Brought you something, too." I held out the other box for Robin. "Stuff can't last till Friday. Thought you might need a snack. . . ." I was babbling, regretting the gesture even before he opened the box with his elegant, piano-player fingers. I should have just stuffed some cannoli in there.

"Holy crap. This is too pretty to eat." Robin's eyes went wide and his smile seemed dipped in glitter dust.

Okay. I lied. Melissa's appreciation was nothing compared to Robin's look of awe. His cupcake was a bit of whimsy I'd been experimenting with. Instead of flowers, I'd shaped spun sugar into butterflies, wings airbrushed and gilded with little flecks of blue and gold.

"Better not let it go to waste." My voice was a bit too gruff, but he was damn well going to eat the chocolate devil's food cupcake with ganache filling that lay under the butterfly.

"Okay, boss." He grinned at me, all teeth and sass. "You able to stay for dinner?"

"Sure I can." I rolled up my sleeves and followed them out to the kitchen. The building had been a factory in its previous life, which meant big spaces but only the bare minimum amenities. Four commercial ranges, each from a different decade, held giant vats of spaghetti.

After we helped the other volunteers get the warming pans filled, Melissa assigned me to the dining room. Food was served cafeteria style, but volunteers staffed the tables, trying to give a more "family" dining experience. Other volunteers circulated among the tables, offering bread baskets and pamphlets about the mission's services. Most people took the rolls and declined the chitchat, but every now and then I'd get a talky table. Sometimes they'd just want to listen to some little story of mine, like a ruined cake or a memory of my dad's burned coffee. I wasn't anywhere near the storyteller Dad had been, but I tried to make things funny and light for my table. Getting people fed, making them laugh—for me it was better than a plate of warm pasta.

Two hours later, the crowd thinned out and I went in search of Robin. I found him sitting on a wooden bench in the entryway with an obviously tweaking teen: disheveled clothing, shaking hands, rambling speech. I listened as he declined Robin's offers of a meal or a bed upstairs for the night.

"Okay, okay. I'll cut you a deal. How about twenty? I'd blow you for twenty." The kid yanked at his dirty blond hair.

"Zach, you know we can't have you soliciting here." Robin spoke softly. "What you need is some help. How about we get you a plate of food, have one of the staff come talk to you—"

"It's the noodles. They keep crawling."

Robin nodded like Zach was making perfect sense, keeping his voice calm and level as he again offered help. This went on for a few more minutes, until Zach lurched away through the double doors and into the thirty-degree night in only his ratty T-shirt.

I was about to go to Robin when his shoulders slumped, his head coming forward to rest on his hands. His slim shoulders shook.

*Oh hell.* My throat tightened. My feet refused to cross the chipped concrete floor. Last thing I wanted was to embarrass Robin. I backtracked into the dining room, chased down a glass of tea and a plate of food. When I made it back out, Robin had collected himself. His face was still all blotchy, but he was taking deep breaths and studying the flyers on the cement-block walls.

"Hey, haven't seen you eat yet. Brought you some before it's gone," I said, awkwardly holding out the plate, not wanting to reveal I'd witnessed his breakdown but knowing the truth was all over my face.

"Thanks." His grateful smile made my insides all warm and squishy. I liked watching him eat. Liked knowing it was our rolls that made him smile in pleasure as he took a big bite. He tucked into the food like he was one of the guests—like he hadn't eaten anything else all day.

Me, I couldn't eat most of the stuff anyway. Didn't really bother me if they kept me too busy to join the guests for dinner; if I manned a table, I was stuck picking at lettuce or soggy vegetables most of the time. But Robin was so long and lean; he didn't need to be missing meals. He wasn't much shorter than my six foot two, but where he was a sports car—streamlined muscles, exotic brown eyes, sleek stomach, and a trim, tight ass—I was built more like a Volvo bus. Despite losing the weight, I still had linebacker shoulders and a barrel chest. Sitting next to Robin, I felt old and clunky.

"Sorry about earlier," Robin said around a mouthful of spaghetti. "Not usually a basket case." His shrewd eyes didn't let me pretend ignorance.

"Sounded like you had reason." I studied the posters on the walls for the various services the center offered: NA and AA meetings, clothing cupboard, referrals to medical care, and support groups. And none of it worth the shiny paper—or the hard-won grants and donations—if the client wouldn't accept help.

"Zach's been in before. Never eats. Never stays . . . he's a disaster."

"And you want to help. I get it." I patted his slim shoulder. The mission was the sort of place that inspired frequent hugs among volunteers. I'd grown up in a big Italian family of huggers and touching people in sympathy was as natural to me as eating cannoli. But this felt different, a charge zinging down my arm. He didn't pull away, so I left my hand there, acutely aware of his heat and knotted muscles. Wanted to rub all his tension away, but that so wasn't happening.

"Just been . . . a hell of week. Man, I hate holidays."

"Word. I loved 'em as a kid, but the last few years, man, they cured me fast." I didn't unload all my crap on him, but I got the pain in his eyes. He turned toward me, and for a second I could have sworn he felt the heat between us, felt the strange electricity, might even be leaning into my hand. But then he blinked and shrugged it off, and the moment disintegrated, as fragile as the butterfly on his cupcake.

"I've always hated them. Shuttling between my folks . . . my brother and I were always in the middle. And now . . ." He shook his head, light catching all the different shades of brown in his shaggy hair. "This week just sucks."

"You need to get out."

"Vic, I told you—"

"Not like that. I got Blazers tickets for next week. Got them from Cliff, so they're likely good seats. You should come with me. Get your mind off your sucky week." I tried to sound a lot more confident than I felt.

But Robin lifted an eyebrow, seeing right through me as usual. "Are you asking me out?"

"Nah." I waved the idea away. His skeptical look already told me to let that hope go. "Just a couple of guys. Catching the game. Probably do us both some good."

"You sure?"

"Sure I'm sure. Cliff doesn't want the tickets wasted."

"That's not what I meant," he said softly. "I don't want . . . don't want to mislead you. I meant what I said yesterday. I'm done dating."

"Not much for it myself." I managed to deliver the half-truth with a straight face. The infrequent hookups I'd had certainly didn't qualify as dating, and telling Robin my stance had recently changed wouldn't serve any good purpose.

"Okay. I'll go. But it's not a date. I'm gonna pay Cliff for the ticket."

"Fair enough."

Didn't matter if it wasn't a date. I knew I'd be counting down the hours until next Wednesday.

# Chapter 3

Wednesday afternoon I was a basket of nerves. I'd seen Robin a couple of times that week, casual conversation at the shelter that probably meant nothing to him but had me searching for hidden meaning in every word. I pulled on a Blazers tee as I stripped off my bakery uniform, too pressed for time to shower. Whatever. Wasn't like I was getting lucky that night anyway. Before my surgery I'd been vain, making sure I didn't live up to the sloppy fat guy stereotype by always being freshly showered and wearing nicely tailored clothes when I wasn't at the bakery.

But these days I always seemed to be running to or from the gym, and I'd gone through so many sizes that my bank account screamed at me to slow down my shirt purchasing. Besides, I didn't want Robin thinking I was reading too much into the evening.

We'd agreed to meet outside the Moda Center. He stood near the main entrance in a beat-up leather jacket and one of the close-fitting tees he seemed to live in. I was glad I'd gone with casual.

"Hi!" His broad smile resurrected every hope I'd tried to suppress. He looked around, taking in the red-and-black-clad crowd clogging the gates. "This is cool."

"You ever been to a game?" I asked after we were in the stadium, following the sea of humanity through the concourse.

"Lakers game long time ago with my dad." He made a face, like it wasn't exactly a happy memory. "But this is way cooler than I remember."

"You wanna walk a bit? See the stadium before the game starts?"

"Sure. And we should get food. I know it's crazy, but I've been looking forward to stadium food all day."

"I'll show you all the food vendors. They have Killer Burgers and

Fire on the Mountain wings now." I tried to match his enthusiasm, but I knew I failed miserably. Time was I could pack away a half-dozen hot dogs and beers, but now navigating the sea of food vendors felt like walking on marbles. I hated eating out. My stomach was so tetchy that I couldn't handle the grease even if I'd wanted to, and despite all the local food favorites, nongreasy was almost impossible to find.

"Oh hell. I didn't think." Robin turned toward me as we stood in line for bratwursts. "You probably can't have anything, right?"

Damn perceptive bastard. Of course, the whole shelter knew about my surgery. I'd had to miss several shifts, and I wasn't exactly coy about stuff like that.

"There's a place over there that's got a salad. I'll grab one." I kept from making a face. I was so damn sick of dry lettuce, but I didn't want to spoil Robin's fun. He bounced on the balls of his feet like there was nothing better than overpriced pork on generic white buns. I distracted myself by thinking about Robin's buns and what I'd like to do to them.

I got the blasted twelve-dollar salad—likely a buck a leaf—and met Robin up at the condiment kiosk, where he was loading his brat with pickles and ketchup.

"You know, I haven't had the chance to tell you how much I admire your changes," Robin said, looking at me. I mean *looking* at me, like he hadn't seen me three minutes prior or weekly for the last two years.

A strange chill crept up my spine, and I couldn't decide if it was a good or bad sensation.

"It's not all me. Surgery and all, you know?" I always felt weird taking praise for the weight loss. I suppose the gym time was something I could take pride in, but after all these months it still felt like a damn root canal, something I did because the doc told me it would prevent long-term problems.

"Still. You . . . look good, man. Really."

"Thanks." I couldn't help grinning at the compliment. He probably meant it no different than telling Melissa he liked her dress or whatever, but I still felt the praise all the way to my toes.

I'd eat lettuce for a year if it meant someone like Robin thought I looked good. Truth was, I'd had an easier time attracting male attention before. It was just a matter of knowing the sites that catered to dudes like me. I might have been way heavier than I needed to be, but I was a big, beefy Italian guy with a hairy chest and a bigger-than-average dick. There were always a few guys into the supersize bear thing. Now, though, I was just another thirtysomething guy with a receding hairline and decidedly average body that didn't translate to great selfies—or much interest on the hookup sites.

Not that I really wanted a hookup anymore. What I wanted was that look from Robin, the one he'd had in line, when it felt like he *noticed* me for the first time. I wanted this not-a-date to be a date. I wanted a gorgeous guy who wasn't ashamed to be seen with me, wanted to be out with someone like Robin, who made jokes about the starting lineup and kept up a steady conversation during the slow parts of the game.

"Sorry," he said as he leaned forward to better see the third-quarter action. Every time he leaned forward our shoulders brushed.

"No problem." I wasn't sorry at all. Just like our easy conversation, touching him felt almost automatic: high fiving for a basket, clapping him on the shoulder. It was all good.

Sometime deep in the quarter, I noticed our legs kept brushing, too. Glanced over at Robin—and oh, hell, he was glancing back.

*Swoosh.*

There's a certain energy when a shot is about to get nothing but net, a charged stillness to an arena waiting to explode. Looking into Robin's eyes felt like that, like every cell in my body was waiting for the chance to applaud. Did he feel it, too? This amped up energy arcing between us? I searched his eyes—

"Ring it up! Blazer three-pointer!" the announcer crackled, drowned out by the roar of the crowd.

The moment was gone; whatever shot I'd had for a second there with Robin had gone wild, clanking off the backboard. Didn't get it back in the fourth quarter, as both the game and the connection with Robin seemed to slip away.

But then, with four seconds remaining, Portland drained a three-pointer for a one-point, come-from-behind win. All around us people were high-fiving like they'd been out on the court.

Without thinking, I hugged Robin. A bro hug. Nothing special until our chests collided and . . . whoa. All that weird energy from earlier seemed to gather into a vibrating ball of potential right in the center of my chest. Robin pulled back first, shaking his shaggy head. But not in a don't-touch-me way. More in a what-the-hell-just-happened? way. And I was right there with him on that.

We followed the crowd to the exits. I put a hand on his back to steer him so that we didn't get separated in the crush of people. I'd do the same with any newbie to the Moda Center, but Robin was the only one who made my palm itch to roam. Like the hug, the touch felt charged with meaning.

"Robin?" A familiar, cultured voice cut across the din of the crowd. Damn it. Twenty thousand people and of-freaking-course Paul the Jerk had to be one of them. Even better, he had some blond twink in tow.

Robin stepped out of the flow of traffic so that the four of us were near a shuttered Sizzle Pie—and the screaming, flaming pizza logo pretty much summed up what I felt about the situation.

"I didn't think you liked basketball, babe," Paul said to Robin, his tone way more *boyfriend* than *ex*. The twink was draped over Paul's back in a pose suited for clubbing. "What are you doing here?"

"Oh, Vic brought me." Robin stepped closer to me. "You remember Vic from the mission, right?"

"Oh, yeah. You're the bread guy." Paul gave me a dismissive wave of his hand. "Been meaning to call you." He fixed his gaze on Robin again. "I need to pick up a few things from your place. Left my good cashmere there."

"Not tonight," Robin said, all airy. He leaned into me a little. "Doubt I'll be home."

*Oh, so this is how he wants to play it.* I was game. I put a hand on his waist. "How about Robin packs you a box?"

"Whatever. Chad and I have plans for the weekend. I'll give you a ring."

Nasty little man. He strode away on a cloud of aftershave and bad vibes.

"Sorry. Didn't mean to put you in the middle of that," Robin said as soon as they were gone. He didn't step away from my touch and I kept my hand on his waist, more of that weird potential vibrating between us. People streamed toward the exits, jostling each other, whistling and whooping their way down the long concourse. But standing next to Robin, I felt like we were the only ones in the stadium.

"I don't mind." *I really don't,* I tried to tell him with my eyes. *Use me however you want.*

"You're too nice."

I couldn't tell whether he meant the playing along or my unspoken invitation. "Nah. You don't know me very well. I'm not that nice a guy. A nice guy wouldn't be thinking how good Paul would look missing a few teeth."

Robin laughed. "I'm picturing him with that stupid sweater of his for a leash."

"Or a noose."

"You're stone cold, Vic. Stone cold."

"Us Degrassis are a bloodthirsty lot."

He laughed again, but it quickly turned bitter. "God, I hate him. Hate this." He flopped onto a nearby bench. "I'm sorry—"

"Quit saying sorry for that dick." I settled myself next to him. A quartet of young guys in Blazers jerseys gave us a disapproving glare. I glared right back with a heavy hint of *I can bench press two of you*, sending them scurrying faster down the corridor.

"I meant sorry for you having to deal with it," Robin said.

"Hey, I'm just glad you didn't run into him and his trick by yourself. Want me to come over when he comes to get his crap?"

"What, and glower and look all menacing? Tempting." His laugh this time was full and hearty.

"I do glower well." I knocked ankles with him, trying to earn another of those laughs. Hearing him loosen up made my chest expand. I really did do menacing well; adding muscle the last few months and shaving my head only increased my thug look. Pretty boy I wasn't.

"You'd do that for me? Play the heavy with Paul?"

"Heavy. Bouncer. Jealous pretend boyfriend. Your pick."

"I'll think about it. I wish things hadn't ended so damn ugly. We started so good. He came with me to volunteer. We hung out constantly. And then . . ." He put his hands on his knees as he surveyed the trash-strewn floor. "Things went south and I should have gotten out weeks earlier, but I really wanted to believe, you know?"

"Yeah." My stomach gave an uncomfortable wobble. I studied the pizza place menu to avoid meeting Robin's eyes. Really, I didn't know. If I did ever get a boyfriend, I couldn't imagine thinking Paul the Jerk was true-freaking-love. But Robin looked so lost and sad, I wanted to offer . . . something.

"Wish I could stop replaying the fight in my head." Robin chewed on his lower lip, distracting me from his sad tone.

"Regrets will eat you alive if you let them. You gotta outrun them. Find something in the now."

"That's awfully profound for you, Vic." Bumping my shoulder, he said it lightly, almost like a compliment. We were sitting closer together now, hips and thighs touching.

"Not the same thing, but when my dad passed, all I could think for weeks was how we argued about midnight mass right before. Probably wasn't the healthiest, but I took on every special order Cliff threw my way. I worked until I was too tired to hear the fight in my head."

I'd also buried my grief under a mountain of cheese and pepperoni and polished off more than my share of six-packs in the months after my dad died. But it wouldn't help Robin to hear how I'd used food and drink as a crutch to make it through.

"Sorry about your dad." He touched my arm, a low sizzle that went straight to my groin. "Work's been slow lately with the holidays, but I should work up a new flyer for the mission. Maybe that would work."

"Sure it would. Hey, you work out?"

"Nah. Play handball with my dad every once in a blue moon, but gyms aren't my scene."

*Damn.* I'd been thinking of offering him a guest pass at my gym. Another chance to see him. But for all I could put in my time on the rower and clang my way through the weight room, no way was I volunteering to get hit in the face with a ball and look like an idiot. Only balls I wanted in my face were the fun kind.

"Still. Just keep looking for distraction." My whole last year had been about the power of distraction. Work. Gym. Getting out with Cliff and James. Anything to keep places like Sizzle Pie off my speed dial. Anything to keep from the long hours alone in my place.

"Damn. I wish . . ." He trailed off.

"What?" The lost-puppy look was back on his face. I wanted to put my arm around him, and I got the feeling he wouldn't shove it away. However, the steady stream of drunken Blazers fans hadn't let up yet, and I didn't need more looks from little punks. So I settled for patting his knee.

"Wish I hadn't been lying to Paul. Wish I didn't have to head home and see him in every freaking room."

"So don't." I glanced at him, trying to figure out what he needed, what I could offer. Something new crackled between our eyes, the potential of earlier giving way to full-on heat zinging along all the spots our bodies touched. "We could get a dr—coffee."

"Not really in the mood for coffee." Robin met my eyes, searching. I hoped to hell he saw what he was looking for.

"You wanna come back to my place? Watch a movie?" *Fuck like bunnies?* That I didn't offer, but I sure as hell thought it. Thought the hell out of what it would be like. All evening it'd felt like we were dancing toward something, like this new . . . awareness between us was a half-court shot, hanging in the air, both of us waiting to see if it would sail through the net.

"I don't date." That sure as hell wasn't a no.

A grin busted out on my face. We were surrounded by cement-block walls, but all I could see was the possibility of a *yes*.

"I heard you. But you need a distraction, yeah? Need to get that bastard out of your head. Why let him have all the fun?"

"Don't want to use you."

"Baby, I am all over the idea of you using me to put that cocky bastard from your brain." I slid closer. What the hell. I put my arm around him. Let the drunken idiots gawk. The area smelled like stale beer and old pizza, but Robin smelled sweet, like cinnamon rolls. "Just come. Watch a movie. You can see about . . . other distractions."

I wasn't very good at in-person sweet-talking. Wasn't sure if I was pushing too far into glower and command. Online, I was good at closing the deal, getting someone to come over. But I'd never wanted a yes as much as I wanted Robin's.

"You're way too nice, Vic." Robin shook his head, even as he leaned into my arm.

"I'm really not." I squeezed his shoulder. If he wasn't going to pull away, I was going to enjoy this moment, however short it was. Maybe there would be another—

"You live far from here?"

# Chapter 4

I lived in South Portland, not far from the bakery, in the neighborhood I grew up in. I liked being able to check on my ma a couple of times a week. We took my car because Robin had taken the MAX to avoid the parking headache of downtown on game night. I tried not to see my old car through his eyes. Admittedly, it was better than it once was—no fast-food wrappers or grease stench, but there was no disguising its last good decade was in the previous century. I'd sold my Explorer and my condo when I went back to culinary school. Now I was back in a more affordable neighborhood.

Like my car, the house's better days were firmly behind it. Luckily, it was dark, so Robin couldn't see the yard that was more weeds and moss than grass. But he couldn't miss the stack of paint cans on the porch or the way the door whined when I opened it. I winced at the noise.

"Sorry. It's kind of a mess."

"It's fine. This all yours?"

"My aunt's. Cousin Manny and I were trying to fix it up to get it on the market before he passed." My neck tightened. Still couldn't explain the arrangement without my gut going all wobbly. Manny had been so gung ho with ideas and plans for the place. Him not being here to help me finish was like a raw scrape I felt every time I picked up a hammer.

"It's nice. They'd be proud."

"Eh." I shrugged off the compliment as I hung up our coats. He was being way too kind. Wasn't much "nice" about an entryway with wallpaper on one side and two different paint colors on the other. But then, Robin knew about Manny. Manny had come with me a time or two to the mission. When he passed, I'd missed volunteering for two weeks. Robin had been the only one not to bug me, asking how I was *feeling.*

I fumbled for the living room light switch, not entirely sure how to play this. With other dudes, they came over and we headed straight for the bedroom, but that wasn't happening with Robin looking around like he was doing a housing inspection.

"This molding original?" he asked, running a hand along the chair rail wainscoting.

"Think so."

"It would look nice in an aqua color."

"Think I'll just stick with white." And shoot me now if we were gonna stand around playing HGTV. I gestured toward the flat screen over the fireplace. "What kind of movie you feel like? I can stream whatever."

"Something funny." He gave me a strange look as he passed me to go sit on the big sectional in the center of the room, like I'd missed a signal.

Chewing the inside of my cheek, I tried to calm the horde of elephants dancing on my chest. *Damn.* What I wouldn't give for a chat window and a set of emoticons to figure out what the hell Robin wanted. I queued up a list of comedies.

"That one," we said at the same time as the preview screen showed a Seth Rogen movie about a dude and his impossible mother.

About ten minutes into the movie, Robin scooted closer to me. "So you really meant *movie* when you suggested it, huh?"

My nerve endings hummed, intensely aware of his nearness, of the brush of his hand on my arm, his scent. I couldn't resist pulling him closer, wrapping my arm around him. "Meant whatever you want."

"Mmm. You're cuddly." He settled in against me with a sigh, stretching his feet out on the sofa. Wasn't the first time I'd been called cuddly. Usually it felt like a poke in all my soft and doughy parts, a reminder that I wasn't anyone's definition of hot. However, I didn't mind it coming from Robin. Hell, I'd be his pillow for the next month if it meant I got him here like this, head on my shoulder, hand idly stroking my thigh. Felt *right* sitting here like this, like we'd done it a thousand times before, crappy comedy on the screen, him curled up against me.

As the movie got more predictable, I let my hand wander down his arm. For all he said he didn't work out, he had nice biceps and my favorite kind of forearms—ropy and lean, with broad hands and long fingers.

"And if I want this?" He ran a finger down my chest, making goose bumps break out down my back. He leaned in, licked his lips and . . . waited.

Damn. He had the sort of game I loved. He clearly wanted me to make the move, but he wasn't at all shy about making it known what he wanted. I didn't play it coy or make him wait. I cupped his face in my hands and closed the distance between us, capturing his lips. Meeting me eagerly, his lips parted and I sank into the kiss. Sank into him. He tasted sweet, like soda and everything else I wasn't supposed to have—including him. The subtle heat that had been stoking between us all evening erupted like Cascades wildfires. Our motions quickly turned hungry and needy and nothing like the slow first kiss I'd been plotting. No, this went straight to need-you-or-gonna-die.

Before I knew it, he was straddling me on the couch, our mouths still fused. Kissing him made my pulse speed up even as my muscles turned to buttercream. Too many guys I'd been with had a no-kissing rule. But with Robin, making out felt like a marquee event. And even more than the soft feel of his lips and the rasp of stubble under my palms, I loved the weight of him on my lap. My dick strained at my zipper, all available blood and brain cells pooling where our bodies connected. His dick prodded my stomach, and I pushed up against him.

In response, he turned almost frantic, all lips and teeth. When I sucked on his tongue, he moaned, long and low. For a second I thought he might be about to come like this, but then he took a shuddery breath.

"What . . . what do you like?" he whispered against my jaw.

"Anything," I said and meant it. I nipped at his ear.

"Anything? You . . . uh, bottom?"

That was unexpected, and my stomach flipped like a drunken gymnast. Truth was, most of the time guys and I had already played out a scene or three in chat, and it was understood that I liked topping. Big strapping dude like me—few guys even asked me to bottom, and the ones who did usually had some agenda to make me feel like crap so I'd largely avoided it. I doubted Robin had humiliation in mind.

"Sure, if that's what you want. But it's been a while so . . . slow, you know?" More like five or six years, but whether he had something to prove or I'd misread his preferences, I was game.

"Yeah." His eyes widened, like he hadn't expected me to agree.

Reaching up, I kissed him again, trying to shut down whatever voices he had going on in his head. I tried to tell him with my kiss that I'd take care of him, get him what he needed.

"Bedroom okay?"

"Yeah." He followed me almost shyly down the hall, footsteps so hesitant I thought he might be about to change his mind. I distracted him with more kisses and by tugging his T-shirt over his head. My bedroom was one of the nicest rooms in the house: big king-size bed and silver-painted walls with bedding my mom helped me pick out. But I didn't flip on the light to show the space off. Much as I wanted to see his golden skin and perfect body, I was content to let the filtered light from the hall hide mine.

Heck, I didn't even like catching sight of my new body in the mirror. It wasn't anything like those magazine before-and-after photo shoots, where the guy looks all tanned and ripped. Sure, I was way more muscular now, but the reality was also a nasty scar from the surgery and the stretch marks and loose skin no one had warned me about.

We shed our clothes between kisses. I kept watching for a flinch or other reaction from Robin, but he seemed wrapped up in the kisses, giving little sighs as each article of clothing hit the rug. I got a little giddy at the familiarity and closeness between us. *So this is what it's like to do it with a friend.* My heart gave a happy thrum. Somehow we landed on the bed, me on top, his erection poking me in the belly. I didn't care who was topping, but I was going to die if I didn't get his dick in my mouth. Sliding down his body, I landed on my knees on the floor, tugging him to the edge of the bed.

His dick was just like the rest of him, long and elegant. I fucking love sucking cock and moaned around his shaft. Fingers petting my scalp, he urged me deeper, and I obliged, milking his cockhead with the back of my throat. He tasted musky and male, with a hint of the sweetness that seemed to cling to his lips and skin. I gobbled him down.

"More," he gasped. His head thrashed against the mattress, fingers clutching the comforter.

My dick throbbed, loving every damn thing about how responsive he was.

Instinctively, I rolled his balls in my palm as I sucked him harder. His harsh moan was more of a bark. Letting my fingers wander back, I rubbed along the tight, smooth skin until I found his hole. Rubbing all around it, I teased more moans out of him, each gasp going straight to my own dick.

"Oh, fuck. Yes." His hips bucked up. I pulled away long enough to fumble in my nightstand for lube, but as soon as I popped it open, he raised up on his elbows.

"Wait." His face twisted, mouth uncertain and eyes cloudy.

"Sorry." My skin heated. I'd fallen into old habits and forgotten how he wanted things to go. I stretched out next to him, running a hand down his tense chest muscles. His heart hammered against his sternum.

"Didn't mean to spook you. Tell me what you need." I lowered my voice, trying for calming.

"Oh, God, I don't know." He pulled at his hair. "What I *want* is for you to fuck me."

"I'd love to." Kissing his neck, I brushed his hair out of the way.

"But I can't. I just . . . can't."

"Okay." I tried to keep up with the flip-flopping. "You positive?"

"Yeah."

"Okay." Cold sweat ran down my neck. I took a deep, steadying breath. That had come up before online, and I'd always run like I was being chased by a rabid dog, but I wasn't going to run from Robin. Wasn't going to be stupid either. "We'll be safe."

"Wait. That's not what I meant. I'm positive fucking won't work. Not HIV positive . . . Oh, God, I am such a mess." He sat all the way up, hunching forward.

I rubbed a hand down his back. His skin felt cool and the air in the room seemed to bring all the chill of January with it. "Hey, it's okay."

"I should be. That's the thing. I did some really stupid shit when I was high. And the rehab my parents sent me to, they kept telling me over and over how lucky I was I hadn't caught something. And now I get all paranoid and twisted around."

I made a soothing noise and kept stroking him. "And now you like to top instead of bottom? That's cool. Told you, I'm a flexible guy."

"No. I don't *prefer* topping. But I'd always been high for fucking before. Always. People kept saying how much better sober sex would be, but either they lied or my body hates fucking sober, and getting fucked has yet to work and it always ends poorly."

"That why you and Paul ended?"

"Yeah." He put his head in his hands. "I kept thinking things would get better, that I'd get out of my head enough to enjoy it. But it never happened and he got fed up with lousy sex. Earlier tonight, I'd had the thought things might be different—"

"They can be. He was a bastard."

"I should probably just go."

"No." I kissed all the way down his spine. "I just want to make you feel good. Fucking isn't on the table, okay? But let me make you feel good."

"Don't want to frustrate you. I can . . . be persnickety. Take too long."

"I'm not in any rush." Seeing him like this, vulnerable and human, made him even more attractive to me. He wasn't the perfect guy I'd spent two years building up in my head; he was maybe just as fucked up as me. I stopped worrying so much about what he was thinking of me and started worrying more about how I could make this good for him. Prove him wrong.

"You're too nice." His muffled voice was almost mournful. The sound went straight to my chest, lodging behind my breastbone. Feeling protective, I pulled him into my arms.

"You think I'm not getting anything out of this? I've got a gorgeous guy naked in my bed and he says it might last all night. That sounds pretty darn amazing. Especially after . . . never mind."

"What?" He raised his head, his face eager, like me having issues would be the best thing in the world.

"You said how you hadn't done it sober. Well, it's not the same thing, but my first time postsurgery was a complete bust. Guy left. Said I didn't look like my pictures. Freaked at the scar. I haven't tried again since." I kept my voice light, but it was an effort. Being here naked with Robin was nothing like that first time. After the dude's wide eyes and abrupt departure, I'd had dreams of being naked in Pioneer Square; felt like everyone could see the scar, like it was a glowing red beacon instead of an angry, pink index-finger-size mark.

"That sucks." He sounded almost happy. I guessed he was feeling some of what I was, like he didn't have to be fucked up alone, like he could give me something instead of just taking.

"Yeah. It does." Taking advantage of his change in mood, I kissed him again. He met me eagerly, licking his way into my mouth. He gave a happy sigh as I stroked his back.

My muscles unwound, my heart beating out a carefree rhythm. Yeah, going slow with him was no hardship at all. Time spun out like a fractal screensaver, kisses seeming endless. I'd be okay if this was all we did. My balls protested the thought, but my soul felt happier than it had been in years, like I'd been an empty cake, waiting for the perfect filling, waiting for my layers to have purpose. Kissing Robin did that—made me feel sure and strong.

Eventually we tumbled back onto the mattress, him on top slowly rocking against me. Even though my body screamed at me to grab his hips, get a hard-and-fast rhythm, and get more of the delicious sensation of our cocks dragging together, I forced myself to match his pace.

"This is so good," he whispered.

"Yeah, it is. Feels so good." His warm body blanketed me, smothered my stupid anxieties over my scar and my skin. All that mattered was lighting Robin up, making him feel as terrific as I did.

"You can come. You don't have to wait." Voice uncertain, he started to tense up.

"I'm not going anywhere." I pulled him harder against me, rewarded by a full-body shudder from him. His cock slid next to mine, tip damp and shaft as rock hard as mine. He bucked harder into my body.

"That's it. You just take what you need." Wasn't usually much for dirty talk, but his little gasps and thrusts made me bolder. "Love how your cock feels. Loved it in my mouth, too."

"Oooh." He made a strangled sound, thrusts getting more intense.

The room felt as warm as our bodies now, sweat gathering between us. I inhaled the scent of sex and men, and that made my dick pulse. My hands cupped his ass, squeezing and pulling, figuring out what he liked, what made his movements more erratic and his moans louder. Tracing his crack, I hesitated, waiting for him to protest, but he arched up into my touch.

"Yes. That."

My fingers burrowed into the warm space, rubbing all around his hole. "You want more?"

"Please." He arched up again. "Finger me. Need it."

"Can I get them wet?" I used my free hand to reach for the lube.

He hesitated, his movements slowing, then nodded. "Just one, okay?"

"Yeah. You let me know if it's too much."

Kissing him, I waited for him to get into it again, rocking us together until I was reduced to counting by threes in my head to keep from coming first. Slowly, I penetrated him, just the tip of my index finger, letting his moans guide me.

"Oh. Oh, man. *Fuck.*" Robin's eyes were squished shut, his mouth quivering.

My head felt fuzzy and light. It meant something—him letting me in, him trusting me enough to do this. Wiggling deeper, I kissed his neck, licking the straining tendons.

"That's it, baby. Fuck yourself on my finger. So tight. So good."

"Yeah." He arched up into my touch far enough that our cocks lost contact.

Pushing deeper, I thrust up against him. Now this was fucking. For all I'd said fucking wasn't on the table, we were doing a pretty damn good imitation of it, thrusts hard enough I knew my bones would be feeling it tomorrow. The suede of the comforter abraded my calves, but I kept the motion going. Anything to get him closer to the edge.

"More."

Hooking my finger, I rubbed his gland.

"Oh, fuck. I think I'm gonna come." His voice broke.

"Do it." I made encouraging noises. Nonsense words.

Then he was coming, shouting and straining against me. Soon as his slick heat hit my belly, I was a goner, my moans mingling with his.

"Jesus. Fucking. Christ." He pulled away from my finger and rolled off me. "That was—"

"Spectacular," I said happily.

"I was gonna go with fast, but spectacular works, too. Thank you. I didn't think . . ."

"I'm glad."

"God, I feel like rubber." His head dropped to my shoulder. "Okay if I crash here?"

"Of course." I grabbed my T-shirt, mopping up as best I could. He was asleep before I even finished tending to him.

Pride and something else, something much more tender, blossomed in my chest, stretching out like fondant, falling over me. I grinned up at the ceiling. He was the first guy who'd ever asked to stay over. Didn't matter if this was a onetime thing for him, it had meant something for me. Holding him as we both drifted toward sleep made my whole body relax, made my mind wander, made my dreams full of impossible wants.

# Chapter 5

Robin was gone when I woke up. Not a surprise and probably just as well. The only breakfast food I had was Kashi and Egg Beaters—stuff that didn't qualify as romantic breakfast fare. Making great use of my expensive culinary education, I microwaved myself some eggs and spinach. As I did my usual five miles at the gym, I told myself not to expect Robin to become a regular thing. I was the rebound guy, not the forever one. But if last night had shown me anything, it was that I was done with sex with strangers. I was done with guys who made me feel terrible after. I wanted sex with friends. Boyfriend sex. Couple sex. I wanted the connection I'd felt looking at Robin, that moment when our breathing had synched, hearts hammering against each other, bodies striving toward the same perfect release.

Even with the disappearing act, Robin had made me feel . . . important. Like he needed *me* and not just my dick.

Saturday was blessedly sunny, the rare January day that inspired long walks and sweaters in lieu of coats, the sort of day that tricked Oregonians into thinking spring was around the corner even though weeks of more rain were sure to follow.

I surveyed the Lambert wedding cake. A massive, six-tier affair, it had taken the whole crew to perfect, but the final touches were all me. Forget the weather; today was simply a scramble to keep up.

"You gonna manage the shelter run?" Cliff asked, taking off his apron. I knew he was probably eager to get out, go toss a ball around with Eddie.

"No problem. I can squeeze it in."

Saturday was the day we usually brought day-old baked goods, along with some fresh rolls, to the shelter. Over the last few months,

I'd fallen into a routine of going in the middle of the week; funny how the more weight I lost, the more important the shelter became to me. But this week, I'd resisted the urge to put in extra time. I knew I'd really be going to check up on Robin, and being the needy one wasn't going to endear me to him. Better to wait for my usual day. Let Robin decide how he wanted to play things.

When I got to the shelter, Robin wasn't the one working the loading bay. Nice as the volunteer was, my feet itched to go find him. Soon as I was in the building, though, Melissa greeted me with a hug. She happily accepted the cookie I'd put in just for her.

"How much longer you have?" I asked, gesturing at her bump. Three sisters and I still hadn't mastered how to talk to a pregnant lady.

"Two months." She gave me a tight smile. "Still don't know what I'm going to do when the baby comes."

"What do you mean?"

"We don't have anyone lined up to be acting director when I go out on maternity leave." Unlike some of the larger shelters, Victory Mission only had a couple of paid employees. Melissa was director, but most of the daily details were handled by volunteers. "I want Robin to take it, but he keeps saying he'll think about it."

"He'd be a good fit."

"Hey, while you're here, could you talk to him?"

"About that?" My mouth twisted. No way was Robin taking advice from me.

"No. Something else." She glanced around the deserted hallway. In the distance, pots clanged as the Saturday crew got started on the meal.

"What?" Bile rose in my throat. Unable to meet her eyes, I studied a poster advertising a free clinic—cheerful thing, undoubtedly Robin's handiwork. Had she found out about Tuesday? Had Robin been talking about it? Maybe I'd played it wrong staying away.

"That kid he keeps working on—Zach—he OD'd today."

The sour feeling in my stomach intensified and my hands clenched. *Fucking January.*

"Shit. Is he dead?"

"No. But he's in a coma, and Robin's walking around like a zombie. I'm worried he's taking it way too personally. He and you have always talked, so I thought . . ."

"Sure. I'll go find him."

He wasn't in either the dining room or the kitchen. I found him in the storeroom, shelving bags of instant potatoes. Alone. I should have guessed. Robin didn't like to be around people when he was in a mood.

"Hey?"

He didn't look up at my greeting, but the jerk of his head said he'd heard me. "Hey."

"You okay?"

"Yeah. Sorry for not calling." Still looking down, his gaze shifted about. He was bluffing, trying to make this about us because somehow that must be easier for him than talking about Zach. His red eyes and shaking hands revealed his true mental state.

"Don't worry about it. It was real fun. But Melissa told me about Zach. What happened is terrible, but it's not your fault—you know that, right?"

"He came in at lunch yesterday looking for me, but I wasn't here. I had a client deadline." Swallowing hard, Robin looked like he might cry any second.

My shoulders tightened, muscles burning with empathy. Seeing him all torn up, ripped up something in me, too. After glancing back at the open door, I took him into my arms. I couldn't *not* hold him.

"Hey, now. You can't go beating yourself up over his bad choices."

"I know that. But . . ." He trailed off, his eyes wide and helpless. I stroked his hair and made what I hoped were soothing noises.

"It's hard. I get it."

"To top it off, Paul came by today. He didn't care about the Zach news."

"Asshole."

"Yeah, well, he wanted to get his things but stopped by here because he says he lost his key."

"Bastard. Change the locks." The hair on the back of my neck went all porcupine. My arms tightened around Robin. I didn't trust Paul. It would be just like him to turn up when Robin least expected it.

"I have to make a request of the super to do that. It makes me all antsy, though, knowing he's hanging around. God, I *hate* this week."

"Sorry." Releasing him, I backed away.

"Wait, Vic. I didn't mean . . . Tuesday was the high point." He grinned sheepishly.

"Yeah?" The chattering voices filtering in from the kitchen kept me from kissing him like I wanted.

"Hey, maybe I should take a page from your book. Stop stewing over Paul and Zach. You free tonight?"

"Not until late." I groaned. *Shitty, shitty timing.* "I have to deliver a wedding cake to Lake Oswego as soon as I'm done here."

"Oh. Never mind." He looked away before I could see whether there was regret in his eyes.

My hands flopped to my sides like limp pasta. My chance with Robin seemed as burned as the smell of that night's tomato sauce. Didn't want him finding distraction elsewhere.

"Wait. You wanna come along? It's at The Foundry. Gorgeous place, but a bit of a drive. I wouldn't mind company."

"You need help carrying stuff?"

"Sure. I could use an extra hand." I didn't really, but I knew how much Robin liked to be needed. And the company *would* be nice.

"All right. Let me finish up here."

Twenty minutes later and we were on I-5 headed to Lake Oswego, an upscale suburb full of Whole Foods and Crate & Barrel shoppers and the sort of money that could finance a January wedding for two hundred at one of the area's more exclusive venues.

"Who the heck gets married in January?" Robin asked as I navigated through the Terwilliger curves to get outside of Portland proper. Saturday traffic was thick, everyone taking advantage of the clear skies.

"Wealthy daughters who want a long honeymoon in Hawaii." I laughed. "There's always some reason to get hitched; we keep busy pretty steady until May, when the orders really pile up. I like this season, though, 'cause I've got time to make each cake extra special." I could feel myself turning red. I hadn't meant to say all that. I surveyed the Airstream trailer in front of us, wishing I could escape my own babble.

"I love that you like what you do." Robin grinned. "All those flowers would drive me crazy. But taking pictures of them? That I can do. Speaking of, you should tell Cliff to let me do a new logo for you guys. The red and white is kind of . . ."

"Classic. Cliffie's dad had that logo first. Good luck getting him to change."

"You ever think about getting your own place? Doing just cakes, maybe? You're too talented to stay an assistant."

"What? And give up bread and cookies? No way." I laughed, liking the chance to talk shop. Robin wasn't asking nosylike, more curious, and that made my chest feel loose and warm. "No, see, Cliff's got two kids, and neither of them wants a thing to do with the bakery. Another year or so and I'll buy into the bakery, then when Cliffie's ready to retire, I'll buy him out."

"Wow. Big plans."

"Yeah, well, not many people know of them. Keep it quiet." Don't know why I shared with Robin. But his compliment made me feel taller, proud of what we were doing at the shop.

"Well, when you become the boss man, you let me do up some nicer materials for you. I could do some real nice wedding brochures and such. And a better logo."

"Will do." My chest and shoulders rose up. I liked the thought of still being friends with him in a few years too much to tell him that I had no plans to change the red and white line drawing logo of a baker holding out a one-tier cake. However, Robin did do pretty work—the midyear appeals letter and brochure he'd designed for the mission were eye-catching and stylish without being pretentious. I'd heard from Melissa that donations had almost doubled. She was right; he would be great at keeping things afloat while she was out.

"How 'bout you? You gonna stay freelance?" I asked.

"Oh, yeah. My folks would love to see me take an in-house graphic arts position, but being my own boss is worth it. You'll see." He nodded, like we were some kind of equals. On the same path.

Warm as that thought made me, we weren't the same. Robin was a trust fund baby of some kind; he'd mentioned private school and college before, and no way could he afford to live in the Pearl on a freelancer's sporadic salary if he wasn't getting some kind of help. My dad had worked construction up until he died and wouldn't have known what do with a 401(k) or mutual fund.

"Melissa says she wants you to think about doing more with the shelter—take over when her baby comes."

"I'll help out whoever she puts in charge, but I'm not a leader." Robin looked out the window. "Tell me more about your house. You really going to sell it?"

*Whoa. Quick topic change much?* But everything else between us was so easy, I didn't want to ruin it by calling him on not wanting to talk about the shelter. After all, the Zach thing had to be weighing heavily on him.

"My Aunt Mary and Uncle Mauro owned it, but Aunt Mary went to live with my mom after Mauro went. She was battling cancer and the house was too much for her. Now the two of them are happy as clams in Mom's fifty-five-and-up complex."

"That's nice they have each other."

"Yeah. Manny and I were fixing the house up to put on the market for her. Didn't want to put it up as is; her and Mauro had remortgaged it enough that we wanted to make sure she got something back."

"Nice of you guys."

"Hell of a lot of work, you mean. It's just what family does." Family held on to the memories of our childhood, bounding in and out of Mauro and Mary's front room. Family held on to Manny's plans. Family held on even as everyone else moved on to lower-maintenance digs. Family held on even when their skill set wasn't exactly up to the task at hand.

A lump the size of Forest Park grew in my throat, but the more Robin acted like my plans for the house were doable, the more my muscles eased. We talked the rest of the way to The Foundry, Robin wanting to play what if and all full of ideas for the house and bakery. Suggestions came as natural to Robin as breathing did to the rest of us.

"See, now this cake should be in a magazine. Get the bakery into *Portland Monthly* magazine or maybe something more national. . . ." Robin climbed up after me into the back of the truck, inspecting the cake like he was the one who'd ordered it. "I love the lime and silver theme. And look at all that drop-line work. Did you freehand all that yourself?"

"Yep." I'll admit it: I puffed up like a proud cat that Robin knew what the fancy icing lines were called and that he appreciated my handiwork. The three-tier cake had white fondant topped with silver drop lines, delicate lime-green flower buds, and silvery green leaves. Our prep guy had filled the layers with lime curd and buttercream.

"Man. Lines like that would make a wicked cool tattoo sleeve." Robin rolled up his T-shirt sleeve, inspecting his bare biceps. "What do you think?"

"I think any ink on you would be . . . nice." Damn it. I could feel my ears and cheeks heating again.

"Nice, huh?" Robin winked at me. Heat arced between us, and I hoped like hell he was still thinking of coming back home with me later.

"So you really need help with carrying?" He raised an eyebrow, tilting his head toward the cart I had ready for the cake.

"You can push."

"I'm flattered, Vic. Really." He laughed, free and easy and no trace of the stress and worry that had marked his face back at the mission. Didn't matter that he could see through me. I'd play the fool any day to earn that laugh.

"Wait. I'm not exactly dressed for this." He looked down at his brown T-shirt.

"Here." I grabbed Cliff's spare jacket from the cab. "This'll be a bit big, but it'll do."

"Look at me, all official." He pulled it on. "Lead the way."

We wove our way through the great hall, past the reception tables and the linen-and-crystal-set dinner tables. Staff scurried around, taking care of the finishing touches for the candlelight reception. The actual bridal party would be back in the elaborate suites off the great hall.

"*Finally.* We've been waiting *hours.* Literally on pins and *needles.*" The wedding planner, a flouncy middle-aged woman named Barbara who spoke entirely in italics, greeted us.

"Sorry." I tried to look contrite; I know where the butter for my bread comes from, and wedding planners can make or break whether a bride chooses us.

"And who are you?" She turned an appraising eye on Robin, her gaze as sharp as the steak knives at each setting. "New?"

"Very." He gave her a charming smile, one that seemed to dial back her pissy level a few notches. "Maybe you can give me pointers."

"I *can.* Let me show you where this *gorgeous* cake is going. Then I'll get Natalie. She's back getting her hair done, but she wanted to see the cake."

*Crap.* While not unusual, it always made me antsy when the bride wanted to come out to see the cake while I was still there. There'd been a couple of bridezillas who'd wanted me to change something on the spot, which no can do. And if the bride really *did* hate the cake . . . well, it was probably best she discover that *after* the ceremony, while liquored up on champagne and surrounded by people saying nice things.

"Don't worry," Robin said in a low voice as Barbara walked away. "She'll love it."

"Who said I'm worried?" My words felt as false as the "Roman" columns framing the dance floor.

"You've got that line on your forehead you get when you're thinking too hard."

I didn't know what exactly to say to that, so I was relieved to see Natalie walking toward us. Her hair and makeup were flawless. Her veil was pinned in place, but the rest of her was wrapped in a giant, fluffy pink robe.

"Oh, it's darling!" she squealed, clasping her fancy manicured hands under her chin like a little girl. "I can't wait to taste it."

"Here." I retrieved a bakery box from the bottom shelf of the cart. "This has some treats for your first morning as husband and wife, but feel free to raid it now."

"Oh, you are the sweetest thing!" Without warning, she launched herself at me, catching me in a giant hug, spindly arms twining around my neck. "Thank you! I knew you'd come through."

"You're welcome." I held both of my arms out to my sides. I was afraid to rumple her and not quite sure what to do with so much perfume and lace in my personal space.

"The photographer wants more candids of you getting dressed." Barbara tapped Natalie on the back. "We don't want to fall behind."

"Enjoy your special day." Robin waved at both of them as they departed. Then, as we wheeled the empty cart back through the lime-and-silver-bedecked room, he let out a deep laugh. "Oh. My. God. Vic, your face when she hugged you . . . epic."

"What?"

"You're this big gruff guy, and here this itty-bitty bride turns you into a big teddy bear. Nice touch with the breakfast pastries, by the way. Classy."

"Yeah, we take care of our brides." I rubbed my jaw. "Hey, you want to look around before we go back? I want to show you something."

"Sure."

We stashed the cart back at the truck and then I led Robin around the main building, past the giant wood deck and down the ironwork stairs to the "garden patio," which was really just a fancy way of saying "pretty slab of concrete with nice ironwork details." It being January, there wasn't much garden happening. The air still had a bit of a bite in it. I shoved my hands in my bakery coat pockets. I should have grabbed my real coat, but us Oregonians like to fly in the face of weather. At least it wasn't raining; the earlier sun had fled, leaving a dreary sky, twilight already creeping in.

"Oh, wow." Robin caught sight of the promenade: a long walkway stretching out to become a bridge over the lake, ending in a huge wooden deck, all surrounded by more ironwork. "Can we go out there?"

"Yeah. Summer, they have small ceremonies out here, or sometimes dancing. Pretty, isn't it?" My steps lightened, my mood as sparkly as the little lights lining the path. This was my favorite part of the venue, and I always managed to sneak down here whenever we had a delivery. Something about the place made me feel sure and certain and insignificant, all in the same moment.

"It sure is. And look at you. Vic, the closet romantic."

"Me? Romantic?" I waved the idea away. "Hardly."

Standing in the center of the deck, though, even I could see the romance. In the dusky light, the lake was gorgeous. The lights of houses on the opposite shore were starting to twinkle, the evergreen trees becoming hulking shadows over gray-blue water so still and shiny it was like a sheet of glass. The gorgeous man by my side, looking like I'd handed him a gift by showing him my spot, made me wish for a little Ella Fitzgerald—something sweet and bluesy that we could dance to. Not that I danced much, but something about being with Robin in such a pretty place made me wish I did.

"Cold?" Robin reached out, touching my face. "Man, the wind down here is something."

"It's something all right." I wasn't looking at the wind or the lake when I said it. I was looking right at him, at his playful eyes and full lips. *He* was something—something that made my heart swell and my toes curl with want.

Reaching out, I pulled him toward me, closing the gap between us. I brushed my lips over his—a little hello, nothing too heavy. But Robin took my dainty, little petit four of a kiss and poured hot fudge all over it, licking his way into my mouth, arms coming around my neck.

My arms knew exactly what to do with Robin, and I crushed him to me. He felt solid, the lean muscles of his back flexing under my hand. He tasted better than any sweet I'd ever had: like pastry cream and coffee and his own exotic spiciness that made me want to lick him all over.

Giving a little sigh, he leaned into me more. The wind whipped around us, catching Robin's hair and my coat and slapping some much-needed sense into me.

"Can't do this here."

"Yeah. I know," Robin said against my lips before kissing me softly again. "Bad idea."

"Come home with me."

"You have to ask?" Robin pressed against me, his hard dick pushing up against mine, even through all the layers of cloth. "Don't know if I can wait . . . I have an idea."

Grabbing my hand, he dragged me back up the promenade, racing across the patio. As we approached the bakery truck, he pulled up short, tossing me a saucy smile. "You know, you have one big . . . truck."

"It's Cliff's. The bakery's. Not mine." God, but Robin made me stupid.

"Size of a camper really."

"You got a point?" I put my palm against the small of his back. I wanted to hold him, wanted to push him into my big, soft mattress and—

"You want to do something naughty?"

"Like what?" My neck muscles twitched. I had a feeling what he might be proposing. On the one hand, I'd never done anything like this. On the other . . . oh, screw it. I was in.

# Chapter 6

The January dusk seemed to flicker with anticipation. There were only a few other vehicles in the back lot, but I suddenly felt department-store-window public.

"Help me put the cart back." He motioned for me to raise the gate to the back of the truck. He followed me and the cart in, then closed the roller door, casting us into pitch black.

"You know, it occurred to me that you didn't exactly see me at my best the other night," he said.

"I don't know. It was pretty darn amazing to me."

"Yeah, it was, but I didn't get to show off my talents." His breath was a warm pulse against my neck and goose bumps broke out down my back.

The space was narrow, barely enough room for both of us and the empty bakery racks. My eyes still hadn't adjusted to the dark, so I shut them, just drinking in the weight of him. He reached around, unbuttoning my white coat and slipping his hands under my T-shirt. His stubble rasped a path down my neck and his dick strained against my ass.

"I . . . uh . . . don't exactly have supplies." I might have been okay with him fucking me in theory, but not in the reality of the tight confines of the truck.

"Relax. That's not the talent I meant." Laughing, he spun me. My back slammed into one of the racks. Without sight, all my other senses intensified. The feel of his fingers on my waist, dipping below the waistband of my chef's pants, the rasp of my zipper being lowered, the scent of his ginger-and-citrus soap, the silky-yet-coarse feel of his hair under my fingers.

I'd spent two years imagining what his hair would feel like: thick and heavy like rope, but so soft and dense. Of course I'd also spent two years imagining what it would be like to have Robin on his knees for me, my hands tangled in that thick mass of hair, his breath warm on my cock.

"Breathe, Vic." Robin chuckled, little puffs of air against my heated skin. And then his tongue was there, snaking up and down my shaft, making me crazy, making me wonder when he was going to—

He swallowed me down in one swift motion.

As the warm, moist heat of his mouth took me in, I had to clutch one of the racks for balance. My head slammed into the metal behind me as he worked his tongue all around my cockhead.

"Fuck. Ow."

"You okay?"

I rubbed my head, testing. His breath was warm against my more-than-willing dick.

"Yeah. But this is a terrible idea."

"Really?" Robin's voice was all innocent as he licked me leisurely. "What was it you said to me the other night? Just let me make you feel good, Vic."

"Ah . . . all right." My stomach went quivery with each swipe of his talented tongue. I reached behind me, using both hands to hold on to the racks as Robin swallowed me again. I tried to stay perfectly still, tried to let him set the pace.

But Robin kept making these greedy moans around my cock, and it felt like white water was churning through me. He swallowed me deep and wrapped his strong hands around my hips, yanking me closer.

"Yeah?" I experimented with moving my hips on my own, sliding deep and then back again. He moaned hungrily, like he couldn't wait for me to move again. "You like getting your face fucked?"

"Come on, Vic. Show me what you want." Robin nodded eagerly.

The motion made his chin graze my balls. Sparks of pleasure/pain lit up my nerve endings, and I had to hiss out a breath. "Oh, yeah."

His thumbs dug into my hipbones as I started thrusting for real. No way was I lasting long, not with an eager throat like Robin's. Myself, I was a licker, but much as I liked using my mouth, I didn't like when guys really unleashed and tried to fuck my face. I liked staying in control, and my gag reflex wasn't quite robust enough to allow much throat fucking anyway.

Robin, however, didn't seem troubled by things as mundane as gag reflexes and oxygen. He hummed low around me, and we slipped into a natural rhythm of me fucking deep and him swallowing hard around me before I slid back, letting him get a deep breath.

"So good." My words got another happy hum from Robin, so I kept talking. "Take it. Just like that."

God, even his deep inhales did something to me: hearing him gasp and knowing he wanted more, knowing he trusted me to cut off his air, even for an instant. The racks clattered behind me, the bars digging into my palm.

"Gonna come."

No more talking. I had to bite my lip to keep from crying out as I came down his throat. It felt like I'd been Tasered, muscles collapsing under the force of the orgasm. The shelves groaned in protest as I slumped down.

"Oh, hell." I uncurled one hand, feeling for his head. "That was . . . something."

"Something, huh?" Robin's rough voice echoed off the metal walls. The bumpy metal floor had to be killing his knees, but he sounded all blissed out.

"I'm not so good with adjectives." I laughed. "Fabulous. Good. Amazing. Damn, you're good at that. Give me a second and I'll show you—"

"Nah." Robin cut me off, and I could feel his shrug against my thigh. "That *was* incredible. Best endorphin rush I've had in a long, long time. I kind of want to just ride that wave a bit. Don't want to ruin that feeling with whether or not I can get off."

"Hey. I told you. I'm a patient guy—"

"Which is why I can wait for your house. Your bed."

"All right. Bed it is." I pulled him up to standing and kissed him. The faint taste of spunk didn't put me off; instead it turned me on, getting me even more interested in getting him to my bed.

"And I want a coffee drink on the way to your place." His voice was ragged. I should have felt a bit bad for going rough on him, but he sounded all smug.

"You can have whatever you want as soon as we get out of here."

"Crap." He pulled away, and I could feel him turning around, his head moving back and forth. "Are we trapped in here? I didn't think about it when I pushed you in."

"No. There's a latch release on this side, too."

"My God. Can you imagine needing to pound on the truck until wedding guests helped us out?"

"You can laugh. I'm the one who'd be facing a pissed-off wedding coordinator. Delay to her schedule and all."

We both collapsed in a fit of laughter, Robin's deep chuckles working me over like a massage.

We grabbed sandwiches and coffee drinks on the way back to Portland, and Robin came with me while I dropped the truck back behind the bakery and collected my car. Hell of a lot of maneuvering, but Robin didn't complain, seeming game to go along with whatever the night brought. In a fit of hopefulness, I grabbed some breakfast pastries from the store. I parked in my usual spot in the garage out back of my house and brought Robin into the house through the kitchen door.

As we came in, I threw my hat on the hook and my bakery coat in the laundry basket I kept under the row of hooks.

"Jeez, I need a shower," I muttered.

"Excellent idea." Robin clapped his hands together. "Lead the way."

*Heck.* I'd almost forgotten he was behind me.

"Uh. Okay." My feet did a nervous shuffle.

This was a new one for me. I'd never showered with another guy before. Never really thought about it as sexy until Robin peeled off his shirt right there in my kitchen, his golden skin gleaming. My hands clenched, ready to sponge him down. Yeah. Fuck my reservations. I couldn't wait to get him wet.

I led him to the main bath. Manny and I had put in new tile and painted, but the claw-foot tub was original. Big sucker in theory, but not so much when confronted with the reality of two dudes over six feet.

Any concerns I had fled as Robin skinned out of his jeans. Good lord, he was pretty to look at. Hard, lean muscles, bare chest, but a little trail of brown fuzz started right around his belly and worked its way south. Strong thigh muscles and a dimpled ass. People around the shelter liked to joke that Robin should model or be in the movies, but that ass was made for a porno.

"So how does this work?" Robin hopped in the tub and inspected the faucets. It was one of those old-fashioned things where the switch to flip the water to the shower was hidden. I had to reach around him to pull it, my fingers grazing his warm chest.

Watching the first droplets of water roll down his lean muscles, I licked my lips. I would've been perfectly happy to watch Robin bathe, but apparently I was supposed to join him. I got out of my clothes as quickly as I could, trying not to think what I looked like in the bright overhead light. There was no hiding behind a darkened room this time; every part I wasn't crazy about was on display. My stomach sucked in and my shoulders rolled back, my neck was all tense, like the right viewing angle might help things. *Fuck.* I knew I was being ridiculous, but I couldn't seem to turn off the spastic bunnies hopping around my too-thick middle. I hopped behind him, hoping he hadn't been looking too hard.

"I like this tattoo." Robin touched my chest. Of course he'd been looking. He was *always* looking.

"Thanks. Getting it redone." My voice was too gruff, but I was a bit tetchy about how the weight loss had fucked with my tats.

"This one's cool, too." He touched the band around my biceps. That one still looked half decent, especially now that I had bigger guns to show it off. "You ever think about getting a neck tat?"

"Nothing visible was allowed when I worked mortgages, but Cliff wouldn't care. Maybe someday. But first I gotta fix the others. Make 'em look decent again." I shifted around, shivering, not sure exactly how this two-guys, one-nozzle thing was supposed to work. Maybe this was one of those things that was a lot sexier on film than reality; reality was cold and slightly cramped.

"What are you talking about? All those NBA guys the other night—you can't even tell what most of their tats are because of how their muscles distort them. It doesn't matter really. Ink on muscles is hot period." Robin's appraising glance warmed me up, made me a little less self-conscious.

My biceps flexed under his roaming fingers. *Muscles.* He saw muscles. I *had* muscles now—firm pecs and defined guns. I resolved to lift a little more next week.

His hand swept over my stomach. It was a soft touch, but I still winced. Six-pack abs were never going to be a reality for me, and no amount of "cuddly" compliments could make me okay with having my stomach touched.

"If ink's so hot, why don't you have any?" I twisted to reach for the soap, dislodging his roving fingers.

"Needles." He shivered. "Hate needles. And honestly, that fear probably kept me alive, so I'm not in a huge hurry to get over it."

I buried my face against his neck, glad he was alive and here with me. He turned, letting the warm spray hit me, too. And then he was kissing me, and I wasn't so cold anymore, and I saw a glimmer of the appeal of this.

We didn't try to get it on in the tub, though. That didn't seem to be the point. Instead, we made out under the warm stream of water, kissing and touching and pressing together. Eventually Robin reached for the soap, lathering me up between more kisses. He washed my chest, his fingers dancing against my scar.

"Does it hurt?" His voice was as soft as his hand.

"Not anymore." Didn't *hurt* precisely, but my stomach lurched. No one other than me and the doctor had touched the scar. I hadn't shown it to anyone save that one bad hookup. But Robin wasn't flinching away in horror. Instead, his eyes were kind and curious.

"Can you . . . feel it?"

"What? The band?"

He nodded. "Sorry. That's rude."

"Nah. It's okay. No, not really. I mean, I'll get a really sick stomach if I eat too much or the wrong stuff."

My fingers drummed against the tile wall. I grabbed shampoo and motioned for him to let me lather up his hair. Not that he needed it, I was just eager to get my hands tangled up in it again. And okay, I was also eager for a change of subject. Talking about what I could and couldn't eat depressed the hell out of me. And nice as his touch was, him petting my scar and washing my saggy stomach gave me weird prickles down my back.

But Robin's hair, slick with shampoo, sliding between my fingers—that was the furthest thing from a downer. Massaging his scalp and neck, I tried to work out some of the tension I felt in his muscles.

"Sometime will you let me watch while you shave your head?" Robin's eyes were closed, his voice all relaxed.

"Eh. Sure." He seemed so comfortable, talking like this might be a regular thing, like he would be happy simply to watch me get ready, like we were a real couple. It was only too easy to picture a morning like that, and I had to look away. Robin was talking just to talk; he didn't know how much I wanted that, and I couldn't let him see.

After he was all rinsed we kissed again, long and slow. And I might not have been willing to let him see my eyes, but I knew it was in my kiss—how much I wanted him, and not only for tonight. Our cocks slipped against each other, but it was a slow, almost accidental slide. Like the rest of him, his cock was long and slender next to my thicker meat. It would have been easy to wrap a hand around us both, but I liked holding him under the water, my hands still in his hair, his arms around my waist.

"Aaeeoo." Robin pulled away with a grimace as the water went cold.

I fetched us both towels, but instead of handing him his, I toweled off his shoulders and flat stomach. More touching. I wasn't ever going to get tired of touching him.

He laughed and I looked up, surprised at how young he looked with his hair wet and slicked back. He looked seventeen, not—

"Hey, Robin? How old are you?"

"A bit late to be asking if I'm legal, isn't it, Vic?" His laugh echoed off the white subway tile walls. "I'm twenty-three."

"Oh, heck." My stomach went sour. I'd guessed twenty-seven or so. Not that young. I felt suddenly old and kind of creepy.

"Why? How old are you?" He was laughing again, and the wide grin didn't make him look any older.

"Thirty-three," I mumbled at my feet.

"See, not so bad. Paul was thirty-five."

"Hardly want to be in the same category as him." The sourness in my gut spread, chasing out all the warm happiness of the shower.

"Oh, come off it. I dig older guys." He grabbed the towel, rubbing his hair and then shaking his head like a puppy. His hair fell back into more of its usual shag. "Now kiss me again. That was hot in the tub."

I pulled him to me, but not without a few misgivings. He was so damn young. And Paul was an opportunistic asshole and I *so* didn't want to be lumped in the same category as him. But Robin was warm and hard and smelled like my soap, and all reason fled as soon as his lips touched mine.

Robin kissed my neck and jaw in a rather determined fashion, cutting a quick trail down my chest. I grabbed his arm right as he was about to sink to his knees.

"No?" He looked at me through long lashes. "I thought you liked it in the truck."

"Loved the truck. Your mouth is too fucking talented. But it's your turn now."

"We can try fucking," he said, but he didn't sound all that confident. He looked young and uncertain. Much as my body was clamoring for the chance to fuck, my brain wanted better for Robin.

"Nope." I kissed him lightly. "I don't want something you have to *try*—I want what you *need*."

"I don't know what I need. That's the problem. I know what I want, but my stupid body doesn't cooperate."

"What do you mean?" He'd hinted at it before, but I still wasn't sure what he meant.

"It can take me a really long time to get off. It's like my neurons don't understand what to do without a buzz. And sometimes orgasm just doesn't happen. My brain won't shut off. I've been sober three years and I still haven't managed to figure it out, and I feel guilty and terrible—"

"Breathe, Robin. It's okay." I rubbed his shoulders. "Nothing to feel terrible about."

"You don't know what I've done, Vic." He looked at me with big, sad eyes.

"You turned tricks, yeah?"

"How did you guess?" His eyes went wide. "Did Paul tell you?"

My heart squeezed, like a piping bag oozing out sympathy. I wrapped a hand around his neck, pulling him closer. I'd guessed as soon as Robin mentioned sobriety. I'd been around the shelter long enough to know what kids did to survive.

"You were what? Seventeen? Eighteen? On the streets?"

He nodded. "My folks cut me off because they thought it would help if I didn't have access to their money. But it didn't. Not until I finally let Melissa talk me into calling home, taking their help to get clean. And in the meantime . . ."

"You did some stuff you're not proud of. I get it." I kissed him lightly.

"You really don't care?" His head tilted to one side, appraising me.

"Why should I? That's not who you are now." Possessiveness made a bitter stew in my gut, but empathy kept it from reaching toxic levels. I wouldn't say I was *thrilled* about the idea, but mainly Robin's revelation just made me want to hold Robin close, smell his hair, tell him he was safe now.

"Yeah, but don't you think it's . . . *ironic* that now I can't seem to relax enough to fuck when before . . ." He waved his hand dismissively, banging against the sink.

"Paul make you feel bad for that?" I frowned. I wanted to put a serious hurt on everyone from Robin's past who'd ever used him or hurt him. Paul would be an excellent starting point.

"God, I shouldn't love it when you look like you'd like to eat him for breakfast. I really shouldn't." Robin's laugh was a nervous little thing. "But yeah. I told him about my past, thinking it might help him to understand, but it just made things worse. Sex between us was . . . problematic."

"He was the problem." I said it emphatically, gripping his shoulders tight. "Doesn't matter what you did in the past. Look, I've done all sorts of shit I'm not proud of. But that's not who I am now. And it's not who you are either. You deserve to go as slow as you need. Get the time you need. It's not a fucking race."

"I love your glower." Robin kissed me, a quick brush across my lips. "And I'm a mess and you don't care."

*I care too much.* I couldn't say that, even though my heart felt tight in my chest and my stomach felt all twisty. I really did want to pound Paul for making Robin feel bad about his past. He'd been a kid. A kid under the grip of an illness I'd seen drag too many others down. A kid, all alone and scared. How could I judge that? My knees felt unsteady, unable to support the weight of my heavy heart.

I kissed him back, deepening it, trying to tell him with lips and tongue and heart that all I cared about was that he was safe now. Robin sucked on my tongue, making the same needy sounds he had in the truck, sending heat straight to my dick.

And yeah, my ego perked up a bit, too. I wanted to be the one who made things better for Robin, wanted to be the one who made sex good for him again. There were plenty of areas where I was a fuckup of epic proportions, but maybe I could give him this.

# Chapter 7

I tugged Robin toward my room. We lost our towels somewhere along the way.

"Now you're going to stop looking at some clock," I said as I pushed him onto the bed. "Or worrying about anything other than feeling good. And we're not fucking. I don't want you even thinking about that."

"You're serious about waiting, aren't you?" He reached up and touched my face.

"Damn right." I nodded. *Waiting.* It was such a beautiful, magical word that meant more shared nights and shared meals and shared kisses.

"I liked the truck," he whispered. "When you took over. I kept wishing I could see your face. I wanted to see if you were glowering like this. Your scowl is fucking hot."

"Yeah?"

"Felt like I was flying when you fucked my throat. Like I was high or tripping. It was awesome." He reached toward my cock, creeping across the black and gray comforter. I batted his hands away.

"Didn't I say no?" I gave him a real good scowl. "You want me to take charge? Want me to tell you how to get done?"

"Oh, fuck yeah." His voice was all breath. He reached for my cock again, and I put a little heat in the slap I gave his fingers. I tossed the comforter to the maple footboard with way more force than I needed to, simply to watch his muscles draw up tight, his eyes going wide.

"Then lay on your stomach. Right now."

He scampered to obey, and it was a beautiful thing, long limbs uncurling as he threw himself down on the bed. Some tension seemed to roll off him. He liked playing like this, and truth be told, I did, too.

My muscles burned, amped up like after a big set at the gym. My pulse raced, ready for the next challenge. I straddled his lower thighs, pinning him in place. He liked my muscles and my scowl and my meanness, and hell if that didn't make my insides go as gooey and warm as caramel.

"I'm going to lick you all over, and the only thing you get to say about that is, yes, please."

"Yes, please." His voice was dusting-sugar soft.

I rubbed my hands down his back and arms, trying to get him even more relaxed. Then I started with his ears. I took my time, outlining the shell of his ear with my tongue, sucking on the lobe, discovering all the little spots behind his ears and neck that made him shiver and moan.

"Oh, my *fuck.*"

"I haven't even started yet."

Moving on to his neck, I licked up all the lingering droplets of water. I took little bites along his shoulders. Licking and sucking and biting my way down his back, I traced his spine with my tongue.

He hissed, his whole body rolling.

"Yeah? You like that?" I sucked up a love bite right at the base of his neck, right below where his shirt collar would be. The air in the room was cool, but it made me hot to think about the air licking against his abraded skin.

"That. More of that."

"What did I tell you?"

"Yes, please."

I did a whole line of bites down either side of his spine. I fell into the zone I did when decorating a cake, finding a rhythm and going with it, making something beautiful without overthinking it. I simply licked and sucked and nipped and followed my intuition.

"Fuck me." Robin's muscles quivered under me.

"Nope." I bit him a little harder at the base of his spine. "You gonna try and tell me I'm taking too long?"

"God no."

"Good, because I plan to take my own sweet time when I eat your pretty little ass." And with that, I licked from the base of his spine all the way down his crack before settling in and attacking his hole.

"*Vic.*" Robin shamelessly pushed his ass up to meet my mouth.

"Don't you try to hurry me, boy." My pulse was as heated as my words. I love rimming. Love driving a guy insane and incoherent with nothing more than my mouth. I like sucking dick, too, but there's something about the noises a guy makes when he's getting tongue-fucked—makes me feel Empire State Building tall.

Robin went from moaning to whimpering to a sort of chanting to humping the bed and whining. God, the whines. Low and needy, ending on a higher squeak, they made my dick leak and my hands tremble.

"Yeah, you fuck my bed, baby. You fuck it hard as you need to. I'm just gonna keep eating this ass." Spreading him open, I used a hand to tease his balls a bit, rolling them around.

"*Oh, fuck.* Don't stop. Dontstopdontstop," he chanted, the bedsprings creaking from his thrashing around.

"Yeah, that's it. You just let it feel good."

I had no idea how long I licked and worked him like that. Didn't matter. I wasn't stopping till I heard him howl. And howl he did, humping the mattress, arching that ass up into my mouth until I had to grip his waist, hold him down, make him take more of the sensations I was forcing on him. Then he started rubbing and grinding on the bed in little circles, and I knew he was close. I got my index finger nice and slick and worked the tip of it next to my tongue.

That did it. He came on a shout, bucking and trembling all over. I licked him through it, getting the most beautiful whimpers from him, until he was curled up, shuddering. I rubbed him all over, soothing him down. Kissed his shoulders.

My lungs burned and my dick throbbed, desperate for attention. Hell, I'd almost come watching Robin go. I got a hand on myself and pulled Robin closer, wanting his nearness. Nothing more. Just him there.

"You . . . can . . . fuck me." His voice was hoarse and he didn't even raise his head.

"Who's in charge here, baby?" I put the command back in my voice.

"Not me," he said sleepily, nuzzling into one of my pillows.

"That's right. And I'm gonna come just like this. Gonna spurt all over your ass."

"Yeah. Do it." He sounded more interested now, bumping his hips into mine. "Want to feel you come."

"Yeah?" I rolled so I was covering him, my dick wedged along his damp crack.

"God, you are so hot." I kissed his shoulders. "Such a hot boy."

My heart pounded like my first time on the treadmill, my body feeling just as uncoordinated. My thrusts against him were rude, jerky things with no finesse, but it didn't take more than three or four good thrusts before I was shouting, too, coming all over his back.

"That was fucking amazing," I whispered afterward, rolling off him.

"No, that was more amazing than fucking." He chuckled, moving around so that he was settled in against my side. I grabbed one of the towels, made a futile stab at cleaning us up before giving up and grabbing the comforter from the end of the bed. Pulling it around us, I let myself fall asleep holding him.

"You want brunch?" Robin asked, stretching. My sheets pooled around his waist. He'd stayed the night and hadn't fled. I counted that as a genuine Sunday miracle. It was well after ten. We'd woken a few hours earlier, but another round of sex had led to a nice sleeping-in. We'd tried sixty-nine, and yeah, I came first, but it wasn't exactly a great hardship to get to play with Robin's cock a bit longer. I saw what he meant about sometimes getting all tangled up in his thoughts and not getting there, but I'd simply kissed him until he'd been too breathless to think, then kept playing with him until he'd shot all over our chests. Then we'd drifted back into another sticky sleep.

What I needed even more than food was a shower. Not to mention restaurants were damn problematic for me. I couldn't handle the huge portion sizes or the grease.

"I brought you some pastries back from the shop. You want those while I shower first?" I rolled toward him, propping myself up with an elbow.

"You did that for me?" He blushed, a pretty pink blooming on his cheeks. The morning sunshine made his hair glow, showing off all the shades between gold and chestnut.

"No biggie. We've always got extra stuff." Sitting up, I waved his question away. Didn't want him thinking I was getting too attached.

"That was nice of you, but I don't really like sweets first thing in the morning. But there's this place on Alberta I like to go for brunch sometimes. They do a vegan buffet—it's all superhealthy stuff and I think you'd find some stuff you can eat."

"Really?" I wasn't sure what shocked me more—that he wanted

to go out with me or that he'd thought about what my dietary needs might be.

"Yeah. Come on. It'll be fun. And we can shower together again."

I wasn't half as into that as he was, but I did like him rubbing all over me. Sundays I usually shaved, taking advantage of the extra time to get my head nice and smooth. Robin watched this like it was a matinee, moving around to get better viewing angles.

"Can I do it sometime?" He leaned against the sink, blocking my light.

"Uh. You have a shaving kink or something?" I'd noticed his chest was extra smooth. If he asked to wax me, all bets were off. What I lacked up top I had in spades on my body, but no way in heck was I letting anyone near me with hot wax. I did have some lines I wouldn't cross, even to indulge Robin the Curious.

"Nah. I just really dig that look on you. Even more than when you used to wear it really closely cropped, which was hot, too."

*Whoa.* Robin had noticed my hair back when I first started volunteering? Back before I'd had the surgery? That did something to my insides—made them all wobbly, like gelatin that hadn't set up right.

"Don't go shaving your own head." I tugged lightly at his wet hair. "Be a shame to waste all this pretty."

And then we were kissing and touching again, and it was another hour before we made it out the door. The vegan place had nice strong coffee and a bunch of odd dishes. But they were all helpfully labeled: low-fat, organic, gluten-free, no soy, etc. Gotta love the Northwest, where you apologize for sticking gluten and butter in your baked goods.

But I managed to find some low-fat raisin toast and "scrambled" zucchini on the buffet.

"Hey, Vic!" A cute Asian dude called my name. Robby. He was one of the coffee-cart guys who contracted with the bakery for pastries.

Behind me, Robin scooted closer. And stood up taller.

"Who's your friend?"

I made the introductions. The coffee-cart guy, Robby, laughed at how similar his name was to Robin's. Robin didn't laugh. *Jealous.* Robin was jealous. My heart did a little tap dance of petty happiness.

'Course Robin had nothing to worry about. Robby had proved my gaydar was for shit; I'd been dealing with him for a few years now and hadn't known he was gay. But he introduced his boyfriend, David, a nerdy-looking dude in a polo shirt.

"How nice to meet you!" Robin got a whole lot friendlier as soon as the boyfriend entered the conversation. We all ended up sitting together at one of the long wooden tables that lined the side of the coffee shop.

"How do you like the food?" David asked me.

"Eh . . ." I struggled to find diplomatic words. He and Robby were obviously regulars at the place.

"Bread's not as good as yours." Robin patted my knee.

"Few breads are," Robby said. "You should have Cliff send over some samples. I'm friends with the owner here. He outsources the baked goods."

"It's okay," David said to me in a low tone. "I'd kill for two slices of bacon right now."

I laughed, and then things were easier, the four of us making small talk and joking.

That was weird. And not weird like the strange food weird. Weird good. Because it was like Robin and I were a real couple on a real date, doubling with friends. Robby and David had an older home, and that got Robin all into amateur-decorator mode. Soon paint swatches were spread on the table and the guys were talking lighting fixtures. I grinned more than I had in years and tried to follow the conversation. I felt weirdly proud of Robin, like he was mine to show off. Like, *Look at how brilliant my boyfriend is. He solved your problems in a snap.* I had a brief flash of introducing Robin to Cliff's brother James and the rest of my friends. Not at a bar obviously, but I liked the image of him hanging with all of us, of more meals like this. It wasn't simply the sex—which was out-of-this-world amazing—it was being with Robin, having him as a part of my life. It would be only too easy to get used to this, and I had to remind myself to enjoy it like the rare sweets I allowed myself, not to go thinking this would become my regular fare.

# Chapter 8

I was in the middle of decorating a retirement cake when my phone vibrated, but I gave up a few seconds of concentration to glance down at the screen. I didn't need a cheesy ringtone like "You Are the Sunshine of My Life" to know the message was from Robin. Since Sunday we'd kept up a regular stream of text messages.

*You need something like this for your foyer.* He'd sent a picture of a light wood table.

I wasn't so sure that the still half-done entryway warranted a fancy name, let alone a midcentury modern sideboard, but it made me smile that Robin was thinking about me and my house as he wandered around Southeast Portland's shops on Tuesday morning. His work was slow again, so he was out shopping and taking pictures for future design projects.

A few hours later, another text came in.

WANT TO COME OVER AFTER WORK TONIGHT?

My palms started sweating and I had to make myself wait a few minutes before replying. *Sure. Want me to cook?*

He replied almost immediately. *That would be nice but not necessary. Paul wants to get his stuff. You still game for being my pretend boyfriend?*

Ouch. That stung a little, made my shoulders tight and my hands tense around my phone. Made sense that Robin wanted a buffer between him and Paul. And I had been the one to suggest carrying on the ruse. But I'd kinda hoped we were on our way beyond that.

*Anytime,* I texted back, because the alternative was not seeing Robin, and that would suck way worse than me being a little put out over labels.

I showed up at six with a bag of groceries. I'd showered after work and put on a nice shirt. If Robin wanted a pretend boyfriend for the night, he was going to get a classy one, not me looking like I was just there to fuck. I wouldn't mind showing Paul exactly how a guy like Robin should be treated.

Of course the smarmy bastard beat me there. Probably came earlier than he said just to fuck with Robin. When Robin let me into his tenth-floor studio, Paul was already there, sitting on a red couch next to a small box of odds and ends: two shirts, a toothbrush, a book, and some other crap. Nothing he couldn't have lived without.

"Sorry I'm late," I greeted Robin with a quick peck on the cheek.

"You brought dinner!" Robin's tone was overly chipper and his smile two sizes too small, but the lingering kiss he gave me was far less fake.

"You staying?" I sent Paul a good long glower. "I only brought two steaks."

"Paul was just leaving, weren't you?" Robin said, not sounding terribly sure. I hated how Paul seemed to zap his confidence. Robin stayed close by my side. I set the groceries down on a nearby stool and put an arm around Robin.

"Robin, you don't have to be nasty." Paul shook his head, like he was scolding a dog. "We could still be friends. I want to *help* you."

"No, you couldn't," I spoke up.

"Babe. Are you really going to let your thug here dictate who you talk to?"

"I don't think we can be friends. Not right now." Robin's hand worried the pocket of his jeans and his eyes stayed on the dark hardwood flooring. "And Vic's not a thug."

"Yeah, I am," I said, keeping my tone overly polite while my eyes attempted to incinerate Paul, sending him a clear don't-fuck-with-me message.

"Fine. Fine. I'm going." Paul stood up, brushing invisible dirt off his perfectly pressed khakis. "But, Robin. Babe. You can do better. Really."

My fists clenched and I stepped toward Paul. It was like I was fifteen again, a hotshot Richie Rich kid looking down on me. *Fuck that noise.* I hadn't put up with that crap then and I wasn't about to start now. That Robin could do better was an undisputed fact. That Paul didn't get to talk to me like that was also an undisputed fact.

"You wanna mess with me? Seriously?" I got up in his face, using the extra fifty pounds and four inches I had on him to look him over like the spineless gym rat he was. All pretty boy and no substance.

Paul swallowed hard, his eyes going to Robin. Robin shrugged, a little smile tugging at his lips.

"I'm out of here." Paul stalked out, but I didn't breathe easy until I heard the ding of the elevator arriving on the floor.

"How was that? That enough scowl for you?" I turned toward Robin.

"Oh, yeah." Robin's mouth pursed, like he'd just eaten something supertasty, a satisfied smile tugging at his lips. "You could have kissed me more, though. Little more PDA would have been nice."

"Yeah?" I kissed him again, this time just for me. He tasted liked soda and the now-familiar taste of himself, the familiarity of it making warmth uncurl in my gut. There was a comfort in knowing his scent and his taste. "Turns you on when I threaten to make a cutlet out of your ex?"

"Is that so wrong?" He laughed. His eyes were full of dirty mischief. "Not like I wanted you to throw a punch or anything. I . . . I didn't want to feel backed into a corner by him, you know? I didn't want to agree to his stupid let's-be-friends plan. *He* was the one to end things."

"You still love him?" I'd wanted to ask that for days.

"Love?" Robin made a dry, bitter sound. "No. I'm pretty sure I was more in love with the idea of a boyfriend than the actual boyfriend. Actually, the more I hang around you, the more I realize what a controlling jerk Paul was."

"You keep standing your ground with him," I said, trying not to let on how pleased his admission made me. "Now: Where's your stove?"

"What are you making us?" He started to look in the grocery bag, but I shooed him away.

"No peeking." I'd also brought along a little something for after dinner, if things went my way.

"As far as the kitchen, that's it." He motioned to the far end of the studio, which held a single short row of cabinets and an island with a cooktop and a breakfast bar.

"I don't cook much, so I don't have much in the way of pans and stuff." After showing me the layout, Robin grabbed a plastic cutting board in the shape of an apple. "What can I do to help?"

"I got this." I plucked the cutting board from his fingers.

"Can I get you some water? Or soda? I have diet." Robin got two glasses out before I could decline.

"Water's fine." I unwrapped the steaks. "This is a nice place," I said as I mangled some garlic. Robin's knives were for shit, but his pans were top of the line. The studio was one long, open space, with the living area on one end, the kitchen on the other, and a bed tucked into an alcove near the kitchen area. A second alcove off the living area held a computer station.

"Eh." He made a sour face. "It's through my dad. He's part of the property management group that owns this building."

"Ah." I suddenly wished I'd brought nicer food to cook. Damn; I'd known Robin probably came from money, but there was money and then there was Donald Trump or Lex Luthor money.

"After I got sober I finished up my degree at the Art Institute, then my dad gave me this as a graduation present."

"Nice dad." Mine gave me a pat on the back and a pen set when I got my associate degree. Didn't live to see me graduate culinary school, but my ma gave me a set of nice knives.

Robin watched me roll the steaks. "Oh, wow, that's fancy."

"It's nothing." I was doing a steak roulade with spinach and cheese. It looked far harder than it was. Ditto the rice pilaf I was planning to plate it with.

"Come on, you have to let me help." He drummed his fingers on the granite counter. "Salad? Lettuce be your sous chef?" He held up a wilty head of romaine from his fridge.

I laughed, catching him for a kiss. "Fine. You can do salad, but I brought my own greens. And you don't want to be my sous-chef. Trish is always getting on me for terrorizing the assistants."

"I don't believe that."

"I made one cry by making him redo a birthday cake at midnight. But he misspelled the kid's name." I got the rice cooking with a little onion and garlic.

"So, am I like the only one who gets to see your nice side?" Robin peeked around the cooktop.

I thought about that as I seasoned the rice. I was civil to darn near everyone, scary to more than a few, and helpful to people who needed it, but nice? It wasn't really a word people used with me. But something about Robin made me sweeter, made me want to be the nice guy.

"Is it weird if I say yes?"

"No. It's sweet." He leaned in, kissing me on the cheek. "Man, that smells amazing. I can't ever have you meet my parents. My dad will want to fire poor Posy and hire you to be his personal chef."

My hand tightened around the stirring spoon. *Meet the parents.* I'd suffered through each of my sister's parade of boyfriends, but I hadn't ever been the one to bring a dude home to meet my family. But maybe . . .

"You close with your parents?" I asked.

"Eh. My dad's okay. Things were really strained between us when I was younger. They're slightly better now." The twisted look on his face said they still weren't on great terms.

"My old man couldn't deal with the gay thing. We fought all the time about my leaving the Church." A decade's worth of guilt and doubt lodged under my shoulder blades, throwing me right back to those arguments. I squeezed the lemon for the steak too hard, making juice hit my face.

"My dad took it personally when I came out at fourteen—like I'd chosen to fuck up his life. That was when I started using."

"I'm sorry." Such an inadequate expression for such a shitty thing. "I used to hide from mine—stayed in the kitchen with my mom and grandma so he couldn't go on about me being a pansy or whatever."

"Year I came out my mom eloped with her masseur. Housekeeper was this German lady who hated me. So no kitchen to hide in." He smiled wryly. "But it's ancient history now."

He looked impossibly young and full of hard-earned wisdom at the same time. Old soul, my nonna would say. My chest tightened. For all my dad had given me a hard time about religion and manhood, he'd been around my whole childhood—full of rules and questions and game playing. My mom too. No one could ever accuse the Degrassi kids of being neglected.

"Yeah. And families do come around. Mine is pretty great now, even if they weren't at first. My little cousin Lance just came out. Whole family's been really good to him. Guess I taught them well."

"To pioneers." He raised his water glass to me. "And to not being teenagers anymore."

"Amen." I threw together a quick vinaigrette for Robin's salad, using a fancy glass when I couldn't locate any measuring cups or little bowls.

"Man. You even brought your own vinegar." Robin smiled up at me. "Didn't trust my kitchen?"

"I wanted to make my—you—a nice dinner, not play *Chopped*." I laughed.

"You know how to spoil a guy, Vic." Robin gave me a sad little smile. I reached across the counter and ruffled his hair.

"You're fun to spoil. And it's just steak."

"Steak. Rice. Real salad dressing. And I spied a bakery box over there. You'd think this was a real date."

I could have demurred, but instead I decided to swing for the fences. "Why can't it be?"

"Oh, Vic. That would be a terrible idea." Robin pushed away from the counter, went to stand by the large picture window.

My chest felt squashed, like the time my little sister jumped off a couch and landed on me, cracking three ribs. My whisk hit the counter with a clatter and I stalked after him.

"Why not? We get on good together. Why not date? See where things go?"

"Because I'm on the rebound. I'm not really in a position for a relationship." His voice shook.

"But you can't deny we have fun together. So let me be your rebound guy." I wrapped my arms around him. He didn't pull away, instead sinking into me with a gratifying sigh.

"Oh, Vic. You're almost too sweet."

"Sweet doesn't have half the plans I do for after dinner." I kissed his ear. "Brought something I think might help you. If you're game."

"Oh, I'm always game. And that's what I mean—you really want to help me with my fucked-up sex problems?"

"Rather self-serving of me, but yeah, I do. I'm not entirely convinced that your issue isn't simply poor taste in dudes, Paul being exhibit A. But yeah, I want to make you feel better about sex. Because you deserve that. Doesn't matter if it's me or the next guy. You deserve to feel good about fucking again."

"Yeah." Robin sighed and tilted his head to give me better access to his neck. "Vic, the benevolent baker who moonlights as a sex therapist. And rent-a-boyfriend."

"Hey, the bodyguard thing comes free of charge. I'll come and look tough for Paul any day."

"I'm not going to break your heart if we keep doing this? Casual, I mean? The whole rebound thing?"

"Nah. My heart's way tougher than that." *I hope.* The organ in question gave a strange little flutter. Below us, the city spread out, buildings and roads and river looking pristine, as much an illusion as my words.

"Good." He gave me a funny look, like maybe I'd said the wrong thing. "Because I do want to keep doing this."

He wiggled around until we were face-to-face. "And not just because whatever you're making smells amazeballs. I . . . I like you, Vic."

"I like you, too." And then I had to kiss him because the alternative was to keep looking into his deep brown eyes that saw too much.

# Chapter 9

After dinner Robin loaded his space-age–looking dishwasher while I put away the food. Like a real couple would, splitting the chores without even discussing it, simply falling into a routine. Problem was, I wasn't sure how real couples slid into postdinner sex. I mean, I *could* show Robin what I'd brought, slap it on his little dining table, but that seemed a bit tasteless.

"You want to watch a show?" Robin motioned at the large flat-screen TV set up by his couch. "Or there's probably a game on."

"Game, if you won't be bored."

"Oh, I won't be bored." Robin gave me a look like I was denser than the pound cake I'd brought him. *Oh.* So this was how a date crept toward sex. Robin flipped on the Blazers game and we ended up on his long leather couch. His place had lots of color to it—red couch, blue computer desk, expensive-looking abstract painting by the door, Moroccan bedspread that reminded me of a cake I'd done the summer before.

Robin cuddled right up to me, half in my lap. Now *this* was how to watch a game. Only thing missing was a beer—but a lapful of Robin quickly pushed that thought from my head. The Blazers weren't even up four points before Robin straddled my thighs, grinning down at me.

"Tell me what you brought."

"It's a surprise." I slid my hands under his gray T-shirt, lightly tickling his sides. "And it's all the way over there." I gestured at the kitchen.

"I don't like surprises." He did a fake pout. "It's not poppers, is it? Because I know that doesn't count as a high to some people, but I—"

"Relax, baby. I know better than to bring you anything like that. Brought you a toy."

"Oooh." He started to get off my lap, but I stayed him with firm hands.

"No you don't. Not yet." I leaned up to kiss him. "Wanna make out with you a bit."

We kissed and stroked and cuddled, and pretended to watch the game until Robin was shirtless on my lap, our dicks grinding through the layers of fabric while I licked and nibbled at his flat pink nipples.

"God. You . . . are . . . really good with your mouth." Robin's breath came in little huffs.

"Oral fixation." I raised my head and smiled at him. "It's why smoking was such a bitch to quit. And why I love sucking dick. Lose your pants."

"Yes, sir," he said with a laugh.

My dick throbbed. I stretched an arm out along the back of the couch, liking this control thing. I kept my pants on because there was something extra dirty about him naked and undulating on me and me still fully clothed.

My mouth tingled, and I knew what I wanted next. I got him to raise up on his knees so his cock was level with my mouth. I played, sucking only on the tip until his hips rocked and he cursed softly. Then I swallowed him back. The angle let me take more than I usually could, and I used that to my advantage, rubbing my tongue all over him while he was deep in my mouth.

"*Oh*. Fuck. Vic." He freed one hand from the back of the couch to clutch at my head.

Working him until his thighs trembled and he was breathing in a series of broken moans, I released him abruptly with a light slap on his ass.

"You want more?"

"God yes."

"Go dig in my bag over there. Bring me back what looks interesting to you." He trotted over to the kitchen, which was a fine sight to watch, his tight ass bouncing and his muscles flexing. Loved how his ass was bare, his leg fuzz not starting till partway down his thighs.

"I'm assuming it's not the vinegar or lemon?" He dug through the bag. I knew when he found it because his eyes went wide. He held up the box. "Beads?"

"Oh, yeah. I was thinking about how you can take a little of my finger. Thought maybe we could play with those. See how much you can take. Work on getting your muscles to learn to relax."

"Ass exerciser?" He gave an almost girlish giggle. "I'm game, but I'm not sure if it'll work. I've tried a dildo a few times and I can't really take it. Stupid—"

"Stop beating yourself up and come here." I put a little of the command he liked so much in my voice, slapping the couch for emphasis. "And bring the lube I stashed in there, too."

"Gee, Vic, you really *do* come prepared."

"Get your ass over here." I tried laying it on a bit thicker, just to see what he'd do. And his response was gorgeous—eyes going wider, cheeks pinkening, chest expanding as he inhaled. He nodded and scampered over. Oh, yeah. My boy liked to play.

"Now, you get up on me so I can eat your ass."

"Not sure I can balance . . ." He straddled me again, facing away from me this time.

"You figure out a way, boy, 'cause I'm gonna lick you open."

He leaned forward, bracing himself on the heavy coffee table, long back muscles and ass displayed like an erotic photo shoot.

I inhaled sharply, taking in the sight. Holding him steady with my hands, I buried my face in his tight cleft, licking my way to his hole. I licked and sucked until he was whining again, those high-pitched noises that told me he was losing his mind.

*Good.* I was too, my cock about ready to bust out of my pants.

Grabbing the lube, I oiled up the beads, then went back to licking, getting him nice and soft before I worked the first bead in. The toy was a string of graduated black silicon balls, the first no bigger than my pinky and the last about two finger widths around. Not quite as wide as my cock, but enough to provide good stretch. I'd played with a similar toy on my own and had a feeling Robin would really like the sensations it gave.

He took the first bead easily, pushing down, seeking more. Working the second in, I slid my finger in alongside, working the beads up toward his gland. I got the third bead to pop through the tight ring of muscle, but then Robin started panting like a marathon runner, his thighs tightening. I withdrew my finger but left the beads in place.

"Sssh." I ran my hands up and down his back and sides. "I've got you. You're doing so good. You took three beads, baby."

"Uhh-nuhh." He made a low, guttural sound.

A low, warm feeling gathered in my gut. His trust as he worked to follow my commands was like the buzz of a good microbrew.

"Flip around." I gave him a light slap on the ass and he moaned. When I'd played with beads myself, the shifting around had felt both weird and awesome, and judging by his moans, it was more awesome than odd for Robin.

I went back to sucking his cock, fingering the strand of beads every so often. Not yet pushing more in, just wiggling and letting him get used to the sensation.

"You want more?"

"Yeah. Wanna try."

Sucking hard on his tip, I pushed the fourth bead in. This one was wider than my index finger, and Robin panted around it, air hissing from between his teeth.

"You can do it, baby. Just relax those muscles. Think of how good it's gonna feel."

"Oh, yeah." He bore down a little and that did it, the fourth bead popping in until the fifth rested right against his tight little hole. "Oh, *fuck, fuck, fuck.*"

God, his whines were almost enough to make me shoot in my pants. "Gonna give you one more, sweet thing. You can take it."

"Can't." He arched back anyway, leaning into me. With all the windows in his place, it felt even more like he was giving me a show, putting himself on display for me.

"Yeah, you can. Relax for me. Bear down again."

"Oh. Oh. Oooh." The fifth bead slid in, and he easily took the sixth and seventh, too. I wiggled the strand while going back to sucking him. He tensed, and for a second I thought he was going to shoot. Sucking harder, I worked my tongue along the sensitive ridge of his foreskin.

"Sorry. Right there. God. Can't." He gasped and clawed at his hair.

"Not going anywhere. And you still got two beads to take." I nudged the next one against his hole. "You can do it. Show me how good you can take this one."

He whimpered and shook but slowly bore down as I wiggled the bead in, his body seeming to suck it in.

*So fucking hot.*

I released his hip, freeing my cock before my zipper did permanent damage.

"You wanna try . . ." he whispered.

My dick pulsed in my hand, the tip already damp. Yes, I *wanted* to fuck, wanted to be right where those beads were, wanted to be locked in his tight heat. But more than that, I wanted to do right by Robin, wanted to make him fly.

"You're thinking too much again." I licked up his cock. "You've got a job to do right here." I wiggled the strand of beads, making him gasp. "If you're a good boy, though, I'll let you suck me after."

"Now." He eyes were wide and wild. "Now. I want you to fuck my throat while I've got the beads in."

Oh, hell, that image was so hot I almost shot on the spot.

"One more bead, baby. One more bead and you can have that." I nudged it in. His body was rigid, but gradually he let it in, cursing low.

I rearranged us so that I lay back on the couch and he hovered above me, almost in a sixty-nine position.

"Wanna be able to play with your new toy while you suck me."

I was hoping like hell I didn't shoot first, but as soon as my dick hit that velvet throat I knew I wouldn't last. The contrast of cool couch leather and burning-hot Robin made my head swim. He gripped my hips with long, strong fingers, pulling me deep and moaning around my cock. He pulled at me until I started rocking and thrusting. Holy hell, did Robin ever love to get his face fucked. His whole body shuddered on every deep thrust, throat milking me like a fist.

I wiggled the beads, popping the last few beads out, then gently sliding them back. His sucking grew more frantic, his body arching and straining. I was torn between wanting to watch him and wanting to give in to the pressure building in my balls.

"Oh. Christ. *Vic.*" He pulled back, gasping, his voice sounding like radio static. "So close. Fuck me hard."

I wasn't sure if he meant throat or ass, but I went for both, thrusting my hips as hard as I dared and sliding the toy in and out until I felt his balls lift and his legs tighten around me.

He flat-out screamed around my cock, and as soon as I felt the first wet splash against my chest, I pulled the toy out, knowing it would push even more pleasure through him. Releasing my cock, he panted and shook, and I stroked him through the last of it with my fist. He sank into me, his head on my belly.

I felt as tall as Robin's building, as light as a Macy's parade balloon, Robin's breathing and the pounding in my head the only things tethering me to earth. I brought my wet fist to my cock.

"Hey. Lemme . . ." Robin turned his head so that he sucked the tip while I worked the base. Only took a few strokes before I was coming hard, orgasm pounding through me. We were a sticky, exhausted mess, and happiness radiated from me. The orgasm didn't wring me out as much as it lit me up, made me feel floaty and light.

"Hey, Vic?"

"Yeah?" I barely lifted my head.

"I think I like dating."

I liked it too, far more than I should. My heart was pounding, but not over the single hottest fuck I'd ever had—which it so was—but because of how I was feeling now. Like fondant that had been pulled too thin. I could rip in two with the wrong tug. Robin made me feel things. I wanted to carry him over to his bed, wrap him in the quilts, cuddle down with him. I'd told him I was strong enough to withstand simply being his rebound fling, but I knew now I'd been lying.

# Chapter 10

"Robin's not here," Melissa said when I dropped off a load of rolls on Saturday. I'd been surprised to see her, not Robin, at the loading bay. Last three nights, Robin and I had spent all tangled up in my sheets. He'd been right: dating was a hell of a lot of fun. Having someone to cook for was a nice thing. Having someone to fall asleep with was even better. And waking up to Robin? Well, that was pretty much perfect.

Saturday Robin had headed out to the shelter while I headed in to work to finish up a few cakes. I'd spent most of my morning humming to myself while I decorated a birthday cake and two retirement cakes. And yeah, I'd been counting down the hours until I made the delivery to the shelter.

"He not show?" I tried to keep my voice neutral. I didn't want to go all overprotective boyfriend when I wasn't sure how open Robin wanted to be around people at the shelter.

"Oh, Robin was here. It's that Zach kid." Her sigh echoed off the metal loading dock and her eyes were red. "Such a sad case. His parents were by earlier. Brought big carafes of coffee with them. Wanted to talk to anyone who knows Zach."

"They trying to find out who sold him his stash?" My shoulders tightened. I'd be pissed and ready to burn down the city in their shoes. Following Melissa, I carried the cases of rolls back to the stockroom.

"Nah. I think it's more that they're reaching out, looking for people to talk to, people to tell them more about how he was living the last few months." Melissa lined up the boxes of rolls with the other baked goods in the storeroom, then started in on unpacking boxes from a dolly.

"He still in a coma?" My gut churned, a toxic stew of worry for Robin and concern over Zach. I took a box of cans from Melissa and started sliding them onto shelves.

"No. It doesn't look good." She paused in her work, gnawing on her lower lip.

"*Shit.* Pardon me."

"No, it's okay. Anytime one of our guys gets hurt it's hard, but it's really hard when it's a kid."

"Was Robin really upset by the parents?"

"Not exactly. He kind of bonded with the mom. He went back with them to the hospital."

The queasiness in my gut morphed into a tidal wave of worry, bringing with it a vicious need to get to Robin.

"Shit," I said again. "He's into this thing too deep."

"Yeah." She sighed, sinking down onto a stack of boxes. "Robin was around Zach's age when he first came around here. Tweaked out of his gourd most of the time, but occasionally I'd get him to eat something. Got him talking a few times. Then Christmas time . . ." She shook her head.

"What?"

"Friend of his named Tim died. OD'd. Kid was younger than him. We were all real worried about Robin."

"Yeah." A chill raced up my back. Whenever something like an overdose happened, things could go either way—could scare someone straight or could push him down an even more dangerous path.

"But then a miracle happened: I got Robin to call his mom for the holidays. I'd been working on him for months to call home. Or get him to accept a referral to services. *Anything.* His mom talked him into giving rehab one more go. And he's made it three years now." She wiped at her eyes. "But I'm worried he's taking this Zach thing way too personally. Seeing himself or his friend in Zach's situation."

"Crap. Yeah, I'm worried too," I admitted. "You got the hospital info? I think I might go check on him. Make sure he doesn't need anything."

"Yeah. You're a good friend, Vic." She smiled at me through misty eyes. "For what it's worth, you'd be way better for him than Paul ever was."

"We're not—"

"Cliff's got me down for a ten that you guys get together. Don't go screwing with the betting pool." Melissa's smile was a bit too wide, like she was forcing herself to grab for a joke when what she really wanted were more tissues.

Me, I wasn't too thrilled about being the gossip of the day. Soup, bread, and a side of the when-will-Vic-get-laid betting line. No, thanks. My back stiffened like week-old sourdough. I regretted ever telling Cliff about my resolution.

"Cliff needs to learn to shut his mouth."

"Oh!" She clapped her hands together, her face brightening like I'd let something slip. "I knew there was something there!"

"Nothing to talk about." Cliff might be my best friend and my boss, but I was gonna put a serious hurt on him next time I saw him.

"Oh, come on, Vic. I've had a sucky week. We all have. Don't hold out good news." She made a pleading face that probably won her all sorts of donations and confessions.

"I'll see." I straightened a row of cereal that didn't need it. I really wasn't one to kiss and tell, and having never had a boyfriend before, fake or otherwise, I didn't know how to handle all this curiosity. Flattered, I guess, but mainly I wanted to get to Robin. Check in on him. Part of me didn't want to confide in Melissa because I still couldn't believe a guy like Robin would want someone like me. He was young and beautiful and kind, while I was old and cranky and decidedly not so beautiful. And it didn't matter how many orgasms we shared or how many public places we went together, it was a hard feeling to shake.

I got the hospital info from her and headed over after I took the truck back and grabbed a few things from inside the store. I texted Robin on my way over, but he didn't respond.

I found him in the ICU waiting area, sitting next to a small blond woman with messy hair and red eyes. He spotted me as soon as I entered the seating alcove, an uncertain smile peeking out of his worried face.

"Vic? What are you doing here?" he asked. Robin and the lady both stood up as I approached their section of the waiting room.

"Melissa at the shelter said you were here with Zach's folks. Wasn't sure if they'd eaten, so I brought them some food." I held out the bakery box.

"I'm Tonya, Zach's mother. Thank you; you're very kind. His dad's in with him now, but he'd thank you, too."

"You good on coffee?" I asked her. "Want something not from the cafeteria?"

"We're good." She gave me a weary smile. "Do you know Zach, too?"

"No," I admitted. "But I'm so sorry he's hurt."

"Vic's my boyfriend." Robin moved closer to me, which surprised me. "The one I was telling you about?"

Robin was telling strangers about me? I felt more than a little guilty for the flip in my stomach and the lightness in my knees.

"Oh. Of course. The baker. How . . . lovely." Tonya looked away. I didn't take it personal. Lord only knew what sorts of emotions she was battling, or how the family had handled Zach's being gay. Or his using. Had they been like Robin's family and cut him off financially? Emotionally, like so many others?

Tonya seemed to drift off into her own world, going back to sitting on a vinyl bench, fiddling with her hands. All the machines and monitors on the floor emitted a steady beep-beep-blip-blip drone, each noise more lonely than the last. Over at the nurses' station, a group of blue-clad nurses talked in hushed tones. I felt a swift urge to call my own mother. Tell her I loved her and figure out a way to say thanks that didn't sound all cheesy. I'd call her as soon as we were done here. Maybe I'd mention Robin. For the first time ever, I had a guy I wanted the family to meet. She was joking just the other week that Trevor and I were the last two Degrassi boys unattached.

"You wanna walk with me?" I asked Robin. "Get you a coffee or a soda?"

"I'm not thirsty, but I'll walk a bit." He bent to say something to Tonya, who nodded absently.

The glassed-in patient cubicles surrounded the nurses' station in a horseshoe shape, but I headed in the opposite direction, down the main corridor.

"The doctors don't think he's going to make it," Robin said as soon as we were out of earshot.

"Oh, man." I didn't have words for how much that sucked—for Zach, for his parents, for the world, and for Robin, who looked like a boulder sat on his shoulders, pushing him down, locking his features in a grimace.

"His folks are all alone." Robin's voice was strained. "Everyone else gave up on him a long time ago."

"Real nice of you to come sit with them."

"I suppose. You don't have to stay."

"Hey. If you're gonna be here, I want to be here, too." My sour stomach called me a liar. I hated hospitals. Couldn't wait to get out after my surgery. They reminded me of death; the smell of antiseptic and old coffee in the hall was taking me back to the bitter, ugly days when I lost my dad and Manny. I didn't *want* to be there, but I *needed* to be there for Robin, to stand witness somehow to the pain I saw in his eyes.

"I'm probably going to go soon." He chewed on his lower lip. "I'm not sure I'm doing much good."

We came to a sky bridge with little benches by the glass walls. I tugged him over to one and sat down next to him. There were enough people needing comfort on this floor that I didn't think twice about wrapping an arm around him.

"I'm sure you're doing more good than you think, but you want to come back with me? Let me cook you some dinner, relax a little, and then see if you need to come back?"

"Ah. Thanks, Vic, but I'm not feeling up to that."

"It's okay that you're feeling down. You can just veg out on my sofa. Let me cook for you. You shouldn't be alone."

"Oh. My. God." His shoulders stiffened and he scooted away from me. "Melissa got to you, didn't she? Look, I'm not at risk of relapsing. I'll go to a freaking meeting tomorrow if it gets people off my case."

"Hey. Whoa." I reached for his hand, but he yanked it away. "I don't think you're about to relapse. I think you need . . . some comfort. Let me take care of you, baby. You can help Zach's parents more with a good meal and some rest in you."

"Ah . . . thanks, Vic." Some of the fight went out of his face and he let me take his hand. "I just really need to be alone. I'll call you later or something."

The "or something" made my stomach cramp. "Are . . . are you through with us?"

"What?" He shook his head. "No. I just need some space tonight. Trust me. My mood is too black for me to be good company."

"You don't have to be good company," I said softly. "We don't have to—"

"Can we just drop it?" Robin's eyes were bright. "I said I'll call. Maybe brunch tomorrow?"

"Okay. It's a date." I clenched my hands to keep them from shaking, kept them clenched the whole way back to my car. My brain felt clogged, like frustration and worry were making ordinary tasks impossible. Ended up sending my mom a quick text because I wasn't sure my brain would cooperate for a call—didn't want to end up unloading all my shit on her. It took me three tries just to unlock my stupid car door. I wanted to trust Robin, wanted to trust he'd be okay, wanted to trust we'd get through this together.

It was a crappy date for sure. Robin barely picked at his food and the easy conversation of a week ago was gone. We were crammed into one of the long tables, surrounded by young families and weekend hipsters, with no real space for me to touch Robin or talk frankly.

"You going back to the hospital today?" I asked, wishing I could force more food on him. He dragged the same piece of toast around uneaten scrambled tofu.

"Yeah. Probably. They don't have anyone else. At least I can fetch stuff for them. Listen."

My hand moved restlessly at my side. Damn people, penning us in. I wanted to wrap Robin in my arms. Protect him from the oncoming hurt. His kindness was what had attracted me to him to begin with; he was so darn selfless. But it also had the potential to cut him open, leaving him vulnerable and hurting.

"I can come too."

"Nah. You don't need to." He picked up a strawberry, considered it, then set it back down.

"I want—"

"They're not the coolest about the gay thing. That's part of what I was listening to them about. They weren't the most accepting when Zach came out to them. They feel guilty and they're working through it, but I think seeing us together might be hard, especially us happy with each other."

I'd gotten that impression too, and ordinarily I'd say that other people's discomfort with my sexuality was their own damn problem, but grief-racked parents got a little leeway.

"We're happy?" I asked. Robin seemed anything but, with listless eyes that didn't meet mine.

"Zach thing aside, you really have to ask?" He offered me a weary smile. "Maybe I can come over after the hospital?"

"Anytime. Even if it's late. Especially if it's late."

We finished breakfast and walked a bit on Alberta afterward, but it was like there was a spatula between us, shoving us apart, filling us up with unpleasant emotions and uncomfortable silences.

# Chapter 11

*B*uzz. My phone skittered across the ottoman next to my feet. I grabbed for it.

YOU UP?

It was nearly eleven and I was pretending to watch *The Walking Dead* and pretending like I wasn't being attacked by a horde of worries about Robin.

*Yes. Coming over?* I replied.

He knocked on the door thirty seconds later.

"That was fast," I said as I let him in.

"Didn't want to wake you." He jammed both hands into his jeans pockets, his shoulders hunkered in his coat, looking young and alone in the half-lit entryway.

"You didn't. You look like crap," I said baldly, rubbing his arms. The damp, chilly night seemed to cling to him. "You eaten?"

"Yeah. With you, remember?"

"That was almost twelve hours ago."

"I think there was a Snickers bar in there somewhere." He shrugged, looking sheepish.

"I'm gonna make you a sandwich."

"You don't have to—"

"I'm going to make you a sandwich," I repeated, using my "mean" voice and a stern look. "And you're going to eat it. And say 'Thank you, Vic.'"

That got a tiny laugh from him. "Thank you, Vic."

I led him back to the kitchen.

"I'm not sure how I'm supposed to eat with you looking like that."

"What?" I said before I looked down and realized I'd answered the door wearing nothing but plaid pajama bottoms. "Oh, hell. Let me grab a shirt."

Cheeks heating, I detoured toward my room, but he stopped me with a hand on my arm.

"I was teasing, Vic. I meant you look good. Distracting." His hand came around to tease the drawstring of the pants. The red plaid pants were too baggy and had ridden low, something Robin exploited with his fingers, teasing along the waistline. With all the expense of getting new clothes, pajamas had fallen to the bottom of the list.

"Yeah?"

"Yeah." He looked up at me, a strange, almost tender expression on his face. "You don't see it, do you?"

"See what?"

"How hot you are?"

"Hot? Me? Nah." I brushed a kiss across his head. "You know you're getting laid later regardless of how thick you lay it on, right? I know I'm not good-looking—not like you."

Robin did laugh, then, a full, rich sound that filled my narrow hallway. "No, Vic, you're definitely nothing like me."

"See, I told—"

"You don't have to look like me to be smokin'. You look like The Rock and Vin Diesel had a love child. I could work out for two years and not be as jacked as you."

I felt like I'd gobbled a package of Red Hots—that burning rush of sweetness. I looked down at my chest and arms. Yeah, I guess I was getting more ripped than I realized. No more man boobs was nice. But no matter how many hours I put in at the gym, I couldn't seem to outrun my teenaged self, who'd worn a shirt even while swimming. Hell, even my thirty-year-old self had kept a shirt on for most hookups. It felt weird, Robin's eyes on me like I was steak and he was waiting for someone to hand him a fork.

"Lemme make you that sandwich." I headed for the kitchen and got a pan on to preheat before I turned back and around and found him smirking at me. "What?"

"You're cute." Instead of grabbing one of the stools at the breakfast bar to watch me cook, he came around to the sink. "It okay if I clean?"

"Sorry." There were some dishes from my solitary dinner in the sink and some boxes out on the counters. At work, neatness counted, down to the last drip of icing, but at home, living alone, I got a little lax.

"Oh, no, it's all good." Robin ran hot water for the dishes and grabbed soap.

"I've got a washer." I pointed to the ancient thing on one side of the sink.

"It's okay. I want to do them this way. I *need* to clean right now. Need to do something."

"Yeah. I've been there. You want to talk about it?" I had a little bread and a little low-fat cheese and some meat left over from my dinner. I started him a toasted sandwich.

"God no. I want to scrub and scrub and not think about anything. Growing up, we always had a housekeeper. There wasn't a lot for me to do. But she was nice, from Sweden. And she used to let me work alongside her. I loved it." His face got dreamy and far away. "Sometimes I just need to get something *done*."

"I hear that." I'd been there, in the first terrible days after Manny passed. Drove around Portland for hours, thinking and wondering and hating and raging. Then I'd come back home and desperately want some small task to occupy even a piece of the hurt I carried around.

Robin attacked my dishes with similar vigor, soaping up a pot so hard I feared for the enamel.

"Lord knows I never run out of shit to do around here." I flipped the sandwich, covertly studying him. Messy hair fell in his eyes and his skin was pale and pasty.

"You really going to sell the place?" He had that HGTV-renovation-show gleam in his eye again, no doubt cataloging all of the kitchen's vintage charm—and many flaws—from the original cabinets to the ancient appliances.

"That's the plan. Was never supposed to take me long to get stuff done, but with Manny passing and my surgery, and me not being the best handyman . . ."

"Why not buy it off her yourself? Then you could take your time. Do it right."

"Nah." I waved my spatula, dismissing such silliness. "Place like this? It needs a family. People. Not some single dude bumbling around."

"Families are good." He looked up from scrubbing the chipped Formica counters. His sad tone made it sound like they were anything but. "You could always give it one, though."

Shoulders drawing up tight, I paused in pouring soup into a pan. If only it was so easy. *You up for it?* The words were right there, trapped behind a thick tongue that wouldn't move. No doubt Robin was picturing me and some faceless dude, while I was seeing a future I'd never have, at least not as long as Robin kept insisting that this was only casual.

"Yeah, not happening," I said, laughing like he'd been joking, like he hadn't pushed a little sliver of need right into my heart.

"See, I never understood my dad's obsession with new development. I mean, I know it makes his company a shit-ton of money. But old places like this? They have a soul."

"Truth." I wished I had his pretty way with words. Wished his words didn't unearth feelings in me I didn't know what to do with. Wished I could make the unhappiness and tension drain away from Robin's face. But wishes weren't worth much. I finished cooking the sandwich, plated it. It was hardly gourmet, but it was good, honest comfort food, the best I could do with a limited pantry.

"Here you go." I motioned him over to the little table in the breakfast nook where I took most of my meals.

"You're not having anything?"

"Nah. It's late." There was a time when that hadn't stopped me, but those days had long past. I grabbed a chair to keep him company. Watching Robin eat was its own form of nourishment.

"This is amazing." He licked his lips around a glob of cheese. "You're such a good cook."

"It's just grilled cheese and tomato soup." My cheeks heated from the compliment.

"Yeah, but it's *good*. Oh, man, I hadn't realized how hungry I was." He devoured the sandwich and drained the soup.

"More?" I'd happily make the man ten meals if it kept that sated look on his face.

"I'm good." He patted his stomach. "Good, but tired. It's okay if I crash here, right?"

"You have to ask?" I knew this thing between us was still new, but we'd slipped so easily into near-nightly sleepovers that I'd missed him like crazy the previous night.

"Good." He gave me a smile that was more sleepy than seductive. "Can I shower?"

"Of course. Take all the time you need. You can even take a bath, if you'd rather."

I got him a fresh towel—the best, fluffiest one I had. Robin used water for stress relief in the same way I used work as an escape. And if that's what he needed, I wanted to give him a good escape. I used the dimmer switch to lower the bathroom lights. "My sister got me these stress-relieving bath crystals for Christmas. No idea what Joanie was thinking, but you can have at them."

I set them on the tub and turned to find him looking at me oddly. "What?"

"No one's ever . . . you're good at taking care of people." He gave my arm a squeeze on his way toward the tub. "Guy could fall in love with you, almost too easily."

My hand gripped the sink, almost tight enough to crack it. *Do it. Just do it.* Words, pretty and meaningless, gathered in my mouth, only to be promptly discarded by my brain.

"I'll . . . uh . . . leave you to your bath. Or shower. Whatever." *Smooth, Vic, real smooth.* I beat a hasty retreat out of the room.

"You still up?" Robin slid beneath my sheets, smelling vaguely like the ocean.

"Yeah." *And how.* His naked body slid against mine as he cuddled in.

"Good." He curved into me, stretching for a kiss.

My hands tangled in his damp hair. His warm mouth was a sexy contrast to his cool skin. While he'd been in the bath, I'd lectured myself that he might not be up for sex and to let him sleep, but all those good intentions fled with the first hot flick of his tongue against mine.

Both of us were on our sides, him rocking against me. Eager to feel his skin against mine, I wiggled out of my PJ bottoms. I honestly didn't miss fucking; rubbing off like this with Robin was simply too good to feel even a pinch of disappointment. The slide of his cock against mine always sent little shooting stars of pleasure up my spine.

"Vic," he whimpered, pushing into me.

"I got you, baby," I whispered. Snaking a hand between us, I wrapped my fist around both of us and started stroking. The intensity of his kisses ramped up, with little whimpers and shudders in between slow, deep kisses. He thrust up into my hand, and his movements felt different tonight. There was a quiet desperation behind them, and I tried to match his intensity, give him what he needed. I cradled him to me and with my lips and hands and cock, I urged him to let go, to let me take care of him, to let himself feel good.

"Oh, fuck, Vic." His moan echoed off the plaster walls, his body straining toward mine.

"Yeah." I felt my lower back tighten, my balls tingling. "Come on, do it."

"Mmm." A strangled sound escaped from between his gritted teeth. His head tipped back, every muscle tight.

"Yeah, that's it. So beautiful." Watching his face sent me over, and I stroked through it, expecting him to come, too, but his body stayed tense. I shifted so that my hand stroked only him, using the slickness to work him off faster.

"I can't." His muscles sagged, going limp, but with frustration, not orgasm.

"Yeah, you can." I kissed him, still working him with my hand.

"God, it's right there." He tensed again and I sped up my strokes. *"Hell."* His curse wasn't one of pleasure.

"Sssh." The mellow glow of my orgasm faded, replaced by concern. I smoothed the hair back from his head. Could practically feel his brain cells chugging along. He needed to stop overthinking this. Grabbing his hand, I brought it to his cock, then started kissing my way down his chest. "Show me how you do it."

"I can't." He rolled away. "Just one of those nights when I can tell it's not happening, no matter how much I'd like it to."

"I bet you could if I suck you off." I tried to pull him back, but he resisted my embrace.

"Leave it, Vic."

"I feel bad—"

"Don't." His tone was curt, but he reached for my hand. "Just . . . hold me? I'm too tired."

My mouth tasted bitter, like I'd grabbed salt instead of the sweet sugar I'd been craving. But one look at his tired face curved against my pillow told me I wasn't winning this one. I gave in and snuggled up to his back, the way he liked to sleep, with me draped around him. Sometimes we slept the other way, with him using me as a sort of giant body pillow, but most nights we ended up like this.

His breathing softened and he was asleep in seconds. Me, I lay awake a long time, feeling like shit because he hadn't gotten off and feeling worse at how he seemed to be retreating, skating farther and farther away from my grasp. And I couldn't stop the sinking feeling that he'd found himself on ice so fragile, I wouldn't be able to yank him back if he fell.

# Chapter 12

I hate redos. Hate everything about them. Hate trying to decide whether to fix or scrap. Hate watching good things fall in the trash because they aren't quite perfect. I cursed as I tossed the heap of mangled fondant and cake that was supposed to be the Caldwell anniversary cake.

"What the heck is with you?" Cliff asked, looking up from the line of cupcakes he was icing. "Boy problems?"

"Nothing I wanna talk about, and nothing I want to hear back around on the gossip loop."

"Oh, come on, man, can't you see that there are a whole lot of people who want to be happy for you?"

Shoulders going rigid, I shook my head. Melissa had said almost the same thing, but I wasn't sure I trusted it. Wasn't sure I trusted me. Wasn't sure I trusted Robin anymore. He hadn't come over Monday night. I knew Robin's unhappiness had little to do with me, but it still felt like my fault that he wouldn't let me in.

I grabbed two fresh vanilla sponge layers off the rack, put them on my station, filled them with buttercream and raspberry jam as per the order sheet, and dirty iced the stack. Just as I started rolling the fondant, Cliff came back over, leaning on my table.

"You know, back when I was running after Trish, I didn't take no for an answer."

"Isn't stalking illegal?" I didn't look up as I carefully draped fondant over the cake.

"I don't mean literally. I mean, I courted her. Didn't let her turn me down."

"Look at you being Mr. Matchmaker." I made a shooing motion with my piping bag.

"I'm just saying, you should woo the boy. Take him—"

"This isn't something dinner at Piazza Italia will fix, man. I don't need to seduce Robin. I just need him to feel better, okay? I need him not to shut me out." *Hell.* My hands clenched, squeezing the piping bag too hard. Hot pink icing glopped all over the nice white fondant. Hadn't meant to say any of that.

"Knew it. You're in love with that boy." Cliff said this cheerfully, like the revelation wasn't supposed to tear me open, leaving me raw and exposed, like half-baked bread.

"We're just friends with benefits." I scraped the excess icing off the cake and tried to salvage the mess. "And that better not be repeated."

"You can trust me." Cliff held up his hands. "But that's what I mean. Since when do you wait for someone to ask for help? You gonna start waiting for Melissa to call before you run bread over to the mission? Gonna wait for Trish to tell you some cake's too heavy for her? Gonna wait for me to ask before you do the run to Caldwell's tomorrow?"

"This isn't like that . . . he doesn't want my help." I looked away, trying not to show how much it killed me. I'd thought I could be Robin's rebound guy, but truth was, I was a damn crappy rebound guy. I didn't want to be Robin's casual, feel-good fuck. I wanted to be his everything. I wanted to get him through the pain of Zach being hurt—and not by waiting on the sidelines.

"Vic." Cliff held out a hand. "Let me fix the cake. It's Tuesday. Robin will be at the shelter. Don't let him shut you out."

"You just want to win your bet."

"No. I want you to win yours."

I headed over to the shelter because Cliff was right: I was a take-action kind of guy. Holing up and waiting for Robin to call me—that wasn't my style. Nothing good would come of letting Robin hide away. Even if he didn't want me, he needed to know he wasn't alone. And yeah, despite what I'd told him, I *was* worried about him and sobriety. Not quite the same as Robin's issues, but I knew how loss and temptation could get tangled up.

When I missed Manny the most, I could smell pizza and taste microbrew, and the memory of sharing an entire pie together would give me the urge to bury the ache of missing him under something heavy and carb-loaded. And then I'd hit the gym, clanking barbells extra hard until the urge passed. I didn't know what Robin used to beat back temptation. But I wished I did—it didn't have to be me, or involve me. I simply wanted to help ensure he had his weapon of choice.

When I got to the shelter clumps of smokers sat out front like always, but they were talking in hushed tones. An anxious vibe seemed to roll off the building, like the foundation had tilted since I'd been there last. I checked both the dining room and the staff room, but there was no sign of Robin—or Melissa, for that matter.

A few volunteers were in the kitchen, starting the dinner prep, but Robin wasn't among them. They, too, seemed on edge, talking in low voices and looking up at my arrival, then quickly looking away. No shouted greetings or hugs like usual. My heart clattered in my chest, insides all wobbly as I got a very bad feeling.

*Please let Robin be okay.* I said a quick prayer to the same God I'd fought my dad so passionately over.

I headed through the deserted storeroom, out to the loading bay. When I peeked around the side of the dock, I saw Robin's dark hair.

*Thank you.* Relief, sure and swift, swept through me, but as I stepped through the door, I saw the rest of him, and rage replaced every last drop of relief. He was sitting on the edge of the dock and Paul was holding him, his arms around him.

*No.*

My muscles froze, literally seized up, my throat closing, my arms paralyzed.

I knew I should call out. Say something. Keep going forward. Pull the two of them apart. But I couldn't do any of that. The ache in my chest was too big, the pain too large to bear. He'd found his weapon and it wasn't me. Instead, I fled, through the storeroom, through the kitchen, through the hall until I reached the entryway benches and collapsed, my head on my hands.

I wasn't sure how long I stayed like that, but I raised my head at the sound of Robin's voice.

"Vic? What are you doing here? Did you hear?"

"I saw," I said, somehow keeping my voice level.

"You—what?"

"I saw. You and Paul," I said, focusing on dirty footprints on the linoleum, not able to look at his beautiful face. "I get why you'd pick him. It's okay. I want you to be happy. I get—"

"You get *nothing,* Vic." Robin's voice was harsh enough to make me look up. His eyes were Arctic Winter chilly. "Zach is dead. Melissa's with his family right now. *Dead.* And Paul found me—and oh my God, how could you not speak up if you saw him touching me? Did you stay long enough to see me push him away?"

Relief and shame and grief bundled together, overloading my nerve endings, filling my head with buzzing static.

"No," I said softly, holding out my hand. "I'm sorry—"

"Sorry? Vic, I wanted *you.* I wanted your arms. Zach is dead—"

"I know, baby, you said. And I'm here now." I stood up, taking him in my arms, but he jumped back, crossing his arms over his chest.

"What? You think that makes up for not believing in me? For coming here to check up on me? For thinking that I would let Paul— *Vic, why can't you trust me?*" He put so much pain into the question that it felt like a whip, stinging my skin, making my eyes smart.

"Last few days, you've shoved me away. I thought maybe we were through. Figured you didn't want me anymore." It felt like coffee grounds clogged my nose and throat. That. That was why I hadn't sought him out. That was why it had taken a kick from Cliff to get me here. I'd been afraid, pure and simple. I hadn't wanted to hear him say—

"Well, we're sure through *now.*" His face was stony, his eyes gone from blue to almost black.

I froze. On the inside and the outside. Like I'd been zapped with a freeze gun from a sci-fi movie, some funky weapon that spat out paralyzing pain. I shook my hands out, forcing my blood to keep circulating, forcing myself not to let him walk away before I could speak.

"Wait." My voice croaked. "Robin. I'm sorry. I jumped to conclusions when I saw you and Paul, but you're hurting right now. It's not a good time to make rash decisions—"

"It's the perfect time because I can't do this, Vic. I can't do the casual thing with you—"

"I don't want casual. I want you. And I do trust you." My heart threatened to pump right through my sternum. I leaned on the bench for balance. Should have told him that days ago. Stupid fucking fear again. Been too scared to tell what I really wanted, and now I was about to lose him anyway.

"I don't believe you," Robin said flatly. "And I can't handle *any-*

*thing* right now. I can't handle Paul. And I can't handle you. And I really, really can't handle that Zach is dead."

"You don't have to handle it. Let me—"

"Let you what? Wrap me in cotton? Protect me from myself? I don't need that."

"Let me love you," I said softly. "Let me hold you. You're hurting."

"No. Don't you see? If things between us keep going, it's going to hurt, so much more than it does right now, maybe even more than losing Zach. More than losing my friend Tim when we were both on the streets. And I can't risk that, Vic. I can't let you in and care about you and then find out you don't trust me or have my back."

"That's not fair." I let go of the bench, pulling myself back up. There was nothing I wouldn't do for him. Have his back? I'd fucking carry him on mine. And I'd thought he knew that.

"Fair? Fair? There is *nothing* fair about today. Nothing. And I'm sorry, Vic. I can't do us. Not right now. I just need some space. Time to think—"

"I can give you space." It killed me to offer, but I'd give him whatever he needed. Even now, I'd strap him to me, carry him across the city. "Just don't shut me out. I'm sorry, so sorry about assuming the worst when I saw you with Paul. And I'm so sorry about Zach. And you can have all the space you need to grieve and be mad, just please, *please* don't shut me out." My voice fucking broke and I stopped.

I'd never begged.

Not once. Not when the bullies had me cornered as a kid. Not when I lost the job at the mortgage company. Not when I fought with my dad. Not even at the hospital, losing Dad, then Uncle Mauro, then Manny. Never begged the universe for a second chance.

"I'm sorry, Vic." With that, he turned on his heel and fled through the double doors, out onto the street. I chased after him—I wasn't making the same mistake twice—but he was nowhere to be seen. Just smoke and blank faces and the lingering sense of loss that pervaded the whole shelter—the sense I hadn't quite picked up on because I'd been so focused on Robin, so certain that it was about him and me and—

And I was a self-centered bastard. Robin was hurting and he was doing what he always did, pushing away people who wanted to help him. All I wanted was to find the right words for an apology, the right words that would make Robin listen, but I had nothing. I picked up my phone, debating texting him, but I had no idea what to say.

I typed, *Stay safe,* but then deleted it, because that sounded like I didn't trust him.

Then I typed, *I'm sorry. I don't want to lose you,* but deleted that just as fast. I didn't want to be a needy, stalker boyfriend.

Then I typed the truth: *I love you and I'm sorry.* I knew I wouldn't send that one either, but I stood there and stared at my screen for a long minute. It was the truth.

I loved Robin Dawson. I'd loved him for a year at least. I'd loved him since before I made my New Year's resolution, since before my surgery. Probably loved him since the first day we pulled up to deliver bread and he was on the loading dock, shaggy hair and sunny smile.

My resolution had never been about finding a guy, any guy to try a relationship with. It had been about finding the balls to go after Robin. And I'd lied to myself and said I was okay being his rebound guy, that I was okay being a pit stop for him on the road to something better, when he was *my* destination all along.

I loved him. I loved his kind, generous heart. I loved the way he looked at my falling-down house and saw so much potential, the way he looked at my future and similarly saw a world of possibilities. I loved the way his face looked when he ate something I'd made, and I loved how he felt in my arms. I loved his fragility. I loved that he cared so deeply about things. And yes, he was right, I did want to protect him from the world. Was it so wrong to want to be his safe place? To want to comfort him?

And now I wasn't going to get the chance. My chest ached and my throat burned. Not since the horrible day when we lost Manny had I felt such agony. My whole body felt consumed by grief and I knew one simple very profound truth: I wasn't ever getting over losing Robin.

I thought of all the times I hadn't told my dad or my uncle—bless their cantankerous souls—or Manny what they meant to me. Life was too short for Robin not to know that he was loved—that it didn't matter if he came back to me, if he never spoke to me again. He was loved.

I hit send.

# Chapter 13

I didn't really expect Robin to text back, but I kept my phone next to me all Tuesday evening. Came in, set my phone on the counter with the ringer turned all the way up, got my mail. Stack of junk, but the top piece grabbed my attention.

*Buy One, Get One Pizza! Call Happy Slice today!*

I held that shiny flyer in my hand for a long time. Carried it and my phone to the couch. I thought about how badly my stomach would ache, how I'd most likely puke if I ate as much as I wanted right then. Thought about beer, and how I *had* puked the last time I'd tried one. I could go straight for hard liquor and a fast drunk, but that felt . . . disrespectful to Robin and everything he stood for. If I was wrestling with my demons that night, he must surely have been wrestling ones twenty times larger. And I wanted to believe with every fiber of my soul that he would win. That he would be safe that night, and the next night after that.

I pushed up from the couch, let the flyer flutter to the ground. I marched to my entryway. Surveyed it. Tried to see what Robin saw— the foot-thick crown molding details, the vintage light fixture missing two bulbs, the dusty hardwood floor. I pushed all thoughts of pizza from my head and put all my focus into cleaning that entryway.

I removed all the half-empty paint cans and the trash. Swept it clean. Put new lightbulbs in the fixture. Washed the trim. Next night, I went to Home Depot after work. Rented a steamer and spent the next four hours stripping my entryway of the peeling wallpaper. The next night I primed the walls. I ignored Cliff and Trish when they remarked on the bags under my eyes and my groans when I hefted flour sacks. The labor at home felt good. Right, even. Necessary.

I was piping a wedding cake when my phone rang. I dropped my icing bag and leaped across the room to answer the call.

"What happened to 'all phones should be on vibrate,' Vic?" Trish asked, trying to imitate my deeper voice and failing. Yeah, I'd cracked down on a couple of the assistants last year. Ordinarily mine never left vibrate. I hate loud ringers. But this wasn't an ordinary week.

I made a shut-it gesture and picked up the phone. "Hey?"

"Hay is for horses, Victor Degrassi. I raised you better than that."

"Hello, Ma." I drew out my syllables.

"You coming for dinner Sunday right?"

*Hell.* I'd forgotten that Sunday would have been my dad's sixtieth birthday. Ma wanted to have a family dinner. Seemed kind of morbid to me, but even if he and I had had more than our share of words, I'd still loved him. More to the point, I loved my mom. Wasn't about to disappoint her, no matter how shitty my week was working out.

"Yes, Ma. I'll be there. What kind of bread you want?"

"A nice sourdough." She said this thoughtfully, like she didn't request a round sourdough for every family meal.

"I'll do a cake for dessert, too. I'll see what's on order for Saturday. Work something in."

"You're a good boy, Vic. Something chocolate, maybe? I'm not supposed to say, but Tessa's got an announcement. Some good news."

"And her good news has her craving chocolate?"

"My lips are sealed."

"Ha."

"You respect your old mother."

"You're gonna outlive us all, Ma." *I hope.* My gut flipped helplessly, knowing how little hope was really worth these days. God knew we didn't need any more bad news. And Tessa having news should have made me happy—I'd put money on buying booties before the year was out. But instead, it made me think of Melissa and her dilemma regarding her maternity leave and Robin's reluctance. And thinking about Robin made the burning spread from my shoulders all the way down my back, my muscles going slicing-wire tight.

"And Vic, we've got to talk about Mary's place."

"What about it?" I paced back and forth in front of my station.

"Spring's coming. Time to call Cousin Carol's husband. Get the house on the market."

"It's not ready—"

"Mary says she can make do with a low-ball offer. Her expenses are way less here. She just needs not to be worrying about the house. Needs not to have it hanging over her head."

*Her and me both.* A deep, sinking feeling gathered in my lower stomach. The house had been hanging over my head ever since Manny passed. I should have been clicking my heels at the chance to be free, but instead I felt a deep weariness, a sense of failure clogging my lungs, almost like I could hear Manny laying into me.

"Yeah. I'll talk to her Sunday, Ma. Come up with a plan."

"And Vic—you need to move on, too. We all miss Manny—may he rest in peace—" There was a pause, and I knew she'd just crossed herself. "But you need to get your own life back. Your own place."

Three days earlier and I would have told her about Robin. Told her how there were good things happening in my life. Told her I wasn't missing Manny so much these days. Told her how the house didn't feel so daunting anymore.

But today, missing Robin hurt even more than missing Manny. Made me feel old and cranky. And the thought of letting go of the house, of letting go of all of Manny's plans to restore his mom's place, that was its own kind of pain, a burn right below my breastbone.

"Yeah, I hear you, Ma."

Friday dawned clear and cold. I'd already told Cliff I wouldn't be in. After the last few years, I knew the drill by heart. I vacuumed out my car, then ironed the one pair of black dress slacks that fit me and a gray dress shirt. Put in my dad's silver cuff links. Put on the same black and silver tie I'd worn to Manny's funeral and my dad's. Then I drove to the shelter and picked up Melissa, who wore a simple black dress with flats.

Next, we drove out to Troutdale to Zach's memorial service. Much as my heart was breaking for Robin, I wasn't going solely for him. I was going for Melissa and for everyone who'd tried so hard to save Zach. I was going for his poor parents and the lonely road they walked. I was going because the crowd was likely to be small and because I knew that not even the large crowds at my dad's and Manny's funerals had done a damn thing to stop my grief. I was going because Zach mattered.

And yeah, I was going for Robin. Robin, who wouldn't return my texts. Robin, for whom my love wasn't enough. Robin, who'd tried harder than anyone to get through to Zach. Robin, who loved deeply and silently.

"I asked Robin if he wanted to ride with us," Melissa said as I got on I-84.

"What'd he say?" The hairs on my neck stiffened like soldiers ready for incoming bad-news grenades.

"That he'd be fine." She said *fine* like it had twenty syllables. "He's been fine all week. I'm pretty sure, fine, okay, yeah, and no are the only words he's spoken to me in days. I'm worried about him."

"Me too." As the city gave way to suburbia, with miles of houses and neighborhoods, my worries mounted.

"I asked him to go to one of the meetings at the center and he just shrugged."

"Hell. Sorry."

Melissa laughed bitterly. "After this week I think we're all entitled to a little cursing. He's shut you out, too?"

"Yeah." Bile rose in my throat and my stomach churned with a bitterness no amount of antacids could fix. My worry for Robin was an all-encompassing ache, and my memories of him, of what we were together, of what he was shutting out, seemed way too fragile to share. "You mind if I turn on some music?"

I turned up the radio, tuning it to a bland, easy-listening station. We passed the rest of the drive in near silence.

The funeral home was a long, low-slung, oversize ranch-style building with tasteful arborvitae and manicured walks. An older gentleman in a black suit had us sign the guest book, then ushered us to the small chapel. I'd been right; the crowd was sparse, maybe thirty people, most of whom looked like Zach and his mother. A few people I recognized from the shelter, including a quartet of young guys in ripped jeans and dirty parkas. Robin stood talking with them, looking achingly handsome in a gray suit. He'd put some product in his hair and he looked older. More aloof and regal.

Melissa went over and hugged him, but he held himself stiff as a broom handle. I wished I could be like her and swoop in for a hug, but instead I hung back. The rest of the world probably couldn't see it, but I could tell how Robin was propping himself up: spine tight, eyes narrow, hands clenched. I could picture him drinking his coffee black, listening to that electronic crap he liked, psyching himself up to be here. The look in his eyes said he wanted to run but didn't dare.

Melissa and I paid our condolences to Zach's parents. Zach's mother seemed as fragile as one of my sugar flowers, looking decades older than when I'd seen her last. We made our way to the tiny chapel and sat in the same row of folding chairs as Robin, but he didn't once meet my eyes.

The same gentleman who'd been overseeing the guest register gave a short welcome. A high-school friend read a short speech scribbled on a sheet of notebook paper. After the words had been said and more than a few tears shed, the crowd slowly filtered out. Hardly seemed like enough for the magnitude of the loss. Robin went over to Zach's mother, saying something to her in low tones. She waved him away.

"Robin." Melissa stopped him as he walked past. "You okay? You want to get some coffee?"

"Nah. Thanks, though." He shook his head. His eyes locked with mine and I felt something pass between us. It wasn't heat precisely, or even need. Wasn't apology or understanding, but there was this near-palpable awareness. In that instant, I saw all the pain he'd tucked away, all his sadness and longing. I thought he was going to let me in, acknowledge my presence, but then he glanced away.

"There's a meeting tonight at the center," Melissa added. "Maybe you could mention it to Zach's friends over there?"

"Will do."

"And maybe you can come?"

"I'll see." He walked over to the group of guys from the shelter, not looking back at us.

"Okay, I've gone from worried to flat-out panicked," Melissa said as we walked back to my car.

"I'm not worried about him using. You shouldn't be either," I surprised myself by saying. In that spilt second when Robin had let me see inside him, I had glimpsed a spine of steel. I wasn't worried about Robin using, not like Melissa was. I was worried about how else he might torture himself, because what he was wrestling with seemed larger than grief, larger than Zach and the tremendous hole he'd left behind.

I'd also seen something else in his eyes, something that made it so I wasn't shocked to find his car idling in front of my house when I arrived home after dropping off Melissa at the center.

"I'm still mad at you," he said as he came loping up the broken sidewalk.

"Fair enough," I said cautiously.

"And I'm really, really not fit for company today."

"Okay." I unlocked the door, let us both into the house. If Robin noticed the work I'd done on the entry, he didn't say anything.

"But please don't send me away." He said it like sending him away would have been possible for me, like it was possible I could ignore the agony in his eyes. My heart thudded painfully.

"Never." I reached for him and he came readily, with grasping, greedy hands. He pushed me hard into the wall, kissing me with a desperation I could feel all the way to my bones. His teeth scraped my lip and I tasted blood, but it did nothing to deter my own rising lust. His need was a visceral thing, clawing at me, yanking at my tie and buttons. He was on his knees with my belt undone before I realized what he was after.

"Hey, wait—"

"Don't say no." He looked up at me, his eyes huge pools of pain and need.

*Never.* My stomach muscles tightened. I could turn down the sex easily. But him? That raw hurt rolling off him? Never.

"Bedroom . . ." I barely had the word out before he was swallowing me deep, his hands demanding on my hips. I knew what he wanted and I couldn't deny either of us, rocking my hips in slow glides.

But he wasn't satisfied with that by half, yanking on my hips, moaning around my cock.

I fisted my hands in his hair, which made him moan more. I yanked lightly, trying to get some control back, get him to slow down before I came in thirty seconds.

"Oh, fuck, do that again." He pulled back long enough to look at me with pleading eyes. Yeah, I knew what he wanted.

"You want more? Want me to fuck your throat?"

He nodded. "Go hard."

"Okay, baby." I grabbed his hair harder, pulling him down my cock. The slick drag of his tongue made my whole body shudder. "Ready? I'm gonna go deep now."

He moaned, long and low around my cock, inhaling hard. He trembled under my hands.

Oh, God, I wasn't gonna last with the way he was so hungry for it. I started fucking him in earnest, pushing forward into the tight heat of his mouth, grabbing his head, holding him there until I felt his throat spasm, then letting him slide back for a deep gasp before he was scrambling forward again.

"Doing so good. Such a good boy."

He whimpered around my cock, and it was the sexiest fucking thing ever. I tried to read his gasps and moans and licks to give him what he needed. I pushed deeper, making us both moan. My balls lifted and I felt a warning tremble in my dick.

"Gonna come. You want that?"

"Can . . . you . . . go again?" His voice sounded like it had been through a food processor. "Come now, but go again in a bit?" His eyes were wild and glassy and his words were warm against my dick. I would have promised him damn near anything to get off.

"Oh, yeah, baby. I'll take care of you after, I promise." My words sounded rough and slurred, like I'd had three shots of Jack.

"Better." He dove forward again, swallowing hard around me, stretching so that his lips brushed my pubes. Then his tongue came out, just the tip, just enough to sweep along the top of my balls.

"Oh, fuck." The angle meant I felt his teeth a bit more, but the novelty of the action made up for the pinch. His tongue retreated and the pressure around my shaft eased. He inhaled big and I went deep. I held him there extra long, feeling the spasm around my cock, feeling the pressure in my balls build again. When he pulled back for a breath, I was ready, hands urging him forward again as I shot down his throat.

It wasn't wave after wave of release so much as like a pressure valve had been opened. I still had a helluva lot I wanted to do to him, even as euphoria surged through me and rendered me stupid for a few moments. My shirt was unbuttoned, my pants opened and a mess. Robin's nice pants had paint flakes all over them, and I'd rumpled the shoulders of his dress shirt something awful.

"What would you like, honey?" I touched his hair. He rested his head on my thigh. "A shower first, maybe?"

"I want you to fuck me." His voice was strained yet firm.

My stomach dropped lower than the basement and I swallowed around the lump of sand in my throat.

# Chapter 14

Robin stared up at me, his eyes full of expectant defiance. He also looked turned on as fuck, his lips still swollen, his cheeks all pink, his hard dick outlining his suit pants.

*What are you waiting for?* My body chugged toward yes, even as my logic said "hold up a minute."

"I don't want to hurt you. Not when you're like this—"

"You always want to know what I need. I need *this*. I need you." He stood, pulling his shirt off and unbuttoning his pants.

"Okay." My body won that round but fast, but my mind still had doubts. "But slowly, all right? Maybe we should play more with a toy first?"

"Stop being so nice, Vic. Just stop. Fuck. Me." He dropped his pants, leaving his clothes in a heap as he strode naked toward my bedroom, giving off a shit-ton of attitude.

"Wait." I caught his arm at the door to my room. I didn't have to fake my scowl or the gruffness in my voice. I was pissed that Robin had decided to use me for hate sex, and I was even more pissed at myself that I wasn't ending this.

"What?" He looked up at me, his voice full of swagger, his eyes full of hurt. That. That was why I wasn't throwing him out or calling this off. I would cut off my own fingers to spare him pain. Lord knew I'd do whatever he needed—even if it meant hating myself for it later.

"Who's in charge here?" I glowered at him, the full-on stare down that made idiots like Paul turn tail and run and made Robin hot, but I wasn't aiming to turn him on just then.

Robin looked like he might be about to protest, then bit his lip. "You are. But I—"

"But nothing. *You* are going to trust me to give it to you, okay?"

"I don't want to be coddled." His rebellious stare demanded action from me.

Anger and lust formed a potent cocktail, racing through my veins, making my steps unsteady. Oh, he'd get action all right, but on *my* terms.

"Fine. No special treatment." I dragged him by the arm over to the bed, pushed him onto it, and stood over him. "But we do this my way. I am *not* going to hurt you. I am not going to let you goad me into hurting you. Understand?"

"Oh, yeah." He was looking at my mouth. I knew I was frowning mightily down on him, but judging by the sway of his hard dick, that worked for him.

"You can have all the angry, rough sex you want, but you *will* feel good, understand?"

"I don't want—"

"To feel good. I get it." I stroked the hair back from his head. "But you will tell me if it hurts too bad or if you need to stop."

"Goddamn you. Just *do* it already." His whole body shook.

"Fine." The word shot out of my mouth like a rocket, as nasty as any I'd ever spoken. I shoved him back on the bed, flipped him so that I was pinning him to the mattress. "This what you want?"

"Fuck yeah."

"No prep? Just go?" I kept my voice hard and mean and leaned into him.

"Yes." He shoved his ass up at me.

"Sorry. You're not in charge." I pushed him back down. "I am. And I'm going to play with you a while. Not because you like it. Or because it will make you feel good. Or because you deserve it. Nope. I'm going to play with your ass because *I* like it."

I had never once fucked someone dry and I wasn't about to start with Robin. I grabbed the lube and a condom from the drawer in my bedside table, set both aside. His whole body was wound tight as a roll of bakery twine. Beneath me, his ass clenched so tight I could bounce quarters off it—yeah, didn't matter what bravado Robin was spewing forth, he was asking for a serious hurt if I tried to enter him right then, even with lube.

He rolled his head to the side, cursing softly. His mouth twisted, and in that moment, I saw the truth in his eyes. He *wanted* to fail.

He didn't want rough sex because that turned him on, because a hard, dirty entry got him going. No, he wanted this because he wanted to fail.

He was asking for something he knew he couldn't do. Maybe he wanted the pain and the begging and the disappointment and the having to stop because somewhere in his subconscious he thought he *deserved* to fail. Perhaps he couldn't or wouldn't let himself fail by relapsing, so he thought he'd come here and fail at sex again. However, I knew Robin, and behind all that was a deeper need—a need not to have to think, to be so overwhelmed with sensation that whatever else was going on in his head would shut off.

That I could do.

"On your knees."

My tie still dangled from my collar and I pulled it loose before stripping off my shirt.

"You trust me, right?" Without waiting for an answer, I wrapped the tie around Robin's head, blindfolding him.

"Oh, yeah." Robin's voice sounded breathy and far away. "I've never—"

"Me either, but this is what you need, baby." I kept my voice firm, knowing that what he needed was me in total control, not me asking him if he was all right with it.

"Okay." Robin's head fell forward.

I stroked a hand down his back, doing that for several moments until I felt some of his tension ease.

"Only thing you're going to think about is this." I traced patterns on his back with my tongue, trying to keep him guessing about where my tongue would land next even though we both knew where it was heading. His skin tasted sweet, like cookies, with a hint of salt and something more primal.

Kneading his shoulders and neck with my hands, I bit him. The contrast in sensations got a long moan from him, and I kept that up—rubbing and biting. His back was going to be a mess of hickeys later, but I couldn't say I was sorry about that.

"Fuck me." He pushed his ass back into me, his feet tangling in the covers.

"Oh, I'm just getting warmed up." I laughed, a low, dirty sound I'd never made before. I shifted so that his ass fucked nothing but air and he had to guess where I was.

"Fuck. You."

"Not on the agenda. I'm in charge, sweet thing. Only me." Capturing his mouth in a kiss, I teased him a little more. Moving around again, I kneaded his ass, watched him shiver as he guessed what was coming. I drew it out, rubbing and tugging his ass cheeks, blowing softly on his hole.

"Oh, God, *Vic*. Do it."

"When I'm ready." I gave his ass a light slap. Then, holding his ass open, I ran my tongue up and down the crack, barely skating over his hole until I felt the muscle quiver. I attacked him, licking and sucking and working him with my mouth until I gradually felt his tight hole soften, let me in. His whines were high-pitched, feral sounds as he rocked back onto my face.

My hands shook as I reached for the lube. Even after rimming him until he was incoherent, he was still so tense. I circled his hole with my lubed-up index finger, putting a little pressure on it until he rocked down to meet it.

"Jesus. So tight."

"Sorry."

I slapped his ass again. "No apologizing. Feels good. Gonna feel so good on my cock."

"Yeah." The bed squeaking, he rocked his hips, fucking himself on my finger. I lined up a second; with all the fooling around we'd done, I'd never given him more than the one finger because he'd tensed up both times I'd tried to go to two, and I hadn't wanted to hurt him. But this time, with me biting his shoulders and whispering encouragement, he slowly rocked back on both fingers.

"Yes. That's it, honey. Take it. Take it so good."

"Ready. Oh, *God*. So ready."

I got the condom on and myself slicked up, then positioned myself right at his entrance—

And he immediately went full-body stiff, his shoulders shaking with tension.

My heart squeezed, every bit as tense as his body. I had to resist the urge to tell him we'd stop. *No.* I wasn't letting him fail and I wasn't stopping until he'd proven his inner fears false.

"You can do it." I used my slick finger to tease his hole again. "I've got you. Slow, okay?"

Removing my hand, I tried again with my cock, pressing forward, soothing his back with my free hand, making reassuring noises. He rocked his hips tentatively back.

"That's it. Just take what you can." My cockhead finally breached his tight ring of muscles, his ass gripping me like a vice. It was just this side of painful how tight he was. Holding myself still took every ounce of concentration I had, but I did it, my thighs burning, my lower back clenching under the strain of waiting.

It was worth waiting to watch Robin's spine undulate, his head stretching toward the ceiling as he arched his back, working himself down my cock by millimeters.

"*Vic.* Oh, God, Vic. *Vic.*" He whimpered my name over and over as he slid farther back. "I need . . ."

"Yeah, baby. Take whatever you need." I stroked his neck, his sweat-drenched back, his ass, anywhere I could reach.

"Move. Oh, please, move." Sweat rolled down his back and he made little grunting noises as I rocked into him. "Oh, God. Like that. *Please.*"

I thrust more, feeling the tension ebb, the clench of his muscles lessening enough to let me slide back. Slowly, oh so slowly, I built a rhythm. A few times I felt him start to go on edge, but I wrapped an arm around his chest, my hand over his heart, steadying him. Through it all, I kept up a constant stream of praise.

"So good. Can you feel? You're taking my whole cock now. Doing so good."

I wrapped my other hand around his waist, searching for his cock, relieved to find him still rock hard.

"More." He rutted into my fist. "Need more. Harder."

"Mmm." A low hum of pleasure escaped my throat as I picked up speed, choosing an angle that nailed his gland over and over.

Body quaking, he let out a series of low moans. His body kept tightening—not like pain, more like he was thinking about coming but backing off each time he got close.

"You feel so good. Just let it go, Robin. Just feel. No thinking." I held him close to me while I thrust.

"Oh, God, Vic. So close. I want to come. Need to come." His voice was broken, each word punctuated by a deep shudder.

"You can do it, sweetheart. It's right there for you." I sped up my hand on his cock. "Letting me fuck you so nice. Taking it so hard. So fuckin' perfect."

"I can't . . . I can't . . . I can't." His body arched and strained.

"Yes, you can." I soothed him with words and hands and kisses along the back of his neck. I was trying to hold back myself, but the flutter of his muscles, sucking me back on every upstroke, made my heart pound.

"Oh, Jesus. Vic. I need this. Need you. Go hard. Please."

I obliged with deep, pounding thrusts that made the bed shake and him cry out. I stroked him faster, trying to get him to tumble over before I did, but I was fast hurtling to the point of no return.

"Vic. Oh. Jesus."

The broken, ragged sounds coming from his mouth undid me, made me crazy and unhinged. I felt my orgasm start in my toes, build itself up, need rising higher and higher with each thrust, restraint dropping, until I couldn't hold back any longer. Pounding into him, I came in a furious rush.

"Oh, hell. Sorry." I dropped kisses all down his spine as I came back to myself.

"It's okay. Don't think I can anyway—"

"You can," I said firmly.

"I don't need to . . ."

"Shut up," I told him bluntly as I pulled out. "I'm in charge. I'll tell you what you need." I flipped him over so that he was on his back now, with my fingers pressing against his hole, finding their way in much easier now. "And what you need is this."

I dropped my head and swallowed him deep, pressing against his gland with my fingers, working his head with my tongue. I glanced up; the tie had gotten all twisted up in his hair. His eyes were still squished shut, though, with moisture leaking out the sides. He was building toward something, something bigger than just an orgasm, something that was threatening to rip him to pieces.

And I knew instinctively that that's what he needed—he needed me to send him soaring, to force him to accept this release, to see him through to the other side. To not give up on him. He bucked against my hand and mouth. His body tensed, like he was about to shoot, then went slack right as I thought he was about to go.

"Come on, baby. You can do it. It's right there for you."

"Don't have to . . . We can stop . . ." Tears were rolling down his cheeks now, but his body kept fucking my hand.

"No one's stopping. I'm here just as long as you need. Only thing you need to worry about is fucking my mouth. Fuck my fingers too, honey. Make yourself fly."

I swallowed his cockhead again, using every trick I knew and some I invented, as my tongue worked the sensitive underside of his shaft. Curving my fingers, I pressed up hard on his spot until he howled.

"Unnh. *Vic.* Fuckfuckfuck. *Vic.*" Heels digging into the mattress, hands yanking my sheets loose, whole body arching like a bow, he went off, stream after stream filling my mouth. It was too much to swallow in one go—I had to pull back and work him through the rest of it with my hand, but I kept stroking until he was completely still.

My chest pounded like I'd climbed Mount Hood, and I felt that kind of victorious. Stretching out next to him, I took him in my arms. As soon as his head hit my chest, he started shaking like a baby bird. His face was wet with tears and I rubbed him all over.

"Sssh. It's okay. I've got you."

"Oh, Vic." His voice cracked and he trembled in my arms, tears spilling faster. He scrubbed at his eyes. "Crap. I'm sorry. I don't mean—"

"It's okay. You're fine." I pressed a kiss on the side of his head. "You go on now."

It seemed like that was it—like his tears had been waiting for permission to fall freely. Sobs wracked his body, and I knew without asking that this was the first he'd cried. Knew it wasn't about me or the sex—all that was just a conduit, a way for the fountain of grief inside him to find the surface.

My own eyes burned and stung. All I could do was hold him and let him sob it out. Seeing another man weep like this was profoundly humbling; seeing strong, capable Robin reduced to a sobbing mess gutted me. My chest was damp where his face lay and my hand cramped where he was clutching it, but I kept holding on. I held on through his sobs, through his curses, through his sniffles and whimpers as the tears ebbed. Held on tighter as he started to talk.

"Why, Vic? Why? Why doesn't Zach get a second chance?"

"I don't know, baby, I really don't."

"But I did. Why me?" Robin sat up, scrubbing at his hair.

I had to think on this one; part of me wanted to tell him it was because he was special, because God had other plans for him, because it wasn't his time. But instead, I went for the truth. "Because you were lucky."

"I don't want to be lucky," he whispered. "It was supposed to be me. *I* should have died. Me. Not my friend Tim. Not Zach. Me. I should have died."

"But you didn't, Robin. And that's good—"

"There should be a reason, right? A higher purpose why them and not me? And Vic, I've spent three years since Tim died, and I still haven't found the purpose. I'm not good enough."

"Yes, you are. You're one of the best people I know." I pulled the covers up from the foot of the bed, draped them around his shoulders. His skin felt clammy with tears and cooling sweat.

"Tim was the funniest guy I knew. And so good with animals—he could get alley cats to cuddle up with him. And Zach was an amazing musician. I never knew until his mom told me, but he used to write songs on their piano. They should still be here."

"Yeah, they should." The sting in my eyes intensified. Manny should still be here. And my dad and Uncle Mauro and everyone else taken too young.

"I thought . . . I thought maybe Zach was my purpose," he whispered. "I thought if I saved him, if I got him off the streets, that would be a sign that I was on the right path, that I was here for a reason."

"You *are* here for reason—you're here for *you*." *And me,* I silently added. But I knew it would be too much to add that right then. My love for him was a physical ache. I felt each pained breath of his, each tug on his hair, each tear.

"It just *sucks*." He punched one of my pillows.

"Yeah, it does." I took a deep breath—so much emotion coursing through me, it was hard to talk. "It's never fair. Ever. Manny taught high school. He talked about getting his PhD so he could be a principal. Look at me. I bake things. Manny changed people's lives."

"Zach was so young, Vic. So young."

"I know."

"It could have been me." And then he was crying again, softer this time, and I held him tight. He sagged in my arms and I laid him down on the bed, cuddled him against my chest.

After a while he was silent, and I thought he might be sleeping, but his eyes were open while he held on to my arms.

"Sorry." He caught me staring at him.

"No more sorry." I brushed his hair out of his face.

"I should probably go." He didn't make any move to remove himself from my arms, so I squeezed him tighter.

"No. You can go back to hating me later if you need to, but let me love on you a bit right now."

I expected an argument, but instead he yawned. "Okay."

# Chapter 15

We napped for a few hours. Well, Robin napped. I mainly watched him sleep. I'd lied, of course. He couldn't go back to hating me. I was going to fight for him with everything I had. Eventually I crept from the bed, started a pot of soup. Got a loaf of bread ready to go with it. Bit of a novelty, baking something at home. But Robin needed some comfort food—a nice pot of minestrone and a baguette would be perfect for this cold, dark day.

Grandma Degrassi used to make this soup whenever someone had a bad cold, but I associated it with being in her kitchen, chopping carrots and green beans for her, picking basil off the plants on her windowsill. Her kitchen was where I went when I wanted to get away from the world. Whenever my dad would start in on his "real-man" lectures, Grandma would slip me another cookie and shake her wooden spoon at my dad. *Not in my kitchen, sonny.*

She'd lived with Aunt Mary and Uncle Mauro in her later years, and this kitchen still felt more like hers than mine. Decades of family meals came from this stove. I stirred in some garlic and wished I had something better than soup to offer Robin's soul.

"That smells amazing." Robin came to the door in only his boxers. "Sorry for sleeping so long."

"Don't—"

"Say sorry. I know." He laughed tentatively, like he was seeing if the sound still worked. "Still. I can't believe I passed out so long."

"Bet you haven't been sleeping well this week." I gave him a pointed look.

"Guilty." He looked around. "Is that smell bread?"

"Yeah. Just plain." I opened the oven to show him, and his face lit up like I'd revealed a seven-layer chocolate cake.

"Oh, man. The Swedish housekeeper I told you about made the most amazing baguettes. She was nice. She'd give me big pieces with lingonberry jam." He looked up at me with big, hopeful eyes.

"I might have some marionberry in there." I motioned at the fridge. "No lingonberries. But I could go to IKEA later. . . ." I stopped as I realized how ridiculous I sounded.

"Have you always been such a nice person?" Robin grabbed a sponge and started scrubbing down the counter.

"You keep saying I'm nice." I shook my head. "I'm not. Sophomore year I broke three of Richie Klein's fingers for calling me a queer. When I was your age, I went to one of the bars with some friends. Three guys started hassling us."

"You took on all three? In a bar fight?" He paused in wiping the counter, his eyes going wide.

"Only one of them needed stitches, but yeah. I narrowly avoided assault charges. I'm just saying—I'm not nice. I have a temper on me. Day before my dad died, I told him to go to hell. We were arguing about the Church again. I was sick of it. Told him where he could go and left my mom's. Never saw him again." My voice got a little raw at the end. Even years later, I could still remember how red his face had been as I walked away, still hear him calling after me.

"Man. That's rough. But that doesn't make you mean. I mean, yeah, you have this stare that says *I will steal your soul if you look at me wrong*. But you, my friend, are a *nice* guy."

I shrugged. I wished he was able to see that *he* was a nice guy, too. The timer for the oven went off, and Robin grabbed two of my pot holders.

"Can I get it?"

"You eaten all week?" I laughed at him. "Yeah. You can get it."

"Ow. Oooh. Ow." He tried slicing the hot loaf as soon as he set the pan down.

"Here, pretty boy." I pushed him onto a stool. "You have to give it a minute."

"Pretty boy, huh? Is *that* why you're so nice to me? 'Cause I'm pretty?"

I looked him over, not sure if he was joking or serious or what he might be fishing for.

"You're fucking gorgeous. And I think you know that." I ripped him off a hunk of bread and set it on a little plate with some butter and the jam from the fridge. "But if you're asking me if that's the only attraction for me, the answer's no. You're good people, Robin. Even if you can't always see that. You're good people."

I didn't have pretty words to tell him how he was the nice guy—far nicer than me. I didn't have the words for how selfless he was. All I had was my grandmother's soup and her words for people you wanted to have around.

"It's talking with you." I tried and failed to find some decent words. Grabbed some bowls for soup and the ladle.

"Pardon?"

"The attraction? You being built like a Hollywood A-lister doesn't hurt, but it's how we talked together. Always have. Right from our first shift together. That's the attraction for me. How the talking made me feel." All right, now I just sounded sappy. I sloshed the hot soup onto my hand. "Fuck."

I waved my hand, and Robin captured it, brought it to his mouth. He blew on my finger, then dropped a kiss on the inside of my wrist, right where the soup had landed.

"Vic?"

"Yeah?"

"What if I don't want to keep hating you?"

I sank onto the stool next to him, my knees turned into butter.

"Then don't." I knew my voice sounded too gruff. "Simple as that."

"I was a shit to you." He kissed my hand again.

"You were hurting. Grieving."

"I saw your text," he said softly. "The one from Tuesday."

I couldn't say anything, could only nod helplessly.

"I probably looked at it a hundred times that night."

"Yeah?"

"Looked at it a hundred more in the last few days. I wanted to call you. Wanted to come over. But I . . . I'm a mess."

"You got all fucked up about me not trusting you, but Robin, you gotta trust me, too. Trust me with your black moods and your anger and your sadness."

"You saw what happened today when I unloaded on you."

"That was *good*; you got to let all those feelings out. I want your mess. Bring it on."

He cocked his head to one side, considering. My chest pounded like a drum solo. I didn't have to consider. I knew.

"I'm serious. Bring it. You think you have something that's going to push me away? Bring it. Bring all your mess. I *want* to help you through things. Want to help you clean up things. Want to help you discover there's no mess at all."

"You're . . . Vic." He chewed on his poor lower lip something awful. "I could fall in love with you. So fucking easy. Hell, I think maybe I already am—"

"Then do it. Go ahead. Fall in love with me."

"You're serious." He dropped his bread to the table. "I get depressed sometimes—"

"Figured that out already. Not scaring me off."

"I'm on the rebound."

"From Paul the Shit? He doesn't worry me. What, you wanna sleep around more? Get your single sex on?"

"You know I don't. With you it's just . . ." He inhaled sharply. "I've never had anything like what we share."

"I know. Me neither. Never been so good."

"Even with my issues—"

"Baby, the only 'issue' "—I used air quotes—"you have is thinking there's something wrong with you. I get that you have moods. They don't scare me away. And we could not fuck for another six months and I'd still be right here."

"Six months, huh?" He scooted closer to me. "A whole six months of no sex?"

"I was thinking no anal, but sure. No sex. I'd still be here. I'd still want you."

"So you're saying it's safe to let myself fall in love with you." He seemed to spin the words over in his mouth, test them out.

"I'm saying I love you." I put my hand over his. "And yeah, it's safe to fall in love with me."

"I . . ." Voice cracking, he trailed off. For a second, I thought he might cry again. My throat got tight and my eyes smarted. If he cried, I was a goner. I got off my stool, came around, and wrapped my arms around him. "I want to believe."

He took a deep breath, his slim ribs expanding, his muscles rippling in a way that made me regret promising I could live without sex.

"Then believe. Believe in us."

Instead of replying, he leaned up and kissed me. The softest brush of two lips against mine, but there was so much emotion behind it. I kissed him back, deepening it, telling him with my lips and tongue and hands how I felt. Somehow, we ended up on the floor, and it was a long, long time before we came up for air.

The soup went so cold I had to dump our bowls back in the pot and reheat it.

"What time is it?" Robin asked.

"Five-thirty." I pointed to the clock on the microwave.

"Okay. NA meeting's at seven at the center."

"You're going to go?"

"Yeah." He nodded slowly. "Melissa's right. I . . . I need a meeting after the week I've had."

"You want me to go, too?"

"Nah. I can just call you . . ." He stopped, looking me over like he was trying to decipher a code. "You're serious about going over to the mission with me, aren't you? I mean, you didn't just offer to offer, right?"

"I never offer just to offer." I ladled up fresh soup.

"I know. It's one of the things I . . . I love about you. And you're right. If we're going to do this thing, I need to stop shutting you out simply because I think I'm going to feel shitty after going to the shelter."

"Damn straight." Joy as warm as the soup gathered in my insides. Him deciding not to shut me out felt almost bigger than those three little words. "But, Robin, why go to the center if it's going to make you feel that bad? There are other NA meetings tonight. We can find one for you. Maybe you should take some time before going back to the shelter."

"No." He laughed, a dry, crackly sound. "You've told me all about your family over the years. How big and crazy they are?"

"Yeah."

"Well, the shelter is family to me. It frustrates me and infuriates me, and lately, it depresses me, but it's still family. I don't want a different meeting. I need to be with my family tonight."

"Then we'll both go. And I'll tell you more about the latest with my crazy family on the way."

# Chapter 16

"You came!" Melissa rushed Robin as soon as we walked into the staff room, her face going soft and open and her arms holding him an extra-long time in a hug. "Can you help me get set up? I've got to move some stuff around."

"Sure," Robin said.

"Good. I'll check on cleanup in the kitchen and be along in a minute."

As we came down the hall, I noticed a kid hanging around the meeting-room door. One of Zach's friends from the funeral. Same ratty parka and unwashed black hair and scared expression.

"Robin." I stopped him with a hand on his elbow, nodding in the direction of the kid.

"I should . . ." His shoulders stiffened, like he was holding his breath. "I should go talk to him. Right? Invite him into the meeting?"

"Yeah." I knew he had to be thinking of Zach and how he'd offered so many times in so many ways. But he needed to get back to the part of himself that could reach out, even when—especially when—it might hurt.

Earlier, Robin had called the shelter his family. Wasn't until we walked in the door that I realized that's what it was for me, too: family. As my own family had gotten smaller, as each loss in my life had mounted, the shelter had become more and more important in my life, kept me from shutting myself off, made me take chances on people again.

"I'm going to see if they need help cleaning up in the kitchen," I said, wanting to give him space. Robin needed to do this on his own.

"Okay."

I was partly down the hall when I heard him ask, "Todd? You wanna help me get the chairs set up for the meeting?"

I slowed my footsteps, waiting . . . waiting . . . waiting . . .

"Yes," the boy said softly. "I can do that."

I skipped the rest of the way to the kitchen.

After the meeting, Robin spent a long time talking with Todd. He and Melissa got him hooked up with a bed for the night and with referrals to services in the morning. The evening breeze had a crisp bite to it on the walk back to my car. Since it was a day for firsts, I chanced reaching for Robin's hand. He looked over at me, a little smile tugging his lips, then nodded. Something warm expanded in my chest.

"No guarantee he'll show in the morning," Robin said as I unlocked the car door for him.

"Nope. But it's a start."

"Yeah. It's a start. Felt good just to have him show." Robin settled back in the passenger seat, looking more at peace than I'd seen him all week.

"Yeah. You did that, you know?"

"Me?" Robin sat up straighter. I took the Hawthorne Street Bridge to get out of Southeast. It was late and the twinkly lights of the city looked friendly, like little promises that tomorrow wouldn't be quite so ugly.

"Yeah. I saw you at the funeral. You were the only one who went over to those kids. Talked to them like they were people. Made them feel welcome. You got him to that meeting." I reached over and squeezed Robin's knee.

"Is that enough?" he asked in a small voice, his eyes on the city whooshing past.

"Is what enough?"

"If I get him there? If I get him and Adam and Skyler there, is that enough?"

"All you had to do was get *you* there. That was enough. That will always be enough." Conviction laced my words, made my voice deeper. My hands tightened on the steering wheel. *Hell.* I wished I wasn't driving. Wished I could hug on him. Make him see what an incredible, courageous success he was every damn day.

"Thanks."

"Melissa's right: no one loves that center as much as you. No one.

And that shows in everything you do there. There will be other Zachs, you know. But there will also be other Todds." We wove our way through my neighborhood. A few houses still had Christmas lights up— cheerful middle fingers to the cold reality of January.

"That's what Melissa was telling me. She also said again how much she wants me to take over while she's on maternity leave. Says I should do it to prove something to myself."

"So do it. You're not overloaded with clients, right?"

"No, time's not the issue. I'll be there every day regardless. It's more . . . I don't think I deserve it. Like I put in the time there because I *have* to, because something inside me will die if I don't. I don't do it so that I can get paid eventually, or so I can be in charge. And even if I *was* in charge, who would listen to me?"

"Everyone. Everyone would listen to you," I said firmly. "People respect you more than you give them credit for. You know every bit as much as Melissa does *and* you know how to connect with the kids."

"Yeah. Maybe." He sounded far from convinced as I parked the car. Strange how coming home with him seemed as normal as breathing right now.

"No maybe about it. And see, here is where you get the advantage of having a thug boyfriend. Someone there's not listening to you? Not respecting you? I'll make sure they do." I shut my door extra hard for emphasis.

"You are *not* a thug." Robin playfully punched my shoulder.

"Oh, you just wait and see what happens if someone disrespects you." I gave him a fierce scowl, tried to live up to how Robin saw me like an action hero.

His mouth quirked. His eyes seemed caught between amusement and arousal.

Heat flared between us, settled low in my groin. Him digging me acting all mean was something I still hadn't gotten used to—felt strange, like taking credit for something I saw as a flaw. *Oh. Bingo.*

"You ashamed about the shelter?" I asked as we came in the house. I headed to the front to check my mail.

"Ashamed? Of course not. They do great work—"

"Not that. I mean, do you still beat yourself up because you needed them? You still trying to make up for the help they gave you?"

"No." He leaned against the living room wall. "Okay, maybe a little. I mean, who wouldn't be? You seem to be the one person in the world who doesn't care that I used to be a junkie who lived on the streets and turned tricks for three months. But everyone else? Oh hell yeah. I think they still see me as a guy who needed—who *needs*—the shelter."

"No, I think *you* still see you like that. Everyone else sees you like the success story you are. You are why the shelter exists. You are the reason people like Melissa roll out of bed and come to work. You're an inspiration. And that's why you should take the job. Tell your doubts to go fuck themselves; you're not that kid anymore, Robin."

"Hey. What did you do to your foyer?" Leaving the wall, he followed me into the entryway. "This looks amazing. I should have noticed earlier—"

"You were a little busy." I raised my eyebrows, giving him a pointed look. "Stop trying to change the topic. You've been looking for your purpose—the shelter is it. Not saving particular people—the shelter itself. That part that feels like family—that's your purpose."

"You really think I should do this?" He flopped on my couch. Not through with this by half, I followed him over, joined him on the couch.

"No. I don't think you *should* do it, but I think you *need* to do it. I think it will exhaust you and wear you out and put your emotions through the wringer. I think it will challenge how you see yourself, and I think it'll be hard and a hell of an adjustment. I think you need to do it for *you*."

"Okay." He took a deep breath, nodded. He settled in against my side on the couch. "I'll tell Melissa yes, but on one condition."

"Yeah?" I tugged him to me, both of our legs going up on the oversize ottoman in front of the couch.

"I'll give the center job a shot if you tell your Aunt Mary you want the house."

"That's not a condition." I'd told him on the drive over about the call from my mom. "I can't keep the house."

"Because it will be hard and exhausting and put your emotions through a ringer?" Robin said in an imitation of my deeper voice. "*Baby,* I don't think you should buy the house, I think you *need* to buy the house."

"The house needs more people—"

"So give it that." Our gazes met. Held. "You've got friends. Make a place you want to have people over. And you've got me."

"I've got you?" Everything felt warm and fuzzy, like I was wrapped in a blanket of contentment. I had Robin. Nothing else really mattered.

"Yeah. I can't promise to go all badass if the house starts mistreating you, but I'm down with hard work. You keep saying how the house needs someone to love it, but Vic, that's *you*. Look at that foyer. That's love right there."

"Okay. It's a deal." The warm feeling expanded, every muscle and bone feeling *right*, feeling settled for the first time in over a year. I'd been so focused on what I couldn't give the house that I'd never stopped to think about what it might give me.

Robin pulled me close for a kiss. "I think making love is way better than shaking on a deal."

"Oh, yeah."

And then he was on my lap and we were kissing, and that's what it was, *making love.* We'd had friends sex and casual sex and makeup sex, but for the first time I understood why people called it making love. Always used to think that was such a bs term—like what could you really make out of bodies and sweat and jizz and moaning. But with Robin, I saw the truth. You really could make something.

It was in the way Robin's strong fingers clutched at my shoulders, it was in the way our lips slid together like they had a thousand times before, the way we moaned at the same instant when our bare chests collided. His hands swept over my stomach, brushing by my scar, and for the first time, I didn't flinch; instead, my body arched into the touch, into the love he so freely offered. We made something out of the pile of clothes on the floor, out of the groans and gasps as we tumbled back together onto the cushions, made something out of the rub of bodies, the murmured promises our lips and hands made. Robin's joy when he came ripped through me, too. It was the easiest, fastest I'd ever seen him go over and that right there—the joy that throbbed in my chest—that was what we made. We made joy and comfort and pleasure and love.

"You made a cake for your dad's birthday?" Robin asked on Sunday morning as he noticed the large bakery box on the counter.

"Yeah. Triple chocolate with a chocolate buttercream. My sister better be pleased."

"Isn't that a bit . . . morbid?"

"Eh." I shrugged and grabbed a carton of eggs to make breakfast. "We like cake. And everyone loved my pop. My mom doesn't need a lot of excuse for a Sunday dinner."

"You loved him too?" Robin asked. "I mean, you've said before how he was kind of mean to you—"

"He was my dad. We didn't see eye to eye on a lot of stuff, mainly the Church. But he was still the same guy who used to give me piggy-back rides to bed every night. And no matter what, he had my back. When I was around twelve or thirteen—right when he was always lecturing me about needing to be a real man—this one day, these older kids cornered me in the alley behind our house. Called me a fag and a nelly boy. There were four or five of them and I was ready to fight, but it was gonna get ugly real fast."

"That's terrible."

"But then, all of a sudden, there was this *roar.* And my dad chased them off. Gave them a piece of his mind. Called all their parents. 'Course the next week he was back to lecturing me, but I never doubted that he had my back."

"I'm sorry he died so young." Robin put his arms around me.

"Yeah, well, young's kinda relative this week." I buried my face in his ocean-scented hair. "He was just starting to come around on the gay thing when he passed. Made his peace with it, he told me. Things were better between us, except for Christmas, when we argued about why I couldn't just fake it and go to church with them. But he was a good dad. Saw all four of us graduate high school. Saw the girls married." My voice got a little thick. "So, yeah, I baked the man a cake."

"I love you, Vic." Robin kissed my cheek "I really do."

"You going to see Zach's parents next week? I thought I might do another batch of soup for them. Maybe a really hearty kale and pumpkin." My voice shook as hard as my hands. I didn't know what to do in the face of so much love and trust. Unlike the day before, Robin said it so confidently, so *defiantly* that it made my guts tremble, too.

"What's wrong?" Robin asked, tightening his arms around me.

"Nothin'. Just when I made that stupid bet with Cliffie, I didn't really expect you—"

"Hold up. You made a bet with Cliff about *me?*"

*Oh, hell.* My shoulder blades squeezed together, trying to hold on to the nice moment. But it was too late. Me and my big mouth had ruined things.

"Only a stupid thing. Not a real bet. More of a New Year's resolution. Over whether or not I could get you to go out with me."

"Is that all this was, then, a bet? A challenge?" Robin stepped back. His face was stony and closed off. "You landed me, so now what? You collect your fifty or whatever from Cliff and go on with your life?"

"You know it's not like that. I was into you for you so long. Both Melissa and Cliff could tell. This was more about a . . . push. Something to give me courage to do what I wanted to for two years."

"Two years. Wait. You were into me before Paul?"

"Oh, yeah." I nodded. "I mean, I didn't wish *harm* upon you guys or anything—"

"Don't lie." A trace of humor crept back into his voice.

"Okay, I wished harm on *him,* but mainly I wished happy on you. Even if it was with that bastard."

"Why not speak up sooner? Before Paul, I mean. Like a year ago?" He said it so reasonably, like all I would have had to do was ask.

"Because I hadn't had my surgery yet." Frustrated, I slapped the counter behind me.

"Oh." Robin nodded, considering. Then he crossed back over to me, wound his arms around me. "Vic? You don't really believe you had to have the surgery to win me? Or a stupid bet, right?"

"Dunno," I mumbled into his hair. I didn't want to hear this. I didn't want to hear that Robin would have said yes to the old me. Didn't want to hear that I'd put in all those hours at the gym for . . . for what? "Why else do you think I did all this work?"

"For you, Vic. You did it for you."

I took a deep breath, considering. For most of the year, my changes had been for Manny and for my mom—didn't want her to have to go through the pain of loss like Aunt Mary.

"I didn't want to die," I whispered, and Robin held me tighter. I'd spent the whole damn year chasing death—the grief of it, the not wanting to die young, all of it. It had all been about what I lost.

But up until this moment, I hadn't once thought about what I'd gained. Maybe I hadn't realized it, but I'd done it for me. Every mile on the treadmill, every breakfast of egg whites, every follow-up appointment with my doctor. Robin was right—it was something I'd done for me.

"I wasn't ready for you," I said slowly. Robin might have said yes to the old me—but the old me wouldn't have had the courage to believe him. "But I think I loved you. Even then."

"You're trying to make me cry again." He poked my stomach. "Stop that. I don't want to meet your family with red eyes."

"They're going to love you. Trust me. I'm more worried they're going to jump all over you like cocker spaniels at the door."

"Well, as long as they don't try to sniff me, we're all good."

We really were. Much as I was nervous about talking with Aunt Mary, telling her that I wanted the house, I felt like things in my life were exactly as they were supposed to be, maybe for the first time ever.

# Chapter 17

"That's your best design ever." Trish came up behind me, but not even her presence was enough to make me drop my concentration. Everything about this cake had to be perfect. Every drop line needed to be spot on, every butterfly perfectly placed.

"You actually gonna eat a piece of that?" Cliff came up next to Trish. The June sunshine filtering in through the large window wavered a bit.

"You're in my light." I didn't look over at either of them, needing to finish the last few lines.

"Of course he's going to eat it," Trish spoke for me. "He wouldn't make Robin eat it all by himself, now would he?"

"*He* just needs to finish the cake, thank you very much."

"I don't know. Mr. Personality here, Robin might just take the cake and go."

"You're not helping." Lines complete, I made a shooing motion with my free hand. Neither of them looked remotely interested in leaving.

"Sweetie." Trish came over and touched my arm. "Are you seriously worried that he's going to say no?"

*Yes. Very.* "'Course not." I tweaked the position of a butterfly.

"That boy's nuts about you," Cliff said firmly. "You haven't started a project at your place in the last six months that wasn't his idea."

"Don't I know *that*. Home Depot might as well start taking direct deposit of my check." Last few weeks, I'd been hitting the gym less because of all the yard work Robin had scheduled. Hours and hours of boulder and moss removal and terracing with plans he'd found online. But another week or two and I'd have the first vegetables from the garden we'd carved out of the rocky hillside.

"You got the welcome-back cake done for Melissa?" I asked Trish.

"Yup. It's in the walk-in. I stuck a few of the butterflies you discarded on it." She gestured at my work space, which was littered with butterflies and flowers I hadn't deemed quite perfect enough for Robin.

Robin thought I was at work on Saturday to finish up a cake for Melissa. Tomorrow afternoon the center would be holding a party to welcome her back—and to celebrate Robin's new position as codirector. He'd grown during his time as acting director, found new confidence and showed more inner strength than a lot of people had given him credit for. And when Melissa decided she only wanted to come back part-time after the baby, he'd been first to suggest they share in the running of the center, letting her have more time with the baby and him more time for his graphic design clients on the side.

"All right. I guess this will have to do." I studied the cake, still not satisfied. The fondant was the blue of Robin's eyes, the piping a chocolate brown that reminded me of his hair, and the combo gave the cake a hipster vibe not unlike Robin himself. The piping was open lattice work—the sort he was always admiring on my other cakes. I'd gone over-the-top ornate with multiple levels of crisscrossing lines on each of the three small tiers.

"Take it to him already!" Cliff ordered.

"And text me what he says," Trish called after me.

At home, I fussed, making a nice Dungeness crab salad for dinner with bread from the bakery and the few greens from my garden supplemented with produce Robin had grabbed at the farmers market.

"That looks amazing." Robin came in the door and hung his keys on the pegboard next to mine. "Are we celebrating with sledgehammers later?"

"You." I shook my spoon at him. Somewhere, the ghost of Nonna Maria smiled at me, standing there in her kitchen, waving a wooden spoon while talking smack to my boy. "I sign the papers yesterday and you're already in full-on demo mode."

"Yup." He stole a cherry tomato from the salad. The plan was to take down the wall between the kitchen and the dining room before starting the bulk of the kitchen remodel. I hadn't wanted to actually bash through walls until my name was on the mortgage, all official-like. Aunt Mary had cried when I'd told her I wanted the house. My biggest battle had been forcing her to take a fair price for it. But as of 4:51 yesterday, the house had been mine alone.

But not for long, if I had my way.

"Hey what's this?" Robin gestured to the box on the breakfast nook table.

"Dessert." I squeezed my hands to keep them from shaking. "Let me show you."

"You're going to eat dessert?"

"Yeah. It's a special occasion." I lifted the box off the cake, set it aside.

"*Vic*. That is stunning." He walked all the way around the table, crouching down to get a better view, rising to peer over the top. "It's like a little baby wedding cake!"

"Yeah, see, we do this thing for our brides at the store; sometimes to help them better visualize the full, I'll do a miniature. Help them see what they're getting." Hands sweating, I felt as nervous as one of the chickens Robin had admired at the farmers market.

"And what am I getting?" he said softly, coming to stand in front of me.

"Well, later you're getting a sledgehammer," I joked, to prove to myself I could still form words. "And me. You're getting me. I realized something at the lawyer's office yesterday. I didn't like the look of just my signature on all the papers. Doesn't seem right for this to be just my house."

"It doesn't?"

"Nah. When was the last time you went back to your place? Two weeks ago? A month?"

"Maybe three." He laughed, a nervous, tinkling sound. He reached for my hand and I went willingly. "What are you after here, Vic?"

"I want this to be your home, too—because it already is. And I want to make you a wedding cake. Like this, but bigger. More butterflies. Probably big enough to feed a hundred or so."

"Can this cake be delivered to The Foundry? Because I think . . . if you're making me a cake that big, I want it delivered there."

"You mind if my family shows up to help eat it?" My voice, usually so strong and sure, was wavering like a high-wire act gone wrong.

"Sure. We'll have mostaccioli and dancing for them. Vic?"

"Yeah?"

"This is possibly the most convoluted proposal ever. And I love you. Can you please just ask?"

"Robin?" I gulped hard. "Will you marry me? I know it's only been six months, but I don't want to wait to have this be your home for real. To have you be . . . mine." I looked at the floor, not him, as I finished.

"Vic." He raised my chin with his hand. "Are you seriously worried I might say no?"

"Thought maybe you'd hate the cake."

"Oh. Yeah, that's a *real* possibility." He kissed me full-on on the lips, a loud smack. "Yes. Yes, I will marry you. And I want a New Year's wedding. We both deserve some good holiday memories this year."

"Yeah, we do."

And then there wasn't a whole lot left of talking as Robin was kissing me and I was trying hard not to cry, and then he was crying, so then I was crying, too, and it was a beautiful mess. A beautiful, glorious mess in a house that was finally a home again.

# Delivered Fast

# Chapter 1

The delivery boy had sweet buns. Not to mention prize-winning rolls. He wore a pair of those fancy over-the-ear headphones and shimmied around the white bakery truck, his hips and ass working in time to what was apparently a killer beat. Even the way he climbed into the back of the truck was a choreographed dance. I wasn't usually one to get distracted by eye candy, but that ass . . .

I'd propped open the service door at the rear of my coffee shop about fifteen minutes earlier, hoping to coax a cool breeze into the stuffy storeroom where I'd been working. I leaned against the door frame, appreciating the unexpectedly fine view in the alley.

When the guy emerged from the truck—headphones around his neck, carrying a stack of pink boxes—I pushed away from the door and met him at the edge of the concrete steps. I tried to play it cool, like I hadn't spent the last five minutes perving on his world-class bubble butt.

"You're not Vic," I said as I ushered him into the hallway that led back to the kitchen and storeroom.

"Nope. I'm Lance, Vic's cousin. I'll be handling your deliveries from here on out." His smile—a wide, toothy grin—was almost as adorable as his butt. The only resemblance he had to my usual beefy delivery guy was in the chiseled facial features and light olive skin. He looked like he'd be right at home playing World Cup soccer for Italy with his wide shoulders, lean torso, muscular thighs and legs. And that ass.

Which I was going to stop thinking about right the hell now. He was too young—I could see that even more clearly under the fluorescent lights of my kitchen. Early twenties, if that. His gelled-up black hair fell across his forehead in artfully bleached strands. Too high maintenance for my taste.

"I'm Chris O'Neal. Here, let me help you with those." Taking part of the stack from him, I showed him the metal racks where I stashed recent deliveries.

"Nice setup you've got here." Lance looked around the cramped but efficient kitchen area.

"Thanks." Most of The People's Cup square footage was devoted to the coffee bar and seating area in the front, so I made do in the back with my organization system, which bordered on the obsessive. I'd installed floor-to-ceiling shelving on every wall, including over the cooktop and counters. The center prep table was where most of the action happened, and its broad expanse was covered with the beginnings of several dishes for tomorrow's Sunday brunch.

"I've been here before with friends from PSU—for your Sunday thing. And during the week once or twice to study."

I made a noncommittal noise. *Great.* A college kid. As if I needed to feel like more of an old, cranky perv.

"Let's get the rest of the boxes." I herded him back out to the alley. I was eager to get him and his distracting ass on his way. I had several more hours of staging work ahead of me to prepare for Sunday's buffet. During the week we were just another coffeehouse, but we were known all over Portland for our Sunday brunch.

"So are you the owner? This all yours?" Lance asked as he got another load of boxes from the truck.

"Yeah. Mine and my partner's. Business partner." I fumbled the stack of boxes he handed me. Why had it felt so necessary to make that qualification? Like the kid would be in any way interested in my messed-up business relationship with my stubborn bastard of an ex.

Despite his pretty-boy looks, the kid was probably straight; he had a confident swagger girls his age likely found irresistible.

"I've been to your other place, too—the one in Northwest. Did the delivery there earlier. I like this location better."

"Me too," I said, my voice drier than gin. "Randy give you any issues?"

Randy had his location; I had mine. Our relationship had turned into something out of a bad chick flick, except there wasn't any cute ending coming.

"Randy? Nah. It was some girl named Becky, with a nose ring and huge gauges."

I nodded. That sounded about right for Randy's taste. And I was *not* going to care whether he was banging her or how long she'd last as an employee. His shitty employee turnover wasn't my problem. I'd washed my hands of what happened at the 23rd Street store.

"You want a cup of coffee for the road?" I asked before I could stop myself. It was the same courtesy I'd always extended to his cousin and to most of our other delivery people, but somehow my offer felt tinged with more than politeness.

"What do you have on offer today?" His grin was more than a little wicked.

*Wouldn't you like to know?* I bit back the flirtatious retort. And what the hell was up with that? I did *not* flirt. Hell, anything other than bitter and grumpy hadn't been my MO for months now.

"We've got a fair-trade artisanal Guatemalan roast and a small-batch single origin Ethiopian Duromina that's been flying out."

"I'll try the Ethiopian. Thanks."

"Here, follow me to the front and I'll grab it for you."

Late Saturday afternoon the front of the house was almost deserted. The coffee bar ran along one side of the high-ceilinged room and seating dominated the rest of the space—long wooden communal tables in the back, a few smaller tables in the middle, and couches up front. Two die-hard regulars worked on laptops in the cushy chairs by the front window, while Brady, the barista, wiped down the coffee bar.

"How's the leg?" I asked Brady as I cut behind him to the line of carafes with the day's roasts.

"Hanging in there." His pained expression belied his words. He'd had a nasty skateboard wipeout the day before and still had road rash on one side of his face and his left arm.

"Want me to close?" It'd put me further behind on prep, but I hated seeing Brady in pain.

"Nah." His shrug made him wince.

"Okay. Just don't play hero ball. We're slow. Take a break if you need to." I pulled a cup of coffee for Lance. Grabbed one for me, too; I had a long evening ahead. I came around the coffee bar to hand Lance his cup.

"Are you one of those coffee purist guys who'll laugh if I ask where the creamer is?" Lance asked, accepting the cup.

"It's against the wall." I pointed. "And yes. Total coffee purist, but knock yourself out ruining the best cup of joe in town."

"Ha." As I watched him ruin the Ethiopian with a huge dose of coconut creamer and four sugar packets, I smirked. His usual drink was probably a blended mocha. "I'd better get the truck back to the bakery."

"I'll walk you out." I followed him back to the kitchen, working double-time not to look at his butt.

Pausing at the service door, Lance gave me that toothy grin, filled with sass and challenge. "Too bad your barista's hurt. He's cute. You and him a thing?"

Okay. Not so very straight. I ignored the flip in my stomach and the sudden interest from my dick. This news did not involve me.

"Brady? God, no. I don't mess with employees." *Or delivery people.*

Lance's smile got wider, more feline. *Hell.* I'd fallen right into whatever fishing expedition he'd been on. Couldn't be about me, though; I was probably a good twelve or fifteen years older than the kid.

"Brady would probably be flattered. He'll be working the breakfast shift tomorrow. You should come back around with your friends."

"And you? Will you be around?" His brown eyes glinted with predatory intent. His eyes were the exact color of my favorite roast—earthy and dark, with all sorts of possibilities.

Stomach fluttering, I braced a hand against the prep table. I'd always been drawn to confidence, and this kid had it in spades. "I'm always around. You take care now."

"Here." Lance fished in the pocket of his white bakery jacket and came up with a pen and a business card. He scribbled something on it and offered it to me. "In case you need something before next week."

I took the card. "I've already got the bakery's number."

"And now you have mine." He gave me a little wave before leaving.

Lord, that boy was trouble, but I was too old and jaded to get distracted by a nice ass and full pink lips. I hoped.

# Chapter 2

I made sure to let one of the baristas handle the midweek deliveries. I saw Lance in passing a few times but managed to keep things to me grunting out a greeting, then getting really busy in the kitchen or my office. Come Saturday, though, I was flat on my back under the big stainless sink, getting soaked by water that was spewing from the jumble of pipes. Dealing with cute delivery guys wasn't as big of a concern as being able to serve and prepare brunch tomorrow, the shop's biggest day of the week.

"Hey! Chris? You here?" Lance's too-chipper voice was like salt on my freshly scraped nerves.

"Over here." I blinked against the water spraying in my eyes.

"What the heck?" I heard shuffling sounds, and then Lance's face appeared next to mine. Way, way too close to mine.

"Just leave the stuff and go. I'm kind of in the middle of something here."

"I can see. But why haven't you turned off the water?"

"Can't you see that's what I'm trying to do?" I tried again to tighten the pipe with my shitty excuse for a wrench.

"I mean the water to the building? If you want to stop the spraying, you've got to shut off the main water."

"I was getting to that," I lied. Damn. I'd been so frustrated when I discovered the massive leak under the sink, I'd launched straight into damage control with buckets and my wrench and hadn't stopped to do the one thing that made sense.

"Tell me where it is. I'll go do it."

"Basement storeroom. The stairs are in the hallway."

"Got it. I'll be back."

"Shit. I'd better go tell Brady we're done for the day." I slid out from under the sink and took my wet and dripping self as far as the kitchen door, hollering to Brady to put up the CLOSED sign and head out.

"You need me to stay to help mop up?" Brady limped over to the door, his long black ponytail swinging behind him. His skateboarding injuries seemed a bit better, but he was still hobbled and had traces of bruises and scrapes on his face.

"Just clean the bar and go." I didn't need Brady getting underfoot while I sorted out the problem.

"You sure?" Brady frowned. *Hell.* He'd dragged himself into work hurt. We didn't really talk about personal stuff, but I knew he'd been jockeying for extra hours whenever he could.

"I'll pay you for the lost time." I rubbed the bridge of my nose.

"Okay. Water's off." Lance joined us in the kitchen. "Now let's check out your pipes."

Brady made a snorting sound.

"Get cleaning," I grumbled, then turned to Lance. "You don't have to stay. I've got it."

"Yeah, you seemed *totally* in control when I found you." Lance rolled his eyes at me and headed back over to the sink, which had blessedly stopped spewing water. He whipped off his bakery logo jacket and handed it to me, like I was his damned assistant. "My old man's a plumber. At least let me take a look."

"I said I've got it."

Ignoring me, he got down under the sink. "Shit, it's wet down here. Okay. I think you've got a busted seal on this pipe, but the bigger issue might be your disposal."

"Hell." Both of those things seemed beyond my minimal plumbing skills. "How the fuck am I going to get someone here before tomorrow? *Crap.*" I paced toward the other side of the kitchen, glaring at the wall phone, wondering who the hell I could call as my shoes made ominous squishing sounds in the puddles. Even if I managed to get things fixed, I had a long night of cleanup ahead.

"Relax."

I turned to look at him, my back muscles tightening, anything but relaxed.

Lance's hands gripped the sink's lower edge as he pulled himself out from the watery hell and stood, his smile as easy as his body's graceful motions. "I've got this."

I shook my head. I hated being dependent on anyone; it was why I mainly worked alone. Asking for help always made me feel like I was eleven again, managing to disappoint my father by failing some simple task. Over two decades later and I still pictured his scowl as I muddled through a problem.

Ignoring me, Lance fished an iPhone with a shiny red case out of his jeans and hit a button. "Hey! Pops! How's my favorite dad?"

Whatever the reply was, it made him laugh.

"Listen, I'm over at The People's Cup on Alberta, and they've got something of a situation going on—a plumbing emergency. You think when you're finished up on that job you could head over here? As a favor?"

The reply made him laugh harder. He had the best kind of laugh, deep and hearty.

"Yeah. I'll be there. No problem. See you soon." He ended the call and turned to me. "My dad's on the way."

"Thanks." The word tasted like sand in my mouth and was twice as hard to spit out.

"What? Grumpy man knows that word!" Dark eyes going wide with good humor, he put his hand over his chest.

"Grumpy man?" His cuteness made me feel even more ancient.

"If the scowl fits . . ." He gave me a flirty little wink that had me wondering just how much sunshine he was sprinkling all over Portland. Did he flirt with everyone like this? Not that I was interested. Or jealous.

He squeezed the hem of his soaking T-shirt, wringing out some water, giving me a glimpse of tanned, toned abs. I looked away.

"I think your shirt is toast. Wait here." I ducked into the supply closet and grabbed a T-shirt from the box of People's Cup shirts our baristas all wore, which we sold up front for a little extra income. A free shirt was the least I could do for Lance. Seeing as my own shirt was plastered to my back, I grabbed a second for myself.

"Catch." I tossed the shirt at Lance. Before I could direct him to the restroom, he whipped his damp shirt off over his head.

"Oh, cool! Can I keep it?" Instead of immediately putting the shirt on, he held it out in front of him, like the black fabric and white block lettering was fine art.

"Sure." My own attention was riveted on the masterpiece of his chest. His face might be boyishly charming, but his body was all grown man: sculpted pecs and tight abs, with a tasty treasure trail of hair.

I might have made a growling noise. I hoped not, but from the way Lance's eyes widened, it was safe to say that my reaction didn't go unnoticed.

"Damn." Lance glanced down at himself. "I've really got to make time to get back to waxing."

"Don't." The word was out before I could stop it.

"Yeah? Well, of course, *you* like the fuzzy look." Laughing, he gestured at my beard.

Yeah, fuzz was something I had in spades, and something I dearly adored in other men. It was part of why I didn't usually go for twinks. Toned, tanned, and smooth didn't work for me as much as rugged, rough, and furry. I suppose if I had a type, I'd say it was guys like Randy. Silver foxes: guys with chiseled jaws and graying temples and hairy chests. Baby-faced boys like Lance hadn't cut it for me even when I'd been his age.

So why in the hell was my jaw currently on the floor and my tongue hanging out like a cartoon dog presented with a steak? Lance wasn't my type. But try telling that to my dick, which was jumping up like said dog. *Bad dick.* I looked away, counting jars of coconut oil on my shelves, while Lance pulled on the too-big shirt.

I turned my shirt over in my hands, wondering how much of a loser I'd look like if I ducked back into the supply room. I was seriously regretting my choice not to go upstairs to change. "Oh, come *on.*" Lance rolled his eyes, like he knew exactly what I was thinking. He reached out, tugging my wet shirt away from my torso so he could peek underneath the damp cotton. "Oh my god. You have more ink than just your arms. You have to let me see."

"Stop that." I batted his hands away.

"Awww." He shot me a hurt look, like I'd just squashed his pet bumblebee. "I love your sleeves. I wanna see the rest."

"You like tattoos?" I asked, pulling off the soggy shirt. Other than tequila, the fastest way to get me out of my clothes was to talk ink.

"Oh, yeah." His teeth worried his lip as he took in my art: full sleeves on each arm, a scene that snaked up my torso, and another starting over my shoulder and continuing across my pecs "You like fish or something?"

"I guess." I leaned back against the counter, trying to look casual. All of my tats were fish and water scenes. Big fish, little fish, a dolphin, lots of waves. The only nonfish piece was a little surfer dude riding the wave over my shoulder.

"They're like your spirit animal or something, huh?" His fingers twitched, like he was desperate to trace what he was looking at so intently.

My skin sizzled from his invisible touch and my cock was more than half hard, but it wasn't just his worshipful gaze that was turning my crank. It was how he backed up his swagger with insightful comments; he got that my tats were more than just whimsy, and there was a certain amount of respect in his tone. I dug that way more than I should have. "You like tats so much, why don't you have more?" I asked. Lance only had the one I had noticed—some sort of cat leaping across his left shoulder.

"Moolah." He rubbed his thumb and forefinger together. "Three I've got were pricey enough. All my money's got to go to school now, and for saving for graduate school in the fall."

Three? Oh, he did *not* need to tell me that. Now I was going to go nuts wondering where the other two were.

"Graduate school, huh? It figures, you being such a smart-mouth and all."

"Funny. I'm applying to physical therapy programs right now. When I'm done with school, I'm getting some *serious* ink done to celebrate."

"Man after my own heart." I said the words lightly, before I really thought about them, before I saw the knowing smile they inspired from Lance.

"You have one of those?"

"Nope." My heart wasn't available for the taking; Randy swore up and down it was made of coffee grounds, and the lovers I'd had before him would probably agree.

"Hey, can I take a picture?" He got out his phone again.

"What? Why?" I held up a hand. The counter's chilly stainless steel seeped into my voice.

"Because they're hot." He gave me a *duh* look. "And so I can show—"

"That'd be a hell no." I stared him down until he put the phone away. I tugged on my shirt quickly, my neck going hot and tight.

"Dude, if I had your ink, I'd be taking a selfie every day just because."

"*Dude,* if I were still nineteen, I'd find a better use for my phone than putting pictures of myself all over the Internet."

"Twenty-two. I'm twenty-two." He scratched his ear. From the cute pink blush on his cheeks, I figured the good people of Instagram and whatnot had been treated to more than a few pics of his stellar bod.

*Thou shalt not Google the hot twink,* I lectured myself before that idea could take hold.

"Hey. Didn't mean to offend you." Lance put a tentative hand on my shoulder.

I made the mistake of turning into his touch, bringing our bodies much too close together.

"You want me to stick around after your pipes are fixed? Maybe we could get some food?" His hand moved from my shoulder to rest against my chest. His voice was full of his usual swagger, but there was something uncertain in his eyes, like he was bracing for my rejection.

Which was coming, no matter how much I wanted to continue this flirtation. However good his appreciative gaze had made me feel, it was nothing compared to the electric arc of his touch, a caffeine jolt after a long, long sleepless night.

"No, thanks." I tried to soften my tone but immediately regretted the action because he smiled slyly. Might as well have said *try harder.*

"Why not? You're single, right? I'm not currently hitting it with anyone. We could have some fun."

"I'm not sure we have the same definition of fun." My voice had turned low and husky, not the harsh retort I'd planned. My hand clamped around his wrist to remove his hand from my chest and the heat of his skin branded my palm, a mark I wouldn't want to scrub away later. And seeing him in that People's Cup T-shirt, his usually perfect hair messed up from all the water and clothing switches made me think about sex. About holding both his arms down while I thrust—

The door rattled. I dropped his arm, stepping to the other side of the room while he let his dad in. His dad looked like Lance's cousin Vic—a big, beefy Italian guy with thinning hair and a handshake that threatened to tear my arm off. But he had Lance's Hershey Bar–colored eyes and the same big grin.

Everything was all smiles for the next hour, even as he deconstructed my sink and disposal and took my $150 for parts. He refused to take cash for the labor, though.

"Friend of the family. You'll call us next time you have a plumbing problem, though, right? Degrassi and Sons. We're in the book."

"Dad, no one uses the Yellow Pages anymore." Lance rolled those chocolaty eyes and sighed like a burdened fifteen-year-old. "And you can keep adding the 'and sons' to the Degrassi, but I'm still going to physical therapy school."

"'Course you are." His dad ruffled Lance's hair. "And you're also going home for dinner. Your mom says she sees your laundry in the pile and sees the light under your door but hasn't seen *you* all week."

Lance still lived at home? If I hadn't already been resolved to stay far away from him earlier, I was now. At his age I'd been on my own for several years and had been finishing up my degree while living in a group house with friends.

"*Dad.* Yes. Fine. I'll be there. I wasn't planning on meeting up with my friends until later anyway. Probably around eleven. I think we're going to Slaughters this week." He said the last part slowly and deliberately. He certainly hadn't name-dropped the gay bar for his dad's sake.

"You guys take care," I said, every bit as deliberately. "Some of us have to work early tomorrow. Can't be out raising hell like you *kids*."

Lance licked his lips. "You know, I think it's ten o'clock that we're meeting up. I was wrong."

Grabbing Lance's arm, his dad steered him around the prep table.

"Whatever time you're going out, you better get Vic his truck back and get yourself home for Mom's meal." His dad paused at the door, giving me a speculative look over his shoulder. I waited for him to warn me off his kid, or at least give me the menacing stare Vic had down pat, but he just shook his head like he wasn't surprised by Lance's antics.

And he probably wasn't. Lance seemed like one of those guys who flirted with everyone. I had to give the guy props, though—keeping his game going in front of his old man took a special kind of moxie. One that I found more tempting than my favorite coconut ice cream from Salt & Straw.

If Lance were simply a pretty boy, he'd be easy to resist. But add in *intelligent smart-ass* to the mix and my whole body perked up like someone had parked a Ducati out back and invited me to take a test-drive. But Lance wasn't a guilt-free ride. I was old enough to know that there was no such thing as free, and that the price would undoubtedly be more than I could afford.

# Chapter 3

Somewhere in between interminable rounds of chopping for vegetable hash and mopping up what felt like endless puddles of water, I started needing a drink. I had a fridge full of the local Ninkasi ale upstairs and a bottle of good bourbon that had been my last Christmas present from Randy two years earlier. I didn't have a good excuse to be craving other choices.

I hauled a load of towels down to the ancient machine in the basement. Our building was a two-story brick relic of the 1920s that had been rehabbed lightly during the Alberta Street revival of the early 2000s, but much of the original setup remained—shop on the main level, storage and a battered cast-iron deep sink with a laundry area in the basement, and the apartment upstairs. The building seemed quieter than usual, the basement stairs creakier.

Ordinarily, I looked forward to the relative peace of Saturday nights—just me and my kitchen, no employees needing things, no customers to deal with—it was the calm before the tidal wave of chaos that was the Sunday morning brunch rush. But this week my feet were tapping as I diced onions and my mind was wandering. I kept picturing Lance's eyes, the way they'd traveled over my skin, the way he'd licked his hot-as-hell lower lip . . . My dick twitched.

I reminded myself that whatever heat Lance and I generated probably flared up whenever his twenty-two-year-old self got near a horny, lonely gay man.

*Wait.*

Where the hell had that thought come from?

Horny, sure, because it had been just me and my hand in the two years since Randy and I had split. But I was *not* lonely. I got out . . . some. Okay, not often. But still I got out . . . *never*? Had I been to a bar since Randy and I split? Had I been out on my own in the ten years prior? Randy had been the hub of our social circle. I'd been content to stay at the fringes, his sidekick, but not really close to the ever-revolving group of friends and acquaintances. When we broke up, he'd gotten the friends, not that I'd really made an effort to keep them.

But was I really *that* pathetic that I couldn't go to a bar? Grab a drink? Maybe talk to some people? My urge for a drink returned tenfold as I moved the towels to the dryer. I needed food and I sure as hell didn't feel like cooking for myself. I could zip downtown, get some dinner from one of my favorite street carts, then get a drink. . . .

I wasn't fooling myself. I knew *exactly* which corner I'd end up at, which bar's neon sign beckoned me just as surely as that Ducati I'd pictured earlier. Damn. I had no business coveting the fine piece of Italian engineering that was Lance, but the urge was there, every bit as strong as the craving for whiskey and a few hours to forget about soggy towels and minced onions.

Besides, it wasn't like I had to actually take Lance home or anything. Flirty boy would back the hell down as soon as he saw how ridiculous I looked in a bar full of pretty young things. Maybe I wouldn't end up with the shiny chrome model, but that didn't mean I couldn't go out, kick the tires, maybe find a serviceable Yamaha to spend a few forgettable hours with.

Two hours later I had a clean kitchen, a showered body, and a belly full of Moroccan rice from the street cart catty-corner from Slaughters. The scent of fried food hung heavy in the crisp January air. The black-shirted bouncer at the door for Slaughters didn't even glance down at my ID. I hadn't been carded for buying liquor in years. In keeping with my I-just-want-a-drink plan, I hadn't put on club clothes after my shower—just tossed a flannel over a clean T-shirt and cargo pants.

However, in line for drinks I noticed something: somehow, in the decade since Slaughters had been a regular haunt for me, the gay scene in Portland had gotten a lot more plaid. A lot of guys younger than me sported those pretentious hipster beards, along with little caps that looked like they should be selling newspapers. My beard was because of my cursed fair skin—in addition to freckles that made me look ten, my cheeks got a rash if I shaved too often. So bushy red beard it was. But what was with all these young guns sporting the chin sprouts? Maybe Lance didn't have an unhealthy thing for older dudes. Maybe he just had a plaid-and-beard fetish.

Tons of ink on display, too. What the hell? In my time away from the scene, apparently I'd gotten fucking trendy. I ordered a whiskey. That was probably all trendy now, too.

I wandered around the main bar toward the dancing area. I was *not* looking for Lance. I was just sipping my whiskey and—

Okay. I was a fucking lying leprechaun. My eyes scanned, looking past the baby lumberjacks and the clump of drag queens and the straight girls getting their groove on until I found a group of young guys in the middle of the dance floor. Lance was with four other guys, but he was far and away the best dancer. Others shuffled their feet while Lance moved like he had that day we'd met, dancing like no one was watching, like he was just having fun with his tunes.

He'd changed into a tight black tank top and gray jeans with a studded leather belt. I leaned against the half wall that separated the dance floor from the rest of the bar. Hell, even if he didn't notice me, this was quality entertainment—sipping my whiskey and watching pretty boy shake his tail. I wasn't sure how long I stayed; one song bled into another and the group of friends paired off, some dancing with each other, some heading out for more drinks. Lance danced a while with a blond kid, winding himself around the blond's lithe body, fucking him with his eyes as he did that ass shaking move that kept showing up on bad TV. My dick got hard watching them move together.

Going dancing with Randy had always pissed me off—the way he collected hangers-on and then "accidentally" got too handsy with them. Other guys fawning all over my guy was *so* not a turn-on.

Except when it was. Of course, Lance wasn't my guy, but I still got a little thrill out of how he held himself, how he'd dance away from one guy into another's space. He used his friends and the guys who approached them like props—there to display his dancing chops—but he never lingered. The blond kid tried to pull him in closer, but he laughed and stepped back.

In that moment our eyes met and it was the freakiest thing—like every cell in my body powered up, charged and ready for action. Like all the people around me, and the clink of glasses and throb of bad dance music, all of that just fell away.

And then he was in front of me, all sweaty and eager. "You came."

"Eh. It's a Saturday night. Lots of people go out."

"Even grumpy old men?" He poked my chest. "Dance with me."

"I don't dance."

"You do tonight." He tugged on my hand, his wide smile full of mischief. I slammed the rest of my whiskey and set the glass down.

"You're trouble," I said as I let him tug me onto the floor. "I hate this music."

"What?" Our bodies brushed, my nerve endings sizzling like a griddle ready for action.

"I hate this music," I repeated, my mouth near his ear. He smelled like sweat and hair gel and something sweet that made me want to gobble him up.

"Katy? How does *anyone* hate Katy Perry?" He looked like I'd insulted his best friend.

The floor was crowded with other dancers, dim lighting masking the drunken lurching passing for dancing around us. I did the same shuffle-in-place move that a lot of his friends had mastered, my basic staple for weddings and other rare, usually drunken, occasions. I called it the please-don't-trip-over-me step. Lance, however, treated my body like a stripper pole, gyrating in a way that ensured maximum teasing. He was shorter than me, but not so much that our pairing was ridiculous.

Every time his thick thighs brushed mine or his muscular back rubbed against my front, little drops of sunshine rained down on me. He was a disco ball in human form, and I was happy to let him hypnotize me. His ass rotated like his spine was made of ball bearings. He ground against me until it seemed like one of us climaxing on the dance floor was a fine proposition.

I lost track of time until he stretched up, shouting near my ear, "You want another drink?"

"Yeah." I followed him off the dance floor and down the little corridor that led to the quieter bar area in the back of the club. This lounge area was populated by more couples than the dance floor. A memory passed through me of being one of those pairs, of cuddling and drinking and people watching, a brief whiff of longing. *No.* I did *not* miss that sort of connection. Not even a little. The tables were taken by pairs deep in conversation, so Lance and I stood.

I got my whiskey from the bar and turned to let him order.

"You gonna laugh if I order a sex on the beach?"

"Yes. But feel free." I slid the beefy bartender cash for both drinks.

"I like sweet things." He looked me up and down. "And beaches. And everything that might happen on them."

I had to laugh. I was prickly, yes. Sweet, not so much. "You're looking in the wrong place for that."

"Oh, I don't think so. . . . Hey, what time do you turn into a pumpkin? How late can you stay out?"

"Usually, I'd be sacked out by now," I admitted. "I've got to be up by four to get stuff ready to open at seven."

"In that case . . ." He took a big sip of his drink, then moved directly in front of me, so close our bodies almost touched. "How about we skip to the part where you get all toppy and commanding and tell me how I'm getting done."

Wow. My blood rushed straight to my groin. So much for finding an older, cheaper model. I wanted every shiny, sparkly piece of Lance. Right the hell now. "Who said it's going down like that?"

He batted his eyes at me. He had the longest lashes I'd ever seen on a guy. "You're here. You're not asleep. But, hey, if you'd rather *I* get all toppy and commanding and tell *you* how to get done, I can work with that. Not my usual MO, but I can make an exception—"

I hooked a finger in his belt loop, smashing him to me with enough force that our drinks sloshed. He was a wall of hard muscle, his thighs pressing into me, all strength and heat and hardness, showing me how turned on he was. My dick responded before my brain had a chance to catch up, blood pounding in my groin.

"You're a brat."

"Yes. Yes, I am." He grinned widely, like I'd just cracked some sort of code. "What are you going to do about it?"

"*Someone*," I said, emphasizing the not-me part, "should teach you some manners. And patience. And subtlety."

"Boy. That's a lot of lessons. And we only have . . . what? Four and a half hours? Better get started."

His breath was warm and sweet against my face, his body heavy against mine. I swore I could feel his heart beating. Music from the dance floor filtered back to the bar area and there were people on both sides of us, but everything seemed to go still, the moment dragging out. My brain zeroed in on his lush, full mouth until I had no choice but to kiss him.

I claimed his mouth, no sweet and fruity first kiss—no, this was a rough and dirty fuck of a kiss, one where I told him with my lips and teeth exactly what happened to bratty boys. And he answered me just as enthusiastically, his mouth parting to welcome my tongue, his body arching into me.

Gasping, I broke away. "Go. Tell your friends you're leaving. You drive here?"

"Rode with my friends. You gonna be here when I get back?" He said it shyly, not like the bold guy who had just about sucked my tongue off.

I nodded. A sane man would walk out the door while he was gone, but I'd left sanity behind about an hour ago. I could no more leave than I could help myself from watching his retreating back, ass swaying in his skinny jeans. Nope. Definitely not escaping. I was going to end up doing the one thing I'd sworn not to—bring him home with me.

"You ever ridden a bike?" I asked when he returned.

"Bike? Like ten-speed?" One of his eyebrows quirked. In Portland, where half the city bike commutes, one can never be too sure of these things.

"Like Harley."

"Yeah." He nodded, but he didn't look too terribly sure.

I'd parked across from the barricades the police erected each weekend to handle the happy-go-drunkly Portlanders. I got him the spare helmet from its storage spot. His smile was eager, but his eyes were still a bit wary.

"Just so we're clear, this is a one-time deal, okay? This isn't the start of something." Much as I wanted to fuck, I also didn't want to be the asshole who led the kid on. I could let myself be this stupid once, but a repeat absolutely was not in the cards.

"We're clear." He glanced around before stretching up and brushing a kiss across my lips. "Let's go."

"Here." I handed him the helmet and my motorcycle jacket. All he had on was a cotton shirt over his T-shirt and I didn't want him to freeze before I could heat him up.

Judging from the death grip he kept on my waist, he'd ridden a bike just about never. I took it easy, navigating the slow streets back to Alberta. The wind whipping my body was a pleasant sting, not a harsh slap of bitter cold. It was a mild, dry night, the sort of not really winter that people put up with the rain to get. Gradually, Lance's grip loosened and he leaned into me, his head pressed against my back.

I wanted to keep driving until we hit a little patch of dirt and fuck him under the cool breeze and stars. But I didn't have all night. Instead, I had a ticking clock of hours until my alarm would blare and a whole bucket list of things I wanted to do to him.

Too soon, we arrived at my place. I parked the bike in the alley behind the shop, next to my beat-up Ford truck. I unlocked the service entrance door and flipped on the light for the stairs that led to the apartment.

"You gonna get busted for missing curfew?" I asked at the top of the stairs, trying to remind myself why this was an epically stupid idea, and why it had to be a onetime deal.

"Nah. It's not like that. My parents know how much I want to get into graduate school. I live at home to save money, but they know I have my own life. I've got the basement now. It's almost like an apartment."

"Almost." I turned to face him, and whatever retort I'd been planning died as I looked into those big brown eyes. The wariness was back. He wasn't quite so full of swagger now, and something strange and tender unfurled in my gut.

I needed to cut that shit out right now. I dragged him into the apartment, kissing him before I even got the door shut. Our tongues tangled, picking right up where we'd left off in the bar. He was my favorite kind of kisser—almost rough with intensity and totally committed to it, oxygen be damned. I kissed him until I forgot all the logical reasons why this was a terrible idea, until I forgot how young he was, until I lost track of myself.

He mouthed a trail down my neck. I knew where this was headed and I helped him along, putting a firm hand on his shoulder. His eyes were glassy with need, the crests of his cheekbones smudged with pink. So fucking beautiful.

"Go on, then."

"Oh, yeah." He breathed out a warm huff of air against my chest before he sank to his knees.

He looked up, waiting. I wasn't usually one to get off on power plays and games, but whatever little dance we'd started back at the club licked through me, making my hands more sure, my voice more gruff.

"Get it out."

"Yeah." He unzipped me and slid out my cock. "Oh. My. God. How are you not hitting it every night if you're packing this monster?"

"You ask to take a picture and you can get your ass back down those stairs." I tipped my head against the plaster wall. His awe hit me like a shot of whiskey. I knew I wasn't all that. My dick was thick and long with a broad head, but not porn-star huge.

"Not happening." Holding my dick in one hand, he licked around the head, tracing the crown.

"More," I ordered. "You can do better than that."

"Oh, yeah." He opened those gorgeous pink lips, sliding me into his mouth, keeping a hand on my dick.

"Suck it."

He moaned around my dick, starting a shallow bob with a quick rhythm. He was damn good at coordinating his hand and mouth. I didn't care about whether he could deep throat—all I cared about was getting more of that slick heat.

The rhythm stuttered as he unzipped his pants, hauling his cock out one-handed. His cock was on the shorter side but thick, with a gorgeous vein snaking around the shaft and a plump, uncut head.

"Yeah. Stroke it for me."

He swallowed my cock. *Deep.* I felt him start to gag and he retreated.

"Sorry. Never been with someone so hung." His smile was just as intoxicating as the compliment.

"Here, honey." I helped him out, holding his head with one hand while I started a gentle glide of my hips. He got the idea, his lips dragging hard against me on the upstroke, his tongue working my head on his way back down. Damn.

Pleasure thrummed through me, and the need from two years of celibacy made my stomach tighten and my head swim. Slowing down my thrusts to try to make this last, I let him take over again. Watching him slowly work his cock was its own kind of pleasure—one that warmed me up and made my balls tingle.

"Harder." I liked a lot of friction from his fist, something he fast figured out, going for bonus points by sweeping his thumb against my balls.

"Feels so good. You want me to come this way?" It was almost a rhetorical question; I was about thirty seconds away from blowing, so the only question was whether it was going to be his mouth or his fist.

"Do it." He doubled up on the motion of his hands, pumping his cock with lightning-fast motions while giving me the rough stroke I craved. His mouth was warm and tight against my crown, his bob shallow but perfect.

"*Fuuu . . .*" I gritted out a warning.

His answering moan was all the encouragement I needed, my head clunking against the wall behind me as I shot down his throat, spasm after spasm racking my body as he swallowed around my cock. My knees threatened to give out and I had to push my shoulders hard into the wall.

I looked down to see his head tipped back, his fist all wet. Damn. I'd missed the moment he'd shot. But the knowledge that he'd gotten off from sucking me was enough to make me shudder again. I had to take a few deep breaths to get enough blood flow to my brain for speech.

"Damn. You're good."

"Been a while, but I still remember how things work." He grinned up at me. At his age, *a while* meant anything over a month, but I was still irrationally flattered. Half the club would have been happy to break his dry spell and he'd chosen me.

"You got a sink?" he asked, getting up off the floor.

"Yeah. Bathroom is first door on the right down the hallway."

I went along with him, flipping on lights as we went. Our footsteps echoed on the hardwood floors. Like the shop downstairs, the apartment was long and narrow. A long hallway ran its length from the entry past the small living room, the dining room, the galley kitchen, and the bathroom, ending in the bedroom, which overlooked Alberta Street. The apartment was short on windows and closets, but long on vintage, with the sorts of moldings and curved archways that no one tosses in apartments anymore.

"Here." I flipped on the bathroom light; the switch was in the hall by some genius of prewar wiring.

"That sink is freaky." Lance looked down at it. I'd long gotten used to the separate faucets for hot and cold in the ancient pedestal sink.

"Sorry." I grabbed him a towel from the shelf. "Here. I'll ... uh ... give you a moment."

I backed out of the room, then rested my head on the cool plaster of the hallway wall. I wasn't sure exactly what happened now; we'd gotten off within minutes of getting back to my place and I was totally down for round two, but I'd forgotten the sort of casual banter that could get us there.

Not wanting to lurk outside the bathroom like a weirdo, I headed to the kitchen and washed my own hands.

"You got any soda?" Lance asked, coming up behind me. He swallowed, like he was still trying to get the taste of spunk out of his mouth.

"Yeah. We carry HOTLIPS downstairs. You want me to grab you one?"

"I'm down with hot lips." His look accomplished everything I'd been hoping to find the words for—heat, promise, and mirth all in a single eyebrow raise and curved lips. "Anything but ginger ale."

"Ginger ale tastes worse than spunk to you?" I asked as I headed downstairs, him behind me. Not wanting to flip on the main overhead lights in the front of the store, I grabbed the flashlight I kept by the stairs for this purpose.

"Hey, I'm not complaining about spooge. It just ... lingers. Ginger ale, though? That stuff is nasty."

"Here." I handed him a raspberry soda from the cooler.

"This is awesome. I feel like we're sneaking around." He gestured at the flashlight. "When I was a kid, I always loved the idea of being locked in a toy store overnight."

"I had a picture book about being locked in a zoo after closing. I must have read that a hundred times."

"I think we had that one, too. I remember reading it to my sisters." He smiled at me, and something passed between us, something more than the promise of a repeat. He was right—there was something almost ... playful about being in the dark room, the glow of the flashlight casting interesting shadows over our faces. He took a long drag of soda, his lips locked around the bottle. My cock woke up, getting a bit insistent about the whole round-two thing.

"Wanna go back upstairs?" I asked, heading back to the stairs before I could do something really outrageous, like jumping him in front of the plate-glass window.

"Yeah." He followed me up the stairs, the soda dangling from his long fingers. My nerve endings prickled at his nearness.

"You know," I said as we entered the apartment, "*I* kind of like the taste of ginger ale. And other stuff."

"Yeah?" He stepped closer to me.

"I'd be happy to . . . return the favor." I put a hand on his chest.

"Sounds nice." His brown eyes held all the sinful promise of hot fudge. "But this is a onetime deal right? No way am I missing a chance to try that monster dick of yours. You got condoms?"

"Oh, yeah." My cock went straight from interested to painfully erect in two seconds. I hadn't wanted to make assumptions about what he might be down with, but if he wanted to let me have a shot at that fine ass, I was more than good.

"Bedroom. Now." I plucked the soda from his fingers, setting it on the entry table that held my mail. My pulse pounded in my ears, driving me to tug him down the long hall to the bedroom, racing like a kid with a present to unwrap.

# Chapter 4

"Strip," I said as soon as we got into the bedroom.

"You too." He peeled off the rest of his clothes in a few efficient movements while I was still unbuckling my pants.

"Bed." I pointed to the quilt-covered double bed. Giving orders was kind of fun. If he wanted toppy and commanding, I could deliver that.

God, he looked good spread out on my blue and green quilt, like a treasure washed up on my shore—all gleaming skin and rippling muscles and an inviting grin that made me rip the rest of my clothes off. I loved how his skin glowed in the light from my bedside lamp. My room was small to begin with—just my bed, a single bedside table, and the dresser—but having Lance in it made the space cozier somehow.

I fumbled in the nightstand for what we'd need, tossing the condoms and lube on the bed. My hand hit something else.

"You want weed?" I asked. I was mainly a top, but if I bottomed, I preferred being high. It made everything all soft and floaty. And after the mad dash for orgasm the first time around, a lazy energy strummed through me, slowing my hands and mind. I wanted something more than a quick and dirty fuck for Lance.

"You *have* weed?" He propped himself up on his elbows.

"I own a vegan coffee shop in Portland. I'm pretty sure it's required by my union."

"I've never . . . um. No, thanks." His cheeks flushed and his lips looked like they couldn't decide whether to smile or frown. He kept his eyes on my package, and I couldn't tell whether it was awe or nerves in his eyes.

"It's cool." I stretched out behind him on the bed. "Anything else you haven't done? Now would be an excellent time to tell me if you're a virgin." I'd made my voice as stern as possible. I did *not* need to discover he was a virgin midfuck, and I was *not* going to be his training wheels.

His laugh was exactly the answer I needed. Relieved, I lightly tickled his sides, earning another chuckle. Pulling his back against my front, I kissed the back of his neck, right below where his short hair ended. His skin tasted salty from all the dancing, and I wanted to lick him like a Popsicle from head to toe, searching out more of that earthy taste.

"I've done it plenty. I'm just . . . choosy is all."

"Choosy is good." I liked knowing he was selective far more than I should. I let my hand wander farther south, into his neatly trimmed patch of hair, resting my hand just above his cock, not actually touching it. "And you mainly choose small-dicked dudes?"

"Forget I said anything earlier." His laugh reverberated through him, made him shake against me. He smelled good, like sweat and fruity drinks.

"Oh, no, I'm keeping that compliment." Nestling up close to him, I wedged my cock against his ass. Rocked my hips a few times until my pulse revved like my Harley at a stoplight, ready to take off.

Being with Lance reminded me of long-forgotten moments of discovery—the years when sex had been new, and just being naked with someone was both terrifying and thrilling. I could happily get off like this, rubbing against his ass, savoring the little shivers that raced through him when I bit at his neck and shoulders.

"Do it." Lance bucked his hips into my middle, clearly not on board with my take-our-time mind-set.

"You like getting fucked, huh?" I stroked the vee where his hip and abs met. I'd never really found that area particularly sexy before, but Lance's calendar boy muscle definition made all sorts of usually overlooked areas ridiculously sexy.

"Oh, yeah." He pushed back into me. Boy sure wasn't shy about showing me what he wanted. Grabbing my hand, he put it on his cock. "All last week I fantasized about you fucking me."

His words went straight to my dick, little licks of pleasure as potent as his tongue. I rolled away, going up onto my knees as I reached for the lube, got some on my fingers. I still wasn't in any particular hurry. This was the most fun I'd had in years, talking and teasing with

Lance, and much as I wanted to be buried balls deep in him, I didn't want this playful part to end.

I licked a meandering trail between his shoulder blades. Lord, even his shoulders were defined. I had muscle from lifting stuff for work, and I'd always been a pretty lean guy, but Lance made me feel downright flabby.

"What's your favorite way to get done?" Still on my knees, I worked a lubed finger around his rim, loving his swift intake of breath.

"Are we going to get this going?" He bumped his ass into my hand.

"Haven't you figured out yet you can't boss me around?" I withdrew my hand, leaving him humping nothing but air. "If you're not going to speak up, I'm just going to get a lot more . . . patient."

I asked because I had this ridiculous urge to be the best for him. Wanted to show him things those college boys hadn't. But the more ridiculous urge was this . . . *need* to know more about him; my head was filled with questions, some serious, some silly. All unnecessary for what was supposed to be a fast hookup, but then my brain had always been made of massive fail where casual was concerned.

"Only ever done it on hands and knees or bent over something, but this side thing is totally working for me, if you would please, *please* get it in me." His words were as frantic as his movements. He'd pulled the flannel sheet loose with his thrashing.

I rewarded him by returning my fingers to his rim. My movements got more deliberate as I worked him open.

"Yes. That." He moaned, a raw, needy sound. I added a second finger, following the lead of his insistent hips and hungry eyes as to what he liked.

"More," he protested when I withdrew my fingers.

"So bossy," I chided as I put on a condom and lubed it up. I settled in behind him, maneuvering his solid but surprisingly malleable body until we were both resting on our sides, his back to my front.

"Like this?" His ass nudged my cock, firm flesh sliding against my only-too-ready dick. "I like this already."

I laughed. God, he was fun in bed. "How about you let me get in, then you tell me how much you love it?" I held my cock steady, slowly pressing the head against his rim. "Push back when you're ready."

"Oh. Oh, yeah." He rocked his hips down, breathing hard. "God, you're a fucking monster."

"Want to stop?" I really wasn't *that* hung, but I loved how he made me feel like some sort of sex god, the way he was grunting and straining to take me.

"Hell no." He pushed back a little more, letting me slide deeper. He was tight, but it wasn't a sharp, not-gonna-work pinch.

My laugh this time was so deep my dick jiggled. I didn't think I'd ever laughed this much with sex. Being with him felt so good—like the first spring motorcycle ride, blue sky and green hills and warm sunshine chasing away every last drop of winter rain.

"So huge." His nostrils flared and beads of sweat ran down his forehead. "God, I want . . . love this."

"Oh, yeah. One of my favorite positions." I'd chosen this one because it gave him a fair amount of control and minimized my ability to go too hard or too deep. He bent his leg, gripping his hard-muscled thigh with his big hand to hold himself open, giving me more access to that tight, compact ass. I growled my appreciation and began to thrust in earnest.

His neck arched as I slid nice and deep, and my fingers tangled in his short dark hair. I felt almost . . . protective, holding him cradled like this as I thrust, his soft moans echoing the rhythm of our bodies. His hard cock bounced against his abs, but neither of us reached for it—the moment was perfect just like this.

"Beautiful. So beautiful." My thumb swept along his jaw, the barest hint of stubble abrading my fingers.

"Handsome," he slurred. "Men aren't beautiful."

"You are. Especially when you're getting fucked like this. God. Your face . . ." I'd teased him about wanting a dick shot, but I would have given six months' profits for a picture of his face right then— eyes half-closed in a drunken, fucked-out stare, lips parted, and cheeks flushed, a ruddy glow echoed on his neck and chest.

"Love you fucking me. Love it like this. Feel so close to you."

His words were just sex talk, no more consequential than him ribbing me about the size of my dick, but each one slid over me like a caress, and I could only moan my agreement. Close? More like Vulcan mind-melded. Our breath sped up at the same time and our sweat mingled between our bodies. He answered each of my thrusts with a clench of his muscles, dragging me deep.

"Gonna go harder now."

"Yeah. Give it to me." Arching into me, his shoulders pressed hard into my chest as he met my thrusts. His breath hitched and my hand was on his dick before my brain even had a chance to send the command.

Moaning, he used his arm to pull his leg up higher. Damn, he was flexible, his knee resting over his crooked arm. Our lower legs tangled as I searched for leverage. He thrashed, both shoulders on the mattress now, his body pushing onto my dick and there . . . right freaking *there* . . . I found the perfect angle, the one that made him cry out.

"Wanna come." He gasped. His head tilted toward me, our eye contact almost as intense as the fucking.

"Yeah. Come on, beautiful."

His ass got tighter, his back muscles stiffening. I jacked my hips faster, finally reaching that frantic place where we were both hurtling toward orgasm, racing, so much so that I wasn't sure who tipped over first, just that I was coming and so was he, my fist going wet and slick.

Each of his tremors caused an answering quake in me. I'd fucked in this position a hundred times before and never once been struck by its intimacy, but coming apart while holding him felt like someone had stripped away my top layer of skin, like I had no defenses any longer. And I got to see that same vulnerability in him—all his bravado reduced to quivers in my arms.

My legs trembled like tofu as I got a towel to clean us up. Sprawled on his back in the middle of the bed, he barely moved as I mopped him off as best I could. I stretched out next to him and he gave a little sigh and rolled into my side. With all the sex urgency gone, spooning him felt as cozy as the quilts I dragged up over us.

I dozed a bit, maybe drifted off entirely. Because when I opened my eyes, he was standing by the bed, pulling on his clothes. The air in the room had cooled, but it still smelled like sex. My dick twitched, far more awake than my foggy brain. I glanced at the clock: 12:45. Plenty of time for a round three.

"Hey. You don't have to go. Sleep a bit. I can run you back home before I start the breakfast stuff." It would be a tight crunch, but I wasn't going to leave him stranded.

"Thanks, but I've got to get home. My little sister's running the polar bear 5K tomorrow, and I promised her I'd wake up early enough to drive her and cheer her on."

"Nice big brother." He'd mentioned his family a number of times, always with tons of affection. I wondered not for the first time how different my life would have been with siblings to cheer on and bicker with and all that other brotherly stuff.

"I should be. I've had enough practice. Three sisters and one brother. How about you? Any siblings?" He shrugged into his shirt.

"Nope. I . . . I had an older sister, but she died before I was born." I almost never shared that with strangers, but something about Lance loosened my tongue.

"Oh, man. That's rough." He rubbed my shoulder, a warm, firm touch that made me want to offer up even more of my secrets. An urge that I was going to squelch right the hell then.

"Give me a second and I'll get up and take you home." I stretched, trying to shake sense back into my brain. I needed to remember that his leaving was a *good* thing.

"Oh, it's no biggie. My friends are still up. I've got a ride." He held up his phone.

"They safe to drive?" I'd happily haul myself out of bed if it meant making sure he was with a sober driver.

"Oh, yeah. We always roll with a designated driver." He sat on the edge of the bed. "You still want this to be a onetime deal, right?"

I nodded, not trusting words. I'd been so sure that once would be enough to extinguish my inconvenient lust for him—like how I could crave chocolate but be bored after half a brownie. But Lance was more like a fine, handcrafted Ethiopian roast, something I wanted seconds of before I even finished the first cup.

"Well, thanks." He brushed a kiss across my forehead. "I'm not kidding when I say that was the most amazing fuck of my life."

*Me too.* I still couldn't speak, couldn't admit that aloud. I was the older one, the one who was supposed to be more mature, more worldly. And he'd completely undone me.

"Take care of yourself," I said at last.

"Always do." He laughed, then stilled as he traced my lips with his thumb. He leaned in, kissing me. A soft brush, the way our first kiss should have been.

I reached for his head, but his phone buzzed and he jerked away.

"Gotta head out."

And then he was gone and I was left alone in a rapidly cooling bed. I pulled the quilt up around my shoulders. I'd dug it out of the closet after Randy took the "good" linens with him. It had been a graduation present from my grandmother—the last one she'd finished before she passed. I'd always associated the green and blue pattern with freedom, but now I'd always see Lance sprawled across it.

*Hell.* I'd been worried about how awkward things would be next week, how he might be hanging around like an eager puppy while I tried not to kick him. But now I knew the truth: he wasn't the one who was going to have a problem letting this go.

# Chapter 5

True to my prediction, Lance wasn't awkward when he came to the shop the next week. While my expression was sour and surly, he was all smiles and sunshine when he breezed in with deliveries. He gave me a wicked-ass smile on Tuesday, one laced with the memory of Saturday night, but that was it. No over-the-top flirting. No intimations about what we'd done. Not even a sign that we were anything more than acquaintances.

And hell if that didn't irritate the fuck out of me. Saturday afternoon I was in a black mood as I inventoried supplies, making sure we were set for Sunday.

"Hello, darling!" The voice behind me was *not* the friendly voice of Lance. No, this voice belonged to my bastard of an ex. I swiveled to face him. He was standing in my kitchen like he owned the place. Which he technically did, a fact that took my mood all the way to charcoal.

"What are you doing here?"

Randy looked like exactly what he was—a middle-aged hipster who was more sure of himself than he should be. He wore one of those stupid flat caps and a leather jacket. His goatee was trimmed almost to a point. "I brought by the quarterly reports for the store."

"Late." I took the papers from him and set them aside to take to my office later.

Randy waved away my complaint. "You know, it's interesting. My store is turning almost twice the profit as this one."

"So?" I shrugged, like the news didn't hit me like a sack of potatoes to the gut. "Your clientele is way richer and you get more foot traffic. It doesn't take a fancy MBA to get that."

"Why don't we stop this silliness?" He spread his arms wide, indicating the shop that had a decade of my blood and sweat in it, the store that was *our* dream but my labor.

"No." I knew exactly what he was getting at.

"Let me buy you out."

"You and what cash?" We'd had this conversation every six months since we'd split.

"I've got an . . . investor on the hook." His smug smile said he was banging some kid with a trust fund.

"Not interested." My back muscles went harder than a butcher-block counter, ready for the next knife he wanted to fling in my direction.

Did I love every little thing that came with running the shop? No. Of course not. I got cranky about the hours and the lack of appreciation and all the interpersonal management and the endless cash-flow issues. But let Randy have *my* store? No way. He'd gotten the friends in our breakup, the fancy Northwest location, our king-size memory-foam mattress, the plasma TV, and he'd kept his family. He wasn't getting this, too.

"Fine. Be that way. You mind if I talk to Brady while I'm here? I want to see if he wants to cover some hours. I've got a sudden . . . vacancy."

"Still screwing the help? Sure. You can ask. Just don't steal him away permanently." I wasn't going to let my feud with Randy keep Brady from earning some cash. Brady was still limping around, but he brushed off all my suggestions that he rest.

"He sure is a cutie pie." Randy stroked his goatee.

"Fuck with him and I *will* come after you. I don't care what you do with your help, but he's the best barista I've got." The tiny kitchen felt twice as small with Randy in it, and twice as cluttered. I needed him gone so I could restore order.

"Fine, fine. Speaking of cute, have you seen the new delivery kid for Delgado's? He is *prime.*"

"Haven't noticed," I lied.

"Well, you should. That ass . . ."

I growled, taking a step toward him. "You don't get to mess with him either."

"Well, look at that. Not so blind, are you?" Randy stepped back against the metal shelving.

"I'm serious. You fuck with him, I'm going to fuck with you."

"Oh, my." He looked me up and down, his eyes narrowing. "You've already sampled the goods, haven't you?"

I shook my head. I wasn't justifying his amateur sleuthing with a reply. "Next time just e-mail me the shit. You coming around to gloat isn't very attractive in a dude your age."

Sensitive as Randy was about his age, sometimes it felt good to grab a stick and poke at his weak spots. Lord knew he was a master at discovering mine.

"I'm leaving. Enjoy your new toy." He gave me a princessy wave on his way to the front of the store, no doubt to work his wiles on Brady.

*Fuck this shit.* I went back to inventorying, opening cartons of hash browns with a box cutter. If Randy came on to Lance . . . Well, that much was probably a given. The real issue was whether Lance would take him up on it. Lance apparently dug older, bearded dudes and one-night stands, which made him prime material for Randy's harem, but the thought had me seeing every damn shade of green.

"Ow. Motherfucker." The knife sliced deep into the meat of my palm. I tried squelching the cut with my other hand, but blood oozed between my fingers. Fucking hell. This wasn't what my day needed. I went to the sink and turned on the cold water. I winced, waiting for the numbing cold to do its job. Yeah. It was bad. But I did *not* have time for this. Wrapping my palm with a bar towel, I looked through the meager supply of Band-Aids in the first-aid kit. Nothing that would take care of a megaslice to the palm.

I wasn't going to the ER to wait for three hours for someone to stitch me up. I wasn't helpless. Scrounging around for supplies I had close by, I made a pad out of folded paper towels, then duct-taped it to my hand. There. Pressure bandage and cover in one.

An hour later, Lance looked down at my hand as I opened the door for his delivery. "What the hell is that?"

"Nothing." I stuck my hand behind my back. "Cut myself earlier. It'll be okay." I'd been performing tasks that were nonfood related. Working one-handed had turned my rotten mood even more foul.

"It will not." Lance set the boxes on the rack, then grabbed my arm. "Let me see." He cradled the mess that was my hand in his own lean, strong, perfectly healthy hands. "Oh, sweetie, you've bled through this, this . . . whatever the hell you've constructed."

"I'll get a real bandage when I'm done here."

Lance ignored me, unwinding the duct tape. "You need stitches."

"Do not. It looks worse than it is." I yanked my arm back.

*Doctors.* The word had been going around in my head the last hour. Every time I thought about going to the ER, I talked myself out of it. My body went into seizure-strength shudders at the idea of them *sewing* me. And I'd rather hide out in the deep freeze all night than have Lance see me like this. His concern cut me almost worse than the damn knife.

"It *looks* like it needs stitches. And like you're lucky you didn't sever some tendons," Lance said.

"Eh." I tried to wave off his concern, but moving my hand even that much hurt. "Maybe I'll get some butterfly bandages, or some of that glue stuff. Can't you superglue deep cuts?"

"You are *not* supergluing your hand." Lance gave the sort of long-suffering sigh that only those under twenty-five can manage. "Here. Let me unload the rest of the stuff; then you're coming with me. There's an urgicare right by the bakery."

"I don't need urgicare. If I did, I could take myself."

"Oh, 'cause you're that talented at riding your bike one-handed? No. I don't trust you to take yourself. I don't want to come by Monday to find you with a green hand superglued to your cutting board."

"You won't—"

"No more arguing. Go tell Brady he'll need to lock up." He put his hands on his hips, a fierce look on his face. God, he was sexy like that, and if my hand wasn't throbbing, I might do something stupid like jump him again.

"Haven't we had discussions about you being bossy?"

"Nope." Ruining his fierce look, he gave me a saucy wink. "Get ready to go."

The urgent care near the bakery was in a residential neighborhood, a gleaming new facility that spoke to the property value of the surrounding homes. Zippy Care, they called it, and a receptionist in monster truck–patterned scrubs took one look at my hand and put me on the priority list.

"I'll get a taxi back home," I told Lance as we found a seat in the glassed-in waiting room. We had a view of a little garden with a fountain. I wasn't remotely soothed.

"You will not. I'm here now. I'm not going to leave a friend at urgent care. They're probably going to numb you up for stitches."

"Don't talk about that." My stomach flipped, like I was riding a raft down the Columbia. "I hate needles."

"But you have more ink than anyone I know in real life." His face wrinkled up, like he was trying very hard to be understanding.

"That's not the same thing. Ink I have control over. Doctors . . ." I shuddered. I stopped myself from running off at the mouth about the multiple ear procedures I'd had done as a kid, or how the whole health-care industry had failed my grandmother in her final years.

"Oh. White coat anxiety." He nodded all sympathetically. "Don't worry. My little sister's the same way. I'm great at distracting her and holding her hand."

"Somehow I doubt your sister and I get distracted by the same things."

"Oh, I think I can manage. And afterward, I'll take you back to the shop and you can talk me through whatever prep you had to abandon. I'll be your assistant."

"Why on earth would you want to do that?" I leaned forward, my jeans dragging on the chair's nubby upholstery. The waiting area was trying to be homey, living room–like. I didn't feel like a guest; I felt like a frog waiting for the pot to boil.

"Because we're friends and you're in a jam?" Lance touched my good arm, a warm press that cut past my anxiety and pain to send warmth rushing to my groin.

"We're not friends," I hissed, lowering my voice to a whisper. "Just because we—"

"Why can't we be friends? The other stuff doesn't matter. Seems to me you could use a friend right now." Judging by his reasonable tone, one would think *I* was the kid.

I couldn't really argue with his logic. Most of my social circle had left with Randy. And it was hard to argue in favor of keeping things awkward when Lance was so clearly able to separate out the sex.

"Fine. We can be friends. But I still don't need your help." I crossed my arms over my chest. *Fuck.* That hurt.

"Yeah, you kind of do. Would it help if I said you could pay me? Textbooks were killer this term. I'm not too proud to take money from a friend for a couple hours' work."

"That I can do." I had a feeling he needed the money less than he was letting on, but I felt better about doing it that way. "You can put it in your tattoo fund."

And of course then I had to go and remember that I still hadn't discovered his other two tattoos; I'd been a bit too preoccupied last time for a careful perusal. I should make the bossy brat give me a personal tour. . . .

"Mr. O'Neal?" A nurse in bicycle-print scrubs called my name, interrupting my daydream.

"I'll come back with you." Standing up along with me, Lance didn't wait for me to ask.

"You don't—"

"If you pass out, you'll be glad I was there." He stuck to my side as the nurse led us down a bright hallway.

"No, I won't," I grumbled. I wanted to be alone with Nurse Needles far less than I wanted a scene with Lance.

The exam room was tinier than my little office back at the shop—barely enough for the exam table, a sink, and a side chair. Lance sat quietly while the nurse took my history. When the doctor arrived and started talking about numbing me up, Lance stood and took hold of my good hand.

"Hey. Look at me, not them. What's the yuckiest thing you've ever drunk?"

"Ouzo." I laughed at the memory. "Didn't exactly have that in Nebraska, and no one had warned me it tasted like licorice. I hurled all over Randy's shoes."

"You're from Nebraska?" His hand distracted me even more than his questions. I'd always loved big, masculine hands, and Lance had great hands, broad and capable, with faint calluses along his palms.

"Yeah. Little town outside of Lincoln."

"Farthest I've been from Oregon is Disney World, when I was eight." His smile was a bit wistful.

"Trust me, you're not missing much skipping the flyover states. But you should explore more out west while you can. Make a tour of all the national parks." Back when I'd been his age, I was the king of the impromptu road trip—just me and my bike and barely enough dough for gas.

"Maybe after grad school." He shrugged, but that wistful expression was still there.

"All done with that part," the doctor pronounced. "We'll be back in fifteen minutes when it's all numbed up."

"You're a good . . . son?" the nurse said to Lance.

*Bitch.* If she'd been listening to our conversation, she had to know we weren't related.

"Friends. Good friends." Lance gave her a stare that would freeze a campfire, and she scurried away.

"Ignore her," he said to me, perching next to me on the exam table, as comfortable as if we were on my well-loved leather sofa.

"This friendship business isn't going to work," I said, making no effort to scoot away. He was warm and smelled good, unlike the cold, antiseptic-laced air in the narrow room. I didn't really care what Nurse Judgy thought, but her dig only underscored that I had no business being friends with Lance, let alone anything else—the thirteen years between us seemed as wide as the Grand Canyon. He had years of freedom and beautiful vistas stretching out in front of him, while I'd landed firmly on the side of bricked-in views and bitter responsibilities.

"Give me one good reason."

I glanced at the closed door, then lowered my voice. "We're going to end up sleeping together again."

"Tonight? Because I'd really like that." His smile was more potent than any liquor.

"Should have known you had an ulterior motive," I groused, trying not to let on how pleased yet terrified I was.

"Yeah. You're so sexy when you're bloody and all. But seriously, that's not a reason not to be friends. Why can't we be the sort of friends that get it on from time to time?"

"Because I don't want you to get hurt." He was a good guy, the sort of sparkly optimist I'd never been, and I didn't want to be the thundercloud blocking his sun.

"Look. Can I level with you?" He put his hand on my knee.

I nodded. The warmth from his palm coursed through me, more soothing than the pain shot.

"I know you think I'm some big party kid, but I don't make a habit of what I did last weekend. I'm way more of a friends-with-benefits guy than a one-night stand guy."

"I know." I'd figured that out a bit too late—his odd bursts of nerves, the way the sex had seemed to take him by surprise even as much as he'd seemed to want it. No, he wasn't some club rat, which was only more reason not to mess with him.

"The last few years have been nothing but studying for me. I'm only in town a few more months—"

"Hold up. You're moving?"

"I've applied to physical therapy schools all over, but most of the top-rated ones are in Cali. Fingers crossed that I get into my top five. Anyway, I know I'll come back here after grad school, but I'm looking forward to a few years of sunshine. And since I'm only in town a few more months *and* I'm still swamped with school, I really wouldn't mind having something casual."

"Just two friends? Knocking boots occasionally?" I studied his face. He *seemed* serious enough. And if he was leaving anyway . . .

"I have no time for anything else, and I don't think you do either." Lance's hand kept up a steady massage of my thigh, smoothing over all my objections.

"I don't do relationships," I said firmly. "And I'm a pretty crappy friend. You can ask Randy—"

"Your ex? Met him last week. He's . . . interesting. I don't think he's capable of friendship."

I laughed. "He'd say the same thing about me."

"Why don't you let me form my own opinion?" He ran his thumb along my jaw, leaning closer—

"Who's ready for stitches!" The doctor came bustling in, the nurse right behind him. They clicked on the high-powered lights. I winced, but Lance didn't move a millimeter, simply grabbed my good hand.

"He is," Lance said, with such certainty I almost believed him.

Eight sutures and one long hand-holding session later, we left. Tentative friends, I guessed, even if I was more than a little unsure about the "with benefits" idea.

Okay. Unsure was the wrong word. Eager. Nervous. Salivating. Uncertain. I needed a whole vocabulary list for how I felt about friendship with Lance.

# Chapter 6

Back at the shop, Lance put on some hideous pop music, heavy on the Katy Perry, donned one of my aprons, and made fast work of the prep I couldn't do one-handed. He danced to the music, even when hefting big bags of vegetables. I'd expected the kitchen to feel crowded with his presence. I did most of my kitchen work on my own—late nights prepping stuff for the breakfast rush, early mornings setting up soup and sandwiches for lunch.

But to my surprise, Lance never once bumped into me and the kitchen didn't seem crowded so much as colorful, like a few extra bulbs had been added to the ceiling, casting light in ignored corners.

Ever since he'd made it seem inevitable that we'd be sleeping together again, it was all I could think about. He was a sweet guy, and even if he claimed to want something casual, I couldn't shake the feeling that I'd be taking advantage of him. But even as I tried to urge myself toward nobility, I knew I would end up giving in. I poured coconut cream into the mixer with my good hand while eyeing his bouncing ass. Yup. I was screwed.

"You got help in the morning?" he asked as he diced day-old bread for overnight bread pudding.

"I start at four on my own usually. My kitchen assistants show up at five-thirty, then the rest of the Sunday crew comes at six so we can open at seven. I guess I might need to ask one of my guys to come earlier. Why? You offering to sleep over?"

"Whoa. Sleep over?" He feigned surprise. "You haven't even fed me dinner. I'm not sure I trust you to keep me alive till morning."

"Brat." I slapped his ass, immediately regretting it. "Damn. Fuck. Pain shot's wearing off."

"Poor baby." He grabbed my now properly bandaged hand and dropped a kiss across my knuckles.

"Eh. I'm okay. A beer and a jo—pain pill and I'll be good as new."

He raised an eyebrow. He knew damn well what I'd been about to say. "I'd better stay. Wouldn't want you mixing too many things. But, seriously, dude, I know you have the whole live-on-coffee-and-bean-sprouts-stay-skinny plan down, but the rest of us need dinner."

"Bossy baby. I usually just order something in on Saturday nights. Too much work to make myself something and handle all the prep. Would pizza work?"

"*You* eat pizza? Like with real cheese on it? Or is there a vegan pizza place around here?"

"Sssh." I lowered my voice for dramatic affect—making him laugh was almost as potent as the pain pills. "I'm not strict vegan. That angle was all Randy's marketing idea."

"Do you eat some meat? Like fish or chicken?"

"Not fish." I couldn't hide my full-body shudder. I'd had to clean and eat a whole fish once at Boy Scouts. I'd been close to tears and ended up hurling all over my sneakers. I'd been a total and complete failure as a Scout, tapping out at as a Webelo, much to my Eagle Scout dad's chagrin.

"Oh, that's right." He gestured at my tats. "Your spirit animal and all that."

"I very, very seldom eat any type of meat. Or eggs. Cheese I'm down with. But you can get whatever you want on your side and I'm not gonna freak. I want green peppers and black olives on mine." I dug out my phone and thumbed to Bellagios online ordering screen.

"I love black olives. Have them do those on the whole pie. I want Canadian bacon on my side."

"Done." I clicked send.

"Where are the raisins for the pudding?" he asked as he dumped the first batch of bread in one of the big pans I had waiting.

"I don't usually put raisins in."

"Oh, dude, you can't have bread pudding without raisins. Or rum."

"Rum?"

"My nonna never met a dessert you couldn't add booze to. But yeah, you need raisins."

"What the hell." I searched out the giant tub of raisins from the shelf. "Knock yourself out."

His halogen-bright smile was worth shaking up the brunch a bit for.

"So what's with the fish thing? I mean, you've got the tats, you've got the fish tanks upstairs . . ."

"You noticed my fish? I thought I kept you too busy to be nosy." My hand was starting to throb, but I gave him a look promising I could keep him that busy again. This was why platonic wasn't a possibility—he unearthed a flirty side of me I hadn't experienced before. Something about him made my words more nimble and my movements more deliberate.

"Um . . . dude, you have a bigger fish tank in your living room than they had at the doctor's office. Yeah, I noticed. They're . . . nice."

"I think the word you're looking for is weird." I unwrapped some more loaves of bread for him to chop. "It's a hobby. That's all. I went to college for marine biology—"

"They have a lot of those majors in Nebraska?" Lance chopped far slower than I did, but where I was all speed and rustic precision, he was a laser-tipped ruler, churning out perfect cubes.

"Hardly. I was the weird, nerdy kid obsessed with oceans."

Lance laughed. "There is *nothing* nerdy about you. But what happened? Why aren't you on a boat somewhere?"

"I get seasick. Like vicious, no-meds-work sick. But I worked at the aquarium in Newport for a while. Wasn't as much fun as I'd hoped. Randy worked for a restaurant on the coast. He always wanted to move back to Portland . . . so here we are." I kept my voice light, like the whole thing was just an episode of some stupid comedy, not like those sentences contained some of my most bitter disappointments. Lance was far too sparkly to bother with those.

"Here *you* are. No more we, right? Why don't you split back to the coast? Man, if I didn't have all my family in Portland, I'd want to be on a beach somewhere twenty-four/seven."

"Eh. I don't really know what else I'd do. I like being my own boss." It was hard to articulate how much of myself I'd lost—and found—in these walls. I wasn't about to let Randy take this from me, beach or no beach. "Shitty ex aside, this is a good life."

"Why's he the ex? He cheat with a barista?" Lance scraped this batch of bread into the baking tray I had ready.

"Damn. You met him once and you pegged him that fast?"

"Yeah. He's a hound. So who cheated?"

"Who says someone cheated?"

"Someone *always* cheats." Lance looked at me with the conviction of someone who hadn't witnessed a lot of breakups but who wanted to believe fidelity alone could be enough to keep two people together.

My joints creaked with years of experience to the contrary as I poured the mixture from the blender over the bread in the pan.

"Actually, we had a very open arrangement about that kind of stuff. He had people on the side. I didn't care." *Much.* "Money was what split us up. We started the second store and he was there all the time and I was here, and when we were together it was to argue about finances. Eventually, we realized money was the only thing keeping us together. He moved out. Got a place by the new store."

"Ah." He made a sour face. "I could never do that open relationship stuff."

"What do you mean? Aren't you the one with all the friends with benefits?" I helped stage stuff for Lance to wash at the big stainless sink.

"Well, yeah. But that's not *serious*. I get a boyfriend, it's going to be just me and him." He smiled a little smile, like he was seeing some future version of himself in the soap bubbles and loving what he saw. And like he had absolute faith in his ability to live up to that vision.

I felt as withered as a cartoon villain, a pile of old bones and grudges. I'd been idealistic like Lance once, believing in true love and soul mates and all that crap, but it seemed like it all happened in someone else's lifetime. After all, I'd been the kid who romanticized the hell out of living on a boat only to discover I was allergic to any type of watercraft. Some dreams you just grew the hell out of.

We finished up just as the pizza arrived.

"Let's take this upstairs. I've got some Ninkasi ale in the fridge. Feel free to grab a soda from down here, though, if you'd rather."

"No. I'm all over a beer." He wiped his forehead. "This is intense work. I'm impressed that you pull this off every week."

I took ridiculous pride in that, my shoulders pulling more upright, the pain receding a bit. The pain came back, though, as soon as I tried to grab the door to upstairs with the wrong hand.

"God. This sucks."

"Poor baby. I'll have to take your mind off it in a bit." He gave me an appraising stare, one that made me feel less of a sweaty, banged-up mess.

"I'm counting on it. You can put the pizza over there." I pointed to my glass coffee table. Like the rest of the apartment, the living room was small, but it was my favorite room in the place, with my fish tanks along the far wall and the long brown leather couch along the other. Going to the fridge, I grabbed the beers with my good hand.

"So you're staying, then? I don't want you to feel obligated to help in the morning," I said as I returned.

"I want to." He winked at me. "I better text my mom that I'll be gone."

"Gonna get busted for staying out?"

"It's called common courtesy." He gave me the same cold stare he'd given the nurse. "They don't care if I'm gone or wait up for me or anything like that."

"And you're out to your whole family?" Given that he'd pretty much announced his sexuality within ten minutes of meeting me, I assumed it wasn't a huge secret. But I still couldn't picture a universe where one's parents wouldn't cringe at the implication that their kid might be getting laid—in any orientation.

He grabbed a slice of pizza before answering. "Yeah. I've never not been out. I was ten or so when I told my mom I was going to marry my friend Todd. Luckily, she didn't freak."

"Nice mom."

"Well, my cousin Vic was already out by that point."

"Vic's gay?" I tried to match this information up against what I knew of the man—large, bald-by-choice, tats.

"Very. He's got a hot new boyfriend. They're *very* exclusive." He said it like I might be tempted to go sampling in those waters. "Anyway, my folks were already moving toward being more open when I started talking about wanting to kiss boys and stuff. I told the rest of the family I was gay senior year, when they kept asking why I wasn't taking a girl to prom. It wasn't a big deal."

"Must be nice." I struggled to keep the jealousy out of my voice. It sounded like something out of a liberal sitcom.

"Your folks weren't thrilled?" He sounded surprised.

"My dad gut punched me when I told him. We haven't spoken since. My mom's a bit under his thumb." *That's putting it mildly.* "But we talk every so often. I don't want to make things worse for her, so I don't really visit."

"That's terrible." Eyes going wide, Lance reached out and patted my knee. "My family is huge and crazy, but I can't imagine being cut off from them."

The concern in his eyes made my throat tighten, stole my appetite. I hated talking about this shit. It hadn't been the first time my dad had laid hands on me, but it was certainly the last. I'd screamed the truth in the middle of an argument about my future and ended up with said future crashing down around my shoulders.

"It's not all terrible. Surprisingly, my grandmother was cooler with it than my folks. I stayed with her some in college."

"Yeah." Lance didn't sound convinced, and his eyes still had something suspiciously like pity in them. He was still young and idealistic enough to think of family as a good thing, and to see its lack as an injury. Me, I was doing just fine on my own.

"Jesus, my hand hurts." Even eating the pizza one-handed, my injured hand still kept throbbing.

"Take one of the pain pills they gave you." He got off the couch and got me a glass of water. He didn't even need to ask where the glasses were, getting the cabinet right on the first try.

"Pain meds are going to make me sleepy." I went ahead and took the stupid pill.

"That's okay." He touched my face. "And we don't have to do anything. I'll still stay, even if you're too tired to put out."

"Too tired, huh?" I put down my plate and tugged him over to me. I captured his surprised mouth in a kiss. He tasted like good beer and tomatoes and the memory of our first time—all the sweetness and closeness of that encounter wrapped up in a long, slow slide of lips and tongues.

Breathing heavily, he broke away. "I'm done with dinner. If you're going to pass out after, maybe we should go to the bedroom?"

"Yeah." My limbs already felt heavy and I wasn't sure if it was from the meds or the kissing or simply from hanging with Lance. He was like my favorite quilt—cuddly yet substantial, with all sorts of interesting layers and textures, and I wanted to sink into him.

# Chapter 7

Lance did lightning-fast work of putting the dishes in the sink and the pizza in the fridge, then galloped toward my room. He was obviously comfortable in my space. His easy attitude probably should have put me off, but it did the opposite.

"Now . . . what will make the pain better?" He gave me a kiss as I joined him in the cramped bedroom. "You wanna lie back and let me do the work?"

"Eh. I'm not really in the mood to get fucked tonight—"

"That's not what I meant." He shoved me toward the bed.

Oh, yeah. I could totally get behind laying back and letting him exert himself. I remembered the fantasy I'd been spinning at the doctor's office. "Could I watch you strip?"

"Oh, sweetie, you can watch me do a lot more than strip." He pulled back the covers and stacked the pillows against the headboard. "Get comfy."

I stripped down to my boxers, then arranged myself against the pillows. The low lighting and warm air from the radiator made me feel like a sultan waiting to get serviced.

"Do it nice and slow. I want to see your other tats."

"You missed them last time? I'm wounded. I thought I was memorable." His smug grin said he knew every bit how good he was.

"You were more than memorable, brat, and you know it."

He flashed his abs a few times before pulling his T-shirt off. Pointing to his shoulder, he said, "This is my old cat, Maurice. I wanted them to make it look like he was about to catch something."

"Nice." I schooled myself not to laugh—he was so sweetly sentimental. "Maurice would have loved stalking my fish tank."

"Cats do love fish." He gave me another of his flirty winks. "Now, where do you think my other tats are?" He toyed with the button for his jeans.

"Your ass. Show me now."

"Think you're smart, huh?" He pushed his jeans open, just enough to show me red briefs. My own wardrobe was boringly utilitarian—plaid and washable being the defining characteristics. But that didn't mean I couldn't appreciate Lance's always-ready-for-a-party look.

"Nice. I approve of the slutty panties. Show me more."

Slowly, oh so slowly, he pushed the jeans over his hips. They pooled around his feet and I spotted tattoo number two on his calf.

"A heart?"

"It's for my nonna. Vic got one for her after she passed, so I wanted one, too."

"Sweet. Come show me your undies."

He spun, shaking his ass like he was on the club floor. Boy liked to show off. I could totally work with that. He raised his arms over his head, and I finally spotted tattoo number three, something tiny on his ribs.

"What's that one of?" I pointed.

"Firecracker." His smile flashed like a sparkler. "That was my first. I needed something I could hide from my rents. Someday I want a whole fireworks scene."

"They're more cool with gay sex than with tats?"

"Oh, yeah. Mom says I'll regret the ink when I'm old."

"Old like thirty-five?" My voice was way too cautious. I should have known the cozy camaraderie of beer and joking couldn't chase away my doubts about the age difference.

"Is that how old you are?"

"Yeah. Way too old for you." I rubbed a hand over my beard.

"Oh, darn. I guess I'd better put my clothes back on." He rolled his eyes. "Stop being an idiot. I told you; I've had plenty of guys my age. It's not all it's cracked up to be. Either they don't get how busy I am or they don't know what they're doing or they play games, and I'm kind of over all that."

He knee-walked toward me, then straddled my legs. "Now you seriously gonna turn me down?"

He ran his hands down his torso. His gorgeous, golden, gym-sculpted torso. But it was the smile that did me in—the I've-got-your-number grin that made my insides flop around like a fish in a net. No, I wasn't turning him down.

"You like putting on a show, don't you?"

This smile was like his firecracker tattoo—small but full of fun and mischief. "I guess I do."

"Come closer," I said, crooking my finger.

He presented my face with his red silk-covered package. I mouthed his erection through the fabric until it was obscenely damp and he was breathing hard.

"Jesus. Love how your face feels."

"You like the beard?"

"Yeah. I kept thinking all weekend how it felt against my back." He shivered. "So hot."

"This is hot, too." I ran a hand over his fuzzy stomach. His leg hair tickled pleasingly against my sides.

"Hell, you keep looking at me like that and I won't wax till August."

My neck tightened at the mention of his departure date. Which was stupid. I should be *relieved* we'd put an expiration date on this thing.

"Here." I dug the lube and condoms out of the nightstand and handed them to him. "Show off some more."

"Oh, yeah." He smiled, like I'd handed him the keys to a Ferrari. Still straddling me, he shimmied out of his underwear, his hard cock springing up just out of reach. Then he spun around so his world-class ass faced me. He had the quintessential bubble butt of all the bad club tunes: round and juicy but firm.

Looking back over his shoulder, he grinned at me. "What do you want to see?"

"Get your ass ready for me."

He gave a show worthy of xTube, flexing his ass muscles and spreading his cheeks. My cock went from interested to painfully insistent, my pulse pounding in my ears.

"You practice that in front of a mirror?" My voice had dropped several octaves thanks to his show.

"Hey, don't knock jackin' it to a mirror if you haven't tried it."

A deep rumble escaped my chest. Damn, that was a hot image. "I'd like to be a fly on that wall."

"Anytime, baby, anytime." He grabbed the lube, got his fingers slick, and started teasing all around his rim.

"Fuck yourself for me."

"Oh, yeah." He was a bit more forceful than I would have been, going right to two fingers and sending them deep in a sure, swift motion.

"You like to be full, don't you?"

"Yeah." He tipped his head back, the muscles of his back rippling. "Feels amazing."

"Do three," I urged.

"Fuck." He groaned low, working the third in.

"You ever manage to do four?" My hands were slightly smaller than his. My brain added several kinky thoughts to the list of things I wanted to do with him.

"No, but I've got a big dildo. You wanna see that sometime?"

"*Yes.*" My head swam, like I'd had a triple dose of the painkillers. I liked all this talk about future encounters far more than I should. Somehow we'd gone from one-night stand to friends to friends who might fuck to friends who were going to fuck regularly, all in the space of a few hours.

"Oh. Huuuh." He panted. "Want you now."

My dick flexed against my stomach. No complaints here. Before I could even nod, he damn near wrenched my boxers off. He handled the condom and lube with similar efficiency.

"Fuck." His hands on my dick felt so good I thrust up into his fist.

"Exactly." His eyes sparkled. "Which way you want me?" He hesitated before climbing on.

"I wanna see your face while you work."

"Yeah. Gonna be torture." He laughed wickedly. Sinking down slowly, he rolled his hips and abs like a tune was playing in his ear. A very, very dirty tune.

"Feel so good," I said. His ass was tight and slick and he knew how to work the muscles once he had me deep, doing a flutter that almost made me shoot.

"So full." His head fell back, exposing the long column of his neck. I wanted to bite him right below his Adam's apple. "Damn. You're . . . so good."

He flexed his hips, experimenting until he found the angle he wanted; then he started really working, his thighs clenching me tight as he rode hard.

"You love this, don't you? Love taking a big cock?" Dirty talk didn't do a whole lot for me, but I loved the way it made Lance lose his rhythm, his cheeks flushing.

He licked his lips and nodded. "Uh-huh."

Pleasure gathered, a heavy, liquid sensation in my muscles heightened by the weight of him straddling me, the tight grip of his muscles, and the reckless abandon with which he rode me. No way could I last long with this kind of overload.

"Stroke yourself off. Show me how you jerk it."

I could have used my uninjured hand, but he seemed to have a real kink for showing off, and I was only too happy to indulge it. True to form, he got his palm slick with lube, made a show of spreading it along his shaft, then built a rhythm of fucking his fist as he rode me.

"Wanna come," he panted.

"Do it. God, you look so dirty. Riding me and jerking it."

"Want you to come, too." His voice was a low whine, pleading and needy and sexy as hell.

"I will, beautiful." Simply watching his face was enough to get my balls tingling. His eyes were squished shut and his teeth kept raking his lower lip. The strange connection we'd had the first time was back, and I could feel the closeness of his orgasm even more than my own. The tightness in his thighs and the squeeze around my cock said that he was close, and I encouraged him, using my good hand on his hip and bucking up into him. The bed creaked, groaning as loud as our mingled voices.

"Fuck. Fuck. Feel you. Feel you so much."

"Yeah. Come on. Do it."

I'd had a lot of sex over the years, enough to know that simultaneous orgasm was a myth, but with Lance it seemed the opposite—like it would be impossible not to come together, like the only way I was going to orgasm would be in the same heartbeat as him.

His free hand came down to his hip and grabbed my hand, squeezing hard as he shot all over my chest. And I was coming, too, and it felt like I'd always been coming, like there was no tipping point, just pure pleasure flooding through me, no beginning, no end, just existing right there in that moment with him, eyes locked, hands clasped, pulse shared.

"Oh. My. Fucking. God." Releasing my hand, he scrubbed his hand through his hair. "That about killed me. In the best way possible."

I grunted, unable to speak.

"Bet your hand stopped hurting."

"What hand?" My body seemed to have melted into the bed, as worn out as my flannel sheets.

We both hissed as he untangled our bodies. "Um. Dude?"

"Yeah?"

"You've got cum all over your beard. Sorry."

I laughed. "I'll live. Give me about ten minutes to get feeling back in my legs and I'll shower."

"Cool. I'm gonna grab a towel and another beer. You want one?"

"Yes to both."

And yes, sex with Lance really was that simple. Friendship *definitely* had its benefits.

Lance ended up showering with me to "help keep your stitches dry," which led to another round of sex before we both collapsed in bed, him wrapped around me like I was his new body pillow. It had been over two years since I'd last slept all night with someone. I thought it would be weird—and crowded—but instead I fell into a deep, almost dreamless sleep, only to be awoken by Lance kissing my neck.

"You've smacked your snooze button twice. Rise and shine."

"Are you a morning person?" I eyed him blearily. He was already dressed in yesterday's jeans and a T-shirt he'd stolen from the stack of People's Cup shirts on my dresser.

"Fuck no. I'm going home to take a nap as soon as you don't need me."

*I might always need you.* I looked at him; really looked at him in the dim light of the room, the single bulb catching the highlights in his hair, the world still dark outside the window. He was the brightest thing in my life at that moment.

I shook my head to clear it of such sappy thoughts. He was just a kid passing through my life, and I was a cranky old man who couldn't even put on my jeans without wincing.

"Yeah. I'll get you out of here with plenty of time to rest."

"Cool. I've got a study group later tonight. Crazy busy this week. But you know, feel free to shoot me a text sometime."

"You asking to hookup again?" I curved my good hand's index finger through his belt loop, pulling him toward me.

"Nope."

"No?" I had to look away before he saw my disappointment.

"Nope. I'm telling you *when* we can hookup. I don't have to ask."

"Think you're that good, huh?" I bit his chin lightly.

"No, I think *we* are." He kissed me, a sleepy little good-morning kiss. Nothing special, but my stomach still flipped like I'd tossed it in the bean grinder. Being friends with Lance was going to be hell on my insides.

# Chapter 8

"That's not bacon." Lance looked down at his sandwich. "It says BLT, but I don't see any B."

"It's tempeh. Mock BLT." I leaned against the counter. We'd fallen into a pattern over the last few weeks of him coming by in the midafternoon on delivery days. I usually had a drink ready for him—milky way mocha, extra whip—but I'd recently discovered that he routinely skipped lunch, running from class to work.

"It's . . . interesting," he said, taking an extra-long time chewing.

"It's okay if you don't like it. Tempeh is an acquired taste."

"Yeah. I can see that." He chewed the next bite even more slowly. "Thanks for making it for me."

"Let me make you something else."

"Nah. It's okay. I'm hungry, and my mom always taught us to try new things." He picked a few sprouts off the sandwich.

"I think you have 'try new things' covered." My laugh was a bit dirtier than usual, laced with memories of the previous night, when I'd introduced him to the pleasures of sixty-nining. We always kept things professional at the shop—no afternoon quickies or make-out sessions, no matter how much I wanted to haul him into the storeroom.

I grabbed a loaf of sourdough bread from the rack and the jar of cashew butter. My stitches had come out the week before, and I could finally grab things without pain. He was too polite to ask for something different, but I should have guessed the tempeh wouldn't be to his liking. He wasn't exactly a picky eater, but he had a definite palate of preferences: nothing spicy, no weird textures, but lots of classic American white/carb heavy dishes.

"You want jelly?" I asked as I spread the cashew butter on two slices of bread.

"Yes, please. Strawberry." He set the tempeh sandwich down on the counter, looking at it like it might leap up and bite him back.

"You have another late night? I can make you an extra sandwich for a snack later."

"You're awesome. Yes, after I get the truck back, I've got to run home and keep my siblings from killing one another while my mom goes to a PTA meeting, then I've got two back-to-back study groups. Doubt I'll have time for dinner."

"Aren't your sisters old enough to be left alone?"

"Trinity will be at track meet, and the last time my mom left the twins alone they microwaved tinfoil. Time before that they decided to wash their soccer cleats—took my dad two hours to fix the machine. I told my mom I'd make sure she didn't have to make another major appliance purchase this month."

"You're such a good guy." I handed him his sandwich before wrapping up a second in a recyclable to-go box. He really was a sweet dude—one who seemed incapable of saying no to his family and friends but who also seemed to genuinely enjoy lending a hand.

"Heh. Tell me that at ten, when I'm sick of doing all the work on the group communications project."

"More like you won't *let* them do the work." I knew him pretty well by now. He might grouse a bit, but he wasn't about to let his friends flounder. He was also damn near obsessed with his GPA. I'd been busy toking and chasing guys my senior year, but Lance was determined to graduate with a 4.0.

"Yeah, that. You want me to text you after I get free?"

"Oh, yeah." I smiled at him. I'd come to anticipate his texts; every single one made me smile, even the random ones, like pictures of some dude's tattoos. The ones that came late at night were my favorite, though, because those usually led to him on my doorstep.

"Better get going." Our eyes linked, heat brewing for later. The urge to touch him was overwhelming. I glanced at the kitchen door. Surely I could get away with—

"Hey, boss, we're out of veggie chili. You got more back here?" Brady came in right as I stepped toward Lance.

"Yeah." I retreated to the large pot on the stove. We kept soups behind the coffee bar in large warming crocks so that the baristas could quickly dish out cups of them. "Bring the crock in here."

"Hey, man," Lance greeted Brady.

"You get your coffee?" Brady asked him. I appreciated that Brady's voice was neutral—no teasing. He had to have noticed how often Lance was around, but he wasn't one for a ton of ribbing beyond the occasional knowing smile.

"Yeah. Hey, I got the card of the therapy place in Southwest for you. The one with the sliding scale co-pays?" Lance dug a card out of his wallet.

I'd been worried about Brady's injuries not healing, but leave it to Lance to actually do something about it. An unfamiliar emotion gathered in my gut, making me smile.

"They gonna tell me to stop boarding?" Brady asked.

"Nah. One of the therapists races longboards. They'll fix you up. You might need X-rays, though."

"It's not broken." Brady shook his foot out.

"Get the X-rays," I ordered. "And let me know when your appointment is; I'll cover for you." We didn't really do paid sick leave—all the employees were hourly workers—but Brady had been with us three years now, and I'd make an exception for him. I wanted him out of pain.

"Will do. Let me grab that crock." Brady retreated into the front, leaving Lance and me staring at each other again.

"See you." Lance made a hand gesture for the phone and I grinned wider than I had in a very long time.

It was a little before ten when my phone buzzed with a text.

ON MY WAY HOME FROM THE LIBRARY. YOU UP?

ALWAYS. YOU EAT YET? I replied. My stomach had started anticipating his texts even more than my libido. I'd always had the routine of a very late dinner, eating after we closed the shop for the night at nine. This habit dovetailed nicely with Lance's schedule because he seldom had time to grab food; between two part-time jobs and classes, he was actually busier than I was.

HAD YOUR SANDWICH A COUPLE OF HOURS AGO. BUT I'M STARVING NOW.

I'LL CALL BELLAGIOS. EXTRA OLIVES? I typed. The pizza place probably kept better track of our hookups than I did.

SURE ☺ SEE YOU SOON!

Twenty minutes later, both he and the pizza arrived at my place. It was the same delivery girl as the last two deliveries. She was supercheerful; I was a good tipper and Lance was good eye candy. She didn't try to hide the fact that she was checking him out—and he did look rather yummy. As always, he had a red shirt on, this one a polo with thin silver stripes. His jeans rode low on his hips.

"You guys are my favorite stop." She handed over the warm box of delicious-smelling pizza.

"Thanks." I tossed in an extra five with the tip.

"Oh my god, I am *beat,*" Lance said as he followed me upstairs. "And starving."

"You take a load off. I'll grab plates." I waved him toward the couch. "Beer? Soda?"

"Soda. Thanks." Lance dumped his backpack in the entryway before collapsing on my couch. His shoulders were slumped and his face more pinched than usual. I wanted to rub all that tension out of him.

I grabbed plates, a beer for me, and a cherry soda for him—yeah, I kept a supply for him upstairs now. When I came back in the living room, his head was tipped back against the wall, his legs stretched out in front of him.

"Thanks," he said as I served up the pizza. "Man, you have no idea how much I was looking forward to this. Mom needed me to move some boxes, so I was running late to campus. Then Lisa and Cara talked the *entire* stats study group. I doubt they pass the test."

"That sucks." We ate the remainder of the pizza in companionable silence. I liked that we didn't always need to chat when we hung out—no awkward pauses or expectations.

"I really do want to . . . do stuff, but is it okay if I just chill here for a few minutes?" Lance asked as he polished off the last of his soda.

"Of course." I flipped off the table lamp, leaving the room dim save for the glow of the fish tanks. I pulled him into my arms, letting him sag against me. "You relax as long as you need to."

"Fish are fun to watch," he said sleepily.

"Yeah." I dropped a kiss on his head as I watched my tanks. My new betta fish was hanging out in the smaller tank. It was my latest rescue. Someone had given Brady's sister a fish for her birthday and she'd been trying to keep it in a big glass bowl. Brady had brought it to me when she'd threatened to flush it because it was so much work. It was a fun fish, practically jumping out of the tank at feeding time.

"Mmm. Do that again." Lance stretched up for another kiss. He was a bit like the fish—always so grateful for the little things I did for him. He wasn't needy so much as constantly in motion—he simply needed reminders to refuel and rest.

"We don't have to do anything if you want to fall asleep like this." I kissed his head again. Truthfully, the prospect of holding him all night was almost as enticing as sex. He didn't always spend the night, but when he was this tired, I could pretty much count on the luxury of him next to me until my much-too-early alarm.

"Nope. Kept thinking about you the whole study group." He shifted restlessly against me. "Can't sleep with a hard-on."

"That so?" I moved so I could kiss his neck, licking the spot right below his ear. I dropped to my knees in front of him on the couch, pushing the coffee table out of the way. "How about you let me take care of you for a change?"

"Yeah?" Scooting forward on the couch, he spread his legs.

"Oh, yeah." I unzipped his fly.

He laced his hands behind his head, his eyes closing as I got to work. Not that blowing him was exactly a chore. And as I sucked him off, I tried to push all inconvenient thoughts from my head—how good it felt to take care of him, how much I liked these late-night visits, how much I liked *him*.

A few nights later, I got a text as I locked up the shop after exhorting Brady to make the call to the physical therapy place.

Sorry. Won't be able to come over after all. Don't have car & missed the bus your direction. Call you later ;)

Darn. Ever since Lance had suggested coming over when he'd made the afternoon delivery, I'd been trying not to count down the hours. The prospect of phone sex wasn't really a consolation; we'd done that a fair amount. Even if we didn't have time to get together, we usually had time for a late-night phone jerk-off session. Lance was the master of the artful dick shot, which made sexting that much more fun, but it wasn't a substitute for hanging out with him.

You want a ride? I texted back before I could overthink it. I could be there in fifteen. Just tell me where on campus.

You that eager for me? ☺ ☺ Sure, I won't turn down a ride.

He gave me rough directions to where to meet him near the PSU Library.

I finished up my cleaning and grabbed my spare motorcycle jacket out of the closet. Lance was undoubtedly wearing some flimsy thing. It was a nice night for February; the rain earlier in the day had given way to a chilly but clear evening.

When I pulled up to where Lance had said, I spotted him sitting between two college-aged girls on some concrete steps. I took off my helmet so I could watch them for a minute. He had a textbook open and appeared to be patiently explaining some concept to them. They were leaning forward, giving him their full attention. None of them looked up at the Harley. He laughed at something the dark-haired girl said and pointed to the book. She smiled up at him like he held all the answers to a *Jeopardy!* round.

A streetlamp gave all of them a golden glow, and that light seemed to echo inside of me. That was what Lance did. He lit people up. He was a winner. A keeper really. A few years down the line, he was going to make some lucky dude a very sweet boyfriend. The muscles in my back tightened. I was long past such sentimental days, but hell if my own dark corners didn't long for a little bit more of his light. *Don't get used to it.*

I knew the instant he spotted me, a wide grin coming over his face. He'd been happy with the girls, but now he seemed excited, scooping up his stuff. Today's shirt was a red Trail Blazers basketball sweatshirt—and, as I'd suspected, that was it for outerwear for him. The girls trailed after him. I was superglad I hadn't brought the truck; no offense to the ladies, but I wasn't set to haul his fan club around.

"That was fast!" Lance said as he approached the bike. "This is Lisa and Cara." He pointed to the girls. "And this is my . . . friend, Chris." There was the briefest hesitation, one where I knew what he wanted to say. If it was just to get some distance from the girls, I'd happily let him claim me, but if he was starting to get mixed messages, I really needed to talk to him. But then he smiled at me, all that light directed my way, and I knew I'd be postponing that talk for another evening.

The girls made small talk with us for a few minutes: a few questions about my bike, a whole slew of "one last questions" for Lance about statistics problems. Listening to them banter, I was surprised how much I remembered from my own college days. I could at least make sense of what they were talking about, even if I probably would fail their test. And hell, their class sounded far better than attempting to reconcile payroll. At least they had what sounded like an entertaining professor who made jokes about soccer.

"So we'll see you tomorrow?" The needier of the two, a small dark-haired girl of around nineteen with heavy eyeliner gave Lance a lingering hug. The other girl gave him a quicker hug. She had a unicorn tattoo on her wrist and a much better grasp of stats than her friend. I liked her.

"Yeah. See you." Lance waved to them as they went down the pedestrian path that led into the heart of the campus.

"Here." I fished out the spare helmet and jacket for him.

"Hey. Don't I even get a hi?" He stepped much closer than necessary to accept the stuff, looking right at my mouth.

"Hi." I stopped him with a hand on his shoulder right as he was about to lean in. "You sure you want to do that here?"

I kept my voice light, trying to make a joke of it, but some of the light drained away from his face, his eyes not quite so easygoing, his smile drooping. *Hell.*

"Guess not." He shrugged. He kept the sad panda face as he put on the jacket. "Thanks for this."

He struggled with the clasp of the helmet and I reached out to help him. "Let me."

His mouth was right freaking there and his eyes were still all big and sad and I couldn't help it—I brushed the world's fastest kiss over his lips. I *knew* it was a terrible idea—I needed to be more firm about what the boundaries were in this temporary . . . friendship, not keep flinging myself through them. But the way his whole body seemed to lighten just from a hummingbird-quick kiss made me want to kiss him again, and do it right this time.

"There you go." I fixed the helmet and stepped back before I could give in to the urge.

"Thanks. Man, Lisa and Cara are totes jealous of you." He beamed at me—apparently, one little kiss was worth a stack of gold nuggets to him. Toast. I was absolutely and totally burned-black toast, because all I could think about were ways to make that look stick around.

"Because I get to spend the evening with you?" More like I figured Lisa might happily impale me on my handlebars.

"No, silly. They're jealous of *me* getting to ride off with the hot motorcycle dude. You seriously don't know how hot you are, do you?"

"Guess not." I fiddled with my own helmet strap.

"Hot. Hot. Hot." Lance pointed to my curly hair, which was slightly damp and sticking to my forehead, my beard, and my leather jacket.

"Are you hungry?" I asked in a rush, knowing I was turning pink. Thank God the beard hid most blushes.

"Starving."

"Do you like Chinese food? There's a place on the way back that has good vegetarian for me, but they've got loads of meat dishes, too. We could get takeout."

"They got sweet and sour chicken?"

"I'm sure." I shook my head at him. "I'm going to get a few bottles of high fructose corn syrup. Keep them in the fridge for you. Maybe your medic friends can hook me up with an IV bag—"

"Stop." He punched my shoulder. "I'm not that bad."

"Yes. Yes, you are." My laugh echoed across the mostly deserted street.

"Hey, you think since it's a nice night, we could drive a bit after we pick up the food?"

"Absolutely. The bike growing on you?"

"Something like that." The affectionate look he gave me made my legs go limper than lo mein. *Danger. Danger. Danger.* A red-alert alarm sounded in my brain, but I very kindly told it to go fuck off. It was a nice night. I had a hot boy deluded enough to think *I* was the hot one and who wanted to ride with me. Thinking could wait.

# Chapter 9

One slow night toward the end of the month, I had the urge to make myself something more than a sandwich or wait for take-out with Lance. I got a vegetarian French onion soup simmering, found my secret stash of real Parmesan, and texted Lance.

MAKING SOUP FOR DINNER. YOU FREE AROUND 7?

COULD BE. YOU MIND IF I BRING MY LAPTOP? GOTTA FINALIZE AN ASSIGNMENT BEFORE PLAYTIME ☺ he texted back a half hour later.

BRING IT. I'VE GOT SOME PAPERWORK I CAN CATCH UP ON, TOO. I'LL HAVE TO GO BACK DOWNSTAIRS TO CHECK LOCKUP TOO.

His reply this time was immediate. GREAT. I'M AT THE BAKERY. I'LL GRAB A FRESH SOURDOUGH TO GO WITH DINNER.

"Oh my god, your apartment smells amazing," he said an hour later. He had a baguette tucked under one arm and a backpack slung over the other shoulder and—

"Glasses?" I did a double take. He looked adorable in hipster black rectangular frames. The glasses made him look older—like getting a little glimpse of what he'd look like a few years down the road. My chest gave an odd squeeze.

"Yeah. Couldn't get my contacts in this morning. Too little sleep this week." He looked at me pointedly, the memory of two nights prior flashing between us.

"I'm not sorry." I'd been bleary-eyed myself after the eleven o'clock booty call kept us both up till one a.m.

"You should be." He brushed a quick kiss across my lips on his way to set his stuff down. "You set the table!"

"Yeah. Figure soup's too hard to eat on the couch."

The prewar apartment had an actual dining room, a small affair with a built-in china cabinet that I kept beer steins in. Even though I had a perfectly serviceable table, this was the first time Lance and I weren't eating at the couch. In all the years Randy and I had lived there, we almost never dined together at the table either. Thus, this felt new and kind of weird.

Lance didn't seem to be suffering from the same strange feelings. He grinned at the table and fished out his phone.

"Are you going to make me suffer through Katy What's-her-name at dinner again?"

"We can't all dine on a steady diet of Billy Bragg and Wilco. But, no, cranky, I just wanted to get a picture of the table and the soup."

"You need your friends to see my soup?"

"No, I need them to be *jealous* of your soup. Let me snap a picture of you so they can be jealous of that, too?"

"Not a chance." This was a frequent tease between us. If Lance had his way, his friends would be dissecting my tats while he and I were off making homemade porn; boy never met a camera he didn't love.

I dished up the soup, plating it pretty with the bread and the cheese so he could get his picture.

"Why didn't you go into acting or photography?" I asked. "Why physical therapy?"

"When I was eight I broke my leg pretty bad jumping off the shed roof—"

"You jumped off a shed?"

"It was a dare." He waved a piece of bread at me, like it was a given that he had to accept the dare. "Anyway, I had to go to physical therapy. I had a great therapist named Mark. Cute guy. Probably gay. My first real crush. I couldn't wait to go to my therapy appointments. And I knew then I wanted to do that, too."

"And you never wavered?"

"Well, being a porn star would break my mama's heart." His laugh was even warmer than the soup.

I kicked him under the table, making him laugh harder.

"Better not start selling it."

"Damn. This soup is amazing. Now, you didn't always want to be a chef, right? What changed?"

"I'm not a chef. I'm just a dude with some pots and pans. When we first opened the place, Randy was going to work the food and I was going to work the front of the house. I'd been a barista before, and he'd worked in a lot of kitchens. But we quickly realized that we needed to switch; he's far more personable than me—"

"Ha. Personable as a used-car salesman, maybe." Lance's sour look made me unreasonably happy.

"Well, more suited for the customers than me. We outsourced certain items, but I started doing more and more of the day-to-day kitchen stuff. I worked for a catering company in college, so I had some basic skills. Rest was self-taught."

"My cousin Vic went to culinary school and he's pretty badass, especially with baked stuff, but his soup isn't half this amazing." He helped himself to another bowl out of the tureen.

"Thanks." My chest puffed like a popover, all light and airy in the warmth of the compliment.

"Speaking of Vic, his birthday is Sunday. My family's huge on birthdays. My mom is hosting his party this year because everyone wants to meet Vic's new boyfriend. So I won't be able to come around on Sunday."

"That's fine." I ignored the little twinge of unhappiness in my gut. Sunday afternoons and evenings were slow times for me, and I usually spent the time recovering from the brunch rush—and the last few weeks I'd spent Sunday evenings with Lance. It allowed us to take our time more than usual, hang out after sex, maybe watch a movie on my TV if he came over early enough.

"Actually . . . would you want to come?" He said the words carefully, like he wanted me to think he'd just had the idea, when I could see in his eyes that he'd likely rehearsed the invitation.

"To your family thing? I'm pretty sure your family wouldn't want that." I leaned back in my chair, needing a little distance from the table.

"Why not? You know Vic. You'd like his boyfriend, too—he's real nice. And honestly, if you don't come, I'll be the only person over twenty without a date or a spouse or a whatever."

"I'm pretty sure a too-old-for-you guy covered in tats is pretty firmly in the 'whatever' category for your folks. I don't want them to give you a hard time. And we're not dating. Right?"

"Right." Lance looked down at his soup bowl, not letting me see his reaction.

And okay, I'd cooked the man dinner. I'd set the table, using dishes that hadn't seen the light of day in years. That might seem rather date-like. But we weren't dating. We *couldn't* date.

"We're friends." I reached across the table. "Friends who manage to get naked together pretty often, but friends, right?"

"Yeah. I've brought friends before to family stuff, though—there's a ton of food and people. You might have fun."

"Lance . . ." I trailed off, not knowing what to say. I didn't want to ruin things between us, but I also didn't want to give him the wrong impression.

"Whatever. It was just a thought." He scooped up both of our bowls and headed for the kitchen.

I knew it wasn't a random impulse for him; the tightness around his mouth and the stiffness in his shoulders said this had meant something to him. Part of me wanted to give him that; how hard could a couple of hours of a big Italian family be? And it wasn't so much that *I* cared what they thought of me—I was way too old and crusty to worry about things like that—but I worried about Lance; his family was everything to him, and I refused to bring tension into his relationship with them over something temporary. The sane part of me knew that Lance was leaving soon, and even if he wasn't, nothing could work between us on a serious level. It was better not to build up false expectations. For either of us.

I grabbed the rest of the dishes off the table and followed him into the kitchen.

"You know, I'm going to miss you when you go." I reminded both of us that this thing had an expiration date, that he had a real life waiting for him, and that I wasn't going to be a part of that.

"Ditto. You think we might text some?" His voice was light, but he kept his attention on the sink, not looking at me.

"Sure. You can send me dick shots until you get some surfer on the line and forget all about P-town." I laughed, trying to force some humor into what was becoming a cement shoe–heavy conversation.

"Not going to forget Portland. My whole family's here. I'll be back." He looked up, his brown eyes murkier than a February puddle. "My mom wouldn't let me stay away for good. Speaking of, oh my god, I'm so behind with school this week from all the crap she's had me helping with for the party."

"Yeah? Tell me about it." *Tell me* anything *that lets this awful ten-*

*sion break.* I couldn't allow myself to decipher the subtext simmering between us.

He told me about cleaning ceiling fans and moving couches, and I listened to him vent as we took care of the dishes. Some of the weirdness between us seemed to drain away.

"It still cool if I study here?" he asked as he wiped down the table.

"Of course. Are *we* cool?" I hated that my uncertainty came out in my voice.

"Sure." He gave me a quick peck on the lips. "I'd better get to work so we can get to the friends-who-get-naked part."

I worked on bills for a while, then went down to check to make sure the evening crew had cleaned and locked up properly. When I came back upstairs, I found Lance stretched out on the couch, his laptop precariously balanced on his chest, his eyes shut.

"Hey, sleepyhead." I kneeled in front of him, gently setting the laptop on my glass coffee table. "You get your assignment sent?"

"Yeah." He rubbed his face, knocking his glasses askew. "Probably crap work, but it's done."

"Let's get you to bed." I tugged him off the couch. "And it's okay if all you want to do is sleep—"

"I'm tired, not dead." He tackle-hugged me in the hallway and we tumbled onto my bed in a heap of laughter and flailing limbs. I ended up on top of him, looking down. God, he was so gorgeous. Even tired, with red eyes and crease marks on his cheek from the couch, he was perfect. Cupping his face, I kissed him.

"We're good, right?" I looked into his eyes.

"Oh, yeah." He returned my kiss, and all I could do was hope he was right. However, later, as I herded him into my bed and pulled the quilts up around us, doubts tumbled over inside my brain, like beans jumping around in the hopper, my emotions waiting to get ground up into dust.

Sunday, I was out of sorts the whole day, harsh to my kitchen crew and making stupid mistakes, like almost burning the scrambled tofu. Lance hadn't come by Saturday night—he'd barely had enough time to grab a cup of coffee when he made his delivery. His mother needed help with the food for the party and last-minute cleaning.

What would it be like to be that close to one's parents? To be twenty-two and still living at home? By choice? To be out and still be welcome around the whole family? I had a feeling his family might not be quite so cool with him seeing an older, tattooed hippy freak. But the fact that he assumed they would be cool with it, that he *trusted* they would accept whoever he wanted to bring to dinner? That was a bit staggering.

And I'd turned him down, so I had no reason to be dwelling on it. No reason to be feeling all melancholy. No reason at all to be missing something I hadn't wanted any part of. We weren't dating. We weren't lovers. We weren't falling for each other. This wasn't a fairy tale. We were just two dudes who happened to mesh really well together, getting our rocks off.

Finally, around nine, I couldn't stand it anymore. We hadn't gone twenty-four hours without a text in weeks, but I hadn't heard from him since he'd dropped off the rolls on Saturday afternoon.

I gave up and got my phone out. Looked at it. Put it away. Fed my fish. Checked the water. Cleaned the filters. Stared at the tank, but that didn't have its usual hypnotic effect on me. In the big tank, my large red comet fish was doing his thing of ramming the two small Calico Moors I'd added a few months before. He was in a cranky mood, too. I briefly considered toking, but even that didn't hold any appeal for me. It would just make me hornier and more alone.

I pulled my phone back out. No new messages. *Fine. You win.* I thumbed to Lance's quick dial—yeah, he had a shortcut on my phone. No, that didn't mean we were dating.

HOW WAS THE PARTY? I texted. There. No my-bed-is-so-lonely texts. Ten minutes went by and I flipped on a movie I knew I wouldn't really watch. Then my phone buzzed with a call.

"Hey, I saw your text," Lance said. "Party was good. Lots of people. Tons of leftovers. But there's no school tomorrow and Mom is letting Trinity and the twins have a bunch of the cousins stay for a sleepover."

"Total Degrassi circus?" I settled back into the couch, putting my feet up. Just hearing his voice calmed me down, more even than a joint.

"You have no idea. If I have to kick another twelve-year-old out of the basement, I'm going to punch something. I've got two huge tests Tuesday."

"Pack up your stuff. It's nice and quiet here." *Understatement.*

"I might. I took off work tomorrow so I could study, but that's not happening with the tween explosion here."

"Seriously. You can have the apartment to yourself tomorrow while I'm downstairs. You can study in peace." I watched the comet fish circle the tank, darting under the castle moat, ignoring the school of minnows swimming by. Yup. Nothing much happening here.

"Really?"

"Yeah. Come on over."

"Fine. You want any cake or leftover lasagna or some killer carrot salad?" I heard some rustling, like a fridge door opening. "Oh, and there's some seven layer dip."

"You trying to make me jealous of the food I missed?" Cranky fish found the Calico Moors again but this time swam nicely alongside them.

"Is it working?" He laughed that warm, deep, hot fudge chuckle.

"Maybe. Bring me some cake."

"Okay. I'll be there in a bit. And Chris . . . thanks for calling." He said the last bit so softly I had to strain to hear him.

"No problem. I . . . I missed you," I admitted.

"Me too."

The room felt colder as soon as we hung up, and I went to raise the thermostat. I made sure the table was clear for Lance's studying. Made the bed for once. No, I wasn't eager. Not even a little bit.

# Chapter 10

I was good when Lance came over, helping him get his books and laptop set up and not jumping him at the door. I went back to my movie, actually paying attention this time. Merely having Lance close by settled me down. I turned in before he did, but he woke me up when he came to bed, kissing me on the back of the neck. We made out sleepily for a while, eventually jerking each other off before drifting off.

In the morning, I left him dozing when I went down to open the shop at six. I got the baristas set up for the morning rush. Around nine, I made a large mocha, added extra whip, and grabbed a blueberry muffin. Darting up the stairs, I felt almost like I had a secret—the good kind, like a Christmas present I couldn't wait to open, or news I couldn't wait to share. I found Lance at the dining room table, charts and textbooks spread out. I counted at least five colors of highlighters and three types of sticky notes.

"You want some breakfast?" I asked.

"Oh my gosh, you're the sweetest." He stood up and took the things from me. He kissed me on the cheek before looking deeply into my eyes. Something passed between us, something more than a latte, more than just the use of space, something more than the memory of last night's sex.

"Um. I should probably get back downstairs," I said awkwardly.

"Okay. Is it okay if when I take a lunch break I come down or . . ." He trailed off, looking uncertain.

I had to think for a second. I didn't really care if people knew we were sleeping together—Brady had probably guessed, and the rest should know better than to tease Lance over it. *That* was my real hesitation—I didn't want people giving him a hard time, whether it was his friends or his family or even my employees. It felt like I was walking the thin trail around Multnomah Falls, trying to keep Lance from getting hurt. But his eyes were all eager and hopeful, and I knew that treating him like some shameful secret would cut him deeply and would extinguish that flicker of something magical that had passed between us.

"Sure. Come on down. We've got sandwiches and salads at lunch. I'll be pretty busy in the kitchen, but I'll happily take your order." I smiled at him. Lord, I hoped I was doing the right thing by him.

At lunch, he came down and I made him his favorite cashew butter and strawberry jelly sandwich. For the customers, all of our food on weekdays was grab-and-go—sandwiches, salads, and fruit plates in recyclable take-out containers.

"You have no idea how nice the quiet is," Lance said as he watched me work. "I love my sisters and brother, but our house is always so noisy. Even at school, like the library, it's loud and full of distractions. Friends see me and want to chill—"

"Being popular is such a burden."

"Better than being a hermit, old man. Anyway, I like it here. You never seem to expect stuff from me."

*I like having you here.* "Of course not, brat. Expectations are a waste of energy. And you're great just as you are—you don't always have to be 'on' for me." My voice was thick.

He smiled up at me. The strange feeling from upstairs was back tenfold, delicate strands of some new emotion I refused to name stretching between us. God, I wanted *everything* for him—I wanted the world to see him like I did, to see not only his fun streak but this serious side, too.

"Even your fish are cool. But I was wondering why you don't have any downstairs. You could put a tank in the coffee shop."

"No." I shuddered. "All the kids tapping on the tank. Even adults can't resist tapping the glass."

"And that's bad?" He looked a little guilty.

"Too much of it can scare them. But it's okay if you did it—you didn't know."

"I won't do it again. I was just talking to the big red one—it reminds me of you."

"Old and cranky?"

"Yep. That must be it."

I snapped a dish towel at him.

"That fish always looks like it's thinking. And it's like it's big enough for the ocean. But it's decided to make the tank its home. Even though it doesn't really make friends with the other fish."

"That so?" Trying to hide my smile, I scratched my beard. Lance had just shared more insight about my fish than Randy had in a decade of living with them.

"Something like that. I got bored studying." He looked sheepish. "I'll shut up now."

"No. It's all good. Maybe I should save up for a bigger tank for Scruffy, if he's looking that unhappy."

"How is it we've been hanging out all these weeks and I'm just now learning your fish has a dog's name?"

"Because of how you're looking at me right now. It's not that weird to name a fish."

"Sorry. Maybe I'll bring *Scruffy* some new fake seaweed or something to apologize for tapping his tank."

I laughed. "Get back to studying before someone decides *your* tank needs tapping."

"You want me to start some dinner around seven? Or are you getting sick of me?"

"I could never be sick of you, brat. And sure, cook if you want, but I'm cool with us ordering something in, too."

It was another slow night, so I was able to leave Brady in charge downstairs a little before seven. He didn't say anything, just chewed the mint gum he was using to stop smoking and cleaned the counter in slow motion. But his eyebrow ring flirted with his hairline as he gave me a long look. As I climbed the stairs to my apartment, I was greeted by the smell of tomatoes and garlic and fresh bread.

"What did you order in?" I asked as I came in.

Lance came out of the kitchen wearing oven mitts. "Nothing. I made calzone. Used the last of your cheese."

"You made me calzone?" I hugged him. "That's amazing."

"They might suck. I just needed a break from all the math formulas. My mom talked me through the filling. The dough is just pizza crust."

"Was she worried when you didn't come home?" I asked. He'd called his mom so he could cook for me. My ribs expanded, barely able to contain the emotions rising in my gut.

"She's got four other kids, all of whom are still in school. I'm not sure she even noticed I wasn't home today until I called. And I keep telling you—I'm not a kid. I don't have a curfew or something."

"I know you're not a kid." I tightened my arms around him and nuzzled his neck, but he stayed stiff. "Hey, you okay?"

"Yeah. Too many hours of just me and the books—thanks for that, by the way. The quiet was awesome—but now I'm all snappy."

I wasn't sure whether it was the studying or if there was something else bugging him, but there was no denying the knotted muscles of his back.

"Here." I moved so I was behind him and started rubbing his shoulders. "You stayed in one position too long."

"Yeah. I should have gone to the gym for a break." He leaned into my touch, sounding far less bitter. "Man, that feels *good.*"

"Does the calzone need to cool a bit?" I tugged him toward the living room, shoving my coffee table out of the way.

"It can cool." He watched me with a wary smile. "What'd you have in mind?"

"Let me rub your back?" I grabbed the old quilt I kept on the back of the couch and spread it on the rug between the couch and the TV.

"Seriously? Sure. Why not?" He pulled off his shirt, then flopped on the blanket. "Not like I'm going to turn down your hands on me."

I darted back to the kitchen, grabbing the bottle of olive oil off the counter.

"You gonna sprinkle me with balsamic next?" Lance propped his head up on his hands.

"It's this or use lube. Slim pickings on massage lotion here."

"Oil me up." He let his head rest back on his hands.

I started with his neck, using my thumbs to dig into his knotted muscles. He'd probably be ten thousand times better at this than me—he knew the names of all the muscle groups I was stroking over on the broad expanse of his back—but I wanted to do this for him.

I must have been doing okay because he groaned when I worked the muscles around his shoulder blades. I straddled him to be able to use both of my hands more effectively. I rubbed up and down his spine, trying to do things that had felt good to me in the past.

"Man, that feels so good." His words were muffled by the carpet. "You do this a lot?"

"Actually . . . no," I admitted. "I threw my back out a few years ago lifting bags of trash. Got some massage work done for a couple of months, so I'm trying to remember what the massage therapist did."

"Should have gone to a physical therapist." He sounded both smug and sleepy in the same breath. "We would have gotten you feeling better even faster."

"I'm sure you would have." Leaning forward, I kissed the back of his neck. "You're going to make a great therapist."

"Awww. You really think that?" He sounded a bit unsure.

"I do." I stroked up and down his spine, using a little oil so my hands glided over his muscles. "Look how hard you're working. You're pretty awesome."

"My dad always says it's not how much you want something, it's how much you work for your wants."

"Smart man." I worked his shoulders some more because he seemed to like that the best, sighing and arching into my touch. "You know, you're welcome to do this again. Use my place for studying. If that would help you?"

"I wouldn't want to put you out."

"You wouldn't be." I kissed him in one of my favorite spots, right where his hairline ended. "I can give you a key."

"A key?" His voice went squeaky, and I realized what I was offering.

"No big deal. Just to make it easier for you to study. If you have a key, you can go work out or whatever and not worry about me being around, or you can come over after I'm already in bed. . . ." I drifted off, knowing I sounded a bit ridiculous. I was *always* around. But I wanted him to have the key, for reasons that had my throat feeling several sizes too small and my hands shaking against his back.

"And you'd like that? Having me around more?" He sounded like he was fighting to keep his voice neutral, but hell if I could tell if it was from horror or hope.

"You give the fish something pretty to look at."

"That the only reason?"

No, but it was the only one I was going to admit to either of us. "You cooking for me is a nice little bonus. Can't remember the last time someone did that for me."

"You're sweet. And for what it's worth, no one's ever given me a massage."

"That's a pity." I sat up, kneading the small of his back with my palms.

He pushed his ass up into my groin. "Does this massage come with a happy ending or do I pay extra for that?"

"Oh, that can be arranged." Sex. Sex was good, familiar ground, away from all this new territory I'd unwittingly pushed us into.

"Good. Because I really need to kiss you. Like right now."

I lifted up so that he could roll, and then he was pulling me down to him, crushing our mouths together. The kiss was a rough, living thing between us, consuming all the strange simmering emotion. It was funny—for all the sex we'd had, kissing wasn't usually a huge part of it. We kissed hello and good-bye and occasionally as foreplay, but it was always the appetizer, indulged in and quickly discarded.

But this kiss? It was the entrée. A one-pot meal. It was him more aggressive than he'd ever been and me more desperate and all this emotion pulsing—the key, the dinner, the family stuff we weren't talking about, him leaving—all of it coming out in lips and teeth and tongues. And I didn't need to fuck him. Didn't need to suck him off or get him on his knees. I just needed him here, needed this kiss. Needed his face in my hands, his skin warm and slick under me.

My dick throbbed in my pants. I'd never come from just kissing and grinding before, but I was desperately, impossibly close.

"Close," Lance whispered at the same moment I thought it. I pulled away long enough to strip off my T-shirt.

By some unspoken agreement, we both shimmied out of our pants.

"I want to come just like this," Lance said as I settled back on top of him.

"Me too," I whispered.

"Never felt like this."

"Me neither." Sweat rolled down my back. Me on top of him, all skin and sweat and traces of oil slicking everything up—each sensation felt new, felt pure, distilled down to the essence of what it meant to be humans sharing skin and kisses.

The kissing . . . it was everything. *Everything.* Our lower halves strained, almost violent in our undulations, but our mouths stayed fused. Grabbing my hips, he pulled me even more firmly against him. I'd been inside him before, but in this kiss, I finally felt like I was *in* him. Finally felt like I knew him, in every sense of the word.

And when we came, it was a celebration of that connection. Like all the joy and trust and adoration we shared spilled over until we were both sweaty, sticky messes.

"Yes," he said much later.

My heart was still galloping along and my brain was way too fuzzy. "Eh?"

"Yes, you can give me a key."

"Good." I kissed his temple. His eyes were hooded with spent passion. *You're going to give me a broken heart, beautiful boy.* I knew this to be true, and yet I still smiled at him, still stroked his face and arms. Still ferreted out my spare keys while he served up the dinner. Still slept with him wound around me.

# Chapter 11

Even though things between Lance and me had never been better, they had also never been weirder. There was this unspoken sense that we'd turned a corner in our . . . friendship, but neither of us was bold enough to want to define what that really meant. He was around a lot more, and I had to keep reminding myself not to get used to him being there.

Saturday afternoon, he surprised me by coming back after his delivery to help me with prep.

"I should study, but if I see another chem formula my eyeballs are going to pop out," he said as he helped me dice vegetables for mixed veggie hash in the morning.

"We don't want that." I smiled at him. He was wearing a "Keep Portland Weird" T-shirt and tight jeans with boots. He looked much more suited for a fun Saturday night instead of one stuck in a kitchen with me.

"You know, if you want to go out with your friends or something, I'd understand you needing to blow off steam after your hard week."

"I'm certainly planning to blow *something* later." He looked me up and down, made me feel like I was wearing something far more attractive than flannel and an apron. "You got beer? I could go for some of that ale you had last week."

"We can get some." I wanted to do something nice for him. "Maybe instead of pizza we could go by the brewery."

I'd let him get his carnivore on, maybe bring back some beer for later. In all the meals we'd shared, we had yet to actually eat at a restaurant together. A few weeks ago, I would have worried about what message that would send about our supposedly casual thing, but my desire to do something nice for Lance outweighed such doubts.

"Maybe." He gave me that look again that said he was planning on jumping my bones the second we were done here. That worked for me, too. I chopped faster.

"Hey," he said a while later. "I was curious. When's your birthday?"

"July fourth. My dad was bitterly disappointed that I didn't fulfill my patriotic destiny with military service. Why? When's yours?"

"Two weeks from tomorrow." His smile was tentative.

"You another year old is a definite win." Thick sweat gathered in the small of my back.

"You're not that old." He flicked an onion piece at me, which did nothing to defuse the ticking bomb in my gut.

"Anyway, I told you how my family is huge on birthdays, right? My mom will do a big meal. It won't be just family either—a few of my other friends will be there." He said the last part carefully, like he was trying hard to lump me in with his buddies, but the tension in his shoulders gave him away.

"I'm not sure—"

"I'd really like you to come." His eyes had gone all chocolate Labrador on me, and I had to look away. My gaze landed on his hands, which were shaking ever so slightly. *Fuck.*

"I wouldn't want to ruin your birthday with your family lighting into you for . . . seeing someone so much older." No matter what either of us called it, I was pretty sure neither of us could play things completely platonic.

"If you mean my parents, they already know about us."

"They do?" I whacked a carrot far harder than I needed to.

"Uh, Chris? I've been over almost every day for a couple of weeks. And I'm not exactly ashamed of being *friends* with you."

"More of that common courtesy of keeping them informed where you are?" My knife hit the counter with a loud clatter. *Crap.*

"Something like that." He let out a huff. "They're always interested in my life. Just how family is, you know?"

"I wouldn't know." I busied myself scraping vegetables into the prep tray. For the first time since I'd met him, my kitchen felt too small for the both of us.

"Shit. I forgot about your folks." Dropping his knife, he came behind me, rubbing my back. His sympathy was almost more than I could bear.

"It's no biggie."

"My family's not like yours. You'd like them. I swear. My cousin Dana married this Muslim dude and everyone still danced at her wedding. Some people might tease us about the age difference, but it would all be in fun."

That was what bothered me the most—not that they would make a scene but the possibility that I would like them. I'd liked Randy's family; his mom had always given me a shirt at Christmas and his sister made great coconut cake at Easter. But, in the end, it hadn't mattered how much I enjoyed his family. They'd rolled up the welcome mat as soon as Randy and I started having problems.

Lance was still leaving in August. And his leaving was going to kill me. I could admit that to myself. He was a drug I couldn't quit and I *knew* withdrawal was going to be a bitch, but hell if I could make myself cut back. But what if I actually liked his family? I was already losing Lance. Nothing could change that. And getting more entangled would only give me more things to miss.

I honestly wasn't sure which would be worse—a glimpse of something that would never be or a reminder of all the ways in which I was terrible for Lance.

"This is important to me," Lance said softly, talking to my shoulder blades.

*Aw. Hell.* All my careful reasons galloped away in the face of his sadness. "Can I think about it?"

"I guess." He stepped away, going back to the cutting board, his shoulders slumped.

My gut churned. I remembered being a kid and how much I'd hated "we'll see" answers. And when Randy and I were together, I'd quickly learned that "let me think" just meant "I haven't thought of a good enough excuse." And here I was doing that to Lance.

"Hey." I went over to him, wrapping my arms around him. "Don't be sad. Just let me . . . get my head around the idea. I'm not trying to brush you off."

"Okay," he said to the floor.

"I promise we'll do something special to celebrate no matter what, okay?"

He'd been stressed most of the week with tests, but now he seemed downright morose. And I hated that it was my fault. Hated knowing that I could have fixed things with a single word, but a million small doubts kept me from uttering the one he most wanted to hear.

"It's not a big deal." He shrugged in my arms.

"Would you like to go out tonight?" The thought I'd had earlier of doing dinner out seemed inadequate, but it was all I had.

"You mean dancing?" His voice lightened considerably and he spun in my arms to offer a tentative smile.

*Oh, hell.* I'd meant dinner, but I couldn't disappoint him twice in a single evening. I nodded. "Yeah. We could get a drink after dinner, if you'd like."

"I'd like." He wound his arms around my neck. "Can we go to Slaughters? Some of my friends will probably be there. It would be nice to say hi. I haven't been out with them in ages."

*Fuck.* Deep in my chest, something throbbed. If I made an excuse, he would give me a tight smile. The sadness in his eyes would linger. We'd probably go get a beer, maybe come home and have halfhearted sex. Or he might walk out. The throbbing pain worsened. If he was smart—and he was a fucking genius—he wouldn't stick around with an old dude like me. He *should* be out with his friends every weekend. This could be it—the moment when he'd wise up.

"Okay." Or it could be the moment I said yes, prolonging the pain for both of us.

"Thank you." He kissed my cheek. "It'll be fun. And if Everest and Lane are there, this way you'd already know them at my party. You know, if you come."

"Yeah," I said much too sharply, and his smile wavered. I tightened my arms around him. "Tell me about Everest and Lane. Is Lane the one you were telling me about with the Vespa?"

"You remembered! Yeah, that's him."

We went back to our work, with Lance telling me all about his friends. His movements were noticeably faster now that he had the incentive of going out. My own motions felt as futile as trying to carve a winter squash with a butter knife.

Had I known dress up would have been part of the deal, I would have made an excuse not to go dancing and suffered the consequences. But a long shower with Lance left me sated enough that I let him talk me into wearing a hunter green shirt that had been hiding in the back of my closet. I wasn't even sure it was my shirt, but I wasn't about to go mentioning Randy. The evening already had enough conversational land mines.

"I love this one because the sleeves are short enough to really show off your tats," he said, touching my arm as I grabbed my motorcycle jacket from the rack in the hall.

Yeah, it was definitely Randy's shirt; he was both shorter and a little slimmer than me.

"Is this all because I won't let you post a pic of my ink on the Internet?"

"Yup." He leaned up to kiss my neck. "You won't let me show my friends the hotness, so you force me to produce the in-person version."

"In-person interaction? Does your generation even know how to do that?" I turned to face him, making my eyes go all big.

"I dunno. Do they even let people of *your* age drive still?" He waggled his eyebrows at my bike keys.

And then we were both laughing and kissing at the same time. The ride to the bar was similarly pleasant, and we kept the good mood going until it was our turn to give our drink order. He got his fruity little cocktail, I got my whiskey, and the say-hi-to-Lance-sweepstakes got started.

Lance seemed to know *everyone*. He was like a human mobile hotspot, drawing a small crowd of people who all wanted a part of him. Straight girls, twinks, drag queens, even a few middle-aged fools like me—everyone had a hug for Lance. He seemed to eat up the attention, preening and joking. Through it all, he kept an arm around me, but I figured it had less to do with possession and more with making sure I didn't bolt.

Which I wasn't in danger of doing; while young, his friends were fun. It reminded me of the best parts of being out with a group—I got to chill and watch their interactions and little jokes while not being pressured to make small talk of my own. It was weird how being with Lance reminded me of parts of my younger years I kind of missed—the very things I liked most about hanging out with him were another set of reasons why I needed to let him go. He needed to be free to have this stage of his life without some old hippy holding him back.

After a bit, we danced, the two of us together and then in a group with his friends. That I kind of hated. It made my limbs feel too long and heavy and my head hurt. I felt like a poser dancing with a bunch of twenty-year-olds.

But watching Lance dance was far from a chore. I got another drink and hung out at the rail watching him groove. He laughed and spun and made people around him smile.

*All that sparkle is mine.* Ice water landed smack on top of that happy little thought. *Not for long.* I couldn't own him. He wasn't mine. It was just a beautiful illusion, one from which I was powerless to look away.

Leaving the crowded floor, Lance came and wrapped his arms around me. "You having a good time?"

"Yeah. Just tired. I was thinking I might head out soon."

His giddy smile wavered. "Oh. Yeah. I guess I'm tired, too."

"No, you're not." I kissed his forehead. "Stay. Have fun with your friends. Sleep in tomorrow."

"Oh." He sucked on his lower lip, working it with his teeth. "Would you want me to go home after, or could I come over? Wake you up?"

The sane thing would be to send him home to his own bed. But I could tell from the uncertainty in his eyes what he needed to hear from me.

"Come over. Give me a dirty wake-up. But you'd better put me back to sleep." I tried to make my smile bright enough to push past all his doubts.

"If you're sure . . ."

"You deserve some fun."

"Well . . . okay. But . . ." His eyes darted around the hallway. "You can trust me. You know that, right? I mean, I might dance with some people, but that's as far as it goes."

"You're sweet." I kissed him. Randy would have taken my disappearance as tacit permission to get fresh tail. "And yeah, dance with people. Then come home and whisper all about it to me."

"That would turn you on?"

"Knowing I'm the one who gets you at the end of the night? Hell yes." I'd never had this particular fantasy before, but now my dick throbbed and I couldn't wait for him to crawl into my bed.

"Okay, then." He gave me a nervous little grin. "And uh . . . the same goes for you, right?"

"What? No hooking up with other people?"

He nodded, hope and uncertainty at war in his eyes.

"You don't have to worry about that, beautiful."

"Good. I . . . don't think I share well."

"You won't have to." I gave him a lingering kiss, sweeping my tongue into his mouth. He tasted like fruit and rum and like *mine.*

I headed home a bit weirded out—I had never in any of my relationships, whether years' long or quickie short, promised exclusivity to someone. But as much as I knew I was disappointing him with the birthday thing, I knew I could easily give him this. Hell, I hadn't so much as looked at anyone else since our first hookup. As I walked up the steps to my apartment, a ticking clock echoed in my brain, its chime reaching all the way down to my marrow, counting the seconds until this was over. But until that moment, knowing he was mine, all mine, almost made the coming pain worth it. Felt like I was stockpiling all the joy of spring against the reality of a long cold winter without him.

# Chapter 12

Sunday night we were sprawled on the couch, his head in my lap while he read a psychology textbook. The TV was tuned to a survivalist show on Discovery, but mainly I was focused on the warm weight of his head and the silky feel of his freshly showered hair under my hand. He'd pulled the quilt I kept on the back of the couch over us and the coziness wrapped around me like a drug. I'd never thought of myself as a particularly snuggly person, but Lance made it something I craved, something that warded off more than just the chill of a drafty apartment.

"I have a question," Lance said, looking up from his book and breaking my pleasant fog.

"Yeah?"

"Do you ever think . . . maybe we could keep things going?" His eyes were like a puddle I'd encountered once at a truck stop in rural Washington—looked all harmless and almost cute until I stepped in it and found myself up to my pits in deep mud.

"What?" My heart started galloping, like I'd chugged two of his favorite extrasweet mochas. I'd been dreading this question. "You'll be in Cali, right? Or some other state?"

"Yeah. But it's only for three years. I'll be back after that, most likely."

"Three years is a long time."

"Not really." He looked away, studying the cracked leather of my couch. "There's Skype and texting, and I'll be back for all the holidays—my mom'll kill me otherwise. But anyway, I was thinking, there's really no good reason to stop this . . . friendship. If I go away, I mean—"

"If. There is no if. You *will* get into your top schools," I said firmly. My heart couldn't handle *if.*

"Some of the people I know online have acceptance letters already." He frowned. I patted his chest.

"You'll get into one of your picks. And yes, there *is* a reason not to do the long-distance thing. It's called your life."

"Well, what if I want *this* to be my life?"

My heart cowered behind my ribs, its shaky rhythm rattling my chest. I couldn't trust myself to speak for several moments.

"No. You're going to school. Explore a new city. Meet all sorts of new people. Make friends. Go party. Do all the things you've dreamed about for years. You don't need to be tied to Oregon." My voice was thick as oatmeal and about as enthusiastic.

"I don't want to stop . . . being friends," Lance said softly. "I hate thinking about that."

*Me too.* "Brat, I'm always going to be your friend. And I'd like to hear how you're getting on." Happy things would make me miss him more, but silence might suffocate me. And I knew Lance, knew he'd feel better about being able to text, even if the day would eventually come when he wouldn't.

"This . . . this is special, right?" His fingers twined with mine. I pressed our joined hands against his chest, like maybe together we could feel what was right below the surface of this conversation.

"You have no idea." I had to squeeze my eyes shut. "But that's just it; you need to be free to find . . . special at school, too."

"What if neither of us ever finds this again?"

*I won't.* "You will. You'll find even better friends wherever you're heading. You'll find guys who love Katy Perry and going out dancing and bacon on pizza. And I'm not going to hold you back from that."

"I'm not itching to party or anything." His grip on my hand tightened.

"I want . . ." I had to swallow hard. "I want you to look back and have this time be an amazing memory, not a burden with an ugly ending."

"I don't think it would end ugly."

I opened my eyes. He was so earnest. So sweet. So damn tempting. I would be the worst kind of heel to take advantage of his blind trust.

"I *know* it would. Distance never works. And honestly, most relationships don't either. I'd rather part friends."

"Yeah." He looked far from convinced, his eyes distant and sad.

"Look: I'm going to treasure every single moment between now and August." More like I was going to hoard the memories like squares of a quilt I'd use later to wrap myself in, make myself a blanket cave I might never leave. "And then I want you to go off to the next adventure of your life."

His eyes squished shut and his mouth was tight, his lips a barely visible line. All it would take would be a single tear and I'd be promising him stupid, selfish things. I leaned down and kissed him. I tried to put everything into the kiss—how much I cared about him, how much parting was going to kill me, how much I *already* missed him. He smelled like my shampoo and tasted like my beer and felt like *mine*. But he wasn't. He couldn't be, but I drank up the illusion, greedy for every last drop he could give me.

Eventually, kissing led to touching, him in my lap, us grinding all that emotion out. We made our way to bed, shedding clothes as we went, still kissing. Always kissing. His lips turned punishing as I fumbled for supplies, and still I couldn't stop kissing him, couldn't stop my lips from tracing the chiseled angles of his jaw, couldn't stop my hands from exploring every inch of him.

"Give me everything," he whispered as I pushed inside.

"Always." I held his face, watching him the whole time.

"I need you." His hands dug hard into my shoulders.

"You've got me."

We'd had a lot of sex in our short relationship, but this was making love. I'd never say the words out loud, but my body couldn't lie. Love glimmered off every touch, every glance, every thrust. Our bodies joined in a way that was sweet and slow and more than a little sad. I tried to memorize his face as he came—the way he kept his eyes open until the last second, the way the tendons in his neck went taut, the way his lips formed my name. The end seemed to be sneaking up on us, coming faster than I was ready for.

# Chapter 13

Two days later, Lance came in around six, while I was covering for Brady's dinner break.

"Hey, beautiful. What can I get for you?" I readied a cup for his usual.

"Nothing." He glanced down at the cup in my hands, shrugged. "Uh. Something decaf, I guess."

"Did you eat?" I asked as I got him a cup of decaf, leaving plenty of room for him to doctor it up.

"No. Not hungry." He kept shifting his weight from foot to foot.

"You okay?" I reached across the counter to touch his wrist.

"Yeah. I just . . . when does Brady get back?" His gaze flitted from the counter to the customers sitting at the window table to the tin ceiling. As he rubbed at his neck and winced, the pained expression emphasizing tiny, tired wrinkles around his dark eyes, I got the impression that his skin had shrunk in the wash and he was about to claw it off.

"Probably fifteen minutes. Why? You need to talk?"

"Yes. No. Sort of?" He gave me a crooked smile. "Not anything *bad*. I just . . . need you. But I can wait."

*Ha.* He held himself so tight he might shatter if the edge of a table hit him wrong.

"Tell me now," I said, keeping my voice low. Dread gathered in my stomach. "Not many customers right now. Tell me what's wrong."

"No. Not like this." He gestured to the counter between us. "I'll go study." He grabbed his coffee, and before I could force whatever it was out of him, he went to a table by the window. He took out his psych textbook but didn't flip the pages. He kept looking down at his battered red backpack, his eyes wide, wary, like the red nylon was holding a bomb or something equally horrible that might explode in his face. My back muscles stiffened.

I straightened the display of tea and made the world's fastest lattes for a pair of students. The students claimed a couch. A trio of knitters showed up—regulars who always ordered drinks as complicated as the scarves they produced. I messed up the triple shot Muddy Leprechaun twice because I was distracted by Lance. His table shook from the motion of his knees—he kept crossing and uncrossing his legs and jiggling his feet. He was a ball of nervous tics and I wasn't much better.

Finally, Brady came back, readjusting his ponytail and taking his damn time walking over. At least he wasn't limping anymore, but I was too impatient to manage even a greeting for him.

"On break," I barked before he had his apron tied. I kept my own apron on and hurried over to Lance's table.

"What is it?" I plopped down opposite Lance.

"We should go upstairs." He shoved his unread psych textbook back into his bag.

"Tell me right now." I couldn't manage the walk back to the stairs. The way he was holding himself and the wariness in his eyes terrified me.

"Okay." He bent back to his bag. "I got mail today. An e-mail actually."

"Yeah?" I knew the wait for acceptance letters had been driving him nuts. "Bad news?"

"No." His hand shook as he put a hand out on the table. "I got into USC and University of Miami and San Francisco State."

"Your top three schools?" I smiled so wide it hurt. Pride, this lovely, lush emotion, anesthetized my nerve endings. "You got into USC? The number-one physical therapy program? You did it!"

"Yeah."

"What did your folks say?" I grabbed his hand and squeezed.

"I haven't told them yet. I wanted to tell you first."

"Really?" It made me ridiculously happy to be the first to hear his good news—but something was off. He wasn't smiling, wasn't acting like he'd just won the graduate school lottery. Instead, he looked like a condemned prisoner who'd run out his last appeal.

"Why aren't you happy?" I didn't look around the shop before I stroked his arm. Only thing on my mind was how to make him feel better. "Isn't this what you wanted? You've talked about USC since we met."

"That's just it. I'm going to turn them down. I got into Pacific University here a week ago. Before the USC letter arrived, I'd already decided to accept the offer."

My brain felt fuzzy, pride and happiness wearing off, leaving cold panic. My center of balance lurched, the same way it did as soon as I stepped onto a boat.

"No," I said firmly. "You're not. You wanted a few years of sunshine. You wanted to go to the best graduate program in the country. What's changed?"

"You know what's changed. Stop playing dumb."

"Nothing's changed. You are *not* going to turn down USC for me." I gripped the table edge, trying to stop the seasickness washing over me.

"When the letter hadn't come yet and I'd decided to be okay with staying here, I was so . . . happy. I realized that maybe I don't want USC as much as I want to be with you."

"Lance." He'd been right—we really did need to be upstairs for this. But I didn't trust my legs to stand. Wasn't sure I could even trust my voice. My dearest, most secret desire was a reprieve on the August end date. He was dangling it in front of me with his earnest words and hopeful smile. And it was the one thing I couldn't let him give.

"This was never supposed to be anything more than a fling," I said in a desperate whisper, my voice wobbling. "You can't give up your future for a fling."

"It's not a fling." He shook his head. "We keep pretending, but we both know it's not." He paused, looking right at me. I felt like I was a fish, trapped behind glass in a too-small tank, no place to hide from his knowing gaze.

I couldn't say anything. Couldn't even nod or shake my head.

"We have something . . . special. And you said you wouldn't consider doing the distance thing. I'm not giving up my dream. I'm just . . . adjusting it."

My stomach heaved, the coffee I'd been sipping all afternoon rising in my throat. In his words, I heard an echo of my younger self when I'd "adjusted" my vision of the future to meet Randy's. I saw myself at twenty-four, in love with living on the coast, in love with my handsome older chef, and questioning what I wanted to do with my life. Time sped up, ten years passing in the blink of an eye. I saw myself struggling to manage the constant stream of customers, up late testing recipes, trying to teach myself enough to stay afloat. Saw Randy morphing and changing. Saw Randy's approval becoming a stingy, rationed thing. Saw us fighting about stupid stuff, saw me getting more bitter and withdrawn with each year.

I couldn't let that happen to Lance. Lance was sunshine and dancing to Katy Perry and sips of cherry soda. I couldn't be the reason he woke up ten years from now and didn't recognize himself or his life. My legs tensed, the muscles finally remembering what they were for. I could *not* fucking stay sitting a second longer.

"I can't do this here." I stood, making my chair drag along the tile floor.

The knitters all turned their heads. I felt the weight of their gaze like a slap. Like they knew how tempted I was to let this beautiful boy hijack his future. I was vaguely aware of Lance saying my name, but I couldn't stop my feet. I headed through the kitchen door. I stumbled around the prep table and slumped against the sink, letting the coolness of the metal leech into my bones. My stomach heaved again, and for a horrible second I thought I might retch for real.

The kitchen door swung open and I knew it was Lance, but I couldn't look up at him. I focused instead on his footsteps against the linoleum, counting the steps until he was next to me.

"Is here better?" His hand hovered above my back, barely skimming along my flannel shirt. Didn't matter—I still felt his touch like a steel blade.

"No." Actually, it was worse. The spectacle and audience of the front room was gone, but back here there was no escaping my churning emotions. And every corner of the room held memories—his first delivery, helping out with the sink disaster, all the times he'd hung out and talked to me while I worked. So much evidence of us being real and good and everything Lance wanted to believe in.

But I couldn't let him continue to believe—couldn't let him deceive himself into thinking that this was worth giving up his dream.

"There's no point in your staying." I didn't have to try to make my voice harsh; each word felt like gravel.

"No point? I love you."

The fish tank I'd felt trapped in exploded, glass nicking every nerve ending I had, icy water gushing over my heart. All the emotions

I'd been trying to keep at bay came rushing in. He'd been dancing toward this the other night, but I had hoped, lamely, that he wouldn't be able to find the words.

"You don't. You're young. This is all hormones and good sex."

"You love me, too." He said it like an accusation. "You can play the young card all you want, but I know love. I'm surrounded by love—my folks, my bosses at the bakery, my grandparents, my cousin Vic. I know what love looks like. And when you look at me—I *see* it. And I know that me leaving has been holding you back—"

*Oh, hell.* Had he really been spinning it that way in his head? "You leaving has been the *only* reason I've let myself indulge in this . . . fantasy."

"Oh." His face crumpled, like I'd socked him in the stomach.

"Look." I rubbed his arm. "You might think you love me, but you love my ink and you think I'm hung. Attraction isn't love. But someday, you'll—"

"If you tell me one more time about the forever guy I'm supposedly going to meet at school, I swear I'll deck you. I don't love you because you're hot. I love you because . . ." His face screwed up, and I couldn't tell if he was thinking or trying not to cry. "Because you're a fish who turned into a rock—"

I let out a shaky laugh.

"It's like this—you'd like to be out swimming in the ocean, and you're still not exactly sure how you ended up *here*. But you're not pining for your ocean—you've forged a whole life for yourself. You're the rock for everyone around you—your employees, the customers, the suppliers, even me. You're the guy they can all count on—even if maybe you'd rather not be. But inside? You're still the fish. And you prop me up with sandwiches and places to study and reminders to sleep, but you never judge me or try to change me. You give me this quiet, safe spot to recharge. And sometimes I get lucky, and in that quiet place we make together, I get a glimpse of your fish. That's what I love about you—when you let your guard down and I see the fish behind the rock."

I took long shuddery inhalations through my nose. Fish, no matter how mysterious or exciting, were a hell of a lot of work, and I refused to saddle him with all that responsibility right as he was ready to take flight. He was starlight, and I wasn't going to be the heavy rock tethering him to the earth.

"I care about you, too. And that's why I can't let you do this. I care about you too much to let you fuck up your future."

"Well, luckily for both of us, you don't get control over my signature. I'm going to choose us—"

"No." I dug my nails into my palm, hard. "Whether you choose USC or Miami or Oregon, we're done in August. So you might as well go with your top pick."

"Then we're done now. No waiting for August. No 'savoring the moment.' Fuck memories, Chris. I want *you*. I'm not going to spend the next four or five months watching you play martyr to my future. Not when we could have one together."

"Okay." I had to force the word out around all the other words in my throat. The promises I wouldn't let myself make. The begging for a little more time. The pleading for him to see how this was right. The declarations of love that wouldn't change a damn thing.

We stood there staring at each other, each second dragging out like a decade that wouldn't ever be.

"I've got books and crap upstairs. I'm going to get them," he said. *Please stop me*, his eyes said. *Please say something.*

"Did you drive or bus today?" I asked.

*I love you, I love you, I love you*, I tried to say with my eyes, knowing it was probably my last chance to do it.

"What the fuck? Why do you care whether I have to haul my shit by bus or not?"

"I care about you. That's not going to stop. I . . . I'm going to miss you. Like crazy."

"You have no idea how much it hurts me to hear that. You're going to *miss* me? Then why the hell won't you fight for me? Fight for us?"

"Because I love you." My voice broke. "And I know what it means to sacrifice something for a relationship. And I'm not going to let you compromise on your future."

"You don't love me. If you loved me, you would want to be with me. Stubborn bastard." With that, he fled up the stairs.

I wasn't sure how long I stood there, white-knuckling the sink to keep from chasing after him. The worst was knowing he wanted me to. Hell, he was probably up there grabbing his stuff in super-slow motion, hoping I'd come up. That was what I loved about him—he was such an optimist and he wanted to believe in people. I knew he believed in me—believed in us. And that was why I had to do the right thing by him and let him go.

"You okay?" Brady poked his head in the kitchen door.

"No. Go away." My words were way too curt, but it was that or unload on the poor kid.

I was never going to be okay again. My insides felt scoured out. Nothing anyone said or did could change the fact that I was going to spend the rest of my damn life missing Lance.

# Chapter 14

I got righteously drunk that night on a bottle of scotch I'd been saving. World-ending soul suck seemed as good an occasion as any. Or at least it did at eleven p.m., when I was faced with the prospect of sleeping in a bed that still smelled like Lance. At five a.m., with the worst hangover of my life, each footstep down the stairs made my head pound.

I did the opening prep on autopilot—seriously groggy, cutting-corners autopilot.

Around six, Brady showed up, coming in the front entrance. He waited patiently under the front canopy for me to unlock for him. Outside, the weather was dark and nasty with a heavy drizzle. He stamped his feet off on the big mat.

"You look like crap," he said as he grabbed an apron from the hooks behind the coffee bar.

"What are you doing here? Thought it was supposed to be Trina." I arranged trays of pastries for the glass display case next to the coffee bar.

"Sick. She texted you but said you didn't reply."

*Fuck.* I'd turned my phone off last night, afraid that if Lance tried to call I'd lose all my resolve and end up begging for forgiveness.

"Hell." I dropped a turnover on the floor.

"No offense, boss, but you're kind of a mess." Brady stepped back from me, like he was afraid to get a good whiff of me.

"Heh." I made a noncommittal sound, even though I totally was a sloppy, dragged-out mess. My center of gravity kept tilting, like the worst of the hangover hadn't even hit yet. Hell, I still might even have been slightly buzzed.

"Go back to bed." Brady took the tray from me. "Go sleep it off. I can handle the morning shift."

"Nah. Can't leave you guys—"

"We'll be fine. Marty and Alyssa will be in soon. This place can run without you for a morning."

"Okay." My head hurt too much to argue.

"And maybe when you wake up, you'll figure out how to fix things. You guys are good together."

"Not talking about this with you. And no, not fixable."

"You were happier with him than you ever were with Randy."

"Thanks." *For making things worse.* I rubbed my temples, trying to keep my brain in my head. Heading up the stairs, I felt adrift, like I'd swam so far away from happy, I'd never find my way back. Lance thought I was a fish and a rock and all sorts of pretty metaphors, but truth was, I would have given anything in that moment to be an ostrich.

When I woke up from my much-needed nap, I did something I almost never did and made a pot of coffee in my own kitchen. I wasn't ready to face anyone yet. Dug out my French press and some single-origin beans I had in a sampler one of the local roasters had sent over. Took my coffee with a chaser of painkillers for my head.

Still walking slowly, I went to feed the fish. The new betta fish bobbed up to the surface as soon as I sprinkled food in his tank. Likewise, the Calico Moor twins chased their flakes with the sort of vigor I couldn't summon. But Scruffy was nowhere to be found in the big tank—not by the castle and not in the feeding frenzy at the top. Finally, I discovered him at the bottom of the tank, not swimming. I'd owned fish enough years to know that these things happened, but I still got choked up as I disposed of him and readied his friends for a full water change.

I took my time cleaning the tank. Dragged stuff to the bathroom for a full rinse, cleaned the castle and the rocks. Paid extra attention to the filters. I clung to the task, every single bit of its minutiae, like it was a life raft keeping me afloat.

I couldn't lose any more fish. Sometimes fish deaths came in clumps—something in the pH of the water or an illness- -sometimes they were just a fluke. I needed Scruffy to be a fluke, needed my happy little Calico Moors to keep swimming, but I couldn't shake the feeling that I'd done something to cause Scruffy's death. Had I forgotten to check the water last night? Been too preoccupied to notice what Lance was seeing?

Scruffy was my oldest fish—eight years. He'd started as a tiny guy, swallowed up by my giant tank, but quickly grew to a solid nine inches. He was there through the good middle years with Randy and the bitter end, and through Lance. Randy had never gotten my fish thing; he'd thought some of my tats were cool, but he thought keeping fish was a bit weird and never hesitated to tell me so. But Lance had always accepted my marine fascination as a part of me—asking questions about the fish and what they ate and what they liked. He liked to trace my tats with his fingers while we made love. And he'd noticed Scruffy was feeling off long before I did.

I missed Lance's little observations already—the way he'd have out-of-the-box ideas about routine things. He saw my life with fresh eyes. Made me miss things I hadn't thought about in years, made me want foolish things I'd always disdained. I tried to channel his optimistic spirit; I *had* to believe that he would be happier in the end. Down in my soul, I believed that someone better for Lance was out there. Someone who would come along at the right moment, after he'd had his adventures. Someone young and bright like him, who could make him laugh. And I hated him already. My fists clenched. Pessimism won the battle for my brain. Lance would move on—he *had* to. But me? I never would.

When I finally worked up enough energy to head downstairs, I caught sight of the bakery truck through the window next to the service entrance.

*Oh, fuck.* I wanted to race back upstairs. I went to the kitchen door, intending to take the coward's way out and have Brady handle it, but he and the other baristas were juggling a line six deep.

*Be a man. You can do this. You don't have to say anything.* I gave myself the world's worst pep talk as I opened the back door to discover not Lance but his scowling hulk of a cousin.

"Lance offered to come help me paint trim the next three weekends if I would take this delivery this week. You wouldn't happen to know anything about that?" His glare hit me like a search beam, finding all my inadequacies and failings.

"Not your business." I wasn't going to be intimidated by Vic.

"You know, you're lucky you're such a *valued*"—he spat the word out like eggshells in his pancake batter—"customer of the bakery. Otherwise I'd have to call you out."

"Don't let that stop you." I pulled myself up taller. Hell, I hoped he would hit me. I'd almost welcome the pain.

"You hurt Lance. He looked like he hadn't slept when he came in this afternoon, and he could barely get the words out to ask me to cover. I should deck you for that alone." He stepped up into my personal space, but he didn't hit me.

"Go right ahead. I deserve it." I stood my ground even as my jaw started to brace for impact—Vic was ripped like an action star.

"He's a good kid—"

"I know. And that's the thing. He's a *kid*. And I'm trying like hell to do the right thing by him, so either hit me or back the hell off."

"Tell me about this right thing." Vic's face softened, and he stepped back to lounge against some of the shelving. I hoped it could stand up to his bulky frame. His big brown eyes—almost identical to Lance's—said he was perfectly happy to hang out there all day.

I made a show of putting away the bakery boxes. Two could play this waiting game.

"You're all Lance has been able to talk about for weeks now," Vic said much more amiably now.

"Really?"

"You know Lance. That boy can't keep his mouth shut about things he likes—school, his friends, you. I'm surprised you're not in more of the pics he posts."

"*Fuck.* I never wanted him to get in so deep. This was just supposed to be a fling. And I *knew* it was wrong from the get-go."

"Hey." Vic held up his hands. "No judgment. You're an ass for breaking his heart, but if you mean the age difference thing, I've got almost a decade on my boyfriend."

"Doesn't it feel *wrong*?"

Vic glowered at me, his eyebrows cinching together. "You insulting me? No, it doesn't feel *wrong*. It's the most right thing I've ever had in my life."

There was a sureness in his gaze, an absolute certainty that he was supposed to be with this other person. Like he *knew* he was good for that person, too. My ribs ached, tired of holding my throbbing heart.

I had certainty, too; so much of it I felt bloated with the knowledge I was doing what I *had* to by cutting Lance free.

"Well, I want better than me for Lance. Okay? I'm sure whatever you've got going works for you, but Lance is young. Still in school. He doesn't need to be tied to someone like me." And then it all came tumbling out: Lance's getting into USC and his wanting to stay in Oregon and how I was *not* going to let him screw up his future.

"Fuck. I didn't mean to unload on you," I finished lamely. "I'm so, so sorry I hurt him, but he's going to get over this."

"Yeah. Probably," Vic said, rubbing his chin. "But you won't. And what if you're wrong?"

"I'm not." I leaned on the counter, letting the edge dig into my hip.

"Look." Vic's tone had gentled considerably. "I don't know if Lance has told you, but our family's had a lot of loss the last few years. And if there's one thing that death has taught me, it's that there are no second chances."

"Which is why—"

"You want the best for Lance. I get it now. I really do. But you have to ask yourself, at the end of the day, when you're looking back at your life, are you going to be all smug and self-righteous that you let him go? Or are you going to wish like hell you'd tried to make it work?"

"It doesn't—"

Vic held up a hand. "Don't answer right now. Think about it. Really think. And then think about whether it's possible you're wrong. And think about what Lance's answer would be."

"He doesn't know what he wants." I ripped a hand through my hair. "He's young and—"

"Now you're making me mad again. Lance is the smartest person in our family. You don't trust him to know his own mind? Don't trust him to make good choices? Maybe you're right, and you don't deserve him."

"I don't," I said lamely. I was going to have bruises from the counter tomorrow, but I needed its pressure to keep me upright. Lord knew my spine wasn't up to the task.

"Here." Vic fished a piece of paper out of his pocket, set it on the counter. "Wasn't sure if I was going to give you this, but I suppose it's *possible* you might manage to dig your head out of your ass. Here's his address. He tell you about his birthday?"

"Yeah." I squeezed my eyes shut.

"You're going to be seeing me, not him, all week. That's the deal I worked out with him. Turns out I really hate painting trim. But Chris?"

"Yeah?"

"Think about what I said. People want to believe life is full of second chances. But that's not really the case. Sometimes we only get one shot to get it right."

I kept my eyes shut, rubbing the bridge of my nose. I heard the door slam, heard the truck start, and I still kept them shut. I didn't have to be told to think about Vic's words; they were already a part of the jumbled mess of thoughts in my brain.

I tried to imagine telling Lance yes, letting him give up USC to stay in Oregon. It wasn't a *terrible* school—still top 100 or something—but it wasn't Lance's dream. We'd have a good run of months, but what would happen when he'd hear about some seminar at USC? Or when the fall came and he was stuck here for another rainy season? Wouldn't he eventually come to resent me?

Then I imagined doing the distance thing. The issue wasn't whether I could trust him—one of my favorite things about Lance was how darn loyal he was. No, the issue was him carrying around his cell phone, glancing down at it when he should be admiring the sunshine around him. Turning down drinks with new friends because he had a Skype date with me. Rushing back on break instead of going with his buddies on a trip to Mexico.

I wasn't sure what miracle Vic thought I could work. The only options I saw were ones bound to end in heartache.

# Chapter 15

"I'm out of here, boss," Brady said, coming into the kitchen, where I was doing the Saturday prep work.

"Fine." I didn't look up from the bread I was dicing.

"Bakery delivery come?" Brady asked carefully.

"Yup. Vic came by a few hours ago." I pointed at the metal shelves holding the bakery boxes. Vic had glowered at me and shook his head but saved any more lectures. Didn't matter. I saw the judgment in his eyes, same as I saw in Brady's. They both thought I was an ass for hurting Lance. And I was. I totally was. Just hell if I could see a way out.

"You okay?" Brady asked with a heavy subtext of *why haven't you fixed this yet?*

"Yeah. Told you I don't want to talk about . . . things." I wasn't sure why Brady was riding me so hard to talk. Brady's personal life was locked up tighter than the ancient safe in the basement. His limp was better these days, but there was a tightness to his expression. I wasn't sure whether pain or personal stuff was plaguing him, but I tried to give him all the hours he was clamoring for.

"But maybe you should talk to someone? Like what about Robby?"

"Maybe," I said, just to shut Brady up.

Brady was my longest current employee, but before him, my best employee had been my friend Robby. He had his own coffee cart now, a bustling business in a downtown office building. I hadn't seen him in forever, though, other than in passing on Sunday mornings. He had a boyfriend now: a nerdy, bookish type who made him sickeningly happy. No way on earth was I dragging my relationship problems over to him.

"Okay." Brady gave a long sigh. "Whatever. Maybe you can find a way to be something other than rain clouds and mud puddles to-morrow?"

"I'll try," I said, even though I knew it was an impossibility. To-morrow was Lance's birthday. I knew Vic was pulling for me to do some big Hollywood gesture, like show up with an apology. Instead, it was more likely I'd drag myself through the shifts, same as I'd been doing all week, snapping at random people.

I watched Brady head for the service exit. He was right—the em-ployees really did deserve better from me. For the hundredth time, I thought about Vic's questions. I thought about who I'd been before Lance—and who I was becoming now without him. And I thought about who I was with him. I *liked* myself more with Lance. God, that stung to admit. *Which are you going to regret more?* Vic's words rang in my ears for the next few hours.

Working on bread pudding alone in my kitchen made me miss Lance even more. The silence was deafening. No music. No dancing. I added rum and raisins to the mixture for the pudding. He'd brought so much *new* to my life—made me look at my gray, stagnant routine and change things up, simply because I could. Because it was fun. Or at least it was fun when there was Lance egging me on. Alone in my kitchen? Not so much.

Glancing at my cell phone, I sighed. I'd expected him to text at least once. Ask me to reconsider. Send me a cryptic photo. Wonder if we could still be friends. *Something.* But ever since he'd walked out—okay, ever since I'd pretty much shoved him out—it had been radio silence. Maybe I was the only one in agony. Maybe he was . . . relieved. And if so, I should be *happy* for him, right?

But I wasn't. As I finished my work, the need to see him over-whelmed me. Just see him. Glimpse his face. See whether he was happy or depressed or merely existing, same as me. I had a stupid idea, one that was probably going to end up with me shitfaced and alone at the end of the night, but I had a feeling Lance's friends would drag him to Slaughters for his birthday. I could go, stick to the crowd. One look. That was all I wanted.

Two hours later, I still knew it was a dumb idea, but my feet and heart refused to listen, and I found myself at Slaughters. I did two shots of whiskey at the bar before I even looked around—bypassing sipping and going straight for the nerve-reducing, brain-loosening buzz.

Slaughters wasn't huge by any means, but it still took me a bit to make my not-stalking rounds.

"What are you doing here?"

*Shit.* He was right behind me. And he was alone, not with his posse of friends, though I assumed they were around somewhere. Unless he was here on the make, and *that* thought was enough to make me want another six shots.

"I'm not sure," I said truthfully. He looked tired—new lines around his eyes that hadn't been there a week ago. But he also looked good enough to lick in skin-tight black jeans and a close-fitting red T-shirt with the word "Birthday" in rhinestones. "Lots of people buying you drinks?"

"Some." His usually lush mouth was a hard line.

"Can I?" My buzz made this seem like a splendid idea.

"Why? So you can tell me again how I'm screwing up my future?"

"No. I didn't come here to do that." Someone jostled me from behind, pushing us closer together.

"Why did you come, Chris?" He got right up in my personal space, getting a fistful of my flannel shirt, pressing us together.

"I wanted to see if you're okay."

"I'm fine." He mouthed my jaw, each swipe of his lips going straight to my dick. "See?"

"Yeah, you are." My head tipped back.

"You come here so we can fuck and then you can tell me about the guy I'm really supposed to be with?" He ground his hips into me. His breath smelled like rum and fruit, and I wanted to drink him down.

"No."

"No games. I'm too drunk and you look too damn good and you smell like you." He looked up at me through watery eyes.

"No, I didn't come to tell you about other people. I came here to fight." A crisp new certainty pushed past my buzz.

"Good. I'd like to fight you." He bit my neck.

I pushed on his shoulders. "I mean I came to fight *for* you."

I didn't know until right that second, but as soon as I said it, my bones accepted its truth. I finally had an answer to the question that had plagued me all week—I still had no clue how things would play out, but when my days came to an end, I wanted to remember that I'd fought for him. Fought for us.

# Chapter 16

"Well, damn, Chris, why didn't you say so?" Lance nuzzled into my neck before claiming my mouth in a searing kiss. He kissed sloppy, seriously buzzed. A nicer guy would back off, realize he was too drunk for any sort of conversation, let alone sex. But his mouth on mine felt too damn good. I felt like I'd been starved for his kiss for a decade.

"What the fuck took you so long?" He pulled back from the kiss to glare at me. "You think you can just come here, kiss me—"

"You kissed me," I pointed out.

"Whatever. I am seriously so *angry* with you. I can't decide whether I want to fuck you through a mattress or walk the hell away from you."

"Don't walk away." I pulled him toward me, lined up my mouth with his ear. "You want to fuck me, beautiful?"

A spark of want shot through me. For all the sex we'd had, we'd never tried it that way. He hadn't asked, and it wasn't something I craved enough to ask for—even with Randy, me bottoming had been a carefully negotiated event, usually after I'd toked. But I didn't feel so careful with Lance.

"Yes." He sucked on my ear before releasing it. "But I'm still going to be angry after."

After we fucked, we'd both be sober and screwed in more ways than one. Sex wasn't going to solve everything between us.

"Would it help if I said I'm sorry—"

"No." He shut me up with a hard kiss. We kissed long enough that we got a few catcalls from people nearby. It felt like I was trying to crawl inside him, find the warm spot where his feelings for me hid.

"Take me home." His voice was commanding, a harsh edge to his words. And strangely, it did something for me. Made him seem older, more sure of himself. Made me feel more . . . legitimate in my want of him. Like he wasn't the twinky eye candy he'd first appeared—I'd seen the substance behind the delicious frosting—and it was this *man* I wanted. I was desperate to see the person he'd become, and yet I knew we might only have tonight.

Because I'd been pretty sure I'd get plastered at the bar, I'd left my bike at home. We caught a taxi back to my place. We were quiet in the cab, not even holding hands. But as soon as I locked the door, he was on me. Kissing me hard, he nipped my lower lip with his teeth.

"I might hate you a little. I'm not sure." His words didn't stop him from tugging me down the hallway to the bedroom. Shoving me against the wall, his hands tangled in my bushy hair.

"I love you." I tried to slow his kisses down. "And for what it's worth, I kind of hate me, too."

"You should." He pulled and tugged at my clothes, clumsy and insistent. I countered by undressing him slowly, reveling in each inch of remembered skin. When we were both naked, he pushed me back onto the bed and we tumbled in a heap.

"Oh, God, I missed you. And I hate that I missed you." His voice broke, and I pulled him in for another kiss.

"Missed you too." I inhaled against his neck—I couldn't get enough of his scent. Slightly sweaty, a little bit of rum, a little bit of sweetness, and a whole lot of Lance. "You have no idea how much."

He sat abruptly and leaned toward the nightstand, his bleary eyes narrowing as he focused on the task of opening the drawer and retrieving lube and condoms. He tossed the goods on the mattress and looked down at me, his gaze speculative. I grabbed a pillow and shoved it under my ass. If we were doing this, I wanted to be able to watch his face.

He ran a hand down my chest, then paused, his hand stilling on my stomach.

"I thought I could do this angry, but I'm . . ." His mouth twisted. "Are we going to work things out? Because I don't think I can handle anything that hurts worse than this week. I need to know we're going to be okay."

"We're going to be okay." I reached up and stroked his face. I wanted to believe my own words. "We're going to be more than okay."

I touched all of him that I could reach, all that warm olive skin I'd spent all week missing.

"I love you." I wasn't ever going to get tired of telling him that. "And right now, I really want you to fuck me."

"*Chris.*" Balancing on his arms, he kissed me desperately again. "Um . . ." He licked his lips.

"Yeah?"

"I'm not sure . . ." His eyes darted around the room. "I've never . . ."

"But you want to?"

"Oh, yeah." He swallowed hard.

Letting a drunk virgin top fuck me probably wasn't my sanest move, but such was my love for him—crazy and reckless.

"Here." I grabbed the lube, got a generous amount on my fingers and extra around my rim. I wasn't trying to give him a show, but he inhaled sharply, his expression going hot and eager.

Shifting position, he moved to drop a line of kisses down my stomach, heading for my cock. He swallowed me down at the same moment I got a finger inside my hole. My nerve endings crackled, sparks shooting from deep inside me. Sucking me in deep as I worked myself open, he moaned around my cock.

"Yeah. Suck me." I gave myself up to the dueling sensations of his mouth and my fingers.

"Fuck." Way too quickly, my balls gave a warning tingle. Coming like this would be hot as hell, but it wouldn't get him what he wanted—what I wanted to give him. I pushed on his shoulders. "Too close. Ready now."

"Okay." Kneeling between my legs, he folded his muscular legs under himself gracefully, the big hand on my thigh almost timid. He fumbled the condom on before he gently—oh so gently—pushed my legs back. I bit back a smile. He was so damn earnest. Then his dick rubbed against mine and my smile fled in a rush of heat. Frowning, he adjusted his body, this time rubbing all along my cleft, skimming across my sensitized nerve endings.

"Like this." I got a hand on his dick, guided him forward. Cocking his hips, he slowly entered me. The awkward position probably wasn't ideal for a virgin top, but I wouldn't have traded being able to watch his eyes. They sparkled as he reached some understanding, pushing my hand away. His brown eyes darkened, going almost black when he worked his broad head in. The pinch was tight and deep and far better than I remembered. I locked gazes with him, trying to reassure him that this felt amazing, not wanting to speak and break this spell. His eyes went wide as he tried a tentative first thrust. All his wonder played out in his eyes. I worked to relax my muscles, my eyes still on his.

Seeing his uncertainty fade away was like watching a sunrise—the gradual build followed by a sudden confidence, like he'd been doing this forever. Then he was fucking me in earnest; slow, sure strokes that lit me up from the inside. But this wasn't so much about sensation for me as it was about feeling close to him—closer than I ever had to another human.

Everything between us seemed to be coming out, one thrust at a time—every hour we'd spent apart, every nasty word we'd uttered, every drop of love we'd been holding back.

"Missed you. Missed you so much." He squeezed his eyes shut, closing that window into his emotions.

"Me too. Couldn't . . . live." I put my hand against his chest. It was slippery with sweat and more than a little fuzzy—I loved that he hadn't resumed waxing during our time apart. Loved him. "Loved you. Whole time."

"Never again." His eyes opened, vulnerable and needy and breaking my heart all over again.

"Never." I would have promised him anything right then.

"Tell me. Tell me again." His eyes opened, bottomless chocolate pools.

"I love you. I love you. I love you."

"Other part."

"I'm never letting you go. Ever." I hung onto his torso, tight. So tight.

"Oh hell . . . I'm close."

"Yeah. Ride that edge, beautiful." I loved watching him get close. His face squinched up, his movements getting more erratic. Felt so good inside, knowing I was the reason.

"You're . . . not . . ." He panted, his teeth digging into his bottom lip between each word.

"Wanna watch you go. Come for me."

He held still for a long moment, breathing hard. He got a hand on my cock, but I pushed it away. I didn't want the distraction—all I wanted was to focus completely on him, on what this connection meant, on the energy flowing between us. His arms and thighs trembled, but still he held on to that last thread of control.

I wanted it to snap.

"Want your mouth afterward." I met his eyes, trying to reassure him that I was in this, too, that this . . . union was as good for me as it was for him. "Come on. Let go."

"Yes. Yes." He started moving again, harder now. "Love you." It became his mantra, chanted over and over as his face froze into a mask of pleasure.

"That's it." God, I wanted to see him go, wanted to feel it. His thighs slapped hard against mine, his muscles straining. Eyes locked as tight as our bodies, his hand sought my face, cupping my jaw.

"*Fuck.*" He came on a loud moan, his hips stuttering as he rode it out. To my surprise, my body tensed, his tremors pushing waves of pleasure through me—almost like a mini-orgasm. A strange peace, one that transcended lust, blanketed me. It felt like a space had opened up inside me—a secret room full of new emotions.

He pulled out, a bit too abruptly, and I groaned.

"Sorry."

"I'm not." I pulled him toward me, intending to kiss him, but he wiggled free of my grasp, licking the sweat off my stomach on his way to my dick. The memory of him moving in me and what his face had looked like, combined with his hot mouth, got me right to the edge again. He used his hand on the base while his lips slipped back and forth on all the sensitive spots.

"Gonna . . ."

He moaned around me in response, his free hand fondling my balls, and that was all it took before I was convulsing in the hardest orgasm of my life, my shoulders lifting off the bed with the force of it.

"Oh, wow." He released me with a *plop* and then flopped next to me. He moved in, like he was going to kiss me, then hesitated. I pulled him the rest of the way toward me, claiming his mouth in a sloppy oh-my-god-that-was-good kiss.

"That was . . . totally not what I expected." He smiled almost shyly.

"You liked topping, yeah?"

"Yeah." He nodded slowly. "It was . . . intense. Really, really intense. Did *you* like it?"

"You were great." I patted his face. "Felt so close to you."

"Is it . . . different with us?"

"You mean is this just great sex? You know it's more than that." I wrapped an arm around him. "And no, it's never been this good with anyone else. Ever."

"Then why—why could you just let it go?" He sat up. "That's what I don't get."

Ah. We'd reached the sobered-up conversation part of the evening.

"Because I love you so much. I thought I was doing the right thing."

"I'm still angry. I don't *want* to be angry, but I am. I hate that I was falling in love with you and you wanted to discount that and push me away."

"I'm sorry. It's . . . I got scared. You have your whole life in front of you, and you deserve the freedom to discover yourself. I'm not sure this can last—not sure it *should*—and we're both going to end up hurting so much worse. . . ." All my fears flooded out.

"Why can't it last? Why can't you believe in us?" His voice was thin and strained.

"You'll wise up eventually and end up wanting different things." I picked at some lint on my quilt.

"So that's really it, isn't it? It's not about where I go to school. You don't trust me to stay in love with you. *That's* what this is all about." He pulled the quilt from my hands.

"Yeah," I whispered, my voice small. He'd whittled down everything between us to the one truth I hadn't wanted to confront.

He thought for a long moment, chewing his lip. "My favorite color is red. Has been since I was two and insisted on a raincoat that color. I've wanted to be a physical therapist since I was eight. I hate Indian food. I hated it the first time I tried it, and despite my friends insisting I keep trying it, I still don't like it. I'm not exactly a changeable guy, Chris."

Heat spread up my face and down my limbs, chasing away the chill of doubt. I *wanted* to trust him, but my brain still wobbled.

"Which is why you shouldn't change your dream for me."

"I'm not—"

"But what I *do* know is I can't live without you. And that we should probably figure out the right thing to do together."

That had been my biggest mistake—I'd tried to do the choosing for both of us. I kept trying to shove him in the slot marked "kid," even as my heart and brain knew better.

"Maybe there isn't one right thing. Maybe the *only* right thing is us being together." He grabbed my hand.

I nodded. "It's not that simple for me." I took a deep breath, not sure if I could get this out, but I needed him to understand where I was coming from. "When I met Randy, I was trying to decide between masters programs. My seasickness wasn't getting better, and I wasn't crazy about the politics of working at the aquarium. But I was trying to figure out if maybe a masters in science education might work for me—"

"You teach?" He blinked. "I didn't think you liked kids."

"Don't laugh. Back then, I kind of liked the school groups that came around the aquarium. Knew I loved living on the coast and knew I wanted to figure out something long-term to do with science. I had this small inheritance from my grandmother, but I wanted to make sure what direction I was headed before I picked my next step. Then Randy came along, and he *was* sure. He had this dream with a whole plan. He knew his direction. I loved him." I looked at Lance, needing him to get that. I *had* loved once. I had believed and trusted and all that good stuff. And it had still gone sideways.

He nodded and squeezed my hand.

"So I hitched my dream to his. Left the coast. Pooled our resources, bought this place. I let his dream become my dream. And that worked."

"Until it didn't." Lance nodded, far too wise. "But I'm not him. Or you."

"I get that. But what I'm trying to say is, I love you. Far more than I ever loved him. And it eats me up to think of you giving up *anything* for me. That's why I let you go. Because you *do* have direction. I'm in awe of your focus."

"You're in awe . . . of me?"

"Yeah. And I want you to have everything you've wanted."

"That includes you." He poked me in the chest. "That's what you don't seem to get. My dream has expanded to include you."

"I know. And that's why . . ." I took a huge gulp of air. The extra option I'd been seeking all week came into focus, gut punching me with its simplicity. "Randy's been bugging me about a buyout ever since we split. I think I'll take it."

"No." Lance scooted off the bed. "You are absolutely not giving up your coffee shop for me."

I followed him off the bed and tried to put an arm around him, but he shrugged me off.

"But see, that's just it. This isn't *my* coffee shop. It wasn't *my* dream. It's always going to be a part of who I am, but this isn't *me*."

"You'd do that for me? You'd move with me to California? Just so we could be together?" He turned to face me.

"You were willing to stay here," I pointed out. "How is that different?"

"This is . . ." He shook his head. "Wouldn't that be the same mistake you made before? I don't want *you* to hitch your dream to mine and then regret it like you did before."

I hadn't really thought of it like that. The image had arrived in my brain like a brightly wrapped present I could give Lance. But I opened the box and let myself poke around a bit. Pictured a future with him. I laid the choices out in my head. I pictured staying here and being happy. I tried really hard to picture *happy* and not him all resentful. Then I pictured us in California—something I hadn't really allowed myself to do before.

"Maybe letting you go off to your dream would let me search for mine. Maybe it would be for both of us."

I wrapped my arms around him, and this time he came willingly.

"Man." He took several deep breaths. "I still don't know—"

"We don't have to decide right now. I've got to be up in two hours and we're both still half-buzzed."

"I just want to make sure that *neither* of us is giving up more than we should. I just want you to be as sure as I am," he whispered into my chest.

"I am." But I got what he was saying. He was still working past his anger. He wasn't sure he could trust me again. I'd hurt him again and again by keeping him at arm's length. And this was a huge thing to spring on him. A huge thing to spring on both of us really—I felt as wrung out as he looked. I rubbed his back and tugged him back to the bed. I pulled the covers over both of us and cuddled him close.

"You figure out what *your* dream is and we'll figure out a way to make it align with mine," he said, nuzzling into my chest.

And for the first time in years, I was able to picture a dream. Not even a dream really; more like the glimmer of a possibility. The idea that I might find a dream, one that didn't involve spreadsheets and next week's deliveries and dealing with Randy. The idea that I might find my way back to the person I'd been—or the person I could be. With Lance, it seemed like a world of possibilities had opened.

# Chapter 17

If anything could convince me to get out of the restaurant life, it was having to open the coffee shop on two hours of sleep and hung over. Though this hangover was way better than my last hangover because I had Lance with me. He insisted on getting up when I did.

"Two fuzzy heads are better than one," he said as I started some coffee for us in the French press. Still didn't have my shirt on and my jeans were undone. Priorities, I had them. I'd start the big carafes for the brunch closer to opening.

"Advil?" I held out the bottle to him.

"Advil always makes me sleepy. I'm weird." He gave me that crooked grin of his. "But maybe we could nap later?"

"Oh, I am all over that idea."

Things between us felt . . . delicate. Fragile. Like we'd been transplanted into a new tank together, but we still had to adjust to the water and figure out the landscape. For the first time it really did feel like we were *together,* but there was still so much left unsaid about what that meant. And there was a certain newness to that togetherness—a naked feeling of not hiding behind friends with benefits any longer.

*Click.* I whirled around to see Lance with his cell phone.

"Smile." He grinned and snapped another picture.

"What are you doing? Documenting how bad I look without sleep?" I stepped toward him, but he scurried away from the kitchen doorway, retreating to the living room. His grin made my tired legs chase after him.

"It's my birthday. And I always take pictures of all my presents."

"Oh." My insides melted like a sundae on a hot day. I brushed a kiss across his lips. "Happy birthday. Keep your picture. But no Instagram, okay?"

"Okay." He fake pouted. "Are you coming tonight?"

"To your party?"

He nodded.

"You still want me to?"

"More than anything," he whispered. "If we're going to do this thing, I want us to be a real couple. I want to be able to tell people you're my boyfriend, and I need you to be okay with that. I . . . I need that more than almost anything we talked about last night. Location doesn't matter if you can't be real with me."

"I want us to be a real couple, too. And yes, I'll be there tonight. After a nap." Pulling him into a tight hug, I let myself own the want that had built up for the last two months—I *did* want to be a couple with him. I wanted to feel him wrapped around me on the bike, wanted to go out to brew pubs together and cuddle up on the couch after. Wanted to kiss him good-bye and hello and tell anyone who objected to fuck off.

He leaned into my hug, then abruptly pulled away, staring at the fish tank across the room. He hurried over, squatting to peer into the big tank from several angles. "Oh my gosh! What happened to Scruffy?"

"Died."

"I'm sorry." He crossed the room in three wide steps before hugging me tight, like I'd lost a family member. He was the only one in my life who'd ever gotten what the fish meant to me.

"Eh. It happens." I didn't know what to do with his sympathy.

"Are you going to get a new guy for your tank? Want me to go with you?"

"First, I have to get a tattoo." My neck got hot and my face flushed. "Then yeah, I'll fish shop."

"A tattoo?" His eyes sprung open wide. Grabbing my arms, he held them out for his inspection. "How didn't I figure it out earlier? How many of your tats are fish you owned?"

I scratched my neck. "Not the dolphin. Never owned one of those. But yeah, most of the rest . . ." I waited for him to tell me what a morbid freak I was.

"That is like the coolest thing ever. I want to hear the story of each one now."

"Like right now? We've got to get downstairs." I laughed. God, I loved him.

"While we work, then. And how do you do it? Do you bring the tattoo artist a picture?"

"If I have one, yeah."

He held up his phone again. "I've got an adorable shot of Scruffy with his castle."

And that's how I knew he really was the perfect guy for me.

Brady practically danced a jig when he saw Lance in the kitchen with me.

"I want a raise," he said by way of greeting.

"What?" I looked up from the tray of toast I was prepping. My two kitchen helpers were running trays out to the buffet. They hadn't lifted an eyebrow at Lance's presence, but Brady was far bolder. He was wearing earrings shaped like fangs and they gave him a predatory air.

"I'm just saying. This must be your lucky day. 'Happy days are here again,'" he sang. "And I figure this is probably the best mood I'll ever see you in. Hence the perfect time to ask you to sprinkle a little love in my direction."

Lance laughed into his apron.

"Careful. My head can't handle much noise. You might find yourself on trash duty," I said to Brady.

"Oh, you don't fool me." He squeezed Lance's shoulders. "You're ecstatic to have this guy back. And now the rest of us can stop walking on eggshells."

"Was he bad?" Lance asked.

"Total and complete cranky bear," Brady said, leaning in all conspiratorial, like I wasn't right there in the room. "Scaring the other baristas. Burning stuff—"

"Right here. And last I checked, still the guy who signs your checks."

"My tiny, pitiful check." Brady grinned hopefully at me.

"Get to work." I couldn't manage stern. I smiled back at him, my skin stretching in an unfamiliar way. As my crew made it through the brunch rush, nostalgia washed over me. Could I really leave this behind? What would I do without the shop? Who would I be?

Then someone dropped a tray of scrambled tofu and the coffee ran low and I slid into damage-control mode. Maybe Lance had a point and there was no right answer here.

At six p.m., freshly showered and feeling more human thanks to a three-hour nap, I stood in front of a Craftsman in Southwest Portland. Didn't *look* so intimidating. But my heart clattered like a loose valve bucket on a motorcycle.

"It's just people," Lance said as we walked up the sidewalk. We'd had to park far down the street, and judging by the number of cars, Lance wasn't kidding about having a big family. Bikes lined the driveway, too, including a tandem bike pulling a baby trailer.

"Says you. You have this mutual love affair going on with humanity. 'I'll make you popular. Just not as popular as me.'" I hummed a little.

"Did you seriously just quote *Wicked* to me? And badly, I might add."

"Hey. I'm not all coffee and fish."

"Randy was into musicals, wasn't he?" He gave me an I-know-you-so-well look, and if we hadn't been standing in front of his house, I would have kissed the smugness off his face.

"Guilty." Still battling nerves, I hummed another bar. The house had a wide white porch, and a group of men with beers were hanging out in Adirondack chairs. Darn. There wasn't going to be any sneaking in and finding a quiet corner.

"Stop it. You are not a foul-tempered green witch. And no one is going to hate you."

"Not worried about them hating me. I'm worried about them giving *you* a hard time," I admitted. That was the crux of my thing with the age difference. In theory, I could give a shit about what people thought, but in practice, anyone wanting to give Lance a hard time was going to have to come through me. And there was this small—shrinking—part of me that feared the truth of their objections, feared being too old and bitter for Lance.

"Awww." Lance's whole face softened and he tried to yank me close. His mouth was soft and open, and I knew he was seconds away from kissing me in front of a porch full of Degrassi men. I neatly sidestepped him.

"Okay. Let's do this thing."

"Fine." He grabbed my hand, raised eyebrows daring me to object to that, too.

Then we were on the porch and Lance was introducing me to a lot of people whose names I'd never remember. Italian men are good at doing this whole size-the-new-guy-up stare, and Lance's cousins and uncle had it down to an art form. I wasn't sure how to respond, but I settled for handshakes and trying not to look apologetic.

If Lance and I were going to do this, I needed to stop apologizing for being with him—to myself especially. I braced my shoulders, trying to find my missing spine. Meeting the women was a bit easier. They fussed over finding plates for Lance and me. An aunt took it upon herself to give me a tour of the buffet spread out on the kitchen island, pointing out which dishes were vegetarian.

"I went meat free after my Mauro passed. Now I just have a little fish here and there."

Lance snorted and helped himself to noodles in a red sauce. His mom was clearly from the non-Vic side of the family—a slender woman with delicate facial features who shared Lance's nose and smile. She looked far too composed to have five kids. I thought of my mother and how harried she'd been with just me to handle. Overwhelmed was her default setting. Of course, more than some of that was my dad's doing.

But Lance's mom juggled a constant stream of kid questions while setting out more food. I saw what Lance meant about the chaos level in his house; there was a swarm of tween girls running from room to room, a group of teen boys gathered around a TV in the family room, screaming at a March Madness game, and some babies being passed from adult to adult.

"So. You're Chris," his mom said when there was finally a lull in people vying for her attention.

"Yeah." I waited for the lecture or a warning of some kind.

But she smiled and said, "Finally. We were beginning to worry you were a product of Lance's imagination."

"*Mom*," Lance groaned, but there was a lot of affection behind his protest.

"I only mentioned you here and there." He grinned at me, and his mom mouthed, "Every day." I remembered what Vic had said about Lance talking about me, and how Lance had grabbed my hand in front of the house—he was so free and open with his affection for me. And I'd taken that affection for granted far too long. My knees got a little trembly at how I'd almost lost him.

His mom made small talk with us for a bit before a dark-haired girl pulled her away. I relaxed a little, leaning against one of the pillars in the open kitchen.

"You want a beer?" Lance asked.

"Yes, please."

"I'll be right back." He kissed my cheek, obviously not caring if his cousins looked in our direction. God, I loved him.

He hadn't been gone more than a minute when a blond kid sidled up to me. I recognized him from my trips to the club—he was one of the guys Lance danced with. Younger than Lance by a year or two, he wore a defiant expression that instantly put me on edge.

"I see Lance stopped by the nursing home on the way to his party," he said.

Ah. Here it was, the judgment I'd been waiting for.

"See you left your manners at home," I said calmly.

"You hurt him." The kid pointed at me, like he was thinking of poking me, then thought better of it.

"Yeah, I did. And that's between me and him."

"Dude. The oldest guy I've ever fucked was like twenty-five, and he was kind of creepy." He shook his head. "You're like . . . scary old. Way too old for Lance."

There was something in the kid's eyes, a vulnerability behind his bravado that told me that perhaps his feelings for Lance ran a bit deeper than friendship.

"You're wrong. He's not too young for me. He's a grown guy and he can make his own choices." My chest lightened. For the first time, I owned that. I didn't feel guilty for stealing his future, didn't feel like I was taking advantage of Lance, didn't care about pissing off people like this kid. Lance and I loved each other. That was all that mattered.

"I love him," I said firmly. A kid was this guy, who didn't seem to know what he wanted out of life other than to throw his attitude around.

"Whatever. I give you guys six months." The kid made a dismissive gesture. A few weeks ago, I would have agreed with him. But now? I could see us making it.

"You doing okay?" Lance came back with beers for both of us.

"Yeah." I felt . . . well, comfortable was the wrong word, but, weirdly, my encounter with attitude boy had loosened me up.

"Could . . ." He fiddled with the cap on his beer. "Could you see doing this more often?"

"The family thing?"

He nodded.

I adjusted my picture of the future. Last night I'd been working to see him and me in a new light, one that didn't have an end date. Now I twirled my mental dials again, tried to picture holidays in this house. It would be loud. And crazy. And Lance would be happy—I could see it in his smile, the way his shoulders relaxed as soon as we came in the door. His family meant more to him than I could really comprehend—it was like a tightly knit security blanket that gave him courage to fly out into the world.

He wouldn't be the guy I loved without them. That was what I had to accept. So we would come. And it would be a couple of hours of chaos, and then we'd get to go back to our quiet place, wherever that ended up being. And I could be that for him—the place he came to recharge. He was such a fascinating combination of social butterfly and serious guy. I didn't think I'd ever get tired of trying to figure out all his sides.

"Yeah," I said finally. "I can see that."

"Good." He let out a breath that ruffled his bangs.

"Did I pass your test?" I joked as I slipped an arm around him.

"You already did as soon as you came to the bar." His voice was far more serious than my question.

"You needed me to be the one to make the move?"

"Yeah. I didn't want to . . . force myself on you. Didn't want to push so hard that you gave in just to shut me up." Looking down, he fiddled with his beer, rolling the bottle between his long fingers.

"And I realized I needed to be honest about what I needed in a relationship, and yeah, I needed you to come to me, because I needed to know I wouldn't be . . . the only one in love."

"Never." I tightened my arm around him.

A look passed between us, one with far too much heat for a family gathering. The group around the TV cheered as their team scored.

"Hey. Would you like to see my room?"

"Eh. Sure," I said carefully, then lowered my voice. "But you've got another thing coming if you're envisioning—"

"Relax. There's a pool table in the basement. Kids back and forth. I'm not stupid. I just want to show you my stuff."

He led me down to the basement. It was one large room with a pool table at the end closest to the stairs and a room divider fashioned out of shelving at the other. The shelving created a space for a futon and a desk and a round chair. It reminded me of my college rooms—Spartan, but very lived in.

Over the futon was a huge bulletin board. It had the usual stuff, like a calendar and reminder cards for various appointments, but it also had dozens of pictures—tattoos like tribal armbands and flames, pictures of the beach, a small USC flag above a picture of palm trees and college-looking buildings.

"I totally lied. I pulled you down here so I could do this." He kissed me, cupping my face with unexpected tenderness. "You don't know how many nights I pictured you here. Just like this."

"So this is where all those late-night chats happened?" I felt my cock hardening despite my reservation.

"Uh-huh." He kissed me again, deeper this time.

"Would you like your present?" I asked, pulling away, breathing hard.

"Oh, yes." He fingered my belt buckle.

"Not that." I batted his hand away. Didn't matter how turned on I was; I didn't think I could get it on with him in a house full of relatives.

"I got you something. But you should open it here because your mom might freak."

"I love it already," He held out his hand. I got the envelope out of my pocket. I hadn't had time for much, but I'd managed to sneak this in while Lance was showering.

"A gift certificate?" He opened it, his eyes going wide. "For a tattoo?"

"Yeah. I know it's not the most romantic thing—"

"No, it totally is." He kissed me happily. "We can go together. You can get your Scruffy ink and help me pick one." He waved, indicating his idea board.

Looking at his board again, that wavery picture I'd been working on of our future sharpened again. He was so darn optimistic, and it showed in every sunshine-filled picture.

"I want you to pick USC," I said firmly.

"Well, at least we're both sober now." He laughed. "Is it because you think that's the only way to make me happy?"

"No." I knew better now. He *could* be happy staying. He had more than just me—he had his family and his friends and a whole life here, same as me. But maybe that life wasn't the *only* life for either of us. "I thought I wanted to do this for *you*—"

"The same way you did the sex last night?"

*Damn.* He'd picked up on that. I glanced back at the stairs before I nodded. "But just like with the sex, I . . . surprised myself. It's not about you after all. It's about what it gives *me.* Last night gave me a way out of my own head—a way to see other possibilities. And I think . . . this move might be what I need. Three years to figure out *my* next move. Maybe it's another coffee place, or maybe—"

"Maybe it's grad school." A mischievous smile tugged at his lips. "You could probably talk me into an extra few years of sun."

"I'm way too old for that. But maybe—"

"How old will you be in three years if you *don't* follow your heart? You say you want to discover your direction. You should be open to everything."

"Yeah."

"You'd really do this for me?"

"No." I squinted, seeing that future vision again. "I'd do it for *me.* I want an adventure. For both of us. I want to ride my bike up the 101. I want to eat outside in January. I want to try surfing. I know you're afraid that I'm repeating the past, but this isn't about that."

"What is it about?" He stood close to me, nose to nose, breath to breath.

"The future. Being as open as possible to whatever it brings."

"And the coffeehouse?"

"Brady and the gang will be okay with Randy as boss. They'll survive. And who knows, in three years maybe I'll open a new place. Or maybe I'll find a new dream—one that's just mine this time."

"I still can't get over the image of you in a classroom." He laughed. "I almost want you to pick that one just so I can call you Mr. O'Neal and ask if you've got a ruler in your desk."

"Brat." I kissed him, long and a bit recklessly.

"Okay. I want the adventure, too." He smiled up at me, and it was almost enough to make me forget where we were. But then again, we could be anywhere and I'd still want him. Still love him. Still need him. I'd follow him anywhere, and the most incredible thing of all was that I knew it was mutual. Felt it in his kiss. Saw it in his eyes. He'd follow me anywhere, too.

# Chapter 18

"Hold still," Lance ordered, pushing me back against the hotel room bed.

"I can't. I have restless leg syndrome from eighteen hours in the car." We were in town for his cousin Vic's wedding to his boyfriend, Robin. It was a Christmas wedding and we'd be in town for two weeks, so we'd decided to drive it. A decision I was definitely reconsidering.

"Liar. You're trying to get out of a picture. And I *have* to have one of you in your kilt."

"I don't even have my shirt on yet." The kilt was totally Lance's idea. When he'd discovered I owned one, he'd insisted I wear it in lieu of a suit.

"That's the whole point." He wiggled his eyebrows at me.

"How long do we have before the ceremony?"

"Not long enough." He groaned. "And Vic will kill me if we're late."

"I don't know," I pretended to consider. "You look good enough to risk his wrath."

Lance looked delicious in an unbuttoned crisp white tuxedo shirt and black pants. The edge of his new tattoo of two entwined flames was visible through the gap in the shirt. He was one of the grooms-men, so he got to wear the full monkey suit. And I got to appreciate the hell out of it. His hair had extra product in it, and he had his glasses on; he wore them almost full-time now, the dry California air wreaking havoc on his contacts.

He looked older now. More settled. Acing the first term of gradu-ate school had given him a shot of confidence, not that his ego needed much help.

"I miss our place already." He laughed. "You'd better enjoy tonight."

We were staying in the hotel near the wedding venue tonight, but then the rest of the visit would be with his folks. Chaos central and, surprisingly, I was almost looking forward to it. Almost.

We had a tiny apartment near campus, in a complex with a lot of other graduate students. Thanks to Lance, we already had a small circle of friends, and the place felt more like home with each passing day.

"I don't miss work." I had a job managing one of the campus restaurants. I had my money from Randy, so technically I could have coasted a bit, falling into the life of house husband. But I liked my work most days. It gave me the same vacation schedule as Lance. And it afforded me plenty of time to think about what my next move would be. I'd taken the GRE in November, more or less on a whim. The future felt wide open.

"All right." I grabbed the phone from him. "Lean in. Smile."

*Click.* The picture of us appeared instantly on the screen—him smiling wide, me a bit more reserved. But our happiness practically radiated from the phone.

"Okay. You can post this one."

"Finally." He kissed me, and I hit the shutter again. I wanted pictures of all these little moments that added up to a life together. An adventure.

If you liked *Bundled Up*, keep reading for special sneak peeks at two upcoming romances by Annabeth Albert! Preorder them today!

*Love Me Tenor*, the second novel in the Perfect Harmony series, will be released February 16, 2016. (The first, *Treble Maker*, is on sale now!)

*There's no way he'll shake this off . . .*

Trevor Daniels is feeling aimless. A recent college grad, he's not sure what to do with his useless degree, and his family all but abandoned him after he revealed the truth about himself. But a friend's suggestion that he take his chances on a reality show aimed at finding the next big boy band strikes a chord with him—until the show's producers convince him to act like he's in a relationship with a guy who's not at all his type. It isn't exactly love at first sight for Jalen Smith either—but lust just might push them in an unexpected direction. If only their secrets weren't even more twisted than their sheets, threatening to cost them the win—and each other . . .

Also look for barista Brady's story in *Knit Tight*, the next Portland Heat novella, coming in April 2016.

One of Portland's hottest young baristas, Brady is famous for his java-topping flair, turning a regular cup of joe into a work of art. Every Wednesday—aka "Knit Night"—hordes of women and their needles descend on the coffeehouse, and Brady's feeling the heat. Into the fray walks a tall, dark, and distractingly handsome stranger from New York. His name is Evren, and he's the sexy nephew of Brady's sweetest customer, the owner of the yarn shop down the street. He's also got a killer smile, confident air, and masculine charm that's tying Brady's stomach in knots. The smitten barista can't wait to see him at the next week's gathering. But when Brady tries to ask Evren out, his plans unravel faster than an unfinished edge. If Brady hopes to warm up more than Evren's coffee, he'll have to find a way to untangle their feelings, get out of the friend zone, and form a close-knit bond that's bound to last a lifetime . . .

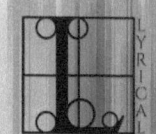

# LOVE ME TENOR

## PERFECT HARMONY

# ANNABETH ALBERT

# Chapter One

@NextDirectionShow Ready to find the next big Boy Band sensation? We are putting together groups now! The winning group gets a record deal, post-show tour & other prizes!

@NextDirectionShow We can't wait for our groups to arrive! Filming starts in June & we can't wait for you to meet our contestants!

The heater was broken again. Trevor shifted around, trying to find a stray bit of warmth from the ancient radiator in his tiny dorm room. The pile of textbooks on the foot of his bed went skittering to the floor as he adjusted the phone to his ear.

"Come on. You're perfect boy band material," Dawn said, her voice all sparkle despite the bad cell phone connection. She was in LA, home of sun and happy people and the best, most terrifying three months of Trevor's life, when he'd played a minor part in the a cappella reality show *Perfect Harmony.*

"A boy band? You want me to be in a boy band?" Here in Iowa, land of reality and final exams and thirty-seven days from homelessness, Trevor couldn't match Dawn's enthusiasm. She had been a production assistant on *Perfect Harmony* but now had an assistant producer gig. *Everything* was awesome in her world, including the new show she'd landed on.

"Yeah. You're exactly the kind of harmless cute that wins over audiences."

"Harmless cute? You mean I look fifteen?"

"Okay. Hot in a nonthreatening manner. That better?" Dawn sighed, and there was a sound of papers shuffling. "Look. I loved you on *Perfect Harmony.* And I'm sorry that didn't pan out for you, but you're photogenic and you've got a decent voice and I *really* have to fill these slots so we can make housing arrangements—"

"Hang on. Did you say housing?" Trevor looked at his gray cement-block walls and college-issued furniture that were only his for exactly thirty-seven more days. And then? Nothing. He'd sent out stacks of résumés, but every other soon-to-be graduate in the state was also looking, and most had way more employable skills than he did. No job had miraculously appeared, and he had no savings for a deposit on a place and no lead on a roommate situation, thanks to what had happened with his family.

"Yes. All the competing boy bands will be sharing a house together. It'll be a big part of the show, and meals will be included, too. We'll pay for you to fly to Vancouver next month. I've got the perfect group to put you in. A bunch of other guys like you. It'll be terrific."

"Not LA?"

"Vancouver is cheaper for filming. I'll get you paperwork for making sure you have a passport. So are you in?"

*No, I'm out. Out, out, out.* Out had landed him in this predicament. He'd been stupid enough to come out to his family at spring break. Now he had no job at his father's church waiting for him, no money, no *hope* of money, and no place to live after graduation. His dad's harsh words still rung in his ears and his mother's bleak face wasn't something he'd forget anytime soon.

And yeah, he could sing, but the ability to harmonize was hardly a meal ticket. He'd put his a cappella days behind him and buckled down at school, but for what? A degree he was never going to use? A family he no longer had to impress?

"Trevor? You there? Can I count on you?"

"Yeah. I'm in." What the hell. He could sing some teenybopper tunes while his life fell apart. At least he'd have a roof over his head. And Dawn said the other guys were like him. Probably fellow a cappella geeks. Yeah, this could work. He pulled his sweatshirt closer around him. Anything had to be better than this limbo land.

### One month later

"You brought your luggage?" The receptionist looked at Trevor like he'd brought a snake to the movie studio offices instead of a rolling suitcase and a backpack.

"My flight was late. And then customs—"

"Fine." She held up a hand, shimmery with the sort of nail art Trevor's sisters weren't allowed to wear. "You can have a seat." She motioned to a seating area with square leather and chrome chairs and a metallic-looking shag rug.

"Wait. Is my group here yet? Stand Out!?"

"Let me check." She glanced at a pink sheet on a clipboard. "No." She made a shooing motion back in the direction of the waiting area.

"Thanks."

The receptionist disappeared back down a hallway, teetering on shoes that put her a good six inches taller than Trevor. The building was kind of a letdown. The whole complex was a series of gigantic gray warehouses, but the inside of this one was like any other office building in America. Or Canada. He'd only been in Vancouver a couple of hours and kept forgetting he wasn't in the States anymore.

His bag made a loud clickety-clack sound as he dragged it across the tile floor to the seating area, but the only occupant in the chairs didn't even glance up. The guy was about Trevor's age, maybe a bit younger. His eyes were half-closed, like waiting for producers to call his name was just *so* boring. He had that jock sprawl, maximizing every inch of the low chair. Trevor took a seat with a good view of the guy. Indifferent eye candy was his favorite kind.

He had this thing for straight guys, particularly jocks. Jocks were his personal kryptonite; they made his knees turn into magnets, headed straight for the floor. And the guy across from him was the deadly, heart-stopping red kryptonite brand of jock. His build was perfect— not too tall, because Trevor was picky about that—but jacked like a Chevy with a lift kit. Hell, even the dude's neck was ripped. Jock's foot moved back and forth in motion with the music pumping in his ears from pricey Beats headphones.

Because dude's eyes were shut, Trevor felt free to continue his inventory of hotness. Baggy shorts. T-shirt for a wrestling team. *Wrestling.* Trevor had to shift around on the slick leather couch before continuing his appraisal. Cheap white socks, but black shoes that probably cost more than Trevor's bike. Rich elitist jock? Yes, please.

The outfit was notable because Trevor would have figured most guys coming to a TV studio would want to dress up a little. *He* had, but of course now his pressed khakis and dress shirt seemed horribly overdressed compared to jock boy and the receptionist wearing a cut-off denim skirt and a tank top that seemed to be made out of nothing more than knotted rope.

Maybe dude wasn't there to be on TV. Or if he was, maybe he was there for a different show from the music reality show Trevor was on. He certainly didn't look like the boy band type. Dude looked ready for an MMA-fighter type show, or maybe working as a stunt double. But if he wasn't on Trevor's show, that meant—

"You done checking me out or you need me to turn to the other side?" Jock's eyes snapped open. They were a startling shade of hazel, almost amber. And at the moment, they were filled with undisguised irritation.

*Oh crap.* Trevor gulped hard. "I don't know what you're talking about." He dug out his phone, giving himself something to look down at. He'd been caught before and it almost never ended well. With any luck, Dawn would show up soon and he would never have to see jock boy again.

"Oh don't be shy." Jock boy had a killer whisper: husky with a hint of command to it. He said it with the air of someone who knew exactly how hot he was. And now he was going to make Trevor pay for noticing.

Trevor didn't look up from his phone, but inside he was squirming in his chair. In a different situation, he'd be more than happy to let this play out until he was on his knees in the restroom with jock boy berating him, but he'd sworn to turn over a new leaf. Plus there was always the risk that jock wanted all the verbal abuse and none of the fun. *No more gambling.*

"Yeah. That's what I figured." The other guy snorted.

"Trevor! You made it!" Dawn came barreling across the lobby, red hair streaming behind her. She was flanked by two nearly identical blond giants—one wore a blue polo shirt and khaki pants, the other a brown polo and blue pants. Both had the same bored smirk on their faces.

"What are you doing with your luggage?" Dawn's smile was replaced by a frown, like Trevor was some clueless kid making her day more difficult. "Why didn't you give it to the receptionist? They're sending all the contestants' stuff over to the house while we tape the intro segments."

"Here. I'll take it." Blond giant number one grabbed Trevor's bags, tossing them like they were a set of hand weights.

"Jalen!" Dawn stepped around Trevor to hug jock boy, who stood up to greet her. "It's about time. I was starting to freak!"

Just his luck. Dawn hung on Jalen the jock like they were old friends, tugging his headphones down to his neck and rubbing his closely cropped black hair. *Oh geez.* Jalen looked a bit young to be Dawn's boy toy; she had to be in her late twenties. But no matter what Jalen was to Dawn, he was now a giant pain in the neck to Trevor. A sick feeling gathered in his gut and his hands tightened.

"Did you meet Jalen already, Trevor?" she asked.

"No," Trevor said carefully. The tension in his muscles climbed to trampoline spring tight—any second now Jalen was going to call him out for creeping on him.

"We're acquainted," Jalen drawled at the same time.

"Um. Okay." Dawn frowned but luckily kept talking before Jalen could reveal way more than Trevor wanted. "So this is Carter. And over there is Carson."

Twins. They had to be twins right? Trevor was already in too much shit for gaping and didn't want to stare hard enough to figure it out.

"So, are we ready to become the next boy band?" Carter spoke like some dude on an infomercial, each word carefully articulated for maximum impact. "I am so ready to win this thing."

The riot in Trevor's stomach grew worse. Win? With Jalen the jock? As in Trevor was now in the same group as jock boy? And the blond giants? For the next six weeks?

"Yeah. Let's do this." Carson came back over. Like Carter, he had a macho, commanding voice, probably a baritone when he sang. Heck. Trevor *really* didn't want to be the only tenor on a team of One Direction wannabes.

"Okay Stand Out!, let's go film your intro." Dawn motioned for them to follow her down the hall.

*Oh hell.* He was really going to be on camera, in a boy band, right freaking now

ANNABETH
ALBERT

PORTLAND HEAT

*Knit*
TIGHT

shine

# CHAPTER ONE

"You're my favorite barista," the girl said with a self-conscious giggle. She was all of eighteen, if that, and reminded me of my sister, with her wispy hair and pale skin.

"Tonight I'm the *only* barista." I took a breath, kept my tone light, and didn't give in to the urge to sigh heavily.

I grabbed a mug to get her latte started. Wednesday nights were our busiest of the week, and I was stuck working alone because my coworker had called in sick. I *hated* Wednesdays, but I wasn't in a position to turn down hours. As it was, our boss had been slashing staff for the evening shifts, citing cost-cutting measures, so he hadn't seen fit to give me a backup.

"You're the best barista I've got, Brady. You can handle it," he'd said on the phone, in his usual offhand manner. He didn't like to be bothered with what he deemed trivial stuff. So I was alone to face Wednesday hell, better known as Knit Night, the weekly event in which a horde of women and their baskets of fibers descended on the coffee shop. But they all bought at least one drink and that meant tips in my jar.

And I was a damn fine barista, something I reminded myself as I put a little flair into making the girl's drink. She came here for this after all—the little bit of a show as I flipped the mug and steamed the milk, the latte-art smiley face I finished the drink with, the winning smile I dredged up as I handed it over. For an instant I made her feel like she was the sole focus of my attention instead of the line of traffic behind her. That was my skill, the one that was going to elevate me from Brady the barista to Brady the national-champion barista and alleviate a whole shitload of problems.

*Buzz.* From deep in my black apron pocket, my phone vibrated against my thigh. Hell. One of those problems was undoubtedly slipping into a crisis state, but I couldn't risk fishing the phone out with a line of customers. I'd have to hope that my sister could hold down the fort at home and that whatever it was could wait for a lull in the rush.

The next order was the girl's friend, another latte, another smiley face, but I made the mistake of glancing up at the door as I worked. The next customer to come in was the hottest guy I'd seen in a very long time. He had artfully styled black hair, the sort of purposefully messy cut that probably cost three digits and took twenty minutes in the morning to perfect. His slim-fitting jeans also looked designer—a rich color somewhere between brown and black and a subtle sheen to the fabric. A fancifully wrapped scarf over a close-fitting, long-sleeved shirt would probably get noticed by the Knit Night ladies, which was exactly what I did not want to have happen.

Our eyes met as I drew the latte art with a stirring stick, and he grinned widely at me. Gorgeous rose-pink lips and perfect white teeth straight out of a dental ad, and—

*Frak me.* I flubbed the smiley face, distracted by my efforts to memorize the handsome stranger. Rather than hand over a squiggly mess, I chucked the cup and started over. The girl didn't seem to care as she was deep in conversation with her friend at the end of the bar.

"Sorry about the wait," I said to the guy when it was finally his turn and he moved up to order. His intent gaze coupled with his polished appearance made me more conscious of my untrimmed beard and scruffy ponytail and made me wish I was wearing something a bit nicer than a faded People's Cup T-shirt.

"It is no problem," the guy said. He had a gorgeous voice—deep and polished, like a shiny piece of ebony. He had the fast speech and clipped consonants of an East Coast accent, but there was a lilt of something more exotic there, too. "I am happy to wait. Very peaceful in here."

Ha. I checked the clock as I tried to think of some flirty reply. The heavy glass door that led to Alberta Street swung open. It was 6:58 and Violet was first as usual, holding the door open for the herd of knitters. Not the steady trickle of a breakfast or lunch rush but twenty-plus women, all obsessed with punctuality and festooned with hats, scarves, and knit vests. Each ordered drinks for here with the sort of lengthy deliberation of someone who only ordered one coffee a week.

An older woman with the look and demeanor of a no-nonsense teacher, Violet made it her business to keep her fellow knitters in line. Knit Night was the brainchild of Iplik, the yarn store just down the street from us on Alberta, but Violet was the weekly event's unofficial hostess. As usual, she started giving her comrades orders about table rearrangement.

The People's Cup wasn't huge by any means, and Knit Night tended to fill the joint up. The space was longer than it was wide, with couches in front of the plate glass window, the coffee bar running along one wall, tables in the middle of the room, and a long wooden farmhouse bench and table for communal seating in the back of the room. The Knit Night ladies liked to turn the couches around and group the center tables together, creating a setup conducive to conversation but a tripping hazard for the rest of the patrons. And the arrangement resulted in an unholy din really, especially on nights when their ranks swelled to thirty or more.

"Remember to keep the aisle clear," I said to Violet and her minions. I'd warned them about creating tripping hazards with their knitting gear, but it was as futile as telling the twins and Jonas to keep their Legos in one area. Like my siblings, the ladies loved to spread out their projects.

"What'll it be?" I swung back to the register, no closer to having the right banter for the stranger, but no longer in a position to care. However, he'd stepped aside for Violet and her herbal tea order.

"I'll be back when the line clears," he said with a wink. He had a leather messenger bag, the sort meant to look like something Indiana Jones would haul around, for which one paid for every crinkle in the distressed finish. He'd probably come in wanting a quiet place to work.

He had the look and accent of a displaced New Yorker—working some cushy freelance job, no doubt. I liked thinking up little stories about my customers, but I didn't bother coming up with a lengthy one for him. He wouldn't be back once he saw how loud Knit Night got. And the ladies were likely to pester him about his intricately knit scarf with its pattern of interwoven cables. One time, I'd made the mistake of wearing a wool beanie I'd found for a buck at the thrift store. *Every* single knitter needed to remark on its construction. Dude was *so* going to be beating feet once Knit Night got underway.

Without a coworker, I was slammed, having to work both the register and the machine. While it kept me hopping, I didn't lose my rhythm until the triplets showed up.

They weren't really triplets. That's what I called them in my head—three middle-aged women who apparently texted each other every week to coordinate their outfits. This week it was cardigans—one yellow, one pink, one green—all in a similarly complex knit pattern. Each woman had long, grayish-brown hair, all carried identical hemp knitting bags, and they all were incapable of making a decision.

"Now, ladies, what are we ordering this week?" the first asked the other two. "I was thinking mochas?"

"Oh, I was thinking chai," said the second.

"Don't we want lattes?" the third asked. They couldn't each order to their own preference. No, they had to agree on that week's beverage, something they couldn't seem to do prior to holding up the line.

"Oh, yes," the first said. "We want some of Brady's art."

I immediately started thinking of what bit of whimsy would make the triplets happy. The smiley faces were better suited for the teen girls, but I could come up with something special just for the ladies. I was good at that, and the detail-oriented work itself always soothed me, even when the shop was busy. But what drove me batty was how the triplets were prone to changing their order as soon as I had it straight in my head.

Yellow gets skim.

Pink gets half caf.

Green gets picky.

Brady gets distracted by the sexy stranger texting on his shiny smartphone in the rear of the store...*No time for that.* I moved quicker, trying to ignore the fact that my eyeballs wanted to track his every movement.

"No, wait." Yellow cardigan stopped me in midpour. "Did I remember to say decaf?"

"Nope." I dumped the cup, ready to start over.

"And mine is sugar-free, too," Pink added.

*Buzz.* My apron vibrated against my thigh again. Behind the triplets, the line was at least ten deep. *Damn it, Renee. Just handle the kids. Please.*

Finally I had the three of them set. Green took a sip, then held out the cup. "Is this coconut?"

"You said nondairy, nonsoy?" I took the cup back.

"I meant almond breve." She sighed, like I should have gotten that at first, and if I wasn't distracted by what was going on back home, I would have remembered to ask her *which* nondairy, nonsoy option she wanted.

"Here, let me try again." I had just finished her new drink, complete with a leaf design in the foam, when a loud crash rattled the whole shop.

A two-seat table had tipped over, sending two coffees flying and leaving two women in tears.

"My Fair Isle sweater!" The younger of the two, a pixie with platinum hair and a hook nose, held up a dripping garment with half a dozen colors of yarn, still on long needles connected by a cable. "I've worked six months on this!"

"I'm sorry!" The rainbow-haired young woman in a roller derby T-shirt had tears streaming down her face.

"You never look!" The first wasn't having any apology.

"Hey, my hat got ruined, too!"

"Ladies." I stepped out from behind the counter, grabbing the mop we stashed against the wall. I approached the mess and tried to inject some patience in my voice as I said, "Maybe if you didn't move the table—"

"And what business is it of yours?" Oh, Miss Fair Isle was pissed and she was turning it all on me and the other knitter.

"Brady! Can we order?" someone called from the line at the counter.

"Did you forget to sweeten this one?" Green cardigan triplet was apparently still not happy, but I ignored her to set the fallen two-top to rights. As I straightened, I noticed a pair of expensive-looking desert boots: the brown leather staples of all Portland hipster men. And as my gaze traveled upward, I took in the handsome stranger who had somehow managed to find his way right into the middle of the Knit Night chaos.

"Is this always so . . . boisterous?" he said with a faint curl to his gorgeous full mouth.

"'Fraid so. Welcome to Knit Night." I finally gave in to that heavy sigh I'd been holding in for the last hour.

"It is not so bad." His lips curled as his gaze latched onto mine, not breaking away.

He didn't move, and I didn't scurry back to the counter like I should have. The air felt charged—

"Debbie. You ruined my Fair Isle! Two hundred dollars' worth of yarn! Ruined!" Anger. That's what the air was charged with. Fair Isle lady wasn't letting it go and was all up in the roller derby girl's personal space again.

*Buzz.* My leg vibrated yet again, this time the steady pulse of a missed call. This just wasn't my night. I had no idea when I'd get a chance to breathe, let alone check the latest message. A solo Knit Night was proving to be a special kind of hell. And, of course, the most attractive man I'd seen in weeks had to be dropped right into the middle of it. I gave him five more minutes before he scurried out to the chain place down the street. They were stealing enough of our business, why not him, too?

"Ladies. May I see?" Instead of fleeing, the man stepped closer to the arguing women.

To my surprise, the angry knitter handed over the soggy garment. "Evren! I thought I saw you over in the corner. You should have joined us! Is Mira with you?"

"I wouldn't miss it." One of my favorite customers stepped out of the line for coffee. The owner of Iplik, the yarn store, she was a neighborhood institution unto herself. And she'd been sorely missed the last few Knit Nights. I'd heard a rumor about some health problems, and I was very glad to see her, even if she did look thinner and frailer, with an elegant knit turban on her head. She was one of the very few people who knew my situation with the kids, and I still got all warm at the memory of the little knit ornaments she'd given me for them at the holidays.

"And what is all this fuss?" she asked.

I loved her lilting Turkish accent, and I realized that was what I'd heard in the man's voice—New York with just a hint of Turkish.

"There's no fuss," Miss Fair Isle said, flipping her long blond hair. She was too busy making goo-goo eyes at Evren. Not that I blamed her. He was handling her soggy yarn balls with such deftness and care that it made certain parts of me take notice. He had long, elegant fingers with blunt tips. Capable grace.

"I think this can be fixed," Evren pronounced, and the whole group exhaled. "Now, why don't we let the man get back to his coffee?"

"Evren, this is Brady, my favorite barista," Mira introduced me with a flourish, emerald tunic top rippling. "Brady, this is my nephew. He's come to . . . help with the store."

"That's great." I forced my voice to be bright and cheery, just like hers. But I knew his arrival couldn't be a good thing—her health must have been even worse than the rumors. "You must be the famous nephew she's always raving about."

Truthfully, I'd pictured someone younger from Mira's stories about her favorite relative. Evren was probably a bit older than me, perhaps in his late twenties. And if I was honest, I'd imagined someone diminutive and round, like Mira was before her illness, not tall, confident, and composed. And hot as hell.

"Perhaps Hala Mira exaggerates." He patted her arm before turning his attention to the bickering knitters. By the time I was back behind the counter, he had the two women sitting next to each other again, laughing, and he'd stowed the soggy mess of knitting in a shopping bag to "fix later." That pronouncement had drawn much awe from the Knit Night crowd.

There had been the odd dude at a Knit Night before, hipster types with scraggly-looking bits of scarf and an eye on a girlfriend or potential girlfriend, but I was still impressed when Evren opened his bag and pulled out a half-knit sock on the needles and a completed sock, which was passed around and oohed and aahed over by the ladies. It was indeed a nice piece of work—at least three colors that I could see, and some sort of complicated pattern that had him pulling out charts and diagrams.

His hands were so sexy that I kept spying on him as I finished the rest of the initial Knit Night rush. I liked watching his long, elegant fingers move rapidly with the teeny needles, liked how he gestured as he passed his scarf around, and really liked when he flipped his ridiculously thick, straight hair off his forehead with a flick of his hand. *Wonder what else he's good at with those hands . . .*

With the scarf on the table, his long neck was exposed, and he had the sort of prominent Adam's apple and faint scruff that never failed to turn me on. Maybe after Knit Night, I could say a few words—

*Buzz.* Hell. Finally, I had enough breathing space at the counter that I could check the texts, keeping the phone hidden behind the counter.

I discovered a series of texts from Renee, each more dire than the last.

*Madison's stomach is upset. Should she eat dinner?*

*She's puking! All over the rug! Help!*

*Fever's 102!!!! Brady!!! What do I dooooooo? :( :( :(*

I could hear Renee's wail just from the text. Yeah, eighteen wasn't a baby anymore and we could all do with fewer hysterics from her, but she was still munchkin-size, with a sweet voice and a sensitive attitude. It was hard to get those memories of us as little kids out of my head. I'd been five when she was born and I'd been the type of older brother who fell hard for the family's new addition—the tiny blond-haired toddler I'd begged my mom to let me push on the baby swing. The too-damn-cheerful kindergartner who'd held my hand so tight on the way home from school every day.

Renee and I had both grown up a lot faster than we'd wanted to when our mother and her second husband died last year, and now we were doing our best to raise our younger half siblings together.

Trying to keep the phone low and discreet, I frantically typed back.

*Calm down. Children's fever reducer in the medicine cabinet. Top shelf. I circled the dose on the box for the twins. Give that. Home soon. Promise.*

Cough. A throat clearing made me look up. Fuck. Evren loomed over me, and he was staring right at my phone.

"Sorry." I pocketed it, shaking my hand off like it was burning. "I don't usually . . ."

"Do not worry about it." Evren made a sweeping gesture. I was already a serious fan of his accent and the little bits of formality that crept into his speech just added to the appeal of that melodic voice. "You looked so serious and concerned. You must have had good reason. I saw nothing."

He patted my shoulder. A simple, friendly gesture, but not one most customers would make. Especially not most *straight* customers. I'd be lying if I said I hadn't been wondering which way he swung since the moment he came in, and the hot sizzle rushing down my arm only intensified those thoughts.

"Thank you." If word got back to Randy, my boss, that I was on the phone, it wouldn't go well. "What can I get you? On the house."

"Do not be ridiculous." Evren pulled out a handsome embossed wallet and slid out his debit card. "Large Americano. Extra shot. Extra sweet. And a chai for Mira, please."

I gently pushed the card away. "Mira drinks free. All the business owners who give us special events and customer referrals like this do. It's how we give back to Alberta Street."

It was a tradition started by my old boss, Chris, and one grudgingly kept up by Randy.

"All right. This time. Next time, I pay." He flashed me a smile full of gleaming teeth. His lips were wide without being overly full and the perfect shade of rose—the same shade as Mira's turban and, unlike the hat, the lips were sure to star in my private thoughts later that night.

"Oh, you planning on making this a regular thing?"

"We shall see, Brady. We shall see." He looked right at my lips as he said the words before he winked. Slow and deliberate. *Damn.* I swear I felt the buzz of his gaze all the way down to my Vans.

He hummed a bit to himself as he accepted the drinks and carried them over to Mira. He made sure she was settled with hers, adjusting a shawl around her shoulders. Oh, man. I was toast. The dude was the definition of masculine hotness with his thick, straight black hair, scruffy jaw, and lean build, and he was kind? And he could wrangle a room full of knitters? I wanted him back every week, and not just for the eye candy.

*Buzz.* I had to pretend to get myself some coffee to sneak a peek. *Fever down but she's asking for you.*

While I had a chance, I grabbed a ginger soda from the cooler and shoved it in my beat-up messenger bag under the counter. Unlike Evren's pricey number, mine was more patches than canvas at this point. Just one more way we were from different worlds. With luck, I'd have time to stop for some electrolyte drinks and broth on the way home, particularly if tips were good. If Madison was sick, Morgan and Jonas were sure to follow. I was on the skateboard, so it would have to be a small trip.

Over at the knitting tables, a loud group laugh echoed through the coffeehouse, Evren's deep chuckle joining in. A low ache gathered in my gut. I should be a normal twenty-three-year-old, free to mack on the hot stranger, stick around and flirt with him after closing, but instead the text had served as a reminder of why none of those things were happening in my life, even with someone as intriguing as Evren. I had three kids depending on me, a sister who should still be a kid, too, and absolutely no room for anything else.